PROMISES TO KEEP

DIANA KNIGHTLEY

Dedicated to the first of my grown kids who reads the series to this point: Hey! Thanks, You! Now I see why I liked you so much.

Note: I left you something special in my jewelry box.

I had spotted her first, wearing what looked tae be one of my dresses, and then had followed her eyes tae see who I guessed was Kaitlyn, though twas difficult tae see her behind a potted palm. I could see the edge of a dress though, one of my dresses, a design by Madeleine Vionnet from 1927. At least my daughter-in-law understood the importance of historical propriety.

So it dinna bother me much tae sign a letter asking Magnus tae come, he must hae been already here.

And his presence complicated everything.

But he had promised tae lay down his life for me — it seemed as if he were going tae get his chance.

CHAPTER 2 - KAITLYN

*W*e were in bed in the guest room of Elmwood in New York. The furnishings were luxurious. The bed had an intricately carved, mahogany canopy, the bedding and curtains were silk brocade. The colors were pale blue and green, a bright version of the colors of the Campbell clan. The ceiling was high and had a painted mural of a blue sky within a circle in the middle. The windows were tall, the lighting was low. It felt like the lush bedroom of a queen, lavish. Everything was antique, but it was all clean, fresh, and well maintained, almost as if the bedding, though clearly from a century ago, had not seen a full century of use. It was the home of a time traveler.

By the light of a small lamp, in the middle of the night, I had my head on Magnus's chest, tucked in under his arm, where I could hear his heartbeat, and draw my fingertips in circles on his skin as we whispered over the news of the day, this time:

Lady Mairead was in trouble.

We were conversing, trying to solve the problem — we just had to think of how.

We had decided to sleep on it, yet here we were... unable to sleep, thoughtful, occasionally asking each other questions, like, "...so the red seal was her seal?"

"It looked much like it, but I canna be sure…"

"…so it was a note from Lady Mairead, right? But then placed into Lady Mairead's safe, but she is asking for help…?"

"Aye."

"How do you think it got there…?"

There was a long pause as he considered, so long that I thought he might have fallen asleep again. Then, "I think perhaps they hae overpowered the butler, gotten the safe's combination from m'mother, and put the note in her safe for me tae find…"

"Then the party is a trap."

"Aye, from top tae bottom, the whole thing is a trap—"

One side of the tall, ornately carved double door, creaked open. Magnus tensed. "Och!"

I sat up with a start.

But it was Haggis, padding into the room. I fell back onto Magnus's chest.

He laughed, "Twas startling, Haggis, ye ought tae knock and announce yerself."

Haggis put his head on the mattress and looked at Magnus woefully, with his tail swinging back and forth, hypnotically.

Magnus said, "I canna argue with ye, ye can come up."

Haggis jumped up, circled, and finally plopped down and put his chin on Magnus's stomach, almost nose to nose with me. His look said, as if to rub it in, "I was invited."

"Your mother, Magnus, is going to be furious that there is dog fur on the bed."

"There is going tae be dog fur upon every piece of furniture. If she survives the drama of her meeting with Agnie, she might never recover from the shock of my insult tae her furnishings."

"If she survives the drama."

"Aye, Agnie is likely feeling verra murderous since I hae killed her sons."

I drew my fingertips around another lackadaisical spin on

Magnus's chest, but then Haggis whimpered so I scratched the dog under his ear.

Magnus said, "Och nae, Haggis, are ye takin' m'strokin'? Tis nae fair."

I joked, "You got plenty earlier, I gave you *all* the stroking."

He laughed, "Twas a great deal of proper strokin', aye, ye are correct Madame Campbell, I hae had m'share, ye may pet the dog now. I will be a grownup about it."

Haggis slunk over Magnus to get closer to me, rolled over on his back between us, presenting his stomach for more petting, and then enjoying himself, rolled back and forth to get comfortable, shoving Magnus away.

Magnus said, "Haggis, ye canna push me aside, what are ye about? Are ye the same dog from the battlefield of yore? Or are ye now such a modern dog ye are rolling around on the silk bedding acting as if ye are the king? Off. Off."

Haggis slowly stood and dropped off the bed, sulkily. He lay down with an exhale, his chin on his paws, a look of recrimination on his face.

Magnus sighed. "Och, Haggis, ye can come back."

Haggis jumped up, licked Magnus's chin, and curled up taking just a small part of the bed.

I put my chin on Magnus's chest and looked up at him. "So if the party is a trap, what does she want — *you?*"

"Aye, I would wager she wants Lady Mairead's son. She would like tae see Lady Mairead suffer by doin' something tae me."

"I do not like the sound of that."

"Nor I, but since we ken about it afore it happens, we will outsmart her. She has a logic, we just need tae understand it, and outwit her."

"...a logic, yeah..." I circled my finger's path around his chest. "Unless there is no logic, unless she's just fury-revenging."

"Now see, but that is the easiest of the enemies, if fury-revenging, she will make a mistake. It will be easy tae defeat her."

"What if she's not logical or furious, what if she's just chaotic?"

He raised his head to look down on me. "What dost ye mean, she is not tryin' tae win, she is just behavin' unreasonably?"

"Yes, maybe we have no way to know what she'll do."

Magnus put his head back down. "Aye, she is a woman."

I batted his shoulder. "Plenty of men cause chaos with fury-revenge."

"I meant I daena understand how tae think like a woman fury-revenging. I daena ken what she will do—"

"Lady Mairead would know, fury-revenge is kinda her thing."

"If she is still alive. If not…"

I said, "I'm very glad you have a plan."

He chuckled, his chest vibrating against my ear. "I daena hae a plan, I only hae a mission, we hae tae deal with Agnie MacLeod."

"What do we know about her?"

"Next tae naething, m'mother keeps many closely guarded secrets. I imagine though that Agnie is verra dangerous as she has lost most everything."

"How will Fraoch deal with this? He's her son."

"He daena ken her. Blood is important, but I truly believe the best family is built by alliances, and any laird will tell ye, an allegiance can be more enduring."

I looked at him. "How does that work?"

"For instance, a prince canna trust a brother if he aspires tae the crown, someone who is an advisor and friend would be more trustworthy. Same holds true for the sons of kings."

My eyes went wide. "You might not be able to trust Archie?"

"Och nae, I canna imagine it, he is a wee boy. He inna conspirin' against me."

"Thank god, that is freaky to think—"

"Eh, but tis difficult sometimes between sons and fathers, I hae tae be a realist. He will be a man someday. Blood ties are complicated."

"You've met him as an adult though, and he liked you."

"True, he admired me and we were friendly, that bodes well for our relationship. But it daena change the point: blood ties are complicated and sometimes allegiances are far stronger and allies more trustworthy. For instance, I might hae tae keep m'eye upon Lochinvar, but I will never worry about Quentin. Quentin and I are aligned, we hae the same goals, and we would die tae protect each other. We hae fought alongside each other many a time and I trust him implicitly."

"What about Fraoch?"

"Fraoch is further complicated — we hae our blood ties, he is a brother and a son of Donnan, but we also hae a long history. I know I should have reservations, but I ken Fraoch is loyal, he has fought for me, he would die for me, and I trust him completely. Many people from the outside would warn me tae be wary. I would be more wary if he and Hayley were havin' bairns."

"And James?"

"I trust James, he is a wildcard in battle, but he will always be on m'side."

"I know Zach is completely trusted by you—"

"Och aye, I would lay down m'life for the chef."

We both chuckled.

"What about... what about Hammond?"

He lay quietly for a long time.

Then he finally said, "I daena understand how he can be devoted and loyal despite the terrible treatment by my mother, but he is. I ken he would hae a possible motive, tae get back at her, yet he remains steadfast, and though I sometimes wonder that he remains loyal, I ken he is — he has been. I hae looked intae his eyes. We fought alongside each other in the kingdom when we were at war..."

Magnus's brow drew down. "That happened dinna it?"

"Yes, you were at war for a long time. In one or more of the timelines."

He nodded.

"When I was in battle with Hammond we grew tae trust each other and I remain that way. I believe he is a true guardian of the kingdom and I believe he is honorable tae m'mother. But... I am still concerned."

Then he finally said, "I daena ken about Hammond."

I looked at his face in horror.

He said simply, "There are many things that hae happened recently: us appearin' at the stadium for instance, mid-battle, that hae the feel of some kind of treason."

"For a long time he wasn't involved in the time travel."

"Aye, but now he kens all about it, and... I am wary."

CHAPTER 3- KAITLYN

*T*hat night there was a loud yelling down the hall from Quentin.

Magnus climbed from bed. "Ye daena need tae get up, mo reul-iuil, tis one of Quentin's night-terrors. I will go check in on him."

I mumbled, "He hasn't had one in a while, but when they happen they usually mean some kinda bad time-shit is going on."

I heard footsteps in the hall, heavy, lumbering, it was Fraoch going to check in. These men could hear in their sleep.

Magnus said, "Sounds like we are all goin' tae check on him, in case he is frightenin' Madame Beaty. I will be back."

I pulled on a robe, in case the noise woke one of the kids and they needed me, but I heard Fraoch and Magnus whispering down the hall. Then I heard Quentin and James joining them.

I put my head from the door and whispered, "What's happening?"

Two rooms down, Archie was looking out. He looked frightened. Magnus told him, "Tis alright, son, the men are needin' tae speak taegether in the hall."

Quentin said, "Sorry, little man, Uncle Quentin had a night-mare, it's all good."

I went to the kids' door. "It's okay Archie, everything's fine, go back to bed, I'll check on you in a moment." The kids were so gosh darn nervous.

Of course they are, our lives are very often a shit-show.

I joined Quentin, Magnus, Fraoch, Zach, and James at the door to Lady Mairead's office. They were looking down on a dark patch on the carpet.

Magnus asked, "Did ye notice this earlier?"

"No, not at… I stood right here." I leaned down and put my hand on it. "It's dry, what do you think it was?"

Quentin said, "Blood. Look, it goes around there, drippings."

"Oh," I withdrew my hand.

"I was here earlier, and dinna notice it." He followed the trail around to the back of the desk where he switched on a lamp. "Och nae, someone has been bleedin' all the way up tae the door of the safe. Tis verra worrisome."

He knelt to feel the carpet, then climbed up and sat in the chair at the desk, with his head in his hands. "Tae get it straight: I received a request for help from Lady Mairead. I spoke tae Fraoch and Hayley about it, because it involves Fraoch's mother—"

Fraoch said, "Call her Agnie. I daena like talking about m'ties tae her, she has never been m'mother in the truest sense of the word."

"Aye, Agnie MacLeod — nae relation worth mentionin' tae Fraoch — she has done somethin' tae Lady Mairead." He pulled the letter from his pocket and placed it on the desk and spread it flat. "I found the letter, discussed the letter, and now after the letter, there is blood."

Quentin crossed to the desk to read it. "And you got it from this safe?"

"Aye, but there was nae blood when I found it."

Quentin tossed the letter back on the desk. "Shit, we need to mount a rescue."

Magnus said, "Aye, we need to rescue Lady Mairead, but we hae nae idea how…" He shook his head, wearily. "But, tis the middle of the night and sleep is necessary. We will discuss it in the morn."

Quentin said, "Good idea, sleep on it, everyone, any good ideas, bring 'em to breakfast."

Magnus switched off the desk lamp.

I checked in with the kids, got them settled, and then we returned to our room and our bed.

Magnus said, "I ken one thing, that blood spot winna there when I went tae the office yesterday."

I climbed in under the covers. "Are you worried? Whose blood is that?"

"I daena ken, but it daena bode well that we hae a plea for help and a bloody carpet and the one is afore the other. It seems as if something desperate has happened tae Lady Mairead."

CHAPTER 4 - KAITLYN

I woke up to the sounds of kids squealing down the halls, the thump thump thump of the dog as he barreled along behind them, and slower, Mookie, grunting and snuffling as he walked by, headed the same way. I squiggled over through the bedclothes to where Magnus lay, and kissed his shoulder. "The army is up."

"Aye, from the sound of it, they are battling outside our walls." Then he chuckled. "My army is up as well."

I laughed. "I see what you did there." I climbed off the bed, crossed the room, closed the door, and locked it. I padded back and climbed into the bed, pulling the covers over us both and wrapping the whole glorious length of his cock—

Bang bang bang on the door. Isla's voice, "Mommy! Zach want go get breakfast."

I said, "Good, we're hungry."

Under the door, we could see the shadows of her feet. I looked up at Magnus and he looked down at me, waiting, the feet were still there, then she said, "Zach say no to donuts."

Magnus called to the hallway, "Isla, tell Chef Zach we will be happy with whatever he wants tae serve."

There was a long pause, then finally she said, "But *I* want donuts, Dada."

He sighed. "Ye hae tae listen tae Chef Zach on it, Isla—"

She was quiet then her tiny voice said, "But you *love* donuts, Dada, I want to get you a present."

He chuckled.

I watched his face. "Whatcha going to do, highlander? Your daughter knows you so well."

"Aye, she is a masterful negotiator. I am thinking I want tae hae a proper good morn with m'wife, yet m'daughter is trying tae talk tae me about donuts and how do I get her away from the door—?" He raised his voice, "Tell Chef Zach that now I think on it I would like some donuts."

She squealed, "Yay! Archie! Ben, Zoe! Dada said, 'Yes donuts'!"

Four kids were celebrating outside our door. Isla said, "Come, Da! We hae tae go get donuts. We need you go with us!"

I rested my chin on his chest.

He said, "I think we hae lost our moment, mo reul-iuil, apparently I am now takin' the bairns tae get donuts somewhere in Manhattan."

"Yep, I think we have lost it, and what an adventure for you." I climbed from the bed.

CHAPTER 5 - KAITLYN

I came downstairs as Magnus, Lochinvar, Fraoch, and Zach were headed out with all the bairns to get donuts from a bakery a few blocks down. I poured a cup of coffee and said, "Man, it is nice to have such a big huge kitchen after the tiny lake house."

We were left with a nice companionable quiet over coffee: me, Emma, Hayley, Sophie, James, Beaty, and Quentin, until soon enough the men and kids returned. They spread boxes full of donuts down the counter, the kids stuffed their faces with sugar-sprinkled, frosted, and glazed fried dough, then they ran off to explore the attic.

Magnus, sitting on a stool in front of a box of donuts, said, "As we discovered last night, we need tae mount a rescue." He rubbed his hands together then plucked a glazed donut up.

Hayley, clutching a chocolate donut, said, "Do we have to? I mean, it *is* Lady Mairead."

"Aye, we hae tae save her. I made a promise." Magnus put the glazed donut back.

I helpfully explained, "But it sounds very complicated

because we don't really know what's happened, plus," I whispered, "bloodstain."

Magnus shrugged. "The bloodstain daena complicate it, nae really, tis more of a sign: we must always remember there are dangerous things afoot." He eyed a cake donut with pink frosting and sprinkles. "But we already ken this, there are always dangerous things happenin'. Lady Mairead must be rescued; we are the ones who must do it. Tis simple. We will approach it as if tis the easiest thing in the world."

I chuckled. "Highlander, are you going to tutor me on positive thinking?"

He took a large bite of the donut and with a bit of pink frosting on his upper lip said, "Aye, ye are too negative, mo reuliuil. Ye hae seen me fight in an arena, makin' easy work of m'opponents. Ye hae seen me rule over more than one kingdom as if I were an emperor, tae cross the ocean like an explorer, tae settle myself…" He looked around at everyone. "Cover yer ears."

Everyone chuckled and covered their ears.

Magnus whispered, "Tae settle m'self between yer legs like a conqueror."

Fraoch took his hands down and joked, "Twas all ye meant tae say? We ken ye are married, we hae heard it comin' from yer bedroom."

Everyone laughed.

I said, "Very funny."

Magnus said, "I hae heard all of ye, the castle halls ring with all yer sounds." He took another bite of donut and with his mouth full said, "I am makin' it *all* look verra verra easy, this will be easy as well."

I said, "Banter aside, you really think this rescue is going to be easy?"

"Och aye." He finished the donut, and wiped his hands on a napkin.

Quentin pointed at the frosting on his lip, and Magnus dabbed at his mouth. "Because Agnie is losin'. I hae killed her sons, Fraoch is on my side, she daena hae any connection tae Riaghalbane, she has naething—"

"Nothing except your mom."

Fraoch said, "If ye think on it, Lady Mairead has probably already escaped. Hae ye ever kent her nae tae rescue herself?"

I said, "She almost always does, and she rarely involves us, but then again, this time she asked for our help. She only asks when it's necessary."

Fraoch said, "True, but even so, likely she grew tired of waitin'. I bet she figured out how tae save herself long ago. She is verra good at what she does. I agree with Og Maggy, this will be easy."

Magnus said, "If what she 'does' is survivin' and bein' triumphant on it, and lordin' it over us, then I agree, she is verra good — so here we are, I am usually thinking from a historical point of view: we ought tae take up arms, rush in, and fight, but we canna loop, and we daena ken what awaits us."

Fraoch said, "'Tis likely an army awaits us, if they hae managed tae abscond with Lady Mairead."

Magnus said, "Aye, our enemy is formidable if they hae found and exploited her weakness, and there is the blood stain, which means there is a time-shift afoot. Is Lady Mairead bleedin'? Or is it my," he looked around and whispered, "butler?"

Zach said, "A butler? Weird… Like a butler was injured… when?"

"I daena ken. I daena hae a butler that I ken of, nae here."

Fraoch said, "Och nae, this is disheartenin'."

Magnus took a bite of glazed donut. "So we hae the historic man, fighting, and we hae the modern man, he would… what would he do, Quentin?"

Quentin was eating a powdered donut with cherry filling. He grinned. "I have some modern ideas, but I would love to hear, first, what do *you* think a modern man would do?"

"I imagine ye would start with a list, usin' yer fancy pens, then ye would spend a verra long time putting yer armaments intae boxes tae ship them tae the battle. Then ye would hae tae calculate how much food ye will need—"

"Speaking of!" I pulled out a drawer and retrieved a notepad and pen. "In case something important gets decided." I wrote at the top: Historics vs Moderns

Fraoch said, "I agree with Og Maggy, when I was in the military camp in the New World m'commander told me, 'Ye can hae a bit of bread *after* the battle,' we had tae fight tae earn our food, because a hungry man is a barbaric man. A *modern* man, on the other hand, canna fight without a proper meal."

Magnus said, "Aye, there is hunger that comes with historic battling. But the moderns will pack coolers of food so everyone can eat cake afore they battle. Then it will all be transported tae the battlefield, with maps and plans, and they will *only* fight if twill be easy tae win."

Quentin's eyes went wide. "*Seriously*, that's what you think modern warfare consists of? Holy shit, I have not been doing my job—"

Fraoch tapped his temple. "Perhaps ye hae been doing yer job too well."

"Maybe, but—"

Magnus said, "I am only joking with ye, Colonel Quentin. I was rescued by a helicopter once, swingin' on a rope away from an exploded castle, afore the helicopter was shot down in a field. I ken modern warfare is brutal and horrific."

Quentin said, "It *is* a lot better with a proper meal first, and a slice of cake whenever possible. But what would I do...?" He tapped on the counter for a moment. "I think I would send two men in, just to gather intel, then I would send the military in."

James asked, "Who are the spies? The Historics wouldn't be able to figure out the time, right? To blend? How about me and Quentin?"

I said, "Quentin can't blend, he's black."

Quentin joked, with his mouth full of donut. "Wait, I'm black?"

We all laughed. I said, "And James hasn't ever been to the 1920s before. I have, I have been there multiple times. I think the spies ought to be me and Hayley, we can blend."

Magnus said, "I daena like the idea of it. Ye would jump intae New York on yer own?"

Quentin said, "James and I will jump first and be there to greet them. I think with four of us, and the mission being to spy, to not interfere — it might be safe enough." Quentin turned to Magnus. "So Boss, you cool with the modern plan so far? We send Kaitlyn and Hayley first, then you go in and rescue Lady Mairead."

Fraoch said, "I will go with Og Maggy."

James said, "Are you sure? She's your... um... it might be a conflict of interest."

Fraoch groaned. "She might hae given birth tae me but she is a vile person and a direct enemy of m'family. I will always take Magnus's side, even Lady Mairead's side against Agnie MacLeod. I will go with Og Maggy."

Quentin said, "Good, the Moderns have decided. Once we've collected the intelligence, then we send Fraoch and Magnus and...?"

We turned to Lochinvar. His mouth was full, his hands covered in powdered sugar. He said, "What...?" and blew a puff of sugar from his mouth.

Fraoch said, "We are plannin' a battle operation, Og Lochie, ye ought tae pay attention."

"It sounded like ye were sendin' the women tae fight..."

Fraoch said, "Nae, we are sendin' Kaitlyn and Hayley tae gather information, then we are sending men tae fight. Dost ye want tae fight with the men or remain behind with the bairns?"

"Go with the men."

Quentin said, "Okay, we will send Magnus and Fraoch once we collect the intelligence, if we need a third it will be Lochie."

Fraoch said, "We always need a third, though Lochie is like a half since he daena ken anything about the modern world."

"I ken enough."

"What's that silver square thing on the table beside yer hand?"

Lochie picked it up and looked at it, flapping the tissue paper sticking up from the top. "I daena ken."

"Tis a tissue box, ye see..." Fraoch reached over and yanked a tissue from the hole in the top. "Ye use it tae wipe yer nose." He tossed it ontae Lochie's lap. "Ye are a half, tis just the way tis."

Magnus said, "This will be easy, the modern way — we hae a plan, we winna leave anything up tae chance. We will be well-armed."

Quentin said, "I like the idea of not leaving anything up to chance."

James said, "I like the idea of being well-armed."

"Kaitlyn and Hayley will spy on the guests, take photos, check the layout of the museum — it is a museum, right?"

Emma said, "Yes, I looked it up. It's on 57th Street and Fifth Avenue."

Magnus said, "Then Fraoch and I will rescue Lady Mairead."

Quentin nodded. "The important part: none of us will be looping, our skill sets will be utilized."

Lochinvar said, "And what do ye want me tae do?"

Magnus said, "For right now, naething, ye will wait with Fraoch and me for the—"

"I daena want tae wait. I am from the past, I am good with a sword and I—"

Magnus said, "Listen tae me, Lochinvar, ye are good with a sword, but this might nae need a sword. I ken it is in the past, but tis nae as far in the past as ye are used tae, there is a gulf of manners that ye daena understand. Besides, ye ought tae ken ye are tae do as I tell ye tae do."

"Fine." Lochinvar pulled the donut box close, grasped one, sullenly took a big bite, puffing powdered sugar everywhere. "Fine, but I winna like it."

Magnus shrugged. "It inna on ye tae like it, I am the boss of it. We just hae tae handle this one thing afore we can go tae Florida."

Quentin said, "I've never known you to be so positive, Magnus, what's up?"

"I hae been positive before — I am positive that we are going tae win. I was positive that I was going tae be king. I am positive all the time."

Quentin said, "Sure, but this sounds different, as if you're being positive about something to *make* it happen, not because you're confident, but because you lack confidence. It's got a modern twist."

Emma said, "Wishful thinking."

Quentin pointed at Emma. "Exactly."

Magnus shrugged. "Well, there are some good things about modern thinking, ye canna forget tae do medieval plottin' though—"

I said, "Man, I love your historical jokes, highlander."

Fraoch grinned. "Ye hae tae make yer battle plans, but if ye can also think positively about the outcome—"

Lochinvar said, "Especially when there are women around, ye hae tae convince them twill be safe or else they will wail and moan about it."

I said, "Lochie! That is outrageous!" I waggled my finger between me and Hayley. "We are going into battle first, there is no wailing!"

Magnus said, "Ignorin' Lochinvar, what we are sayin' is we need to apply some historical *and* modern ideas tae our plannin'."

Fraoch eyed a bear claw pastry, turning it around, admiring it. "There are a great many modern things I like — I really like the do-over button, daena I, m'bhean ghlan?"

Hayley said, "You do, you're begging me for a do-over all the time."

Magnus said, "I like a do-over as well. Tis a little like askin' God for forgiveness, yet tis verra modern. Historically, if men made a mistake, the bears would come and eat their family. Now we hae tae only ask for a do-over and twill likely be better."

James said, "If your family has been eaten by bears, who's giving you the do-over?"

We laughed.

Lochinvar said, "What exactly is a do-over?"

Magnus said, "For instance, ye insulted all the women in the room a moment ago, a do-over would be when ye apologize tae them and they accept it and tell ye they will forget ye said something so stupid."

Lochinvar groaned. "I hae tae apologize? Och nae, I daena like tae, tis a sign of weakness."

Magnus said, "Nae it inna, Lochinvar, ye arna thinking on it right, ye are a young man, prone tae doin' stupid things. Doin' stupid things makes ye look weak. But if ye acknowledge it and apologize ye winna seem weak, ye will sound strong."

Lochie scowled. "I daena get how that works."

Fraoch said, "It works like this: Ye canna care if apologizing is weakness. Ye daena care about it, because ye are too strong tae care. Ye say ye're sorry, because ye are strong and wise and ye ken it daena change ye tae be wrong sometimes. Ye hae wronged someone, ye admit it, and in doin' so ye are seen tae hae strength. Do-over magic. I hae grown verra strong over the years."

Hayley said, "That you have, my love. Me, too."

Magnus said, "Tae apologize tae someone shews yer strength."

Fraoch said, "If they deserve it. If they daena deserve it, ye ought nae. Instead ye ought tae... what...?"

Lochinvar answered, "Kick their arse with... nae with swords, tis not a good idea in Maine or New York, I would kick their arse with my fists and m'boots."

Fraoch said, "Aye, like a civilized man."

CHAPTER 6 - KAITLYN

I went up to our bedroom to begin preparing for my jump.

Magnus was brushing his teeth at the sink. I was taking a long luxurious shower. "I am using all the shampoo and sweet-smelling soaps because who knows when I will get another, I doubt the whole of New York in 1929 has this much hot water."

"It daena matter, ye are nae going tae be there long enough tae worry on it."

"Right." I ran water through my hair and then poured some conditioner in my palm and began working it through the strands.

I said, "Just for the record, downstairs you said something... you *conquered* me?"

"When did I say I conquered ye?"

"You said you settled yourself between my legs like a conqueror."

He took the brush from his mouth and spit in the sink. "Och aye, tis true, I conquered ye so hard, just last night, I conquered ye until ye quivered. Ye ken, I am amazing."

I took the shower wand down from the wall and held it

above my head and rinsed my hair. "I will need to build my fortifications so you don't think I am so easily conquered."

His eyes went wide. He rubbed away some of the steam on the glass so he could see into the shower. "How would that work, mo reul-iuil? Ye would tell me 'nae'?"

"Yes, I would tell you 'nae'."

He looked wary. "Ye wouldna, right? Nae, ye wouldna, ye are incapable of sayin' it tae me, I hae kent ye for many long years, ye are powerless. I conquered ye long ago, as ye ken."

I turned off the water and put my hand through the door. He passed me a towel. "I know you conquered me long ago and I never ever, or at least *rarely* say no, but I can, I just don't do it very often, but I can, I can if I want to."

He chuckled.

I stepped from the shower. "What do you mean by that laugh? You don't think I can say 'nae'?"

"Never, I think if I settle my mouth on yer throat, right here, near yer jaw, nestled there, and if I exhale through m'nose right against yer ear... and then if my finger trails right up yer stomach tae yer... ye winna be able to resist me." He did indeed get very close and trailed a finger up my skin.

"Oh my god, Magnus, is that how easy you think I am? That's all it takes? One finger...?"

I tilted my head back to receive his kiss on my throat.

He laughed, his mouth near my ear. "It takes much less than that, mo reul-iuil, the finger trailin' is for me, for ye all it takes is the breath against yer ear. Next moment ye are pullin' up m'kilt."

I laughed and dropped my towel.

He chuckled again. "All I hae tae do is see ye, want ye, approach, breathe against yer ear, and... I barely hae tae lift a finger."

"Ha! Well, *fine*, I might be that easy, but the truth is, in that scenario, I am just sitting there, minding my own business, and *you* saw me, *you* came over, and *you* seduced me with a breath —

guess what I had to do? Literally nothing. You want me from across the room, so who is conquered?"

He said, "When ye put it that way, it must be me."

CHAPTER 7 - KAITLYN

Quentin and James collected gear and weapons. They were going to a day before Hayley and me.

We found a jaunty Roaring Twenties suit that fit James, but we only had one, so Quentin was going to wear modern clothes and try to stay out of sight. As he packed, Quentin grumbled, "When we came up with this plan, I didn't think about the waiting. I've been on vacation, sitting around for days, literal days. Now our rescue mission involves more sitting around? Great. The only cool part about this mission is I have weapons."

James said, "You also have me. Aren't I enough? My job is to keep you from getting bored and to keep you company. Believe me, no one wants a bored Quentin, especially a bored Quentin with weapons."

Quentin laughed.

"I'm carrying weapons too, in case I need to put your ass down—" He glanced at Beaty, whose face had gone white as a ghost. "M'apologies Beaty, I was just joking. I'm going as Quentin's buddy, I will bring him back safe."

She gulped. "Tis verra hard on me, Master James, that

m'husband must hae dangerous work tae feel comfortable, tis verra tryin'."

James said, "Well, shit, now I am so sorry, I feel about three inches tall."

Beaty laughed. "Twas my turn tae joke, Master James. I fell in love with Quennie when he was the only black man in a castle full of Campbells and he was the bravest and strongest of them all. Now he has risen in the ranks of King Magnus's army and has kept our whole family safe for many years. I am verra proud of his nature. I ken I made him take a vacation and it almost killed him, believe me, I hae learned a lesson."

We laughed.

CHAPTER 8 - KAITLYN

*O*ur plan seemed well-laid: Hayley and I were going to a party. We had memorized maps and scrutinized schematics of the museum, but we also knew nothing was ever well-laid when time travel was involved.

That was literally the one thing I knew. The other thing we knew? We would need dresses.

Hayley and I went up four flights of wood stairs with an ornately carved banister and then down to the end of the hall and up a small creaking stair to the attic and immediately tripped over an overturned box of board games. "Great, the children wreaked havoc up here already."

I scooped up the games and returned them back to the box while Hayley wandered down to the end where racks stood. "So many clothes!"

There was dim light streaming from a window at the end, but I found a switch and turned on a bright overhead light to see.

It was like traveling through time: Lady Mairead had a large collection of fashion from every time period, including from the future kingdom of Riaghalbane. Much of the collection hung in dress-bags. The front of each dress-bag had a tag that listed the year and if applicable, the designer.

"What are we thinking, Hayley — anything from 1920 to 1929?" I flipped a few dresses and found one with a tag that read: 1925, Vionnet.

I pulled the dress-bag from the rack, laid it across the top, unzipped the length of it, and pulled the dress from it. "Wow, this is a gorgeous pale green, such a pretty fabric, and the beading is beautiful."

"If you get a mark on it, Lady Mairead will kill you."

"She always wants to kill me, I will do my best not to give her any more of a reason. Do you think it will fit?"

I held the dress in front of myself in front of the long floor to ceiling mirror that leaned against the high point of the roof. "It might fit, she's smaller, but the way it drapes... it might work."

I pulled my t-shirt off over my head and stepped out of my jeans, leaving them in a pile on the rug. I pulled the dress over my head, the weight of the beading drawing it down... but then it stuck. "Uh oh, it's tight right here, I don't think I can zip it."

"The pale green color looks great on you, matches your eyes." Hayley tried to pull up the zipper. "Squeeze. Suck in your tummy," she jiggled it, "just do it — no... more..." She sighed, "You can't suck in two inches, it's impossible."

"Darn it, I don't want to tear it."

Hayley stood back and looked me over. "But, it's down there on the side and you literally can't tell. What if you wore a wrappy thing? You know, one of those thingies that drapes."

She flipped through the rack and pulled out a garment bag that said, 'fur stole' on the tag. "I doubt this is fake fur, so maybe don't flaunt it until we're in the 1920s when they won't care." She pulled it from the hanger and wrapped it around my shoulders, then tugged it lower.

She stepped back to see. "If you hold your arm to your side, like this, you can't tell the side is open. What if we pinned it too, with some safety pins?"

"She will *really* kill me."

"Not if you save her life first."

"Are you sure about that? Her murderous rage might be stronger than any sense of honor."

CHAPTER 9 - KAITLYN

*W*e waited until dusk and then Magnus and Fraoch walked us to a jump-spot in Central Park. I had already said goodbye to the kids, who were untroubled, because I was going to be back the very next day. Barely enough time to miss me.

I hugged Magnus goodbye.

He said, "Daena be a hero, mo reul-iuil. Ye are tae blend intae the room. Ye and Hayley will witness the events and take photos, if ye can speak tae Lady Mairead ask her what she needs, and please, leave if there is any trouble."

"I know, I'll be careful. I have my phone in my handbag, I'm dressed for the part, under this sweltering coat—"

"It might be verra cold, tis November in New York. Tell Colonel Quentin we said hello from our warm house in the twenty-first century."

"Ha! He'll love it."

We hugged goodbye and then climbed to the top of a giant jutting rock, hidden from most of the park by a clump of trees. We were able to see the backs of Magnus and Fraoch as they hiked a safe distance away.

Hayley grabbed my forearms. "Are we doing this?"

"Yep, we ought to do it before I talk myself out of it."

I twisted the vessel and we jumped.

I woke up with Quentin smiling down on us. "Thank *god* you got here."

"Why? Something going on?" I groaned and rubbed my temples. "And can you talk more quietly? My toes are still screaming and my head hurts from your shrieking."

I quickly added, "No… wait, why?"

"Because James is fucking annoying!"

Hayley mumbled, "Where are we? These big ass trees do not look like Manhattan."

"We're in the deep recesses of the darkest forest. I snuck out to the road, Elmwood is down there, a row of fancy mansions, a bunch of old-as-shit cars, people wearing vintage clothes."

Hayley and I sat up. "It's cold."

"Yep, and the rations are working my nerves — what did Magnus have for lunch?"

"You don't want to know. It was good, but he wants to brag about it himself." I added, "…And don't be too hard on him, he was a long time in the past."

"I know, I know, he's too thin."

He helped us up to our feet. "I think the party is going to start soon, we've got some distance to cover."

We hiked for a while and then at the edge of the park, under a streetlamp, I fixed Hayley's hair and she fixed mine. We changed from our heavy modern coats into fur wraps and applied lipstick and walked along the park path. Hayley stepped in a mud puddle. "Dammit, Lady Mairead is going to kill me, these shoes were… Katie, don't let Lady Mairead kill me."

"We're going to rescue her, I was wrong earlier, she will be grateful. She won't kill you."

Quentin cleared his throat. "You are not rescuing, you are the spies, gathering intel for the rescue. Just discreetly take photos. Don't screw this up, *please*. Don't be a hero. I've got too much melanin to walk into that museum. Don't make me have to do it."

As we made it to the road, he passed us walkie-talkie necklaces he had found on Amazon. "James and I will be able to listen in, but we can't communicate with you. You're on your own. I'll be nearby though, James will be right outside the museum, let us know if there is any trouble."

I said, "Sounds good, we got this, right, Hayley?"

Hayley nodded.

I said, "What's our code for trouble?"

Quentin said, "Magnus uses 'Ice cream sucks'. He thinks it's hilarious."

I said, "Perfect."

Quentin split off from our group.

We began to walk, but almost immediately Hayley said, "I know we are only going a few blocks, but my shoes are awful, can we ride?"

James said, "Nope it's not in the—"

She put up an arm to hail a car, and a yellow and black old-timey taxi slid up to the curb.

James said, "Great — you've already gone rogue."

Hayley said, "Look at our shoes, James, just look at them, this is necessary."

The driver jumped out and helped Hayley and I into the very tight backseat.

James took one look and said, "Yeah, no... I'll jog and meet you there." He tapped the side of the taxi and took off at a brisk walk.

Hayley and I were practically on top of each other, cramped in. It smelled a little bit old and leathery and a lot like body odor. She dug in the seats. "Seatbelts? What the heck, no seatbelts?"

I gripped the handle as the driver pulled us away from the curb and then we were jostling, bouncing, and careening down the city streets, swerving around horse-drawn carriages, pull carts, weird bicycles, and pedestrians crossing wherever the hell they wanted.

Ten minutes later on the other end of the park, we jerked to a standstill in front of the building that housed the new collection of the Museum of Modern Art. I tossed the driver a coin from a stash I had found in Lady Mairead's things, and Hayley and I were let out on the sidewalk out front. We adjusted our wraps and checked each other for hair out of place and makeup gone awry.

James strolled up. "Eventful?"

Hayley said, "We almost died."

I scanned the crowd, people climbing from cars, wearing finery, hoping we blended in — we did, sort of, though our hair was not quite right, too long, not 'done' enough. "We need to get off the street, what if Lady Mairead drives up?"

James went to the side of the building where he would have a view. Hayley and I walked up the grand steps toward the building and inside.

CHAPTER 10 - KAITLYN

*J*t was a big imposing museum structure, an entry with a crowd milling around the foyer. I scanned for the exits, which were right where we had expected. Hayley nodded.

This is going to work.

Lilting notes from a band met our ears, we followed the music out to the sculpture garden. My eyes swept the crowd, but saw no sign of Lady Mairead.

Hayley said, "You stand over there, I'll stand over here."

I pushed through the crowd to stand half-hidden, as discreetly as possible, near a potted palm tree. A waiter carrying a tray of drinks walked by and I thought, "Maybe one," and pulled a cup off the tray.

I took a sip. *What the heck, punch?* A moment later, Hayley's voice emitted from the tiny walkie-talkie strung on a cord, tucked into the top of my dress. "...a drink? Aren't we on a mission?"

I ducked my head to talk into the radio. "I'm a spy, like James Bond, I wanted a drink, but guess what? It's non-alcoholic — stupid Prohibition."

My eyes swept the room as I sipped idly from my cup, then I met Hayley's eyes. She jerked her head to the door.

Lady Mairead, dressed beautifully, entered on the arm of a very handsome younger man.

Hayley turned to hide her face.

I stepped into the shadows behind the palm, put my glass down on a nearby table, fished my phone from my bag and took secretive photos of the room, the entrances, the crowd, and especially of Lady Mairead — where she was standing.

My radio-necklace beeped.

I glanced up, Hayley was gesturing with her head and pointing with her finger.

There was Agnie MacLeod... I recognized her from the restaurant in Los Angeles. She was a bit younger than Lady Mairead, dark-haired, pretty, pretentious-looking, and wearing an outfit that did not fit in. She looked like she was walking a fashion runway in the 1970s, and because her clothes were all wrong, she was the center of attention.

She was ignoring Lady Mairead, while also heading straight toward her. *Bitch.*

Lady Mairead leveled her eyes on Agnie, and the color left her cheeks.

I took photos but then Agnie looked directly at me. *Shit, did she see me?* I stepped back into my hiding place, bumping against a man who had approached. "Madame, I couldn't help but notice—"

"Shhh." I stuffed my phone in my purse.

The walkie-talkie squawked. I clamped my arm across my chest, trying to keep it quiet.

He was a foot shorter than me, balding, a slicked comb-over. "Your dress made a sound, Madame...?"

"Shhh, please, just shhhhh..." There was a crowd between me and Lady Mairead.... I stood on tiptoes, craning to see — yes, Agnie had sidled up to Lady Mairead.

I could see the side of her face, Lady Mairead looked upset.

I glanced around for Hayley but she wasn't at her station.

Great.

I brushed past the man. "My apologies, I have something to…" and skirted the sculpture garden, sticking to the shadows, trying to get a better view.

Lady Mairead had about four men encircling her, it looked as if she was writing something… I crept a little closer hoping to hear where they were taking her, getting very close, hiding behind yet another potted palm tree. I heard Agnie say, "Now ye have signed the letter…"

Lady Mairead said, "Ye promise that ye winna use yer detonations — do ye promise the art is safe?"

The twittering laugh of Agnie, mocking Lady Mairead. "The art being destroyed is the *least* of your worries."

"That is the most of them! Tae destroy these paintings is tae destroy the meaning of history in the world!"

Agnie laughed with the surrounding men. "So overdramatic! I knew ye would sign anything, would promise anything, with your precious artwork in the balance." She tapped an envelope against her hand as if she were thinking about something.

Then she said, loudly, "Did ye get that, Kaitlyn Campbell, eavesdropping incompetently behind the bush?"

"Oh, um…" For a half second I thought, *hide more?* But no, that would look idiotic. I decided to go for haughty condescension as I stepped from around the tree. "Agnie." I nodded. "I see you are being a bitch yet *again*."

She asked, "I will ask once more, did ye hear all of that, Kaitlyn?"

"I heard that you threatened my mother-in-law with some kind of explosives around her art, at her party, which makes you cruel."

"Says the woman whose husband has murdered my sons in cold blood."

"Ha! Cold blood. They were attempting to kill my husband, for centuries they tried — shows *their* incompetence that they couldn't manage it."

She asked, "How's Fraoch?"

I said, "You know what, I am not a fan of you or your bull-shit, Fraoch is fine, he's excellent by the way."

"Tell him I said hello."

"Nah lady, I'm not going to fuck with Fraoch's head, he's too sweet to have you messing with him."

She exhaled. "I have won, Kaitlyn, I have explosives set throughout this party, see that man with the wire from his ear? He's with me, he's rigged this whole place. See the men near the columns? They are also working for me. This is my first step. I destroy Lady Mairead, then I destroy your whole family."

"You seem in a talkative mood, make it make sense for me."

She opened her eyes wide. "I heard ye were dim, Kaitlyn, but this is really too much."

I narrowed my eyes. "Magnus can barge through the door right now, he can barge through the door ten minutes ago. All he has to do is kill you."

"Eh, unlikely, because he winna be able tae kill all the men who are here."

"I only count ten in this room."

"When ye report back tae yer husband ye tell him that when he comes the whole place crumbles down around him. You tell him that from the moment Lady Mairead set eyes on me until now, there will not be enough time for him to set up a defense. The game is lost."

"You have to know that Magnus will never let you get away with this."

"I daena care."

"Of course not, you're all like, 'Whatever, I'm going to destroy the world, I am an agent of chaos,' as if you're a villain who learned how to be evil from Tumblr in the early 2000s."

Agnie directed, "See that painting?"

Lady Mairead put her hand to her throat. "The Van Gogh?"

Agnie smiled. "Aye, watch this." She pushed a button and an ink-black liquid poured down the front, a river with tributaries fanning out, completely obscuring it.

Lady Mairead screeched and fell on Agnie clutching her jacket, begging her, "Please stop!"

I said, "Holy shit, Agnie, that's pure evil."

A furor had gone up and a crowd formed around the painting. Agnie whispered, "Stand straight and stop begging, Mairead, ye are embarrassing yourself."

Lady Mairead straightened up and smoothed down the front of her dress. "Aye, of course, I understand. Please, Agnie, daena destroy any more paintings, *please.*"

Agnie held up the button again. "I said, stop begging!"

Lady Mairead clamped her lips between her teeth. A man sidled up, holding a struggling Hayley. He whispered something in Agnie's ears.

I asked, "And this man, I don't believe we've met?"

Agnie sneered, "This is Ian Campbell."

"Where have I heard that name before?"

Lady Mairead said, "He challenged Magnus. He is a cousin."

"Oh right, Ian the Troublesome. Agnie, I have to say, you keep shit company." Hayley shoved his hands away.

I said, "What do you want from us?"

Agnie said, "Nothing from ye, yet. I will destroy Lady Mairead. Then I will take the kingdom, and then I will destroy yer family. I believe I will begin with yer descendants, yer grandchildren perhaps, and work m'way up, so ye can watch."

The man who Lady Mairead had arrived with rushed over. "Lady Mairead, the paintings! There is some dark political work at foot, we need to leave—"

She said, "Cornie, ye must be strong, I hae tae go somewhere for a moment." She patted him affectionately on the cheek.

Agnie said, "This verra handsome man is with ye, Lady Mairead? Verra interesting. Does General, what is his name — General Hammond? Does *he* know of your young man?"

Agnie jerked her head and two henchmen grabbed a struggling Cornie by the arms and dragged him away.

Lady Mairead's face went even more pale. "Where are ye

taking him? He is important tae history, ye canna harm him, he…"

Agnie brushed that away. "Did ye hear what I said about your mother-in-law's descendants, Kaitlyn? They happen tae be your descendants as well, and Lady Mairead winna be able tae help you. It will be very entertaining tae destroy the Campbells by cutting off the head of the hydra and then one-by-one slicing off the tentacles, the children."

I said, "That's the stupidest plan in the world, if you cut off the head of the hydra, new heads come — the tentacles, what the hell are you talking about?" I looked at my mother-in-law, "You were right, she is an imbecile."

Agnie scowled. "I am talking about destroying your family! Your husband won't forsake his mother — tell Magnus he's next."

Lady Mairead raised her chin. "Ye are ridiculous, your black heart has made ye wretched and a–"

"Ye hae always wanted what is mine."

"Ye stand there in yer out-of-time Gucci scarf, destroying a painting, inside the Museum of Modern Art, great art! Important art! At my party! I have been first in *everything*! Ye are trying tae take it from me, but ye winna win. I am stopping ye if it is the last thing I do!"

Agnie put her finger on the button once more. "It seems as if I am the one winning, Lady Mairead."

"Ye are the most ridiculous woman! From throwin' yerself at Donnan, tae this bullshit, I canna *believe* ye expect anyone tae take ye seriously, least nae me. I am unlikely tae think ye serious, as ye are too far beneath m'consideration."

"Frankly I am tired of speakin' on it. Ye lose another piece of art." Agnie pushed a button. "They must be careful dealing with this one, acid burns."

I swept my eyes around the museum, looking for the — a painting on the far wall, clear liquid rolling down the surface, the paint smearing, dripping, and sliding down.

Lady Mairead clamped her hands over her mouth. "Tis the Cezanne! Nae!"

"Be quiet then, I want naething but silence."

Lady Mairead clamped her lips between her teeth but couldn't draw her eyes from the disintegrating canvas.

Agnie watched her with a smile. "I am sick and tired of all of this, I'm going to destroy another painting." She pushed the button once again.

Lady Mairead shrieked, her face a pallor, her body weaving, weakly she said, "Which one, which one was it?"

"It does not matter, except that it's gone, no one will ever even remember it, except you. All this art, all these historical events, all these people, we will take them from you, one by one." She held up her remote control, pushed another button, and there was a flash of light and a small bang. Smoke rose from a large painting near the back wall.

Lady Mairead screamed, "Nae! Twas one of Pablo's!" She collapsed against one of the guards. "Nae! Not Pablo's!"

Agnie rolled her eyes. "Och nae, Lady Mairead, are ye upset? Ye seem verra stressed out."

She and the man named Ian laughed.

I whispered, "What is it you want to stop doing this?"

Agnie said, "Nothing really, I am going to destroy all these paintings out of sheer malice."

Lady Mairead clung to my sleeve. "Daena press her, Kaitlyn! We must protect the art!"

I put up my hands. "You're right, I'm not here to interfere. Come on Hayley, if our being here is causing the art to be destroyed and it's causing Lady Mairead distress, then I will not be a part of it." I took a step back. "Please don't destroy any more paintings."

Agnie grinned. "Now I have Lady Mairead and Kaitlyn both begging me for the art. Hmm, what should I do...?"

Ian the Troublesome said, "Ye ought tae feckin' destroy it all."

She laughed and pushed another button on the remote. There was a loud bang, like a small explosion — rubble sprayed around, and one of the sculptures tipped forward rocking, rumbling, and then dumping over on its side, broken in half.

Lady Mairead shrieked, but she wasn't the only one, people rushed the doors. The police pushed us toward the walls.

Agnie said, "That was perfect, my demolition man is so good, isn't he Ian?"

Lady Mairead said, "What do ye want me tae do?!"

Agnie said, "I want ye tae come with us, it's verra verra simple."

Lady Mairead's hands shook. "Fine, yes, I understand."

Agnie turned to me, "Kaitlyn, tell your husband that Lady Mairead is just the first of many."

She led Lady Mairead down the hall, accompanied by that asshole, Ian.

Hayley and I watched them go. "What the hell just happened?"

"Lady Mairead was just taken by, and I do not say this lightly, the biggest bitch in the world, and we don't know where or how or when she is going, which means we didn't learn the most important things."

"And no do-over."

"Nope, next time it's Magnus's turn."

We followed the crowd into the large foyer and got in line. The police were searching through bags on the way out. Hayley and I slowly proceeded through the queue.

I whispered, "Do you have any paperwork, proving anything about yourself?"

"No, do you?"

"Nothing."

She whispered, "How do you think they got through this security checkpoint? Where did they take Lady Mairead?"

"I have no idea, but I have a phone in my bag."

She said, "And I'm packing."

We both tucked our walkie-talkie necklaces deeper into our dresses. I created a screen while she pulled up the front of her dress and shoved her gun into the front of her underpants. "Oh man, they are drooping with the weight."

She screened me while I stuffed my phone into my underwear. "Cold cold cold."

"Did you get photos?"

"Yeah, yeah I did. I hope it helps."

We made it to the front doors where the police patted down our shoulders gently, then said, apologetically, "Sorry ma'am,"

We both looked haughty.

They checked our bags, mine in particular because of my yellow plastic Burt's Bees lip balm with a bright red cap.

The officer scrutinized it, sniffed it, and showed it to another man who took the lid off.

I explained, "It's lip color, for ladies."

"Oh, sorry ma'am, we've just seen unexplainable things here tonight, we cannot be too safe."

"True." He dropped the lip balm back in my bag, and told us we were free to go.

CHAPTER 11 - KAITLYN

On the front steps we overheard a man say, "That was a freak storm. It was over before it barely started." A crowd was watching the sky over the back of the museum.

James and Quentin rushed up. James said, "I was listening on the radio, you weren't supposed to make contact, that was so much contact!"

Quentin directed us across the street away from the museum. "What happened to 'Ice cream sucks'? Basically, that whole 'discreetly taking photos' thing, gathering intelligence — that was just thrown out the window? What the hell, Katie, you were talking to her!"

"I know! She saw me, there was nothing I could do! She pulled me into conversation, and now she's taken Lady Mairead. Damn. And I couldn't use the code word because there was nothing you could have done either, I hate to say it Quentin, but that there," I waved my hand toward the museum, "is a *mess*."

We walked briskly down the block until we came to Elmwood and stood looking up at the mansion.

Hayley said, "So after leaving the museum, Lady Mairead will put the letter in the safe asking for Magnus to come?"

"I mean yes, she did, but we are here now, we might have changed the course of events."

We crossed the road and walked down to Central Park.

I said, "The good news is we have photographic evidence, the bad news: I'm not sure what Magnus will be able to do. She said she wants to destroy us... She took Lady Mairead, I don't know where... did I mention it's a mess?"

Quentin said, "Yep, you mentioned it."

All four of us jumped back to present-day Central Park, and once I was able to move and speak, I realized Magnus was holding my hand.

"I am verra relieved ye are back."

"Were you worried?" I mumbled.

"Aye, it made sense when we planned it, but once implemented I thought it might be a mistake. Did ye get us information?"

"A lot of information: photos, direct dialogue, the villain laid out her plan, we ought to have enough, but... my love, it was *also* a big mistake, this is far more complicated than you thought."

"Let us brush ye off and go speak on it."

We traipsed down the hill from the woods and across the wide grassy fields to the park gates. I held onto Magnus's arm and dragged my feet. "How come whenever we wake up from jumping we have to walk a long long way?"

James joked, "Do you really want an answer or are you just bitching? Because we are walking a long distance and I don't have the strength to answer."

"Just bitching."

Then, exhausted, we climbed the steps to the house, and my kids came running from all directions to see us.

I was deposited on the couch with a glass of go-go juice to replenish my vitamins.

Magnus sat across from me. "Tell me what happened?"

I pulled my phone from my bag and passed it to him. He said, "Remind me yer code?"

My head on the back of the couch, I said, "So modern of you to even *know* there's a code. Our wedding date: seven, two, twenty-seventeen."

He typed for a second then sniffed the phone. "Yer phone smells like yer..."

My eyes went wide. "Magnus! I'll have you know, like a *spy*, I had to smuggle the intel out in my underwear."

His brow went up.

I said, "Just be aware if you take weapons or phones or anything into the museum you'll possibly be frisked and—"

Magnus laughed, "I will hae tae put them in m'underwear?"

"Exactly, it's a thing — a thing *spies* do."

"Nae if they are properly wearin' a kilt." He sniffed again and grinned. "I think I will need tae carry yer phone with me for the photos — its prior proximity tae yer gardens will be all I will think about."

Hayley laughed.

I said, "We have a great many *other* things to think about."

"I winna use it as a distraction, mo reul-iuil, but as a focus, I promise." He added, "So this is a photo of the grounds, and there is...?"

He turned the phone so I could explain. "That blurry person in the top corner is Agnie."

He nodded and scrolled through photos. "Did ye see Lady Mairead?"

"Yes, we talked to her, and saw her taken away, we even, I hate to say it, spoke to Agnie."

"Och nae, ye could hae been killed."

"She wasn't really interested in me and Hayley, not right now. I got the distinct impression she just wanted to make Lady Mairead fucking crazy. Do you agree, Hayley?"

Hayley was curled up under Fraoch's arm. "Yep, she destroyed paintings and a sculpture, she seemed to delight in making Lady Mairead miserable. Then she took her away."

I said, "She said to tell you that you're next, Magnus, and that she wants to destroy our whole family."

Fraoch asked, "Och nae, she is malevolent, did ye discover where she took Lady Mairead?"

I shook my head. "No, I didn't."

Hayley said, "She had that dude with her, what was his name... Ian?"

Magnus said, "Ian... m'cousin, Ian? Shews she is losin' that she had tae make an alliance with Ian the Troublesome, the *last* person I intended tae accept a challenge from — he has the least claim tae the throne, the least ability, and the least strength. They *canna* be serious."

"Well, he's her henchman now."

"Did she hae guards with her?"

I looked at him seriously, "At least ten men. Probably more. You can't just waltz in there, they'll have you in shackles in a second."

He brushed off his knee. "Twill be fine, we will go get Lady Mairead, I will be safe. James and Quentin will remain here tae guard the house while we are gone."

Next thing I knew, Magnus and Fraoch and Lochinvar were suiting up to go to the year 1929. We put them in dark pants and white shirts. We found one black tuxedo jacket that fit Lochinvar.

Quentin instructed them on the layout of the park and any issues they might come across. He gave them weapons and some camping gear.

Magnus said, "I will see ye on the morrow, mo reul-iuil." He kissed me goodbye and Quentin escorted them to Central Park to jump.

CHAPTER 12 - MAGNUS

*W*e landed in the twentieth-century without a greetin' party so I needed tae rise quickly. I was first up, guarding, until Lochinvar and Fraoch arose. Twas two days afore the party

Lochinvar muttered. "M'skin is blazin' in pain, m'bones are achin', why does it hurt so badly?"

Fraoch groaned. "The machines are makin' us miserable so we daena do it every day and complicate the world."

We sat with our backs against a boulder, hidden behind a stand of trees, but with a wondrous view of the city. The buildings stretching out before us on a grid. I said, "Tis much smaller than in the twenty-first century."

Fraoch said, "Aye. It looks wee in comparison."

Lochinvar said, his eyes sweeping over the city, "This is excitin'."

Fraoch looked around the woods. "Really, ye think so?"

"Aye, look at the view! There are buildings everywhere, built by men, how did they do it? We can only guess. And we hae food, we just open packages and there it is, how does it get inside the package? Nae one kens. Next, we are going tae battle in a museum, tis verra excitin' — what is a museum?"

I laughed. "A museum is a large building full of art and antiquities. Dost ye ken what an antiquity is?"

"Nae."

Fraoch said, "We are an antiquity, something from the olden days."

I said, "Aye, but usually tis swords or armor, perhaps a pot or a mug from a long time ago. The mug ye used when ye lived at Dunscaith might be sitting in a museum right now, Lochinvar. There might be Moderns filin' past tae see it, sayin', 'Och, look, there is a mug once drunk from by the young Lochinvar—'"

Lochinvar said, "He was a valiant warrior, he never lost a battle."

I smiled. "Aye, the story might go that way, Lochie, it might. But also, the museum holds art, tis verra important tae my mother, Lady Mairead. She collects it."

"Art, such as paintings or sculptures?"

"Aye, ye ken, in the history of the world art becomes near priceless. I once met a man by the name of Pablo, och he was an insufferably numptin' bunghole. He spoke French." I spit on the ground beside us. "He was beddin' Lady Mairead and she was payin' for his food and drink and he was naething but... och, an irritating hassle, but he was a painter, and everyone around him pretended as if he was verra good at it, though I dinna see it. Lady Mairead thinks verra highly of him and she is, I believe, willing tae die tae protect his paintings. We hae our work cut out for us, that they are plannin' tae seize her surrounded by art. She inna going tae be happy, and she winna go peacefully. We will hae tae be very careful."

We slept under the tall trees, talking as we fell asleep.

. . .

The first day we did some exploring, a great deal of sitting and talking. We discussed the photos, the lay of the land, the orientation of the buildin', all the possibilities for how the event might transpire.

The next day, preparing tae leave the park for the party, Fraoch asked, "Why do I hae tae guard the back door?"

"Because if ye go inside ye are going tae get yourself kidnapped or killed by the woman who was yer mother. It inna going tae end well for us if that happens."

He said, "Ye afraid I will turn on ye?"

"Never, but imagine what she might make ye do with a properly trained alligator."

Fraoch chuckled. "I haena ever spoken tae her, she is unlikely tae ken a properly trained alligator is m'weakness."

"True, but a wee bit of torture and she'd have it out of ye."

Fraoch said, "Og Lochie, if she catches ye and tortures ye, daena tell her about the alligators or I will rescue ye tae kill ye."

"I daena plan tae get caught. I am going tae go in, take Lady Mairead by the arm and bring her out tae the road where she will be safe. Then, I will return and kill Agnie and this trouble-person."

I asked, "Where am I durin' all this excitement?"

He grinned. "Ye are watching in awe."

I said, "Och, ye hae a fine idea of yerself, Lochinvar. But if Lady Mairead is safe, and Agnie is dead, it will be well-deserved."

Lochinvar brushed off his pants. "Good, then let us get ready tae go."

CHAPTER 13 - MAGNUS

*W*e walked at a fast clip tae the museum.

Fraoch, Lochie and I stood shoulder to shoulder lookin' up. Fraoch said, "The building looks different."

"Aye, twas big and stone, now tis tall and brick, do we hae the right address?"

Fraoch asked the nearest woman, "The Museum is here?"

She said, as she passed us going up tae the door, "Yes, on one of the upper floors."

I said, "This is a weird time twist."

"Aye, and we studied the schematics of the other."

Fraoch waited at the side of the building, while Lochinvar and I strode up tae the main double doors at the front where a police officer began pattin' Lochie down.

I asked the doorman, "Which way tae the sculpture gardens?"

He looked at me oddly. "There are no sculpture gardens, this is the Heckscher Building—"

"The Museum is here? I thought the buildin' would be more grand."

"Yes, the museum is up—"

"Has it always been here?" I looked up and down the block.

The doorman narrowed his eyes. "Yes, and it is new, this is the *opening*. There's a stair, and an elevator, the gallery is on the twelfth floor."

I said, "Och nae, wait..." I turned and jogged down the steps, returnin' tae the curb with Lochinvar joggin' down behind me.

I told Fraoch, "This is a different buildin' than afore. There inna a sculpture garden."

Lochinvar asked, "What does this mean?"

Fraoch said, "It means our intel is useless. Now what is our plan? We are blind, time shifted, our spyin' did naething."

I glanced around as people were beginnin' tae arrive for the party. "I will wait here on the steps waitin' tae intercede... perhaps I can catch Lady Mairead afore she goes in. Fraoch will guard the back as we planned. Lochie, now ye will go inside on yer own. In case the situation gets away from us."

Lochie looked up at the building. "How do ye even get up tae that great a height? There is naething easy about this."

I asked, "Ye ever taken an elevator?"

"Nae."

Fraoch said, "Then ye take the stairs, but daena worry, Og Maggy will stop Lady Mairead afore she goes in." Fraoch passed me a gun before he left to head to the rear of the building.

Lochinvar entered the museum while I waited beside the steps, hidden in the shadows, until finally, Lady Mairead stepped from a car tae the curb.

Twas absolutely easy how it was workin' so far.

I walked straight for her. "Lady Mairead—"

"Magnus! What on *earth* are ye doing here?"

She glanced at the man beside her, "Cornelius, this is Magnus, an um... friend."

I shook hands with Cornelius.

Lady Mairead said, "Cornie, go on up tae the top of the steps so I might speak tae Magnus alone."

As soon as he wandered away, I said, "Ye invited me, Lady Mairead, ye are about tae come upon serious trouble."

She whispered, "This is the party of my lifetime, I hae been building this collection alongside Abby for years! Magnus, what happens?"

"Agnie is laying in wait for ye."

Her hand went tae her throat. "I daena believe ye, this is my own private business, this has naething tae do with the kingdom — how can she...? Nae, this is off limits tae her."

I said, "I daena think this is true, but either way, she is there, inside."

"Well..." She watched the doors. "I see police, they will arrest her before—"

"She is going tae destroy the artwork — it has already happened, she will use the threat of destruction tae take ye."

"She would never!" Her eyes wide. "Are ye looping?"

"No, we are trying to be smart, we sent Kaitlyn first for information, I am here for the rescue of ye. Lochinvar is inside waiting for ye, but now that I hae seen—"

"Who is Lochinvar?"

I looked at her for a moment. Then I put out my hand. "Lady Mairead, give me the book."

"What book?"

"Ye ken what book!"

She pulled a book from her purse.

I yanked it open, and flipped through. It was missing most of the writing. The book I had seen her with was full and this one was barely used. "Is this new? Is this... how much hae ye written? Does this...?"

The main entry said:

Reyes

. . .

But he was many long years and battles ago.

I glanced at her face, she looked young. How old had she looked last I had seen her? She ought tae hae been... "Ye daena ken who Lochinvar is...? Ye are from... ye are from — what year?"

"I just saw ye in Riaghalbane, ye were—"

Behind the building storm clouds rolled up into the air, rising, roiling, lightning arced down, hitting the roof.

I left her side and raced up the stairs, taking them two at a time until I made it tae the top as Lochie shoved out the door, "Run!"

I followed him, racing down the steps, as behind us there was a loud rumbling, the sound of thunder, but also much more, enough tae make the earth shake. At the corner of the steps, a blast detonated from behind, an explosion shovin' me as I dove over a low wall, landing and rolling on the sidewalk, and though I clamped m'hands over m'ears, I lost all sound except for a ringin'.

From the ground I looked back at the building. Crowds were floodin' from the entrance, screaming, people knocking each other over tae get down the steps tae the road, rushin' toward the park. The rumbling continued, smoke billowing from the windows — the noise growin' even louder.

I scrambled up and raced down the street, through stopped traffic tae the far side of the road, where I turned in time tae watch the top three floors of the building crumble down. Fire billowed from the ground floor, the grounds behind the building were full of smoke and screams. I doubled over, out of breath.

Lochinvar raced up, put his hand on my shoulder, his breath coming in puffs. "Och nae, twas frightening!"

"Where is Lady Mairead now?" We scanned the crowds, the injured and the frightened, the cars surrounded by people, the police pushing everyone away. "Do ye see her?"

"Nae."

Fraoch came racing around the side of the building. He was covered in smoke and ash, his face pitch dark, his eyes beady in the middle where he had wiped on his sleeve. "Och nae!"

"That's what Lochie said."

His breath comin' in bursts, he asked, "What... are we... goin'... tae do?"

I shook my head. "We are outmatched and outplayed. We must reconvene and decide what tae do next."

"Do ye think they jumped with Lady Mairead?"

"Aye, they hae her, we haena stopped anything." I shook my head. "I was speakin' tae her, but twas Lady Mairead from years ago, she is... I daena ken…she is loopin' within her life. She was younger, she dinna ken as much about her history. This is a sad state of affairs."

"How do we ken if we are *ever* talking tae the current Lady Mairead?"

"We daena ken."

We stared up at the building as the rumbling continued, a wall from the top floor slidin' down in a large billow of smoke. The crowd screamed, racing away, pushing past us, buffeting us.

Fraoch yelled over the ruckus, "What next?"

I watched the crowd. "We ought tae go tae Elmwood and see if she is taken there."

We marched briskly down the street tae Elmwood, where I knocked and peered through the window, but the building was dark and lifeless as if nae one had been there for a long time.

We watched the house for a time, then headed tae Central Park, walking through the high grass, up the hill and intae the woods. We collected our things and jumped back tae present day.

CHAPTER 14 - KAITLYN

I went with Quentin to wait for Magnus at the park and it was a long wait, which is why, once the storm died down and I could get close enough, I lay down beside Magnus with my arm across his chest and waited for him to wake up.

He sputtered awake a few minutes later and his head rose to look down at me. "Och aye, ye are a fine sight, mo reul-iuil. I hae arrived in one piece?"

"Yes, you did." I squeezed him in a hug. "But Fraoch looks like he was in a coal mine blast, and... you all smell like smoke and... I just needed to be close."

Quentin said, "Did you have better luck, Boss?"

"Nae, I think we had worse."

I said, "Uh oh."

He lugged himself up to sitting, plucked a piece of grass and tossed it away. "I tell ye, Colonel Quentin, twas nae easy—

Lochinvar groaned and threw his arm over his eyes. "Naething about it was easy."

Fraoch hefted himself up. "I question whether the way of the Moderns is the right way tae do anythin' at all."

I frowned. "It was that bad? But we had all the intel. You

knew the layout and the timing, I mean, you didn't get Lady Mairead, I see that, but even worse than that?"

Magnus said, "Aye, we dinna get Lady Mairead, and the museum building is gone. All the art is…"

Fraoch made a pthhhhtp noise.

Magnus nodded. "Aye, all the art is destroyed, and when I say the museum building is gone, I mean the first buildin' was completely gone. The one ye went tae had a large sculpture garden in the back, ye ken? That building wasna there at all, *instead* there was a tall buildin' and the art was up at the—"

Lochinvar said, "The twelfth floor, I ran up all those stairs."

Magnus said, "The second building was exploded."

"Is that why Fraoch is coated in black soot?"

Fraoch said, "Aye, I had tae run through a fire."

Lochinvar said, "Twas nae easy at all, after I ran up, I had tae run back down."

Quentin stood with his hands on his hips. "So that sounds like a disaster. You blame the fact that it was a modern plan? How would the historic alternative have gone?"

Magnus said, "We ought tae hae run in fightin'. I daena ken if it would hae worked but—"

Fraoch said, "It couldna hae been worse."

We loaded up all their gear and began walking across Central Park headed to the hotel, but then Magnus stopped walking. "Where are we goin', Colonel Quentin?"

"To the hotel."

I asked, "Did you forget the way?"

His face drew up in a question. "What hotel, what are ye talking on?"

"The Park Lane hotel." Quentin squinted his eyes. "What are *you* talking about, Boss? Where did you think we were staying?"

"The Elmwood." Magnus gestured north. "Lady Mairead's house. We were there, we..."

Quentin shook my head. "Nah, are we doing this again? There is no safe house, you lost that bet, fair and square."

Magnus looked distressed, Fraoch and Lochie did too.

I said, "When we drove into New York we went there first, but it wasn't there, my love, just a tall glass building. You don't remember that?"

Magnus turned tae Fraoch and Lochie, "Do ye remember the house — Elmwood?"

They both nodded.

Lochie asked, his voice in a whisper, "What is happenin'? The house is gone?"

Magnus asked, "Fraoch, we were there, right? In the house?"

"Aye, m'stuff is still there."

I said, "I *hate* when this happens."

Quentin shook his head. "We rolled up into New York, rolled up to the house, it wasn't there. I danced around because that meant I won our argument. Then we checked into our hotel: The Park Lane. We've been there ever since."

Magnus exhaled. "How did I get the letter from Lady Mairead, the one that started this whole thing?"

Quentin said, "You went to the bank, you said it was in the safe."

Magnus said, "Nae, there has been yet another time shift. I had hoped we were done with them." He looked at me. "Where did ye get the dress ye wore tae the party?" He dropped all his bags, reached in his pocket for my phone and scrolled through for a photo, he turned it around for me, "Where did ye get that dress?"

I shook my head. "I don't know." I scrolled through photos, "Not sure... the whole timeline seems messed up."

Fraoch said, "But everyone is there though, right? Zach, Zoe, Beaty... Hayley, all the people? We arna missing anyone?"

Quentin said, "Everyone is there, we aren't missing anyone but Lady Mairead."

We picked up our bags and packs and walked toward the hotel.

In front of the Park Lane hotel Lochinvar gaped up at the height. "How many floors up are we goin'?"

Quentin said, "We're on the forty-second floor."

The lobby was very grand, and we were a spectacle because all the returning men were stinky and dirty, but especially because Fraoch was covered in a layer of dark coal from the smoke of some distant fire.

Fraoch didn't seem to notice the stares, while Lochie was gaping at the marble and opulent splendor, the flower bouquets, and crystal chandeliers, he said, "Och, ye are goin' tae love the elevator, Og Lochie. This is goin' tae be fun."

"I canna run up the stairs?"

"Tae the forty-second floor? I daena think ye can."

The doors slid open and we crammed in with all our bags.

Lochinvar grasped hold of the railing as if he might be flung out.

Quentin pushed the button, and the elevator rose.

Lochinvar closed his eyes and began to pray.

I tucked my head to Magnus's shoulder. "I'm so glad you're home, it's always so dangerous, but with a time shift it feels like a very close call."

He said, "Aye," as the doors opened on the twenty-seventh floor, but the person there, on seeing all five of us and three of us disgustingly dirty, said, "No thank you."

Lochinvar tried to exit but Fraoch held him back. "We must go higher."

"Och nae." Lochie prayed even more feverishly as the elevator continued to rise.

. . .

We arrived at the forty-second floor and the kids, along with Haggis with his tail wagging, were waiting at the elevator doors. Archie and Isla leapt onto Magnus. Haggis jumped up and down, maniacally.

Quentin led us down the hall to the sitting room of our suite.

CHAPTER 15 - KAITLYN

*F*irst thing James said was, "Damn, boys, that looks like it was an ordeal."

Ben asked, "Did you rescue Lady Mairead, Uncle Magnus?"

Magnus sank onto the couch. "Nae, I dinna, and Ben, I tell ye, I am nae used tae not rescuin' someone when I set m'mind tae doin' it. I am disappointed."

Ben said, "That sucks."

Magnus said, "Aye, it really does."

I sat down beside him.

Hayley said, "But you saw Lady Mairead, you just couldn't get to her?"

Magnus had both Haggis and Mookie with their chins on his knees. He pet both of their heads. "I saw her on the steps of the museum. I told her nae tae go inside, but there was somethin' off about her. She dinna ken the name Lochinvar, for instance."

Lochinvar said, "And how could she forget me?"

"Aye, and so I asked tae see her book and flipped through it, twas barely filled, and she looked younger but... I had nae time tae investigate further — the museum exploded and Lady Mairead disappeared intae the crowds."

Lochinvar said, "I saw her inside with Agnie, Lady Mairead looked distressed. They were headed up in the…?"

Quentin said, "The elevator?"

"Aye, I think they planned tae jump from the roof. I tried tae follow them, I began tae climb the stair, but then the museum began tae rumble. I worried the building was too tall, and it was goin' tae fall down around me." He glanced uneasily at the windows.

Fraoch said, "I was going in through the back, but then the explosion happened, and a fire erupted from the boiler room. Twas a mess."

Hayley said, "Does this mean we can't rescue her? I mean… I'm not that sorry —" She glanced at the kids. "My apologies, I know she's your grandma… but she has been kinda mean and I… but that was *not* nice of me. She is still a member of your family and we ought to rescue her, no matter what, but we haven't. What options do we have now?"

Magnus said, "We hae nae options, everyone but Beaty, Zach, Sophie, and Emma hae now gone—"

Zach joked, "And the kids."

"Aye, we daena want tae get tae the point where we hae tae send the kids, and we canna go again, we would all be loopin' and—" Magnus gestured toward Fraoch, "as ye can see, he barely escaped."

Fraoch grinned, white teeth in the middle of a smudged dark face. "This was just smoke, I was fine. I just had tae race up some steps, duck when stone was crumblin' down on me, skirt a fire, climb a fence and drop down ten feet ontae a city street where all the people were runnin'. Twas a little like the battle on the shores of Loch Awe, ye remember, Og Maggy?"

"I remember, except there was mist and rain and mud and swords swinging nae smoke and fire."

Fraoch said, "Twas verra alike, in *some* ways."

Lochinvar dug in his ear with his finger. "M'ears hurt, the

explosion was verra loud and I canna get Lady Mairead's shrieks out of m'mind."

I asked, "Was it pain or fear or—"

"All the art was gone."

"Every last piece?"

Lochinvar nodded solemnly. "Twas all confusin' though, I saw one of the paintings, I daena understand why she was so distressed over smears of color." He shook his head. "The sculptures were all toppled and broken. Black ink running down the paintings."

I said, "That happened when we were there too, but we were outside in an opulent sculpture garden. It was tragic how she shrieked while they destroyed the art."

Emma said, "It sounds as if there was less art the second time, right?"

Zach said, "And this sounds dangerously like Lady Mairead was looping. She was young outside and older inside? That's the kind of thing that makes the world go kerflooey."

Magnus said, "Och aye, it verra much went kerflooey, ye hae captured it perfectly, Chef Zach."

Everyone was thoughtful for a moment then Chef Zach said, "Well, Magnus, you missed dinner."

"Och nae!" Magnus hugged Isla and asked, "Did ye save me some, wee Isla?"

She giggled, "No Da, I didn't think you wanted the sad bit of food I had, you need a big proper meal."

Hayley said, "Fraoch needs to wipe down, but then how about we go around the corner to the pizza spot?"

The kids all yelled, "Yay!"

Chef Zach said, "Hey, I already fed you! From a fancy restaurant with a real, not junk, meal."

James said, "That was baked chicken with potatoes, that was not at all pizza and you know it."

Chef Zach laughed. "Fine, everyone go get your shoes on!"

He tossed Fraoch a damp bar towel. "For your face and hands."

Fraoch grumbled, "I think this is goin' tae require a visit tae the washroom or the towel will just rub more dirt on me."

Hayley said, "I don't think I've ever been so proud, my love."

CHAPTER 16 - KAITLYN

*a*s we went down the elevator I whispered to Magnus, "Are we safe?"

Quentin overheard and answered, "I'm armed up."

We walked out in the golden hour, the night being overly hot and humid, the dinner rush, people everywhere, the aroma of restaurants wafting in the air, queues of diners waiting on the sidewalk for seats.

We all crammed into the little pizza shop, ordering slices, one each, just inside the door, with a rough and tumble cacophony of kids yelling, "Me too! I want that too!"

Then we shuffled through to the dining area, sliding together three tables, though there were not enough chairs, but that was okay, some of us stood.

Chef Zach was at the cash register, ordering drinks, passing soda cans over his shoulder. The drinks moved down the line like a water brigade to our tables. Then we all popped open the tops at once and the kids thought it was hilarious.

Cooks in the back yelled, "Two cheese!"

And then "Four pepperonis!" passing them over the counter,

big wide greasy triangles. Emma handed out tiny square paper napkins to sop up the grease.

The owner showed us all the proper fold technique, and the pizza was delicious, but then the kids only had one or two bites, because they were already full. So Lochie, Magnus and Fraoch each ate one, then finished all the kids' pizza, then ordered more.

Finally Magnus sat back and patted his stomach. "Och, I canna eat another thing," but then he added, "Ye ken what we need? Ice cream! Is there an ice cream spot?"

The owner told us about a gelato shop around the corner and down half a block and even though Zoe was exhausted, Magnus got up close to her face and said, "Wee Zoe, yer Uncle Magnus wants tae buy ye some ice cream, would ye please come hae some?"

She nodded her sleepy head on Emma's shoulder and then put her arms out and got up in Magnus's arms, Isla climbed up in Fraoch's arms. And we left the pizza shop for an ice cream shop.

Emma joked, "This is entirely too much food but how can any of us argue with Magnus, he's still thin, and he does like ice cream so *very* much."

We trailed down the sidewalk, as the sun went down, as the night grew dark, and found the gelato spot and took up twenty minutes of their time asking for every flavor in big cones. Then we stood out on the sidewalk and people-watched as we ate our ice cream.

Then we walked home, Zoe in Zach's arms, falling asleep, Isla's sleepy head against Magnus's shoulder once more. The rest of us, trailing behind them, skirting the crowds along the street.

Then we made it back to the hotel.

I said to Magnus, with the light of the city glowing around the edges of the curtains, "Are you worried about her?"

"Verra. And irritated, because this is a trouble of her own

makin'. If she dinna travel around and around in such close loops, tryin' tae save herself from the passage of time, she would be safe right now. I had her, but she wasna the same person, she was from the wrong time..." He added, "But I am still concerned about her, she is dangerous if she is held prisoner. Who kens what she might divulge?"

"I don't think she will divulge anything, I think she is too strong."

"You think she would die afore she would tell it?"

"Yes, she would lay down her life before she would help Agnie in anything."

CHAPTER 17 - KAITLYN

*I*n the morning, sitting around the table with coffee mugs in front of us and baskets of bagels and cream cheese, Magnus said, "We need a plan—" There was a knock on the door.

Quentin went and answered it saying, "Probably Beaty, she needed to finish dressing."

He pulled the door open and Beaty entered. Her pale green hair was mussed, her face, also tinged a bit green, had an ill expression.

Emma said, "Beaty, I wondered where you were this morning, we got your favorite kind of bagels—"

Beaty slumped down in a chair that Quentin pushed out for her; she looked like she was about to throw up. "'Tis alright, Madame Emma, I—" She clamped a hand over her mouth, gagged, twisted away from the table, dove for the trashcan, and retched into it.

Sophie jumped up and held a napkin under Beaty's mouth. "Are ye well, Madame Beaty?"

Emma said, "Beaty! Are you pregnant?"

The entire table did a slo-mo turn to look at Beaty.

She had the look of a sad-eyed puppy, pleading, ill, drawn

face, a pallor. Without answering she clutched her stomach and heaved again.

James clamped a hand over his mouth to keep from heaving himself.

Quentin said, with his eyes very wide, "Beaty, babe, you pregnant?"

She nodded solemnly, "Aye, Quennie, I believe I am."

He threw his arms around her, crouching in front of her chair. "Oh my God, Beaty! We're going to have a baby?"

She nodded, her head rubbing up and down on his shoulder.

Emma clapped happily. "This is wonderful news, how lucky! We're going to have another baby!"

Beaty said, "I need tae lie down."

Sophie put out her hand. "I will accompany ye tae the bathroom, we can get you cleaned up and settled back in bed."

Beaty wailed, "I daena want tae leave the conversation, I need tae... what if the bairns need me?"

Emma said, "Well, you're right, of course, let's get you cleaned up, and we'll get you something that tastes good and put you in a comfy chair, right here, so you can hear the discussion."

As they left, Magnus said, "This is outstanding, totally outstanding! A bairn! Colonel Quentin, I am verra pleased for ye!"

Quentin was beaming as we all hugged him and the men hugged and pounded him on the back. Then we all returned to our seats. Magnus said, "Are ye nervous, Colonel Quentin?"

"No... not really... wait... should I be?"

James laughed. "Only because you're about to be a dad, no pressure, but that's a big deal."

Magnus said, "Ye will hae tae be the moral, ethical, and spiritual guide for yer first son, tis a verra big deal. Any man would be nervous on hearing the news."

Quentin ran his hands over his head. "When you put it that way."

Fraoch said, "Aye, many a man will become a father, but tis the verra rare man who becomes it well."

Quentin groaned.

Lochinvar said, "Nae, Quentin, this is nae a big deal, ye just do what a man does — get yer wife pregnant tae prove she is yers. Then yer job is over except tae give the bairn his first sword and *then* the fun begins." He leaned back wisely in his chair. "Then ye teach the wee lad tae smite his enemy and yer—"

We all groaned.

Fraoch pushed his knees. "Sit up straight, Lochinvar."

Lochinvar sat up straight.

Magnus said, "I was teasin' him with the 'Ye must be the spiritual guide of yer son', but ye hae taken it much too far, Lochie. Ye hae said the most frightening thing of all, that a man is inconsequential except in the creation of the son. Or in teachin' the son tae fight."

Quentin's eyes were very wide.

Beaty entered from the bathroom, and collapsed across the room on the couch. "Ye are alright, Quennie?"

"Yes, we're really doing this?"

She said, "Aye."

Magnus said, "The truth is, Colonel Quentin, ye are a good man, and ye will be very consequential in yer son's life." He raised his coffee mug. "Tae Quentin and Beaty, may yer son live a life full of courage and free from battles."

Quentin raised his mug, we all raised our mugs.

Magnus said, "We fight so our sons winna need tae."

Hayley said, "Or daughters."

The men all laughed.

Hayley said, "Y'all are a bunch of sexist pigs."

Beaty said, lying on her stomach, her face smashed against the pillow, a hand on Mookie, "Shhhh, daena badmouth pigs, Madame Hayley."

We all laughed that time.

Beaty said, "And how come ye are speaking on a son? This is a girl. I ken because I had a fae visit me in the night, she said twould be a girl bairn."

Quentin said, "A fae? Well, either way, it's great."

Magnus said, "When I say our sons, I mean our *children*, I daena want any of our bairns tae hae tae fight." He raised his mug. "Tae a peaceful world for the bairns."

We all drank from our coffees in agreement.

Quentin said, "So speaking of peaceful worlds, you were going to talk about the plan and what we were going to do first, please let it involve riding horses in Scotland."

Magnus put down his mug, "We do need tae go tae Scotland, but ye daena hae tae worry on it, we daena all hae tae do it."

Quentin looked suspicious. "What do you mean, 'we daena all'?"

"Ye hae a baby on the way, 'we' can hae ye take some more time and do another part of—"

"More time! Another part!" Quentin scowled. "That sounds suspiciously like I am not a part of the main plan, and I just spent the longest few days of my life bored out of my mind sitting on a rock in Central Park, after sitting in a lawn chair by a lake. I want to be in the action of the main part."

Beaty groaned, lumbered up, came across the room and curled up on the chair beside Quentin. He kissed the top of her head. She said, "Magnus, I ken Quennie is drivin' ye tae distraction with his whining about bein' bored, but I love him and he does want tae do something that is involved in the main part of it and—"

She clamped her hand over her mouth and retched.

Quentin grimaced, clamped his hand over his mouth, and retched too.

James said, "Don't get me started!" He retched.

Sophie put a dainty hand on her lips and gulped. "Madame Beaty, ye are goin' tae get all of us up-surgin'."

Quentin swallowed, recovered his calm and said, "And what do you mean by 'we can allow you,' Boss? I'm a part of the 'we', don't be having meetings without me. Who's the 'we' that 'can allow me', to what—?"

Magnus said, "Och nae, I meant the royal 'we', Colonel Quentin, because I am the king—"

I patted his shoulder. "My love, lots of people use the 'royal we' not just kings."

"Aye, but I get tae use it especially, as I am the king of all over the place and all through time—"

James joked, "I'm not so sure about that — didn't your kingliness get wiped off of Wikipedia? I'm not sure you get to pull the king card right now."

Magnus chuckled. "I am a future king—"

Fraoch said, "Three hundred years from now."

"I will be someday, so I demand tae be able tae use 'we' tae mean I. Because I say so."

I teased, "Wow, I have rarely seen you so 'kingly' and demanding, it's kinda hot."

Magnus pretended to whisper. "Kaitlyn, I am pretending tae be demandin' tae get Colonel Quentin tae agree tae what we need tae do."

I nodded conspiratorially. "Oh, of course, King Magnus, what do 'we' need to do?"

Magnus said, "We are not sure of the exact plan, but we are once again on high alert."

Quentin said, "Do they know where we, meaning all of us, have the house in Florida?"

"I think we hae tae assume they do — we had tech in Riaghalbane that shrouded our location in secrecy, and Lady Mairead and General Hammond kept it cloaked, but if Lady Mairead is nae in the kingdom then I am nae sure.... Agnie's sons kent where we lived, Agnie must ken."

Quentin said, "Great, that sucks. So where do we go?"

Magnus laid out the strategy. "I need ye, Colonel Quentin, tae take the family tae a new safe place. This hotel is the height of luxury but it is goin' tae be wrecked by all of us. We ought tae take the kids somewhere safe."

I said, "Like a compound."

"Aye. Emma, can ye look for one we can rent or buy for a time?"

Quentin said, "But, I don't want to get sent to some compound, I want to be useful."

Magnus said, "Once ye hae driven the van of tears, full of bairns and animals, tae a compound and kept them safe, ye can tell me how ye were nae useful."

He groaned. "We need to fly," he snapped his finger, "Emma, find a compound near an airport."

Emma began typing on her laptop on the counter near the small kitchenette.

Beaty said, "But ye forget, Quennie, Mookie canna go on a plane! We ought tae go slow, we can stop and see many sights, I would verra much like tae see the White House of America, and maybe tae see the Grand Canyon."

I said, "Your geography is not quite right, Beaty, you'd have everyone going in circles—"

Emma said, "Here's one..." She clicked a button. "It's freaking big, and..."

Magnus said, "Make sure it has stables."

"It looks like it does..." She clicked and scrolled.

Magnus said, "And when you're there, Colonel Quentin, I want ye tae get our munitions in order, prepare for possible trouble — we need weapons."

I said, "Will a landlord rent to us when we've got everyone on high-alert and carrying weapons?"

James was looking over Emma's shoulder at the property. "It says it's for sportsmen, yeah, they'll let us have weapons."

Magnus ran his hand through his hair. "Good, because we

hae Agnie after us, and some fella named Ian the Troublesome, and they are threatening and carryin' on—"

Fraoch said, "We hae other things afoot as well — who was it that moved ye intae the stadium...?"

James said, "Easy, it was Ormr and Domnall."

Fraoch said, "Aye, it could be, but now they are dead, who is holding the technology now?"

Magnus twisted his coffee mug back and forth, "If twas nae Ormr and Domnall, who else could it hae been?"

Fraoch said, "I hae been wonderin', could it hae been Hammond?"

Quentin's eyes went very wide. "No way, he is... no way. No way at all."

Magnus squinted at Fraoch. Then he shrugged. "We canna take any possibility off the table. Hammond has been around for a verra long time, I feel we hae a stong alliance, I trust him, yet... he was at the stadium that day, he might be allied with someone else."

Hayley said, "But what about Lady Mairead? He's loyal to her!"

Magnus said, "She daena return the loyalty. He might have grown tired of waiting for her tae take him seriously."

Quentin said, "And for *that* he would align with your enemies?" He scoffed. "No way, I don't believe it!"

"Nae, I am only sayin' we canna be naive. We hae a cousin with a great deal of power and possibly a grudge."

I joked, "*We* have?"

Magnus chuckled, "Again with the royal we. But it works since I am talking about m'future kingdom." He added, "And *we* are all family."

Fraoch said, "So we will be mindful of Hammond..." He asked Emma, "Where is this compound?"

Emma had her phone to her ear. "I'm calling about it now. It looks like it's about a five-hour drive."

Fraoch said, "Who else is goin' tae ride for five more hours in this van of tears, please God, nae me. The seats are too cramped and Mookie farts."

Magnus listed, "James, Sophie, Zach, and Emma will attend, along with Quentin and Beaty, and all the bairns, tae the compound that Emma is..."

We looked over at Emma, she put up her thumb.

"...arranging for us. Then ye will keep the bairns safe and get the household runnin' while Kaitlyn and I will operate the rescue of Lady Mairead. We need tae check in at Balloch, perhaps go check Paris, we will meet ye at the compound a few days after ye get settled."

Fraoch said, "What about me and Hayley?"

Magnus said, "Tis up tae ye, Fraoch, ye want tae visit Balloch with us?"

He said, "I *would* like tae be able tae fish."

Hayley said, "You were just fishing four days ago!"

Fraoch joked, "Och is this how long we hae been livin' in this hellish cityscape where the sidewalks hae gaping holes that ye might fall intae that would send ye tae the bowels of the earth? It feels like ten years!"

We all laughed.

Quentin said, "I disagree, Fraoch and Hayley shouldn't go with you, we need to continue with our 'no looping' strategy and—"

Magnus said, "Because it worked so well this last time."

Chef Zach said, "But that's not our fault, that's because Agnie is—"

I said, "Pure chaotic evil."

Zach said, "Nice, Katie, well done. Yes, she is chaotic evil, she is everywhere, in all times, one step ahead and her plans are inscrutable. While we figure her out we should be careful and split up our warriors. Hide them away until they're needed."

Quentin said, "That I agree with, we ought to have Fraoch at the compound with us—"

Hayley said, "And Aunt Hayley!"

Quentin nodded. "Of course, and that way if you discover something and you aren't able to deal with it, we can send the next man and then the next."

Hayley said, "Or woman!"

Zach said, "Absolutely, and like we did before, but this time it actually works."

CHAPTER 18 - KAITLYN

*E*mma sat down in front of her laptop. "We got the compound, I'm sending our payment — your 'Lord of Awe' title worked wonders, Magnus, that was a great idea. He said we can sign once we're there, and that he will keep the contracts anonymous."

She grinned. "Also, there's a loch. There's a stable."

Magnus asked, "Will there be enough bedrooms? All I want is a bedroom for each of us."

"It sleeps all of us, look," she turned the screen, "look at the big timbers. It's like a big log cabin with bedrooms all over the place."

"Good."

"Oh and its address is, get this, you ready?"

We all waited.

She grinned. "It's on Attitude Adjustment Road."

We laughed.

Lochinvar said, "What does that mean?"

Fraoch said, "An attitude adjustment is much like a do-over."

Quentin said, "So that sounds like a plan for almost everyone, but we didn't mention Lochinvar. What's he doing, going with us to the compound?"

We all turned to Lochinvar, who was still sitting straight in the chair after being reminded by Fraoch.

Magnus said, "I haena decided what tae do with Lochinvar, yet."

Lochinvar grinned. "Ye ought tae put me where the sword is needed most, as I am the best in the room."

Fraoch groaned.

Magnus chuckled. "We ken ye are good with a sword, Lochie, we daena need ye tae remind us at every turn."

Lochie said, "Ye're irritated with me, Og Maggy, but ye needed m'sword—"

Magnus said, "Afore ye continue, Og Lochie, and firstly, ye canna call me Og Maggy, only Frookie calls me that."

Fraoch chuckled.

Magnus continued, "I am Magnus tae ye, or ye might call me Yer Highness, I will answer tae either. The thing tae consider afore ye continue is that I am deliberatin' where ye will be most useful, ye might think on how ye would survive better in a compound in the middle of nowhere, in the year 2024, with no swords — or would ye like tae go somewhere better?"

"Better," he said solemnly.

"Good, I am thinking ye can go tae Balloch and stay with Sean, ye would be able tae look after them, he can look after ye. I am sure ye will hae plenty of swordplay there—"

"How would the food be?"

Fraoch said, "Shite."

Lochie said, "I daena like the sound of that."

"Good, so ye can see that while I deliberate, ye ought tae shew me some respect."

"Aye, Magnus," Lochinvar said, then added, "Please, Yer Highness, where the food is nae shite. I grew up with naething much and I would like tae eat what I want for a—"

Fraoch said, "Careful, Og Lochie, ye will grow soft and then nae one will need ye tae fight as ye will be fat and—"

"Fat as ye, auld man?"

Fraoch said, "Och nae," he tossed his half-eaten bagel back in the basket. Then he huffed and said, "I daena care what ye think of me, boy, I can still kick yer arse and enjoy a proper bagel." He pulled his bagel out and ate half with one bite and said, with crumbs flying. "Ye need tae be careful how ye challenge me, a little respect for yer elders, this is all I'm sayin'."

Lochinvar said, "I ken, Frookie, m'apologies, I will be on m'best behavior."

Magnus watched their exchange, then said, "I want ye tae come with Kaitlyn and me tae Balloch castle, Lochinvar. I think it would be a good place for ye, and we will give ye a box of cookies tae take with ye."

Lochinvar said, "Is this because of me calling ye 'Og Maggy', Yer Highness?"

"Nae, I can see ye are goin' tae be properly respectful, I hae just made up m'mind on it, ye ought tae be at Balloch. Sean will be able tae give ye a proper lookin' after, he is verra good at being a guide and caretaker of young men, and if ye remain there ye will be able tae intervene with Lady Mairead if she returns."

I said, "That's a good point, if Lady Mairead gets free from Agnie, she will likely go to her children in Balloch—"

Magnus said, "Aye, that is our meeting place, if she inna there, we will need tae check Paris. It will be good to go, we need tae warn Balloch that trouble might be coming."

"Ah man, I didn't even think about that."

"'Tis always a consideration."

Lochinvar said, "I would stay there, for always?"

"I daena ken, I would come for ye in time."

Quentin said, "While you do all of this you must watch your back, I mean it Magnus, if you're on your own, if we aren't there, you have to be cautious. You have a direct threat on your life, and she isn't playing by the rules. You're not being challenged, you're being threatened, you have to be on guard."

"I ken, Colonel Quentin, I will be careful." Magnus added, "Are we all decided?"

James laughed. "Not sure what the hell we're doing, but yeah, we're decided to head to a compound in the middle of an attitude adjustment."

The kids ran by, and overheard. "Attitude adjustment! Attitude adjustment!"

CHAPTER 19 - KAITLYN

A few hours later we had the van pulled up in front of the hotel, its hazard lights blinking, while we carried all the suitcases from our hotel rooms and piled them on the street with Lochie guarding while the bellman brought out carts carrying our luggage and we went in and out for things we had forgotten. James, Quentin, and Zach packed our luggage into the top bins on the van, bickering as they liked to do when working along-side each other.

Archie got hugs from both me and Magnus. He was stoic about having to leave us. There had been a lot of that lately, and I totally understood, but also, he agreed he would be strong for Isla. Plus there was an adventure afoot: traveling across New York state would be fun and Magnus and I wouldn't be that far behind.

He understood we needed to get his grandmother from her trouble. And I supposed on reflection, that it was easier that Archie was leaving us. We knew where he'd be. We would be there too, soon enough.

Isla cried, of course, and I couldn't blame her either, but it was a more grown up kind of cry than before. She sobbed, then swallowed it down, then clung to me, quietly weeping in a morose way, while I stroked her hair. Then finally, she sighed. "You really can't come with us?"

Magnus said, "Aye, we really canna come, Isla, but we will come as soon as we are able tae."

She sighed again. "Fine, but you have to bring me a present this time, Da, you didn't bring me *anything* last time."

Magnus laughed, "I had tae become king of Scots at great peril…? But aye, ye are correct, I dinna bring a present, and just so I ken what I am agreeing to, what kind of present are ye talking about?"

"Something very special, like an acorn or a sea shell."

"Och aye, I will bring ye something very special from our rescue mission. I promise."

I said, "And while we're away I want you to find me a feather."

Isla's eyes went wide. "A feather! How will I find one?"

I shrugged. "I bet you can."

Isla rushed down the sidewalk to tell Ben and Archie she needed to find a feather for us. I stood and folded up in Magnus's arms. "She is going to be okay, right?"

Magnus said, "I think what ye are truly askin' is are ye going tae be okay — are ye able tae be without yer bairns?"

"Yeah… you're right, I hate saying goodbye." I pressed my face to his shoulder.

Into my hair he said, "I could send ye tae the compound with them, but then I am sayin' goodbye tae ye in order tae save m'mother — tis nae fair, daena make me choose."

I looked up at him and took the kiss we both needed. "I will go with you, you don't have to choose between my warm bed and rescuing your bitch mother — you promised your mother to save her, which means, as your partner, I promised her. We will do it together."

∼

Hayley, standing outside the van, asked, "Quick question, since I won't be around to save your ass. Do you have a gun?"

"No. I…"

She huffed exaggeratedly. "You need to wake up every morning and strap your gun on, like me, learn from me."

I said, "You have one right now? Out on the streets of modern New York? Where?"

She patted her fanny pack. "I keep a small pistol on me here. Seriously, sister, you don't? As much as you've gone through, if you aren't packing, that's on you."

I said, "I suppose if a bad guy got me he would probably just get my gun, I don't really trust my abilities."

She scoffed. "How many knives do you have on you? You need confidence. I'd like to *see* a bad guy *try* to get my gun."

"I have two knives on me."

"Bad guys will totally take those two knives, *especially* old-school bad guys."

"The gun is not historically correct, it's—"

Her eyes went wide. "You're planning to load up a six-pack of Coke in a cooler to take to the past! What the hell are you doing with that? Giving eighteenth century kids diabetes is what you're doing, going to start the whole thing a couple of centuries earlier."

"I don't think a six-pack of Coke is likely to destroy the history of the world, but a weapon just might. Then again, the sugar trade was pretty brutal. Wait! Imagine the sugar trade with future guns."

"Imagine the sugar trade with people all jacked up on caffeine with future guns…? I mean, okay, you have a point, weapons in the wrong hands *are* the worst thing, but you know… you aren't getting any younger, your husband, bless his heart, has been fighting legions of bad guys for too long. I think you need to arm up. It's time, wear a gun. You've been through firearms training, I've seen you shoot, you're very good."

"I know that's just in the eighteenth century, this is the twenty-first century, it seems excessive."

"Have you looked around? Besides the crime, everywhere, you're a time-traveling queen, in Manhattan, I don't think there's anything excessive about it at all."

"You're probably right. I'll get one as soon as I can."

We hugged and she climbed into the van.

Goodbyes had been said, most of our family was loaded up in the van: Mookie and Haggis were sitting in the middle seat. The kids were spread out in the two back rows. All the passengers were still very packed in though three of us weren't continuing on.

The van slid away from the curb and we waved, Isla turning all the way around in her carseat to give me a last wave, staring at me wistfully through the back window.

I waved and smiled. Then said to Magnus, "Our Isla has removed her seatbelt."

I texted Emma:

HEY, MAKE SURE ISLA BUCKLES BACK UP

Emma texted me back:

GOTCHA, OOPS! SEE YOU IN A FEW DAYS AT OUR NEW PLACE, STAY SAFE.

Me:

YOU TOO, SEE YOU THEN.

I turned to look up at the Park Lane hotel, no longer full of our kids and friends and family, now just me, Magnus, and Lochinvar, walking up the steps to the lobby, greeted by the concierge, heading up the elevator to our mostly empty rooms.

CHAPTER 20 - MAGNUS

*L*ochie and I walked down the block tae a small corner store. I stood in the doorway first, as I liked tae do, takin' in the sight: so much food and ale and whisky stored within the four walls. The fancy wrappings, the bright colors, and funny words, twas a marvel how this culture, this world, had harnessed food production: they could feed millions and hae food left over.

I glanced at Lochie standin' beside me, his eyes wide. "Tis all for the takin'?"

"Ye hae tae buy it. But aye, if ye hae the money ye can take everything."

"Och, we want it all, I think, sort it later."

"Tis nae that easy, we must carry it tae the jump spot deep within the park, so we will hae tae make it a sensible plan. Kaitlyn told me I must get gifts for Sean and Lizbeth and the bairns as well, so I must be verra sensible."

Lochinvar went straight tae the liquor section and had two bottles of whisky under his arms, the proprietor of the store giving him mistrustful glances. I grabbed a bottle of bourbon, and a vodka with a bit of lime, and two bottles of pre-mixed margaritas. I grabbed a box of salt, thinkin' we could use it for the drinks but then take it tae the kitchen.

I gestured for Lochie tae follow me tae the counter, we placed them there and I told the man, "We are goin' tae want more."

Lochie went tae the cookie aisle and pulled boxes of Oreos off the shelf. Three. Then he went tae the chip aisle and grabbed big bags of tortilla and potato chips. I went tae the candy aisle and filled m'arms with chocolate, sour sugar treats, and gum. Lochinvar found a bag of candy sticks. I unloaded the sweets on the counter and the man asked, "Do you need boxes?"

"Aye, and dost ye hae hardware?"

He pointed tae the far wall, and left tae get boxes from the back while I collected rolls of duct tape for Sean and Liam, and a few flashlights and Zippo lighters for all the men. Carryin' it all tae the counter I passed first-aid kits and picked up three, and some aspirin along with Vitamin C for scurvy. Lochinvar called from the counter. "This smells verra good!"

"What is it?"

"Perfume!"

"Put it on the pile, one for each of the women. What is this?" I held a small bottle out for the man behind the counter.

"Energy shots."

I considered it, but as I wasna sure what it was I decided against it.

I picked up some rubber bands, then noticed an aisle of toys and found stuffed bears wearin' top hats, and shirts that said, 'I love NY.'

I took all of them for the cousins. Some of the boys were much too auld for stuffed bears but I thought they might enjoy the novelty of it. I tossed some water pistols on top of the pile and a rubber ball.

I paid for it, then asked the proprietor tae hold it for me

once he was done packing it, and then went next door tae a green grocer and bought fruits and vegetables and had them packed in three more large boxes, along with steaks, more salt, pepper, ten pounds of sugar and many small bottles of spices.

I ended with a large stack of boxes.

Lochinvar and I gazed upon them. "Och how will we carry it?"

The grocer asked, "Where are you living?"

"At the Park Lane hotel."

"Oh, yes sir, I will have it delivered to you right away, sir."

Lochie took one box of Oreos, tae eat from, as he and I returned tae our rooms.

It was dark when Kaitlyn and I got dressed in basic eighteenth century clothes, something we haena done in a long time.

Kaitlyn said, "I'm so excited, I haven't seen them in so long!"

"I saw them just recently, when I was trying tae get tae yer timeline in the thirteenth century, so the visit was full of fear and disappointment. I am looking forward tae seeing them again with ye alongside."

We met our grocery delivery downstairs, and I bought the flat-cart from the grocer, and tipped him enormously. Kaitlyn said, "What the hell? This is so much stuff!"

I nodded. "Lochinvar and I were a wee over-excited, but everythin' was essential. I daena ken how we would hae pared down."

She joked as she plucked a bottle of perfume from the crate. "This bodega perfume is essential? These teddy bears?"

"Aye, hae ye smelled the perfume, Kaitlyn? It smells as if angels live among us."

She took the lid off and sniffed, then sneezed.

"And the teddy bears are essential." I held one up. "He is wearing a wee hat! The bairns canna live without it, ye ken,

Kaitlyn, what is the point of livin' without bears with wee hats?"

"You sound like Beaty."

"She is verra wise about the necessary things for happiness."

"Speaking of happiness, you got the coffee for Sean and Lizbeth? They're probably desperate now that they have a taste for it."

"Aye, two verra big cans."

Lochinvar pushed the flat-cart, piled high with boxes and bags, while Kaitlyn and I followed it down the sidewalk and then crossed the busy street and through the gates tae Central Park. We walked up the path aways and then pushed the flat-cart up a hill. This took a great deal of exertion, gettin' the presents tae a safe space behind a cluster of trees in a bit of a clearing. M'mother had chosen this spot years ago and had shewn me the location and the numbers tae get here.

We had tae roust a homeless man, restin' behind a large boulder. I pulled some money from m'sporran. "Here, this is tae buy ye a proper meal."

He slurred, "Yesh, thanks," put it in his pocket and continued to sit there.

"I meant for ye tae go now."

He looked at me blankly. "Where?"

"For food, or ye ken, at least down the hill so we can hae a picnic."

Kaitlyn looked up at the sky. "Looks like a storm is coming, you might want to get under cover."

He grumbled as he staggered down the hill, dragging his sleeping bag behind him.

Kaitlyn grimaced. "It smells like piss all around here, gross."

I said, "When we were back in 1929 we had tae live here for a few days. There was much urinatin' here."

"So all around here there are centuries of piss? Wow. Your piss, over here somewhere — a century ago?"

I nodded and pointed. "Near that stone there."

"Now that is weirdly wonderful, do you think that tree grew from your piss? I mean, that's cool. We're in the middle of New York and yet this spot is timeless."

"Except for the trees. Trees always mark the passage of time."

CHAPTER 21 - KAITLYN

I noticed Magnus turned away from Lochinvar to hide the working of the vessel when he twisted it, being cautious.

And I totally agreed — now that we were finding all these brothers we needed to be very cautious, especially with the ones who could fight him in a stadium. As Magnus had said before, *I daena want tae kill him. I daenae want tae kill a brother or a cousin just because they share m'bloodline, tis barbaric. I hae done it enough.*

I could hear him saying it in my head, that push pull between past barbarism and present attempts at being a civilized man: a courageous warrior, a thoughtful king, a good father, a loving husband. He balanced all of that with having to also be bloodthirsty and it was heartrending to watch the struggle sometimes. And it weighed heavy on him.

That heaviness explained my presence now, why I was here. He had promised his mother, taken an oath to protect her, but he needed to be so much more than her warrior — he needed reminders of his humanity, too, and if it had been safe to keep the kids nearby, they'd be here, as well.

Instead it was just us.

I was his human, his humane, influence, to help him beat back the dark as he took on the role of hero.

It was one of the main reasons I had Magnus go to the store, so he could have the fun errand for once: to dote on his nieces and nephews, to be proud of delivering treats to his brother and sister.

I held on around Magnus's arm, tucked my head against his shoulder, while Lochinvar held onto his other. Magnus and I had the gold threads on the back of our heads, but even so... I braced—

CHAPTER 22 - KAITLYN

I woke up first down in the dirt. I mumbled, "Ugh, it never gets easier."

I rubbed my eyes, and realized Magnus was sitting up, arms easy around his knees, talking casually to...

I lifted my head—

Sean was on a horse. He laughed. "How often do I find ye in the dirt, Madame Kaitlyn? Ye ought tae make yer husband care for yer traveling better. He ought tae see tae yer bein' in a proper carriage instead of lyin' in the muck of the forest floor."

I grumbled, "I keep telling him that."

Sean continued, "If I dinna ken any better I would think there was somethin' afoot as I see a storm, so many storms around here, and then people waking up in the dirt under them — tis a magical thing I think."

Magnus groaned. "Ye ken — ye ken what is happening. I told ye long ago, yet here ye are, once again, demandin' the proof of it again."

"I ken ye told me, but here ye are once more, and I think there must be more tae it, beyond travelin' back and forth tae yer kingdom. By the air! How are ye tae be flyin' through the air? Ye daena hae wings! And I hae always wanted tae ken, how dost ye create the storms? Tis yer flatulence?"

Magnus groaned.

Sean laughed. "However it happens, I wouldna choose it, brother, ye are always makin' life difficult for yourself."

Magnus said, "I do wish I was better at makin' my life easy, like ye do, brother, with yer horse, while I am here on the ground without a horse."

"Ye ought tae travel with a horse! Or one of the, as Black MacMagnus used tae call it, aytuvees. How come ye dinna bring an aytuvee?"

His horse stamped.

"Because I am out of my mind."

"Ye hae brought a stranger with ye, pink as a young muc, down in the mud."

I turned to look and there was Lochinvar, groaning. He said, "Och nae, I daena like it."

Magnus climbed to his feet. "Sean Campbell this is m'brother through Donnan, Lochinvar. Lochinvar this is m'brother through Lady Mairead, Sean."

"Pleasure tae meet ye, lad Lochie, we are brothers then."

I said, "Not sure that's how it works."

Magnus said, "Ye ken, Kaitlyn, a brother of Magnus is a brother of Sean in any land." He added, "I think ye will get on well taegether, Sean, Lochinvar is a fine warrior, willin' tae battle with sword in an arena or with axe in a hedgerow with equal dexterity."

"He daena look like much."

Magnus said, "He saved m'life in battle, he is enough." Magnus nudged Lochinvar with his foot.

Lochinvar groaned and slowly rose to his feet. "Thank ye, auld man."

Magnus laughed. "I'm standing straight and ye are still whinin' like a bairn. Who's the one who ought tae be insultin' the other?"

"Tis a fair question." Lochinvar cracked his back and groaned happily. "Hopefully I winna need tae save yer life for a time, ye are on yer own while I recover from the travels."

Magnus laughed. "Weak as a bairn."

Sean said, "Ye hae a lot of gear with ye?"

Our flat-cart full of boxes was tipped over in the dirt.

Magnus said, "Presents for ye and the family, but I think we can take a few of these light things, and we can let Lochinvar push the cart tae the castle, as I am verra auld and require the respect for an auld man. He ought tae be the one tae push it all."

Magnus picked up a light box, passed me a bag, and directed Lochinvar, "The castle is through that way, ye can follow the path and get there soon enough, and I ken how much is in the boxes, danea stop tae eat and drink — all the cookies ought tae be there as they are for the bairns that daena call me auld."

I followed Magnus, and Sean followed us but then looked back. "Och, I canna stand tae watch, the poor lad has tae push all of it?"

Magnus chuckled. "Och nae, Sean, ye are soft."

"There is a present for me on the cart, twill take him forever tae get it tae the castle! I am nae soft, I am impatient!"

Sean returned and peeked in one of the boxes. "Tae make yer load lighter, Young Lochinvar, I will hae my horse carry this one, with the whisky in it. Tis meant for me anyway."

He strapped the box to the back of the horse and then walked, leading the horse beside Magnus and me.

Lochie was way behind, pushing the flat-cart down a difficult path.

CHAPTER 23 - KAITLYN

*W*e came to the castle and Lizbeth raced across the courtyard, "Madame Kaitlyn!" We rocked back and forth in a big warm hug. "Are ye well? Are the bairns well?"

"I am well, the bairns are very well. They send their love, but they are at home with Beaty and — Beaty is pregnant!"

Lizbeth clapped her hands. "Och, I wondered when she would hae a bairn. I am verra pleased for her!"

"Me too."

We hugged again, she said, "I must show ye the bairns, Jamie is near grown!"

I laughed. "How old is he, all of ten?"

She laughed with me. "Och, he will be draggin' a sword around soon enough, if Liam has anything tae do with it. But he is verra good in his studies, a boy of wit, I tell ye. I am verra proud of his lessons."

We stood talking for a moment more then entered the main house to see the nieces and nephews.

Magnus remained with Sean and Liam near the front gate, he didn't relent and help, he just watched, bemused, as Lochinvar gave up trying to push the cart and began lugging boxes one by one to the castle.

The day had been high when we arrived, but then it was late afternoon by the time we were settled.

Magnus met us in the Great Hall, scowling as he took his seat. "Ye ken I hae been tae see the Earl, och nae, he is verra auld, and twas as if I came in and he was still talking from havin' seen me just months ago. He told me again all about his lands tae the east, the crops in the fields, he talked at length on the cold spell."

Sean said, "Tis all he talks about these days. His son, John, is mindful that his father is agin' and has had an eye on the seat for the past year. He is findin' it difficult tae be patient."

Magnus's eyes went back and forth, scannin' the room, then he leaned forward and asked, "Will he be a good guardian of the castle, ye think?"

"Aye, I think so."

"But are ye are worried on yer own line?"

"Nae, I hae three sons now, I hae lived here m'full life, my mother is the sister of the Earl, I am sure that even though John has three sons, we are secure here. This is our home." Sean's words sounded confident, but he did look worried.

Magnus said, "Tis too bad, since ye live here year round that the castle canna come down Lady Mairead's side of the family."

Lizbeth and Sean laughed.

Lizbeth said, "As if there had *ever* been a chance, she is a sister, a woman! There was nae way she was goin' tae be able tae pass the castle down. Imagine!"

I said, "Haven't you had a queen before?" I looked around. "I mean, right? That means the peerage allows for it?"

Lizbeth said, "A queen is *verra* different, the bloodline flows through them, and if there is nae son, the daughter is good enough — tis sometimes better than nae having a secure line."

Sean said, "But in passing down a lordship, lands and a castle, ye canna expect it tae go tae the children of unmarried Mairead, from a match with m'father, who died years ago, a drunken lout leavin' his title tae his eldest son by his first wife... Nae, we daena hae a castle, we must continue our lot here as the familial guests of the Earl and his sons. I am thankful m'sister is such a help tae the Earl or we might hae been kicked from the castle years ago."

Lizbeth said, "He canna run the castle without me, but he needs ye just as well for the lands, brother. Ye do run the lands verra well. We haena had trouble since the battles on the walls and then later, the occupying army from... what was his name, Roderick was it? And then there was Padraig."

Sean said, "Aye, they were following Young Magnus, och, ye hae brought a great deal of trouble, brother."

Magnus held up his hands. "Daena hold it against me, Sean, I dinna mean tae bring the trouble, it just seems tae follow me." He added, "But about the castle, I ken she canna inherit the title, there is nae chance of it — I dinna think twould happen, but Lady Mairead has a way of makin' things work for her. I always thought she would win it, perhaps through a wager with the Earl."

We all laughed. Sean said, "She is verra cunning, and she would love tae take it from her brother, but och nae, if she could take it, her gloating would ring through the castle."

"Where is John, the Earl's son, now? He is here?"

"Nae, he daena like the castle much. He is livin' most of the year in Edinburgh."

"I ken ye hae always liked this castle and the lands."

"Och it is a verra good home for m'sons. I dream someday my sons will hae the run of it. I worry once the Earl is gone, my sons will hae a harder time of it. I am the link that holds us all here in the castle, if somethin' happens tae me or tae m'sons, then my whole line will hae nae where tae go."

"We just need tae secure yer place. I will speak tae the Earl about it, perhaps we can get ye a title, our mother might be able tae do something... and Kilchurn is in ruins, hae they rebuilt?"

"A messenger told me they are rebuilding, aye."

"Once done, tis yers, ye ken, ye can hae it."

"I appreciate it, Magnus, but hae ye seen Kilchurn lately? Tis fine for ye tae say tis mine, tis almost a ruin. Twill take a great deal of time and energy tae build it again. But ye daena need tae worry on it, m'sons are strong, this castle is braw, and we hae a promise that we can live here as the niece and nephews of the Earl for as long as we want. We ought tae nae borrow trouble."

Lizbeth said, "There is always time for Lady Mairead tae work her magic."

"Tis true." A server delivered a plate of what looked like mounds of brown hard bread and placed it in the middle of our table.

Magnus said, "What's this then?"

Lizbeth said, "This is the kitchen's attempt at cookies, Young Magnus, they canna get the recipe right, but ye canna complain or they get verra upset."

"Och nae, tis verra…" Magnus tried to pull up a corner, it shattered into crumbs. "I need a chisel tae get intae it."

Sean said, "Careful, ye may break a tooth, the last batch looked much better."

Lizbeth said, "Twas raw!"

"Aye, but it dinna wound yer gums."

Lizbeth said, "Well, I am nae going tae even attempt tae eat it, because I hae been promised, by the arrival of Magnus and Kaitlyn, proper sweets."

I said, "So many sweets, as soon as Lochinvar is done bringing them up."

I glanced up to see the server, an older woman by the name of Mary, nodding and gesturing for us to eat the inedible cookies.

Lizbeth sighed. "Och, we are goin' tae hae tae partake." She broke off a bit, put the tiniest bit in her mouth and made a large production of chewing and smiling. "Tis verra good!"

Mary beamed, bowed, and left the room.

Lizbeth grimaced and pushed the plate away as Lochinvar

entered, lugging one of the largest boxes. Lizbeth clapped her hands.

Magnus said, "Finally! We hae presents for all!"

He opened a box, and working deftly inside, pulled small paper bags over cans, and passed the drinks around the table. Sean immediately pulled his can from the bag and read, "Coo...Ca... Cal...?"

Magnus said, "Coca-Cola, but the bag is on it so it winna distract from the taste."

Sean said, "Aye, sorry, Young Magnus." He slid the can back into the bag and once everyone had one, Magnus showed them all how to pull up the tab to open it, and then to drink. Coke sprayed and fizzed, and everyone tasted it, and grimaced and shivered and carried on as if it were the worst thing ever, but though they were warm, they continued drinking anyway, licking their lips and smacking.

Magnus pulled bottles of perfume from the box next, giving one each to Lizbeth and to Maggie, then duct tape and Zippo lighters for Sean and Liam. He ran his hand through his hair nervously as he passed the gifts around. Then, rubbing his hands together excitedly, he passed them each a bottle of bourbon, and pre-mixed margaritas for Lizbeth, who asked, bemusedly, "Young Magnus did ye buy us these presents yerself? I believe tis usually Kaitlyn who does it!"

"Aye, I picked them all out. Smell the perfume, ye will like it, I think."

"I daena think I ever had m'brother give me a bottle of perfume before!"

He ran his hand through his hair again, flushing awkwardly. "I wanted ye tae hae something verra fine."

Her eyes were misty. "That is lovely. I think I always assume that the wife will buy the presents. I think tis a fine compliment that ye hae done it for me, thank ye."

"Yer welcome." He placed an extra piece of chocolate in front of her. Lochinvar was farther down the table with a box of

Oreos, ripping it open on the side, and quickly swarmed by Magnus's nieces and nephews, placing one each in front of them. The kids all cheered. Wee Ainsley tasted his first, with all the others watching him wondering how it would taste.

He chewed. "Vewa good!"

The kids begged for more, so Lochinvar gave them three each and told them to run off. They did, cheering.

Magnus said, "Now we ought tae all eat our own cookies and drink our own drinks." He mixed Coke and bourbon for Sean and Liam in glasses that said, I love New York on the side. Sean tasted it. "Young Magnus, this is delicious!"

"Aye, tis verra delicious tae hae such a drink with the sweetness and the fizz, though tis better with ice in it."

Lizbeth said, "Och, how I do miss ice. Twas lovely when I had it in m'drinks! And coffee, I hae a special fondness for it."

I grinned, "Magnus brought coffee for you too!"

Lizbeth clapped her hands. Then she broke a small piece of chocolate from a bar, bit off a very tiny piece, and moaned happily.

Sean said, "Magnus, ye must come tae the nursery and see the new bairn, a son!"

Maggie nodded demurely.

Magnus exclaimed, "Och aye! Another son! How many bairns dae ye hae now, brother?"

Sean finished the last of his bourbon and Coke, slammed the glass on the table, and exclaimed, "Six! She is a fine wife, the bairns keep comin' and most of them sons!"

I glanced over at Lizbeth who pursed her lips.

She said, "Brother, there is a wonderful virtue in making many bairns, tis of course the divine callin' of a good, virtuous wife, but ye might want tae consider slowin' down, else ye will tire yer wife, and what if she lost her good humor?"

Sean laughed. "M'sweet Maggie would tire? Nae, she winna tire! She is a patient, and doting mother, och nae, Lizbeth, that is the blood of Lady Mairead flowing in yer veins tae even suggest it. Ye take after our mother, daena she, Liam? And now that we are speaking on it, when will ye hae another bairn, Lizbeth?"

"God will decide, Sean, and ye ken, the last was a verra difficult delivery for me."

Sean, looking a bit drunk, nodded, "Aye, I ken Lizbeth."

She continued, "Liam and I near lost our son. He is verra fine and that is all we can ask for — a fine son, perhaps there winna be another, but Liam is verra proud of him."

Liam, always quiet, patted her hand.

Sean said, "What of you, Young Magnus, another bairn for ye? Yer Kaitlyn will give ye a son?"

Magnus grinned at me. "How do ye like it, my Kaitlyn, whenever ye come tae visit m'family, m'brother asks ye why ye arna with bairn yet? This is a verra proper question for ye?"

I laughed. "There is no one else in the world who gets so far up in our business, husband, than your brother, always wondering whether *everyone* is with bairn."

Sean laughed, "I appreciate a castle full of bairns, it secures our future — daena ye enjoy it as well, Young Magnus?"

"I do verra much, a full castle is a blessin' — did ye hear that Black Mac is expectin' his first bairn?"

Sean raised his glass, "Tae Black MacMagnus, a good man, a brave warrior, and soon tae be a father — a proper Scottish son!"

We all drank. By this time I was feeling pretty tipsy.

Magnus said, "But for us, we hae seen a great deal of danger and… we arna comfortable bringing a new bairn intae it."

Lizbeth patted the back of my hand.

Sean said, "Well, I am sorry tae hear it, brother, ye are a king of a distant land, ye ought tae rule it well enough tae keep yer bairns safe. Dost ye need me tae go? Dost ye need me tae take control of yer guard, help ye keep the castle fortified?"

"Nae. I daena need yer help in the kingdom, Sean, but if I do I will ask. I will hae ye come, brother, if I need ye." Magnus spun his glass, then he slammed down the last of his bourbon and Coke. "But we hae been talking on these dire issues for far too long."

Sean said, "We ought tae hae some frivolity. Some dancing!" He looked around, "Ian-Dubh! Where is the music?"

The young man named Ian-Dubh, rushed off and returned a moment later with a modern guitar.

I said, "Did James leave that?"

Sean said, "Aye, and he taught Ian-Dubh, tis verra fine when he plays."

Magnus said, "Och, this ought tae be weird."

Ian-Dubh began to play a song that was a little familiar, but odd, and he sang, "Will ye be comin' as ye are…?"

I said, "Uh oh, that sounds like Nirvana."

Lizbeth said, "Aye, tis heavenly tae hear his voice lifted in song."

Lochinvar shoved his end of the bench from the table and stood so abruptly he almost caused Sean to tip over backwards. Lochie staggered toward the man playing the lute in the corner.

Sean righted himself, laughing, and called after him, "Are ye goin' tae dance, Young Lochie?"

"Aye!" Lochie waved his arms clearing a spot and beginning a comical looking jig, his leg kicking in and out, an arm up, spinning, then putting his arms out, then wiggling his hips like he must have seen someone in present day do, jerking around, kick kick kick, wiggle wiggle wiggle. He was not in-time to the music, but then I realized… I turned my head to the side. "Is he doing Isla's favorite dance, the Duck dance?"

Magnus said, "I thought I had seen it afore."

Lochinvar yelled, "I hae a poem! A poem in exchange for a warm place tae stay tonight."

Lizbeth said, "Dear God, he is a poet? I dinna ken it when ye asked if he could stay."

I said, "You love poetry!"

"True, but when poets come tae stay, they insist on reciting their poems, Kaitlyn. They must keep reciting them, endlessly, sometimes residing for months at a time, all the while reciting!"

Lochinvar announced, "This is a poem I ken, about a flower, and it begins..." He held his arms out, "Oh how I love ye, yer flower, m'love, tis pink as a night sky, and O m'love in the springtime, I wish tae sing ye a song... and kiss ye long — in all the world I miss ye, out of time I yearn for ye, yer flower calls tae me..."

He wiped his eyes, "Och, it turned sad."

He continued, "But I would fight for yer flower, how dare he... Och nae! Tis only for me, the yearning, quivering petals," he clutched his chest, "yer sweet sweet fragrance and I would battle—"

Lizbeth's eyes went wide. "Och nae! I will hae tae watch him like a hawk, all the girls will be wantin' him."

Lochinvar was swinging a pretend sword. "...tae protect ye from the scoundrels and the thieves, wantin' tae steal yer glory, m'sweet flower." He bowed, having finished.

Sean chuckled. "We need tae find the young'un a woman or he is goin' tae disrupt the peace of the castle with all his yearnin' and quiverin'."

Magnus said, "I am relieved it is yer problem instead of mine."

Lochinvar strode over to a table with three young women and stood preening with his chest bowed out, while they giggled in his presence.

He had the look of a happy young man for someone who had just been reciting sad poetry about flowers that were a metaphor for vaginas. I giggled.

Magnus looked at me with his brow raised.

I gestured toward Lochinvar.

He nodded with a chuckle.

Then Sean said, "Finally, I think I hae had enough of the drink tae be in the right spirits tae discuss why ye hae come."

Magnus sipped from his bourbon and Coke. "Why hae I come? I hae forgotten!"

"I believe it has somethin' tae do with Lady Mairead, as I haena seen her in a—"

Magnus leaned forward, "When was the last time ye saw her?"

Lizbeth said, "I daena ken, six months ago? More?"

I asked, "Is that rare? Do you see her more often?"

Lizbeth said, "As ye ken, she daena care much for seeing her grandchildren, and most of her auld friends hae died a'ready, so she is out of sorts when she does visit, and she only wants tae come if the Earl is away. She has a way of arrivin' just after he leaves."

Magnus pulled the letter from his Sporran. "Aye, Kaitlyn and I saw her recently, but I believe she has had some difficulties since. She sent me a letter... She says she needs m'help."

He tucked the letter back to his sporran and asked, "Hae ye received any word from her? Any sightings or signs?"

"Nae, but she is probably on one of her adventures, she is often travelin'." Sean added, "Remember when we went tae France lookin' for her, and she had already returned?"

"The high seas and the pourin' rain in the crossing — twas terrible."

"Aye, good times." They raised their whisky glasses. "Slainte."

Lizbeth asked, "How long before ye must leave, Young Magnus?"

Magnus said, "Kaitlyn and I will stay for a few days, as it has been long since we hae seen ye."

There was a commotion, we all turned to see Lochinvar, standing on a chair, swinging his sword in the middle of the room.

Magnus shook his head. "Och nae." He stood as Lochinvar boomed out, "...and then he lunged for Maggy! And if I hadna been there, Maggy would be dead!"

Magnus groaned and rushed Lochinvar and put out his hand. "Give me yer sword."

Lochie said, "Why nae sword, Magnus?"

"Ye are too drunk, ye can hae it in the morn."

Lochinvar hiccupped. "What if a Baobhan Sith comes in the night—?" He hiccupped again, then held the sword out, but when Magnus reached for it, Lochi pulled it away and giggled.

Magnus said, "Lochinvar!"

Lochie passed him his sword and then turned his attention back to the young women.

Magnus returned and slid Lochie's sword under his chair, joking, "And when we leave we will be leavin' the wonderful and untroublin' Lochinvar with ye…"

Sean said, "I am certain the fair lad has stories tae tell on ye, Young Maggy, I think I will enjoy his company greatly."

Magnus moaned again.

Lizbeth said, "Of course we will watch over Lochinvar, and let ye ken when Lady Mairead returns, but honestly, daena worry on her, Young Magnus. She can take care of herself."

The rest of the night was us talking, until finally Magnus said, "Och nae, I hae been drinkin' a great deal, we ought tae retire tae our room."

CHAPTER 24 - KAITLYN

*M*agnus took my hand and led me through the Great Hall to the outer corridor. We walked down the galleries, lined with the Earl's best art and sculptures. Then we went up the staircase, bumping against each other, staggering a little. He laughed. "Och, I would take ye right here, but we are an auld married couple, we ought tae wait for our room."

I giggled. "You wanting me, Master Magnus?"

"Och aye, the poetry earlier..."

"Ha! The quivering flower did it...?"

"Of course, tis the whole point of poetry, ye ken, Madame Campbell, ye are..."

I stumbled a bit on the stairs, Magnus took the moment to bump against me from behind, holding my hips, while laughing. "Nae worries, damsel in distress, I hae ye."

He was hard and erect under his kilt, I could tell because it was poking me, quite urgently.

"Someone is going to come up the stairs and see us!"

He butted his hips against my full skirt-covered bottom. "We arna invisible? What about the cloak — we daena hae a invisible cloak?"

"You were listening in the car when the kids were watching Harry Potter?"

"Aye, they are m'favorite stories."

He lifted me around my waist to the top stair and then we staggered and laughed down the hall to our room and after some discombobulation at the door pushed our way in.

"I missed this room!"

"Me too, we need tae visit more often."

I went to the chamber pot and peed, my head spinning, and then collapsed on the bed. "Master Magnus, remember when we fell in love here?"

"Tis how ye remember it? I thought we fell in love in Florida. We dinna come here until after we were married." He sat on the edge of the bed and took off his boots.

I had my feet dangling off the bed, I put my foot on his thigh. "Mine too, please."

While he took off my boots, I continued. "...and while that is true... we were in love, right from the start, and it was blooming, love all over the place, but then we came here and we had our first big fight and we had to get back together, and then when you were injured and you had the oxygen machine here and we hated each other and—"

He stopped untying my boots, his hand resting on my ankle. "I dinna hate ye, I hae never hated ye. Ye hated me, mo reul-iuil?"

I sighed. "Hate is sometimes a part of love, I think, especially when there are big issues like infidelity, but... I have always loved you, I have never been indifferent."

Magnus looked up at the ceiling and around at the walls. "It sounds a lot like we tried tae fall *out* of love when we came tae this room, I am glad we were never successful in the failin'."

I lay on our old bed, enjoying the scents of the past, the embers in the hearth, smoke and dust, a bit of flame, the smell of the wood, and then the smell of age, the must and damp.

He tossed my second shoe to the side and then climbed onto

me. "I do think this room has been verra good for our makin' up."

I chuckled. "This is true. We have made up here, a *lot*."

He started pulling up my skirts, heavy on me, hot for me, while kissing me with a searching tongue and licks and small nibbles and — I pushed his hand down.

"Och nae, ye arna allowin' it?" His breath was coming heavy.

I kissed him, my tongue licking his lips, meeting his tongue dancing around. His hand pulled at my skirts again. I pushed it away.

"Madame Campbell, please? I beg of ye."

I stretched my arms over my head. "Madame Campbell is in her castle, Master Magnus."

He kissed my neck. "I will storm yer walls."

"Nae, I think ye might want tae ask kindly at the gate."

"Och aye, ye sound a bit Scottish there…"

He wriggled down my body and rumpled my skirt up to my waist and buried his face between my legs, kissing and suckling and licking, and oh my god. My fingers entwined in his hair he drove me to climax with a long low moan.

Ohgodohgodohgod — I pulled his ears to come, *up, please, now,* and he climbed me, chuckling, super sexy, kissing up my pelvis to that bunched up pile of skirts at my waist, and then trailing his lips along the top of my breast above the bodice and then drawing his tongue up my neck to my ear and then sweet breaths while he settled between my legs, then a fidget while he tried to get his kilt up, bound between us accidentally, then his lips grazing mine, our eyes met as he drove into me, again and again and…

Finished, he collapsed down on me. *Och.* His breath was warm against my ear, his voice low and vibrating against my cheek. "Ye were like a pink flower quivering…"

I laughed. "And now we are done, as Lochinvar so poetically said, *now* it has turned sad."

He laughed.

I said, still clutching around his back, "I think we haven't been in an argument in a while, but if we had been that would have just fixed it, that proper bedding of Madame Campbell rocked my world and I feel all full of love for you now."

"Ye didna love me afore?"

"Ye ken what I mean."

"I do, naething like a good bedding tae get a man tae rights, I suppose it works for Madame as well."

"Aye, it does, it really does. And we can store it up, all this good feeling, so that all future arguments will be solved before they get going."

He chuckled against my ear. "This is how it works, mo reul-iuil? We will store up the good feelings and then never feel pain again?"

I teasingly bit his earlobe.

He said, "Och, it dinna work."

"Probably not, though it is a good dream."

"Aye." He rolled off me and lay looking up at the ceiling. Then added, "Ye ken what I want tae do?"

"What?"

"Tis a fair night, and ye hae been bedded well—"

I giggled. "And you, Master Magnus, have been bedded well, too."

"It goes without sayin' — ye allow me in yer gardens and it is all good again."

"So modern! But I thought it was my castle?"

"Yer castle surrounds yer gardens, ye ken, tis the usual way of it, we men are always clamorin' tae get through the gates... but as I was sayin'... we are still mostly dressed, I think we ought tae go up on the walls."

"I would love that."

. . .

We climbed from bed and he went to the chamber pot to piss, his stream sounding like a rushing waterfall. I was used to it by now.

Not so much used to the fact that it would remain in the room all night.

The castle was quiet, an insistent, looming darkness. I felt along the hallways where the torches were out, wishing I had brought my flashlight, but Magnus strolled as if he could see well. "Can you see?"

"Nae, but I grew up here, I remember the dark hallways verra well." He took my hand in his and led me confidently to the stairs. We climbed up, and then out to the walls.

"Ooh, I forgot how awesome it is up here."

"I was a wee bit disappointed they dinna need me tae stand guard, I do love the feel of the stone and the night air, the silence and the comfortin' stillness."

I watched him as his eyes swept around, then he greeted and spoke to the guardsmen, and then I followed him to the wooden steps leading up to the high walls. I climbed first, steep as a ladder, he put his hand under my arse and hefted me as I climbed.

I laughed. "Thank you for the lift, it's not an easy climb in all these skirts."

"Nae an easy climb in my skirts either." We both laughed.

He spread out a blanket and lay down and patted for me to lie down next to him, my head on his shoulder. We looked up at the sky, diamond-encrusted with stars flung across the expanse of deep black.

"Wow."

"Aye, tis a braw night."

"Did you know, Magnus, that there are billions of stars up there? And do you know what a billion is?"

"Is this a trick question?"

"Yes, because a billion is so much more than we think, if you woke up every morning and counted, every second of every day, all year long, without taking a break… it would take your whole lifetime to count to one billion. But it's too late to try, because you're too old, if you started now you'd only get halfway there, if you were lucky."

"Och nae, another regret."

"Ha! I think you have much better things to do with your time."

He kissed the top of my head.

"What *do* you regret, my love?"

He exhaled as he considered. "I think in a man's life he will always regret some things — I regret leavin' ye after we lost our first child."

"But then we might not be here — it's impossible to look back on our past and think about changing one thing, because every little change might change *everything*. We're time travelers, we know that lesson more than anyone else on earth."

"True, and ye ken the other thing I regret, though I daena want tae say it aloud."

"I'm glad you don't, please don't, we don't want to spoil this vibe. Let's not talk about regrets anymore, my love, let's enjoy the stars."

Then I asked, "Did you know we're trying to go to Mars?"

"Who's we? I truly hope tis nae the royal we."

"Oh, not me… This royal we means humankind, the United States, a rich billionaire at the helm."

He chuckled. "Tae visit the small red planet? I think it would be an easy trip. A man will just get on a ship and go."

I raised up on an elbow and looked down on him, "No, Magnus, it's sooo far. Really far. It would take about seven months to get there, a three month wait, and seven months back."

"Och, tis a verra long time. The two months on the ship crossin' the Atlantic with Fraoch was too long — he almost died. They will need lemons."

I lay back down and looked up at the stars. "I would never

do it, not at all brave enough, but it's pretty thrilling that someone will."

"Och nae, ye hae the bravery tae explore new worlds, mo reul-iuil, ye are doin' it almost every day."

"I guess that's kind of true. Do you think the vessels and the other tech were brought here by aliens?"

"Ye mean someone from another planet?"

"Yes, from out there, or do you think humans on this planet invented it?"

He thought for a moment. "Twas men who carried it tae the original place."

"Yes, but maybe they stole it from aliens, like how Johnne Campbell stole it from them?"

His eyes went back and forth, calculating and thinking. "I watched the movie with the kids, ye ken, Star Wars, I think it canna be aliens, else we would be time-jumping and accidentally landin' on other planets."

I looked at his face in horror. "Thank *heavens* that wasn't in the mix."

He chuckled. "Aye, I wouldna like tae end up on a desert planet with two moons."

"Me neither."

"Also, we operate the vessel with our hands, nae our tentacles, or our flippers or... ye ken? It must be human."

I nodded. "So yeah, I agree, it seems like humans, earthbound humans."

He looked at me with his brow raised. "Why are they earthbound humans, mo reul-iuil, dinna ye say that we were headed tae Mars?"

"Oh, I suppose I did."

"Someone verra far advanced in the future built the vessels and the Bridge, they figured out how tae alter time, tae create alternate timelines and tae augment the jumpin' from one tae the other." He shrugged. "They must be verra advanced, and they hae nae missed the vessels, as they haena returned for them."

"Or maybe they plan to return for them but are so advanced, so far in the future, that our hopping around on the timeline back here in the past is of no concern to them. Like, if they were giants, like Jack and the beanstalk, and Jack is worried about the beans, and the giants are just polishing their golden eggs — you know that story?"

"I heard it when I was wee, a visitin' poet told the bairns the story, though twas nae the same as the one Emma reads tae Isla and Zoe. In the one in the past there was a great deal more gore."

"I'm glad that's not how Emma tells it. But yeah, maybe the advanced people who invented the vessels are just doing nothing and plan to come for them later, maybe this whole time, from the year 1557 to now, they've been having lunch. Maybe they're going to have a wee nap and then come down and deal with us." I comically gulped.

He grew quiet.

"Did I blow your mind?"

"Aye, and I feel verra small."

"They might not be literal giants, I might be wrong."

"They must be verra inventive though, they must have a great many resources tae be able tae command such a voyage of discovery, and that they daena care about the vessels means they are well above our means. They must hae wealth beyond our imaginings."

"Or... and hear me out, they came back in time, and didn't calculate on the issue that if they changed the past they might affect the future."

"They would nae be verra smart."

"True, but maybe they didn't know. Maybe Johnne Camp-bell from back in 1557, and the men who came after him, began going into the future and stealing from the tech and maybe they stole so much tech, that they disrupted the timeline. What if they made the invention of the vessels impossible?"

"Ye sound like Zach when he is ravin' like a madman."

I said, "I do a little…"

"If they did make the invention of the vessels impossible, we wouldna hae vessels, anyone can see it, mo reul-iuil."

"Unless it was space aliens."

"Aye, that is the only answer."

"It's always damn space aliens."

Magnus said, "And perhaps when those wee aliens saw me use the vessels, a king twice over, building a large family — they were awestruck by my mastery. Perhaps they said, 'We ought nae bother him, King Magnus has the history of the world all under control.'"

"That is the most likely scenario. Who wouldn't be awestruck by your mastery, Master Magnus? Ooh," I pointed, "look! Did you see the shooting star?"

"I did, twas marvelous."

I nestled in against his shoulder and kissed his chest.

Then he raised his head and listened. Then he groaned and sat up, dislodging my head from his shoulder.

"What?"

"Ye canna hear it, the fight?"

"No… I… wait, what's happening?" I could hear it now, men's voices raised from over in the courtyard.

"The men are brawlin' and likely tis…" He listened and then nodded. "Aye, tis Lochinvar. Och nae, he is going tae get himself killed."

I scrambled up and bundled up the blanket. "You can go ahead—"

"Nae," he ran his hand through his hair, waiting for me to go down the steps first. "Tis night, and if there is drunken brawlin' goin' on, I need tae accompany ye."

CHAPTER 25 - KAITLYN

*A*ll the guards were leaning over looking down on the courtyard.

Magnus glanced down, "Och, they hae given him a sword!" He rushed toward the stair. "Stay close, Kaitlyn!"

I followed him, two steps at a time, holding the walls as we plunged down to the ground floor.

He burst through the doorway to the courtyard where there was a large crowd of men, yelling, and Lochinvar's voice above them all, sounding furious, "Ye take it back, auld man, or I will kill ye!"

Magnus shoved through the crowd to the front and I followed close in his wake to not be separated. We broke out at the edge of the crowd ringed around the duel, near Sean to see Lochinvar facing off against Craigh, an older man, who was an uncle figure to many in the castle.

Magnus said, "Sean, brother, he is verra drunk — why has Lochinvar been given a sword?"

"He called Master Craigh out tae duel, he has called him tae the courtyard and—"

Lochinvar bellowed, "Raise yer sword!"

Craigh yelled, "Och, ye are insolent as a wee—"

"Ye disrespected me!"

Craigh said, "Ye deserve the respect of a hairless bawbag — what, ye want the respect I give tae a hairless pink bawbag, Young Lochie?" Craigh tossed his sword from hand to hand, confidently.

Lochinvar sneered.

Magnus groaned. "Ye canna let Craigh fight him, he will die in the dirt of the courtyard."

Sean said, "The young lad is nae so skilled, Craigh is a fine—"

Magnus was very upset. "Craigh is nae good enough, brother, I told ye, ye canna allow Lochinvar tae arm himself, or tae duel in anger."

Magnus pushed past Sean and stepped into the ring. "Young Lochinvar! Ye need tae put down yer weapon!"

"Nae! The auld man has insulted m'honor!"

Craigh said, "Young Magnus, ye daena need tae interfere."

"Aye Craigh, I do, I canna allow this duel tae stand." Magnus put his hands out, placatingly, and said, "Put yer sword down, Craigh, please, I need tae speak tae Lochie and he canna hear over the storm of the battle."

Craigh lowered his sword.

Lochie yelled, "Are ye afraid, auld man?"

Magnus said, "His name is Craigh, and he is nae afraid, he is bein' sensible. Are ye going tae shed blood in the middle of the Earl's courtyard, Lochie? This is where ye are tae live! Ye canna wage a drunken battle in—"

Lochie's face was blood red, overheating in anger. Spittal flew from his lips as he spluttered, "He started it!"

Craigh raised his sword again. "I am goin' tae finish it!"

The crowd began to chant, "Craigh! Craigh! Kill young Lochie!"

I was wringing my hands, the crowd wanted to see someone hurt and my husband was in the middle of it.

Magnus bellowed, "Craigh, stand down —everyone stop!"

He took a step toward Lochie. "Young Lochie, ye need tae put down yer weapon, ye are going tae draw blood in the Earl's house and ye winna be able tae stay—"

From the portico above us the Earl called down, "Sean, is that Young Magnus, is he causin' trouble again?"

Sean glanced up. "Nae, sire, ye may return tae yer rooms. I will handle it."

"'Tis disorderly, and I winna stand for it. Ye tell the men tae put down their weapons. Tell Young Magnus that there will be nae fighting in my courtyard."

Sean said, "Aye, sire."

I saw Magnus shake his head.

The Earl left the rail and Magnus called to Lochinvar. "See what happened, Lochie? Ye are causin' trouble for me! Ye want tae cause trouble?"

"Nae, I want tae prove tae—"

Magnus took two steps forward. "Ye daena need tae prove anythin' tae anyone, I ken ye can kill with yer sword. I hae seen ye fight. I ken ye would kill any man here."

Men began shouting that Lochinvar wouldn't win a fight against them, but Magnus just waved his hands.

He said, "I also ken ye are goin' tae live here at Balloch — how are ye goin' tae do it if ye hae killed Craigh? He is a good man. Ye canna let him upset ye because he has called ye a pink bawbag. He has regularly called me a disgustin' carbuncle and I haena killed him."

Lochinvar kept his eyes trained on Craigh but the edge of his mouth went up. "Ye haena killed him because ye arna skilled enough tae kill him."

The crowd laughed.

Magnus chuckled. "Och, Lochie, ye are a huge pain in m'arse. I need ye tae drop yer weapon. All these men saw ye were willin' tae duel, there are only two things that will come of this, either ye will kill Craigh and then ye will be hung, and there winna be anything I can do tae stop it. Or Craigh will kill ye, and nae because he wants tae, but tae protect himself from yer brawlin'. These are poor reasons tae die or tae kill, I tell ye, ye ought tae hae more sense."

Magnus took another step closer. "I hae told them that ye are a champion at drawin' yer blade. I hae warned the crowd that ye are a dangerous swordsman, haena I?"

Lochinvar said, "Aye."

"So why daena ye drop yer weapon and—"

"They are laughin' at me!"

"Nae, Lochie…" Magnus took another couple of steps. "Ye remember yer favorite singer?"

"The candyman?"

"Aye, ye ken how he says ye hae tae 'lose yerself'? Ye hae tae lose yer pride, Lochie, ye only hae one moment, right? Ye only get one shot, ye ken?"

Lochie nodded and lowered his sword. "I do like that song verra much."

"I ken. Ye are surrounded by a new family. Ye hae Sean tae be a brother tae ye, tae look after ye. Sean, would ye look after Lochie, make sure he inna goin' tae ruin his opportunity of a lifetime?"

"Aye."

"But from now on he daena get a sword when he has had too much tae drink."

Sean chuckled, "Now that I see his temper, I concur."

Magnus continued with his hand out. "Now kick yer sword over here tae me."

Sean said, "Is he too fast for ye, Young Magnus?"

Magnus said, "Aye, I am warnin' ye, he is fast, and skillful, and verra dangerous with the sword."

Lochinvar said, "Nae, I winna, unless Craigh kicks his away as well."

Craigh said, "Young bawbags, I daena hae tae prove I can hold *my* temper, I hae had m'temper in check the entire time." Craigh sheathed his sword.

Lochinvar sneered but placed down his sword and kicked it skidding through the dirt to Magnus who picked it up and passed it to Sean.

Magnus said, "Maybe he canna hae his sword from sundown tae sun up."

"Like with Drunken Dunlach?"

"Aye, same rules until he is done brawlin' tae prove himself."

Sean nodded.

Magnus called to the two men in the middle of the ring. "Now Craigh, since young Lochie has challenged ye tae a duel, and I hae intervened, what must his punishment be? A whippin'?"

Lochinvar scowled.

Craigh charged him, knocking his breath out, and plowed a right hook into Lochie's face, then a left and right in quick succession, with Lochie stumbling back, and Craigh on him. In three swings Lochinvar was on his back down on the ground, his arms up, trying to stop Craigh's blows.

Magnus and Sean pulled Craigh off.

Lochinvar lay on the ground and held his cheek.

Craigh asked, "Has the wee boy had enough?"

Magnus and Sean told Craigh to calm down.

"Nae, I want Lochie tae tell me he has had enough."

Magnus said, "Lochie, what are ye goin' tae say tae Craigh?"

Lochie raised, leaning back on one arm, the other holding his cheek, dabbing at the streaming blood. He said, sullenly, "I hae had enough."

Craigh said, "Good." He added to Magnus, "Lochinvar will work for me for the month, I could use a strong back."

Magnus said, "Good, Lochinvar will meet ye at dawn after his guard shift."

Sean called out to the crowd, "Everyone can go tae bed or take yer shift on the walls, but ye canna stay here, the battle is over!"

Men cleared the courtyard, heading off in all directions, with just a few hanging around to watch the windup.

Magnus went up to Lochinvar, far enough away that I couldn't hear what they were talking about, his hand clapped on Locinvar's shoulder, he talked earnestly to him for a long time.

Then finally Lochinvar left to go to the stairs and Magnus came over to me. "Och nae, what a night."

"You ready to go to bed, Highlander?"

"Aye."

On our way up the stairs, I said, "I can't believe you used Eminem to talk Lochinvar down!"

"Tis his favorite, James and Zach introduced him tae it, explained the words, and he listened tae it about twenty times a day at camp. Tis a great song, it can be used tae solve all kinds of trouble. Ye ken, Kaitlyn, that feelin' he had when he was on the stage for the first time, twas much like my own feelin' when I was out in the stadium for the first time, the feeling that ye must prove yerself, and this is it — all men feel it."

We made it to the hallway, dragging because I was so tired.

Magnus continued as he led me down to our room, "Twas a bit of a different meaning, as I was askin' him tae stand down, but I kent he would understand — he has proven himself tae me, I ken he can fight. He daena hae tae fight, he has tae keep from going intae that barbarian condition. He has tae pull himself back from the brink and be civilized — it inna an easy path for him but he will get it with practice.

We went down the hallway to our room and collapsed on the bed. I lay on my back, he curled up with his head on my breast.

"He will be okay here?"

"Sean will see tae him. He dinna take it seriously when I first asked, but he understands now. I am glad the row happened afore we left. Sean would hae let Craigh die afore he understood that Lochinvar inna tae be dueling, he is too lethal."

He chuckled and rolled on his back. "Craigh is going tae handle him. Craigh is an arse, he is strict, and he winna take any trouble from a young lad like Lochinvar. He will hae him saying 'yes sire,' and ' nae sire' in nae time."

I laughed. "Poor Lochie, but also he needs to learn a lesson before he kills someone."

"Aye, the Earl would hae him hung from a rope before the next crow of the cock."

CHAPTER 26 - KAITLYN

The next morning I saw Lizbeth at breakfast. "There was trouble with young Lochie, last night?"

I nodded and told her what had happened.

She shrugged as if it was normal. "It sounds just like a fight I saw between Liam and Young Magnus once, tis nae a big deal unless he is too dim tae learn his lesson. If there is a battle he must fight for the Campbell men, nae against them, tis an important lesson."

"Yes it is, I hope he's smart enough."

Lizbeth asked, "Would ye like tae walk with me tae the village tae see Madame Greer? I missed my visit last week, and now she is holding it against me, by refusin' tae come tae the market, so I must go. It has been a long time since you and I entwined our arms for a walk along the path."

"I would love to."

"Good, I am glad I dinna need tae plead with ye, the weather is shite, absolutely terrible. It will feel like rain without rainin' but I need tae go, so I would love the company."

I joked, "The weather is shite? Is it too late to change my decision?"

She teased, "Of course it is, and what else are ye going tae do? Twill be so boring without me!"

I laughed and ran up to my room for a wrap and met Lizbeth in the courtyard where it had already begun to rain.

She said, as we went out through the main gate, "We will be wet as trouts in summer spring once we make it tae her house."

I asked, "How is she? I haven't seen her in so long."

"Longer for ye than for her, Kaitlyn, she feels strongly that she has seen ye just the other day."

"Thank you for letting me know."

She laughed. "Yer carryings on make ye forget yer days of the week, daena they?"

"They do. It is very confusing."

We leapt across a wide mud puddle, and splashed along a wheel-rutted route.

"Your boots are still good, still waterproof?"

"Aye, I am verra grateful for them."

The rain began in earnest. Lizbeth put out her palm and rain quickly collected there, she drank from her hand.

I said, "So last night it seemed as if you were worried about Maggie."

She nodded. "Aye, she has been pale and weak for many long months, och nae, *years*, but I had a long talk with Sean about it this morn — I feel better now, I believe he understands me."

"Oh good, I'm sure that sets your mind at ease."

"Well, she has just given birth tae her sixth bairn, not a year after the fifth, and after his crowing last night... I felt I must speak my piece. It was verra difficult, he was aggrieved with me for stepping out of my place, but I told him he *had* sons, he had heirs, and that Maggie was going tae die if he kept getting her with child."

"I'm impressed you broached the subject."

"Maggie is the best woman for him, she is demure and sweet and kind and bears his brutishness. I told him he wouldna find another wife so easily, the next would likely be young and full of

impertinent ideas and he would be auld beside her, and there
would be those who would laugh at him for lookin' so auld. And
then, as it happens, a man auld and laughed at might begin tae
see his power slip. I told him that when the head of a family has
a proper auld wife alongside him she *also* has power. An auld
wife will help him conserve his family's power. But if he takes on
a younger wife he would hae tae expend energy tae keep her, and
she would be pregnant again many times. He might hae sons
that would battle against his first sons — Och nae, it can be
such a trouble, Kaitlyn. Auld Lachlan has had nothing but
trouble with his young wife and it spills out upon us all. We
came tae a moment though, finally, when Sean agreed that I
made sense, yet he told me that he had tae believe in God's will."

She held a gate open for me to pass through and then
continued on, "I told him that God's will might be that Sean
ought not tae kill his pious wife with so many bairns. We had
tae argue over the amount of sons a man ought tae hae, but I
assured him he had the proper amount. And so, Madame Kaitlyn, I explained tae him how tae pull himself from her afore he
was in the throes. He almost fell tae the ground in a faint."

"Oh my, I truly wish I had been there to see and hear that."

"He told me that I was mistaken on God's plan for us, but I
reminded him that the Earl's first son is not sufficient in his
mind, his second son is inheriting the title, but prefers tae live in
Edinburgh, and so Sean has become the head of the household
and that I was proud of him for it. Sean is a good man, and I
believe that this is God's plan for him, tae be the head of the
Campbells of Breadalbane, if nae in title, in word. If ye think on
it, tis much like how Uncle Baldie was the man who all looked
tae for guidance."

I said, "It is. He reminds me a lot of Uncle Baldie."

"Aye. I told him, 'Ye are now that man, Sean, and Maggie
has been beside ye as ye became that man, ye canna think on her
passing as part of God's plan, ye are her husband—' and he
interrupted me tae say, 'God looks poorly upon us if our fields

are fallow,' and I said tae him, 'Yer fields are not fallow, ye hae had a fine crop of sons, but I believe yer wife is failing in health and ye must be a proper husband tae her.' I told him, 'God would not want one crop over the whole field.'"

The rain poured down on us then and we stepped under a tree for some respite.

"You would make a good minister."

She cackled. "Och nae, what a horror! A woman ministering God's word, Kaitlyn? This is blasphemy!"

"I only meant, you would be as good as one, not that you ought to be one."

"Besides, I wouldna want tae be one, a priest would never see the waning health of Maggie and intervene with Sean. He would see it, like Sean, as God's will. I daena understand how it would be God's will to see the wife die when there are sons here already. Maggie has done her duty, tis time for Sean tae do his."

I chuckled. "And his duty is to pull out?"

"Aye, he has been instructed by his sister on the workings of it, and now tis up tae him. He promised tae do his best tae not get her pregnant so soon, tae give her time. We will see."

I said, "I am proud of you, you're a good sister, and a wise advisor to all."

"I do m'best, I hae a great deal tae make up for in m'mother and her carryings on."

I said, "I brought some candles for Madame Greer, but I have many more back at the castle, I know she will use them so sparingly, and I don't want to overwhelm her, so I will give her three and you can give her more later."

"Ye are also verra wise, Kaitlyn, tis exactly how she would be: if ye give her too many she would be dismayed, if ye give her too few she would be disgruntled."

CHAPTER 27 - KAITLYN

*A*t Madame Greer's cottage, Lizbeth knocked, then entered without waiting.

Madame Greer began exclaiming, "Tis Queen Kaitlyn! The beautiful Queen Kaitlyn! Yer Highness, I am thrilled tae hae ye in m'home once more, did ye pass down the lane?"

She led us into the main room, where there was a chair that Lizbeth and I both refused, a small stool that Lizbeth perched upon while I stood. Madame Greer needed the chair, you could see it in the way she limped as she moved.

"I wonder if m'sister saw ye as ye came along the pass? Did she notice?"

Lizbeth said, "Yer sister has passed from this earth, early last year, Madame Greer."

"Och nae," she stared wistfully from the window at the pouring rain, "it feels as if she is right here sometimes, with her nitpicking and her insults."

Lizbeth nodded. "I ken she was a constant source of trouble tae yer heart, though, as a kind and loving woman, ye miss her desperately. Ye always did take the righteous road."

Madame Greer dabbed at her eyes.

I said, "I brought you some more candles and matches." I

had a bundle of candles wrapped in string. I placed them in front of her. "And a new lantern." I showed her how to open the metal door, put a candle inside, and gave her some boxes of wooden, emergency matches.

I lit a match, put the flame to the wick of the candle, and closed the lantern door.

Her sighed. "It does turn away the darkness!" She opened the door and blew the candle out. "I must use it verra sparingly though." She put the new matches inside of a small box and while the lid was opened I glimpsed matches lined in orderly rows.

I said, "If you run out, Madame Greer, please tell Lizbeth and she will get more for you."

"Oh? That is wonderful, ye both always think of me."

Our visit was short, as Madame Greer grew tired — the rain began to come down in a torrent. And then there was a man's voice outside, "Lizbeth! Kaitlyn!"

We opened the front door to see Magnus and Liam on horses.

Magnus was cloaked and dark. "We came tae give ye a ride back tae the castle as ye arna salmon, ye canna swim upstream."

Lizbeth and I wrapped up in our tartans and Magnus and Liam pulled us up onto the front of their horses, and we traveled much faster up the path to the castle than we had traveled down, but were still so drenched by the end that we had to go to our bedrooms to change into dry clothes.

CHAPTER 28 - KAITLYN

*T*he night was dark, the rain and gloom of the day drew the night close long before we were ready. We sat in the Great Hall for the meal, but the chill was settled on us from all around, we huddled at one end of the table and talked and drank and complained about the cold.

It was gloomy except for our laughter.

Then a herald entered and came to whisper in Sean's ear. Sean announced, "Lady Mairead and a large party hae arrived."

Liam jumped up to inform the Earl, while the rest of us went to stand under the archway to greet her horse-drawn carriage in the driving rain.

A footman held an umbrella over her head as she stepped out. She met us in the covered area and then we walked into the castle down the galleries to the Great Hall as Magnus said, "What are ye thinking, Lady Mairead, traveling in this rain?"

She said, "Ye ought tae blame the rain, this interminable rain, other than yer mother. What am I but someone who must get from one place tae another? If I waited for the rain tae cease I would never go anywhere."

She swept down the hall and settled in the chair at the right of the head of the table.

I said to Magnus as we followed. "This is good news right, she's safe?"

He looked thoughtful. "It might be."

The Earl bustled in, his wig crooked, his clothes disheveled from quickly pulling them on. "Lady Mairead!"

Her brow arched. "Ye are in bed already, John?"

"Nae, there is much tae do, I am just... nae, I was in m'rooms, there has been a ruckus about with the men brawling at all hours, keeping us awake."

"Who on earth is brawling? Nae Magnus?"

Magnus chuckled. "Why, whenever brawling is suspected, does everyone assume tis Young Magnus? I haena brawled all week!"

We all laughed.

Sean said, "Twas Young Lochie." He gestured toward Lochinvar.

I watched Lady Mairead's eyes settle on Lochinvar, she was noting him, as if seeing him for the first time.

I glanced at Magnus, who met my eyes.

We all sat. The Earl, who had hastily rouged cheeks, tugged the corner of his wig to straighten it, and said, "Where hae ye been, Lady Mairead? It has been months since ye visited!"

She distractedly looked down at her skirts. "I believed ye tae be visitin' Edinburgh, I was planning m'visit tae coordinate with yer travels."

He, missing the point, said, "Well I was goin' tae travel before the rain, so ye hae come at the perfect time tae visit with me. Ye hae brought yer husband?"

She raised her chin. "Ye ken I daena hae a husband. Three has been *plenty*."

"I might make arrangements for ye, I hae had a—"

"Nae."

She turned her attention to Magnus. "And when did ye arrive?"

"Yesterday, we brought Lochinvar tae live here at the castle with Sean."

"Good, good, that is wise." Her eyes drifted to Lochinvar and rested there.

The Earl said, loudly, something he was prone to do because he was losing his hearing, but also bored because the conversation didn't include him, "Tomorrow, Mairead, I will expect yer visit tae my offices. I would like tae tell ye about what I hae accomplished on the grounds. I hae made many improvements, though, as ye ken, we hae had many upsets in the long months since ye were last here."

She said, "Of course, who is 'we' having the upsets?"

"The privy council, Scotland..." He took a deep breath, "All of it."

She nodded and turned back to speaking to Magnus, but the Earl continued trying to draw her attention, "...because of it, we are nae needed so often in court."

Lady Mairead said, "Brother, ye voted 'no' on the Acts of Union, ye canna expect tae be useful in determining the future of the Union!"

He didn't seem to hear her. "...I meant tae go tae London, but I nae longer hae close connections."

Lady Mairead looked at her fingernails, bored. "Surely ye can visit with my cousin at Ham House? Lord Campbell would be bound tae put ye up. Twould be for the betterment of the family tae hae ye in court in London. I am sure he would patronize ye."

He waved the idea away. "Nae nae, I daena think I will be making the long trek any time soon, but John might go — he would nae feel the journey in his bones as I do and he, as my son, has the legal right tae represent me."

Lady Mairead's brow arched and she huffed, her eyes resting on her own sons, Sean and Magnus, as he spoke.

She tilted her chin up and said, "If ye need me tae arrange for yer comfort with my ample connections at court in London, just tell me. I was with Her Highness, Queen Anne, just recently."

He flustered. "Och, I dinna ken ye were at court, Lady Mairead! I might hae sent my regards tae Her Highness."

She shrugged, indifferent. "Tis fine, we had much tae speak on. Your name dinna come up, but if it had, I would hae assured her of yer high regard."

He looked confused for a moment, ill-equipped to spar with his sister, then he said, "The hour has grown late, I must head tae m'room." He heaved himself up from the chair and with his steward holding his arm, hobbled from the Great Hall.

There was silence as he went and then a collective exhale and then noise and discussion once he was gone.

Lady Mairead rolled her eyes. "Tis always about his life, and the small town politics of his lands and grounds, the interminable politicking over the nation of Scotland and unions and treaties and 'who will be next in line for his title,' and never, not once, a thought of my life and what my own family might be doing."

She flicked an imagined piece of dust off her skirt.

Magnus said, "When you conquer your next kingdom ye can do it with him in mind."

"Every conquering I hae *ever* done has been tae shew him up, some might call it pettiness but it is the seat of my strength. Remind me tae send a message through tae Ham House that I would prefer they not be hospitable tae his son, John, he is the title holder, he ought tae..."

Her eyes settled on Lochinvar again. "Young Lochinvar is verra handsome, he has a fine jaw."

"It seems almost as if ye are seeing him for the first time..."

"Who, I? Nae, I hae seen him before, but tae see him again.... Now that is something."

Magnus asked, "Where are ye comin' from?"

She waved her hand.

He squinted his eyes, "Because I hae seen ye verra recently."

"Of course, I ken, we were just taegether." She turned tae Sean, "Would ye please refill m'mug?"

Sean jumped up and crossed the room.

She said, while her eyes looked out over the crowd, "Magnus, we ought not tae talk on our adventures when there are those listening who might not understand."

Magnus's brow turned down. "True."

I decided to help. "Didn't you tell me, months ago, that you had a Museum of Modern Art opening in New York coming up — have you been?" To put her off guard I added, "And was it lovely? I know you were looking forward to it."

She narrowed her eyes, then Sean placed the mug in front of her and returned to his seat. She said, "I hae had many art openings in New York — what are ye insinuating Kaitlyn? Nae one likes when a true meaning is hidden. Ye ought tae be truthful and forthcoming in yer word and deed."

My eyes went wide.

Magnus squeezed my hand under the table, meaning to support me — how many times had he needed to do that because of things his mother had uttered, insinuated, threatened?

Lizbeth said, with her eyes wide, "Lady Mairead, ye are in rare form this evening. Ye canna accuse *anyone* else of prevarication when ye are the prime example of it. I heard Kaitlyn ask ye a question, verra politely. Ye are the one nae being forthcoming!"

Lady Mairead turned on me. "Do ye think I hae been tae a certain art opening?"

"I do, I saw you there. I'm wondering if you, the woman in front of me, were actually there?"

Sean said, "What are ye talking on, Kaitlyn?" He laughed. "Lady Mairead was there, ye were there, tis enough of it — Magnus! Would ye hae more cookies?"

Magnus called Lochinvar over from his place at the end of the table.

Lochinvar bowed to Lady Mairead and said, "Lady Mairead

tis a pleasure tae see ye again."

She nodded with a flirtatious smile.

Magnus asked, "Lochinvar, can ye retrieve a box of Oreos from our gear?"

Lochinvar left the room.

Lady Mairead turned to Magnus and said, "So ye are trying tae understand what I ken about the timeline?"

Magnus said, "Sean, Liam, and Lizbeth, could ye leave me alone with Lady Mairead for a moment?"

They nodded and rose from the table.

Magnus said, "We made contact with ye in New York, at a museum, Agnie was there..."

"I daena..." Her eyes narrowed. "I haena done it." She sipped from a glass of wine.

"Good, we can stop it from happenin', right here, right now. Daena go tae the opening."

"What happens tae me?"

"Agnie absconds with ye."

"Och nae! Ye dinna stop her? Ye ought tae at least hae tried!"

Magnus said, "I did try, ye ken who tried first? Kaitlyn. She and Hayley, along with James and Colonel Quentin went tae intervene, then I went with Fraoch and Lochie."

Her hand went tae her bodice. I noticed a tremble in her fingers. "And none of it worked? How could ye be so incompetent?" Her eyes traveled to the table where Lochie was ripping open an Oreo box and passing them out to Sean, Liam, Lizbeth, and some of the other men. "Kaitlyn, ye let him bring Oreos here?"

As if *I* was in charge of the food and Lochie. I hadn't even bought those Oreos! I said, "He loves cookies too much, if we are going to force him to live here in the past when he has already had a taste of the present, we will need to give him some treats."

"Tis the best way tae ruin a warrior — tae give him treats whenever he asks. Ye ought tae harden him with—"

Magnus said, "He is hardened enough."

Lochinvar leaned over a chair where a lovely young woman sat and presented her a cookie with a flourish. I laughed.

"*How* did ye nae rescue me?"

"Agnie was destroyin' the art in front of ye."

"She would do that?"

"Aye, ye were powerless tae stop her. I was powerless tae keep ye safe."

The color left her cheeks. "What was it, one of Pablo's?"

Magnus looked at me.

"I believe she destroyed at least one Picasso, yes. I saw it with my own eyes, and one of those brightly colored ones with the splashes of paint, you know..."

"A Cezanne?"

I shrugged. "Maybe."

Magnus said, "The final time she destroyed most of the art."

"Och nae," she exhaled. "I told ye, dinna I tell ye? She is a horrible person. Anyone who would destroy historically important paintings is the lowest form of person. Imagine destroying a Picasso!"

She patted the back of Magnus's hand. "I will keep all of this in mind. I will solve the issue without it becoming a problem."

Magnus squinted. "I hope ye can but... It has already happened, and ye are dangerously loopin' within yer life."

"Daena be worried, Magnus, of course I can, tae be forewarned is tae be fore armed."

Magnus chewed his lip. "I suppose it is — ye do look verra much younger than last I saw ye. This all seems a great deal like loopin'."

"I told ye, I constrict m'travel tae many jumps within compressed times in order tae nae waste moments, I daena want tae—"

"I ken, ye daena want tae age."

She said, "Ye ought tae heed my warnin', Magnus, ye daena want tae grow auld."

"Lady Mairead, tae not age is tae not truly live."

She shook her head. "Magnus, we hae been given an important power, we ought tae make the most of it, because tis likely tae kill us — we canna live forever."

Magnus joked, "Speak for yerself."

Her brow raised and she took a sip of her wine. "If ye think on it, the best years of yer life would hae tae be the years between thirty and fifty, ye are nae too auld, capable of conquerin' still, and once ye hae seized power, ye hae yer auld age tae rest."

"How auld are ye?"

"Och, who kens? Auld enough tae be powerful, young enough tae be beautiful tae enjoy it."

She turned to me, "Ye ken, Kaitlyn, ye hae amassed a great deal of power and ye are beautiful enough tae keep yer husband happy — twill be fleeting, someday ye will be alone, but at least ye will hae the fond memories of it." She shook her head. "Unlike Queen Elizabeth: she amassed all that power without a proper husband, and rarely a man tae keep her bed warm..." She took another sip of her wine. "I met her, did I tell ye, Kaitlyn? She did hae one lover of note, but I dinna care for him much." She finished her wine and looked quite buzzed.

Magnus said, "Kaitlyn daena hae tae worry on bein' alone, I am her husband—"

"So much honor, Kaitlyn, ye hear how he speaks? Ye will be auld and he will still be there, he says so, ye hae nae reason tae doubt him."

I sneered like a child.

She waved her hand for another glass of wine. Then said, "Speaking of believing Magnus's word, how is yer son with Bella, Magnus?"

Magnus shoved his chair out from the table. "First, Lady Mairead, ye and I hae discussed yer behavior and we hae come tae an agreement. Ye arna tae be cruel tae Kaitlyn, the fact that ye hae forgotten the agreement or ye hae nae recollection of havin' made it, makes me believe ye are much younger in the timeline than ye are letting on, which means, I am nae going tae rehash auld disagreements, nor am I going to allow ye tae banter and keep tae auld scores. Ye might be younger, but yer behavior has grown verra verra auld." He took my hand. "Kaitlyn and I will be moving, ye are unwelcome tae join us."

To me he said, "Grab yer glass, Kaitlyn."

He led me to a smaller table on the side, and we sat, and he drained his ale, then he waved to Lochie, and mimed eating a cookie. Lochinvar showed him the empty box. Magnus said, "Och nae, this is a tragedy, I ought tae call it the Evil Mother and the Lack of Cookies, a play in three parts."

I joked, "Dibs on the band name."

He laughed.

"What are we going to do about her?"

"I daena ken, she is..." His eyes traveled down to the end of the table where Lady Mairead was flirting with one of the younger men from her entourage, hard. "Och nae, she is going tae..."

"I know, I see it, the poor man."

Sean walked up and gestured toward Lady Mairead.

Magnus said, "Aye, we see it."

Sean then gestured toward Lochinvar, flirting with an older woman. "I suppose he will at least get a warm bed taenight instead of the straw-covered floor of the men's quarters where he was made tae sleep last night."

Magnus groaned. "Tis Widow Arthur, Sean, she came here taenight specifically tae catch him. How are ye takin' it so easy? I will remind ye, I gave ye Lochie intae yer safe care, and already he has almost drunkenly killed a man and now is about tae bed a treacherous widow."

Sean shrugged. "Young Magnus, part of keepin' a young man safe is tae allow him tae make an arse of himself."

"Ye must also keep him alive."

Sean laughed. "He is still living!"

"It has been mere hours since we arrived."

Sean watched Lochinvar for a moment and said, "Aye, ye are right, I canna let Widow Arthur get her claws in him. I will return."

Sean stalked over to Lochie's table and spoke, a few moments later Widow Arthur left the Great Hall through the main doors and then Lochie left for the back stair that went up to the walls.

Sean returned with a smile. "I reminded Widow Arthur about her five bairns in the nursery needin' her and sent Young Lochinvar up for guard duty."

Magnus said, "Thank ye, brother."

Their eyes moved over to Lady Mairead laughing with her young conquest. Magnus said, "Anything we can do about this turn of events?"

"What ye arna rememberin', young Magnus, and this is most important, if Lady Mairead is busy, she winna bother with us so much."

"Och nae," Magnus lamented, then shrugged. "I suppose ye are right on it."

Lady Mairead rose from her seat and approached us with her young man close behind. "Magnus, I ken ye daena want me tae speak tae ye, but I intend tae properly say goodnight."

"Fine, good night tae ye."

"And I wanted tae say one thing more..."

"Och, of course ye do, ye must hae the last word."

"If I went with Agnie tae save the art, then I meant it, ye canna override m'decision. I will hae a plan, ye ought nae interfere."

"Ye think ye had a plan, ye think ye hae a way out of Agnie's clutches?"

"Aye, ye ought tae worry about yer own troubles, I am perfectly capable of m'own rescue."

"Ye asked for m'help."

She faltered. "'Tis immaterial, I will be fine."

CHAPTER 29 - MAGNUS

*K*aitlyn was verra drunk as we climbed the stair tae our room. "So let me get this straight, she is not on a regular timeline? She is way younger? That is so unfair. How many times do you think, Magnus, we interact with her when she is out of our regular timeline?"

"I daena ken, perhaps verra often."

She stopped in the stairwell. "Perhaps *all* the times are irregular times!"

"It could be."

"What about when she asked me to marry you, was she... was she out of time then?"

"By that time she understood more about time travel than I — I had barely a clue and she was already amassin' a verra large collection of goods and art. She was verra fast tae learn how tae use the vessels, she might hae been out of time, twould explain how she gained knowledge and riches that quickly."

"Yes!" Kaitlyn began tae climb the steps, bumping intae m'shoulder and then bumpin' off the wall. She rubbed her shoulder. "I'm ping-ponging." She added, "How does she keep it all straight?"

"I daena ken."

She stopped again with her eyes wide. "Maybe she leaves notes for herself! I saw a movie like that one day. What was it called?" She laughed. "I'm drunk."

"I ken, ye are being verra funny."

She turned and clutched the front of m'shirt. "We ought tae read all her notes, and… so we can find her." She hiccupped. "And we ought to get to bed fast, because you, sir, are hot."

I put an arm around her waist and lifted her tae the top of the steps and placed her down.

She said, "Whee!" Then she stumbled.

I tossed her over my shoulder, and carried her down the hall to our room.

She said, "Och aye, this is verra ho—"

I jiggled her up and down and she giggled, "Ho-oh-oh-oht! So hot."

In our room, she was laughing, until I dropped her down on the bed — *clunk*. "Och, nae, Kaitlyn, are ye alright?"

She rubbed her butt. "My love, our bed is not soft enough. Where's our fancy mattress?"

"I think it has been dragged away tae feather another bed."

"Probably the Earl."

"In his defense, he is verra auld, and we never gave him one."

She rolled, attempting tae plump the straw and feather sack upon our bed's planks. "I don't blame him, but I find him very irritating. I hate to take Lady Mairead's side, but he's an arse. Especially if he took our fluffy mattress."

"Aye, me as well, but we will hae tae make do. One of us will be the mattress, the other will be the action for our activities, which role dost ye want?"

Kaitlyn said, "Oh I will be the action, you get on down here, Master Magnus."

I stripped off my clothes, it was verra chilly in the room. "Dost ye want me tae build a fire?"

She wriggled from her skirts, "There is not enough time, Master Magnus, at all."

I climbed ontae the bed and she climbed ontae me. We kissed as I pulled her laces loose and she drew the bodice off over her head, drawing up the blankets and wrapping them around her shoulders as she kissed me. "Brrr, cold."

"Aye, tis verra cold." I felt between her legs, explorin', and fondled her breasts, her skin bumpy with the chill of the air, her shiverin' tae my fingers' touch. My fingers explored her, while she breathed deep beside my ear, a warmth tae my skin, a bit of dew upon her cheek from the effort and exertion, though twas cold, she was warmin' up.

I couldna see her, twas too dark, and we hadna turned on any of our lights or lanterns or even a candle, the glow from the embers barely enough. The scent of ash and smoke, her skin, the fragrance of her shampoo lingerin' in her hair.

The mustiness of the old blankets surroundin' us, a scent that might bother me, but also set the place, the mood — twas an auld, familiar room in m'castle with my wife in my bed. I said, "Och, yer castle gates are welcomin' me."

"Oh yes, they really are, you ready, Master Magnus?"

"Aye, verra ready," and she sat down, takin' me in. An exhale. Then a pull and a glide as she moved her hips up and down under the covers, her whispers in m'ear, speakin' tae me and God and the heavens in our efforts.

She rode on, drivin' us tae a climax, my grip on her buttocks, directin' her, as she rode, her body archin' and then roundin' upon me, and then after reachin' our climax with breathless moans and trembling limbs, she collapsed on me, her hair mussed, her cheek warm, her lips wet. She went from light and energy, tae languid and heavy. We kissed deeply, then she rolled over and off me, draggin the covers with her.

She laughed and teased, "Ya cold?"

"Aye, but ye hae overplayed, ye forgot about the mattress. Now ye hae rolled off, ontae the hard bed, and though ye hae all the covers and I am cold, all I hae tae do is..." I grabbed the edge and yanked, pulling the covers over ontae myself.

She shivered. "You aren't going to share?"

I laughed. "Just one minute ago ye had all the covers and I think ye laughed on it!"

"I regret it so much." She teased, "Didn't I just fuck you very well, Master Magnus — don't I deserve the blanket?"

"Och aye, twas a tremendous fuck." I drew the blankets over her, then patted m'chest for her tae lay her head.

She nestled in and then quickly pretended tae snore. "I wore myself out with all that exertion."

"Aye. Ye were verra exertin', twas verra fine."

She chuckled, then grew quiet, drawing near sleep.

But twas difficult for me tae sleep — after years of the time-line bein' stable, then years of the timeline bein' unstable, there had almost always been one constant: Lady Mairead. Her activities had been orderly. Her motives had been tae further m'power, but now....?

Now she was behavin' erratically. I couldna tell which age she was, when I was dealin' with her — twas troubling.

I considered it all while Kaitlyn fell asleep and then I slid from under her, tucked the blanket around her, dressed, and left the room.

I headed tae the walls, for guard duty; the night air would help me think.

The next morning I was dressing, when Kaitlyn said, "Ow, my head hurts, *why* did I drink so much?"

I chuckled. "Ye were verra fun."

"Good, that was sloppy drunk — I think I wanted to numb myself to the fact that your mother is such a bitch." She moaned and rubbed her temples.

"Aye, she is a terrific inconvenience, but ye are verra generous with her, she is more a witch than a bitch, though I am a modern man and I daena believe in them."

"Good answer."

I said, "I hae been thinking on it, though, Kaitlyn, we should ignore her. We hae tae find her, the real her, whatever she says about it, we hae tae find her anyway. I feel like havin' her kidnapped in front of us is too dangerous a precedent. I canna allow it. It is an affront tae m'power, even if the peace and quiet is a welcome thing."

"How will we find her?"

"Ye said how last night." I grinned.

She looked at me blankly. "I have no idea, was I wise?"

"Aye, ye were verra wise, ye had a perfect plan. Or wait, nae a full plan, more like the start of a plan."

"Great, what was it?"

"Ye said we ought tae read her notes."

"Oh." She blinked, wrapped up in a tartan, the bottom half of her naked and crossed the room tae crouch over the pot tae piss. She said, "And the notes are in her book?"

"Aye, we need tae find her most current book."

She used a tissue tae wipe and stood.

"When I'm drunk I am very wise, who would have thought?"

CHAPTER 30 - KAITLYN

*I*t rained all damn day.

~

The men went out on horses to ride, enjoying the horrible weather. I helped Lizbeth around the castle. Because of the rain we weren't going to have a delivery from the farms, so we had to go in the storeroom to make lists of what was available to tide us over. Lizbeth pulled from her pocket a book, looking much like her mother, and then a pen, a real pen from modern times, looking a little like Magnus. She made a list, a little like me.

"Remind me to bring you more pens."

"I do love them, they are verra sensible. I think if the future holds wonders such as an inkless pen we might do well."

I smiled. "If only you knew of all the wonders. I wish I could take you to Florida someday, to see where we live."

She nodded. "I would love tae see it. I think it must be a magical world, where cookies grow upon trees, the rivers flow with soda drinks, and the pens are endlessly full of ink. I would like tae see it verra much. But..." She blew a bit of hair off her forehead, it was chilly, but she was moving a big sack of oat flour and had a dewy forehead from the work. "I daena think I ought tae — whenever I visit Edinburgh and dance at the balls, or eat at the fine tables, when I return I am verra put out that I must endure all of this. Tis difficult that I hae tae be the mistress of the house, without the title, and I must work in the storeroom, and put up with the stench of m'husband after a day out on the grounds." She put her hands on her hips. "He dresses up verra fine and I do miss it when he is just a man. My point is, Kaitlyn, tae travel makes me feel less inclined tae be grateful for what I hae at home. And I do verra much like my husband, even when he does reek, and I like my bairns, best of course, when they arna underfoot. I like the power of my station, and I admire and enjoy the company of Sean. I can even enjoy an afternoon in Maggie's company, when she is nae complaining. I like my life. I daena need tae see what other things lie beyond. This way I can be properly grateful when ye bring me chocolate and fancy lotions."

"That seems very sensible."

"Och nae," she joked, "I daena want tae be seen as sensible."

Just then a servant came seeking Lizbeth. "There is a envoy here from London, we hae a visit from the young Lowden, the heir tae the Earl of Lowden's title..."

Lizbeth's eyes went wide. "What is this? The Earl dinna mention there would be a visit!"

"He dinna ken, Madame, he is in a tither now, dressin'."

"Good Lord! And the men are out on a ride in the rain, all will be bedraggled this evening and we are down tae the last of the..." She huffed. "Send Cuther out tae the docks, tell him we will need as much salmon as they bring in."

She turned to me. "I suppose we must greet our guests. Someone must go up tae tell mother that her step-grandson has arrived."

"I wonder if they've ever met?"

"Unlikely."

Young Arran and his companions walked into the castle as if they owned the place. They had the look of entitlement peculiar to the nobility. The young women were ostentatious and preening, the men acted as if they ruled everything.

The Earl was in his chambers — I imagined the scene, the young men stifling their laughter at his high wig, his rouged cheeks, and his silly manners. I saw the entourage pass by, the men displaying haughty airs and the lead man, Arran, with a sneer on his face.

Lady Mairead waited in her own office and after the Earl received the group they were ushered into her room. Lizbeth and I were sent for and sat beside Lady Mairead while she made the guests stand, and after introductions, grilled her step-grandson. "How is your father, is he keeping the lands well?"

"Aye, Lady Mairead, m'lord has added tae the north, in a treaty with Munro."

"Good, good."

Then the future Earl of Lowden crossed the room, dragged a chair over and sat down across from Lady Mairead and allowed his legs to splay, looking very pleased with himself.

Her brow raised.

They spoke pleasantries but it was clear they had become adversaries, tension grew in the room.

Then Arran took his leave and he and his entourage went down to the Great Hall. I jokingly said, "Phew."

Lady Mairead looked at me with her eyes narrowed, then said, "Aye, ye are correct, twas a relief tae hae them leave. Och, tae be a man with a title tae give ye a pretense tae superiority."

I joked, "Oh to have the entitlement of a titled young man."

"He will be here for the rest of the day down in the Great Hall, which means, until the men return, we will be the hostesses. I might bow out as much as possible, his smug face reminds me of his grandfather, and it is causing my head tae ache."

Lizbeth rose. "Of course, mother, we will go downstairs — ye should rest, join us if ye are able."

We rose and I followed Lizbeth downstairs.

CHAPTER 31 - KAITLYN

*I*n the Great Hall, Arran and his company had shoved the table to the wall and moved the chairs in a half circle facing the table, as if it were a stage. One of his men was standing on the table, and looked very drunk. Lizbeth said, "Och nae, if the Earl sees this, twill be..."

Arran grabbed her hand and pulled her to a chair then rushed back to grab my hand and pulled me to sit beside him. His brow went up, his fine wig floated like a white cloud above his dark hair. He had his shirt untied and open at his chest. The bottom of his shirt was mostly untucked from his pants — he passed me an ale.

"Oh no, I—"

"Nae! Drink!"

I took a sip, because he scared me and I didn't dare say no.

He sank back in his chair, his legs splayed again, a look on his face that tried to be seductive, but was actually very sinister. He was facing me, not the table where his friend was reciting poetry, which was disconcerting. His friend, I noted, was not as good at poetry as Lochinvar.

Arran's eyes were leveled on my face.

I flushed and he found it amusing.

He hooked a foot around the leg of my chair and dragged me closer, my chair scraping across the floor.

Lizbeth said, "She's married!"

He laughed, "I ken, she is verra beautiful though—" He sipped from a whisky glass. "Your accent is interesting, where are ye from?"

"I'm from the New World." It had been a long time since I broke out that old excuse.

"Intriguing, very intriguing." He leaned forward on his knees and peered up at my face. "It sounds like ye must be verra adventurous."

"My husband, Magnus Campbell, the Earl's nephew, and I do have very many adventures."

He sneered and leaned back, a darkness clouding his face. "I am nae interested in yer husband, Magnus, relation to the Earl." He huffed. "It is disinteresting tae talk of husbands, that is not the way of the day, Madame Kaitlyn. We are glorious men and women of the aristocracy, are we not? We like our pleasures…" He leaned forward placing a hand on my chin. I tried to pull away, but he grasped and held it firmly, scaring the hell out of me. "Ye hae a fine cheek, and it has a high color as if ye are vulnerable — ye are a pleasure, I imagine." His eyes locked on mine, dangerously close.

Lizbeth said, "Unhand her! Or I will go for the guards."

I glanced over his shoulder, Lady Mairead entering the room, but swiftly rushing out again.

Lizbeth said, "You let go of Madame Kaitlyn Campbell right now!"

He let go of my chin with a little shove and then yanked my chair even closer, so that his knee was shoved between mine. He locked eyes with me and pushed his knee forward, obtrusively. I was really frightened.

He said loudly, to the man on the table. "John, continue with the poetry, I do enjoy it."

The man continued reciting his terrible poetry, the room got cold, the light waning — *what time was it? Late afternoon?*

Why the fuck was I in the Great Hall with Campbell men, with strange Campbell men? While all the familiar Campbell men were out for the day, God, what if they were delayed?

Lizbeth strode for the door, I was hoping and praying for her escape, but one of the men stepped in her way. She raised her chin, her best impression of Lady Mairead. "Remove yourself. *Now!*"

He laughed at her.

My heart sank.

I had, yet again, no weapons. I had gotten up hungover and had used my dagger in the storeroom and hadn't put it back in its sheath.

It was lying beside a sack of oats.

Not that I could get to it anyway, with this man's knee pressed against my skirts. He'd have it from my hands in a half-second.

He languidly watched me, the expression on his face best described as pleased with himself, he was a fucking awful person. He said, "What are ye worried upon, Madame Kaitlyn? Wondering about yer husband? I heard a group of men were detained near Fortingall, the rain making the river difficult tae cross. They wouldna make it tae Balloch by nightfall, a few hours more, I suspect. And we, of course, are just paused for a rest, we will have some ale, then ye will show me tae yer room. I am sure ye can be verra hospitable."

He snapped his fingers at the man near him, and he was passed a hunk of bread. He ripped off a chunk and chewed it lustily. "Then we'll leave, yer husband won't even notice we were here."

"Is that because you're so wee? He won't notice because you're so small?"

He chuckled maliciously. "Ye've got the mouth of a brazen

witch." He grasped my knee and pushed it aside. I tried to stand and he shoved me back in the chair.

Lizbeth shrieked, but then, from my peripheral vision, the door opened and men strode into the hall, Magnus at the lead, sopping wet and covered in mud. Sean and Liam right behind him.

A man slammed the doors shut.

Sean bellowed, "Man, ye best get off the table."

The men with Arran backed away into the corner. The man on the table sheepishly climbed down.

Mangus's face went from curious to concerned to stormy in the eight seconds it took him to stalk across the room to Arran's chair.

Arran tried to stand, but Magnus was on him — Magnus grabbed the wooden arms of his chair and slid it back away from mine, then grasped Arran's linen shirt, Arran cowering under him. "Ye will unhand m'wife."

Arran put his hands up, "We were just havin' a meal in the Earl's Great Hall. We were invited."

"Ye werna invited tae frighten Madame Lizbeth Campbell, tae offend m'mother, tae hae yer way with Madame Kaitlyn, my wife! Ye are takin' liberties with the women of Balloch! Ye are a scoundrel and a fool — what say ye tae the charge that ye hae come here, under false pretenses, pretending tae be family, but actin' as a scoundrel touching another man's wife?"

"I dinna ken she was yer wife!"

Magnus picked him up from the chair and shoved him so hard he fell to the ground. "Ye dinna hear her say it? Kaitlyn, did ye tell him ye were married?"

"Yes. I told him."

"Did ye tell him ye were married tae Magnus Campbell?"

"Yes."

"Did he ken I was away from the castle for the day?"

"Yes," I sobbed, by this point the fear of the situation had devolved into tears. "Yes, he told me you weren't coming back tonight, and that he wanted me to take him up to my room."

Arran tried to stand, but Magnus swung his foot back and kicked him hard in the ass. "Ye are a liar, and hae behaved without honor. What were ye goin' tae do in m'rooms with m'wife?"

"Nothing, I—"

"Naethin', yet I can see yer fingermark upon Kaitlyn's jaw — ye put yer hands on m'wife? Enough tae leave a mark? I am goin' tae kick yer arse."

Magnus took off his coat and tossed it tae the side.

There was a voice from the door — the Earl's, "Young Magnus! Are ye brawling again? I told ye there would be nae more brawlin' in m'home!"

"Nae, I am impartin' a punishment, sire, this man, Young Arran, was disrespecting yer title!"

"Now was he? I... I'm sure there must be some misunderstanding."

"Nae, Arran is in yer lands, the lands of the Earl of Breadalbane, inside yer castle, shewin' ye disrespect — much like his grandfather once shewed ye little honor!"

Magnus circled Arran. "Ye came in here as if ye are entitled tae the place, how dare ye? I am going tae kick yer arse because ye disrespected Lady Mairead, ye frightened Madame Lizbeth, and ye deserve tae hae the lesson. Get up and take the fight."

Magnus said, "Kaitlyn, will ye remove yerself from the hall? I daena wish ye tae see it."

I said, "Yes, Magnus." I left through the large wide doors, into the arms of Lizbeth.

Lady Mairead said, "Thank God Magnus arrived when he did, I ran tae get him, as soon as I saw what was happening."

"Thank you."

Inside the shouts and bangs and sounds of furniture being upended and grunts and groans. Lizbeth and I hugged and then let go of each other and pressed our ears to the doors to listen. A second later, Lady Mairead was beside us, with her ear pressed, a look of intense concentration.

A few minutes later, Sean's voice, "Young Magnus, enough!"

The sounds of a struggle, then Magnus's voice, "He and his men must leave, right now! They do not receive one more minute of shelter."

Sean said, "Aye, brother."

The Earl said, "The guards have their horses readied."

Lizbeth said, "What of the women?"

"They will be confined tae a room, their carriage will leave at dawn."

Lizbeth, Lady Mairead, and I jumped from the path of the doors as they were pushed open and the visitors were shoved and dragged from the Great Hall, down the passageway, yelling and groaning. Arran looking dazed and semi-conscious with his face bloodied. Then the crowd of men shoved out through the main doors to the courtyard. By this time it was a big melee, the strangers being picked up and carried out into the rain.

It was horrible to witness, and also a huge relief — both those things were true. I didn't relish the idea of justice being meted out like that, but the dude had been really scary and there was no guilty or not guilty, he had been creepy as hell and had malevolent plans... Relief washed over me — then Magnus was pushing through the crowd toward me.

Aye?

Yes.

"Ye good, Kaitlyn?" He swept me up in his arms, burying his face against my neck in my hair. "Och, I was worried on ye."

I nodded against his shoulder and kissed his cheek. "I'm okay, are you okay?" I pulled back to look, his brow was wet from sweat, his lip swollen, his heart racing.

"Aye," He kissed me, a full mouth, a searching tongue, a 'wanting me' kind of kiss. "Wrap yer legs."

He carried me from the gallery toward the end, one of the

rarely used entrances. I glanced back at the crowd. Sean, watching us leave, chuckling, nudging Liam.

We made it out of the main room into a smaller corridor where Magnus pressed me up against the wall and began pulling up my skirts, kissing my mouth, pressing and searching, pulling and pushing until he got my skirts up.

"I wish I could help."

"Nae worries, I can manage, just hold yerself up."

He got my skirts up in the front and then his kilt up, muddy and damp, against my stomach, then with a firm grip on my thighs, he entered me, fast and hard, breathlessly, *Och.*

To hold me up there was a shoulder, pressing against mine, his forehead pressed to the wall, his hips plowing, with bullish exhales, animal, beast-like, he fucked me hard. Until he came with a moan and pressed against me, in a collapsed-like state. His mouth against my throat, his breath vibrating on my skin. "Och, I feel gratitude, thank ye, Kaitlyn."

"God, I think you just saved my life."

"Ye would hae fought him."

I groaned. "I didn't have my knife."

He chuckled. "How many times will ye hae near death experiences afore ye remember tae strap on yer knife in the morn?"

I wailed, "I don't know!"

He chuckled. "I feel a great deal better."

"Me too. That was necessary."

CHAPTER 32 - KAITLYN

*M*y legs were still up and around him, but he was shivering from the cold and his legs were shaking from the effort. "You're shaking."

He kissed my jaw, lifted me from the wall, and carried me, laughing, to a low wooden bench. He laid me down, sat at my feet, and lifted my legs up tae his lap. He joked, "Yer skirts are like a blanket."

I put an arm under my head, and watched him. He looked shaken.

"Are you okay?"

"Aye." He dropped his head back tae the wall. "I think."

"That was scary."

"Aye, if we haena returned who kens what would hae happened."

I nodded.

"But also, ye ken, I am a grown man, a powerful king, but yet I felt like that young man who was trying tae protect ye, remember? He was a bit lost, in over his head."

"Yeah, I remember."

The corridor was dark and cold, a high, thin window at the

stone end of the room let in a bit of blue moonlight. It fell across his face, setting the mood — noir, sad.

"You are a very different man from those days. Then, you were the son of Mairead, the younger brother of Lizbeth and Sean, you had little consequence, but now you are Magnus, you are important — a father, a husband, a king, though none of them here seem to notice. But you don't feel the need to prove yourself to them anymore, right?"

"Right. But still..."

"Yeah, I know."

His thick strong hand was resting on my skirts, I entwined my fingers in his.

"I am just feeling as if I am disrespected."

"Yeah, that happens when you go home, when anyone goes home. It's easy to be disrespected, no one seems to get how important you are, but I see you, Magnus, I know how important and powerful and humane and generous and wise you are."

"Thank ye, I am verra glad ye are okay."

He closed his eyes and exhaled.

"Another thing we ought tae speak on — are ye goin' tae be okay tae hae another bairn?"

I screwed up my face. "That's a weird question, you mean, Beaty? To have another bairn around us? Yeah I mean, sure..." My voice trailed off.

He was smiling, one of his cocky smiles.

"Is that what you mean?"

"Nae..." He tilted his head back and looked down his nose. "Nae, I meant I got ye pregnant just then and I wanted tae make sure ye were ready for another bairn."

My eyes went wide. "What are you talking about, Magnus? You got me pregnant just then?" I scoffed, "That is not how sperm works, my love. God, you need a science lesson."

He shrugged, chuckling. "Ye daena hae tae believe me, but ye ought tae ken, I always do whatever I set m'mind tae, and just then, I wanted tae get ye pregnant verra much, twas primal, it felt like a bear. I couldna argue with it, and so, I am asking if it was okay with ye that I came tae ye and carried ye down the hall and got ye pregnant. I wanted tae ken if ye were alright with it."

I sighed. "Well, it was very primal, and you did feel like a bear, that much is true. And I will say this, we haven't talked about it in a while, we've been busy and we hadn't planned. As you know I haven't been on the pill for months, and there has been a lot of sex, and I got my last period, that was fine... I mean, I'm not pregnant, I would have noticed if that—"

He shook his head, mockingly, "I am nae sayin' ye would notice, I am saying that it happened just now, do ye notice yet?"

"Magnus, you have no idea. But yes, I am alright with it, I would like to have another, definitely. I would love to have a boy."

"Good." He grinned. "Because I got ye pregnant and we are goin' tae hae a son."

"Ha ha, verra funny."

"How could it nae be a boy, Kaitlyn? I kicked a man's arse in yer honor, I picked ye up and ravaged ye against a wall, I worked at it so hard I grew weakened. Tis for sure a son, tis science, ye ken."

"How do you make a daughter?"

"Candlelight and roses, a good night's sleep after."

"Very scientific."

"Ye are all right with it? I dinna ask afore I did it?"

"I am all right with it. I do think we should start trying to make a baby."

He chuckled and made a checkmark in the air.

"You honestly believe I'm pregnant?"

"Aye, this verra moment, we will be able tae tell him, when he is grown, I was ravagin' yer mother in the dark corridor of the—"

I groaned. "Please, please don't tell the children stories about their conception."

He grinned. "I winna. But I reserve the right tae tell everyone else."

"You are *very* sure of yourself."

"I hae the confidence of a man who beat another, and the humility of a man who is sitting in damp, muddy clothes. I think I am balanced."

He squeezed my hand. "I love ye, Kaitlyn, I am glad ye are safe, and I promise ye I will keep ye safe while we wait for the bairn."

I swung my legs off the bench. "And there is no pregnancy test for miles around, but it wouldn't *even* work tonight, it would take at least a week."

He said, "Trust me. I promise ye are havin' a bairn. I promise ye that I will keep ye safe." His stomach growled.

"Let's get you some food." I stood and pulled him up from the bench and we walked back into the Great Hall.

The room had been put back into order, the longest table placed down the middle, the chairs and stools and benches returned to their places. Food was set on a side table and people were serving their meal onto plates. We all sat down.

Magnus asked Sean, "Brother, what happened when I left?"

"We sent them from the castle, and Lochinvar and some of the young men followed them down the road so they wouldna turn back."

"Lochinvar had a sword?"

"Aye, but none of the men in the party were gunnin' tae fight, tis all good Young Magnus."

The Earl entered and went to the head of the table and sat. He was wearing his long, cream brocade, at-home robe, tied with a sash at his waist. His hair was mussed.

He said, "Magnus, ye are filthy."

Magnus said, "I dinna hae time tae change intae m'dinner clothes, Yer Highness."

"Ah yes, because of the brawl. I am glad tae see it is—"

Lady Mairead pushed her chair back from the table and stood.

A hush went over the entire dining room.

She said, "Brother, I winna hae ye disrespect my sons. Sean has had tae remove a man from yer castle, a man who was showing a great deal of dishonor tae yer sister and her daughter, Yer Highness's niece. Yer niece had tae flee your Great Hall tae seek help and safety. And m'son Magnus had tae beat a man for placing hands upon his wife. It is unconscionable that ye hae allowed it tae happen in yer hall and that ye..."

She drew in air. "I will go tae Edinburgh, I will tell all about how ye are runnin' yer household, about the dishonor ye allow in yer hall."

"That is nae necessary... I daena think ye should tell anyone..."

"Ye want me tae keep quiet on how yer household is run? Ye want me tae be silent on the fact that a man was here with his hands upon yer nephew's wife? That the women of yer family were in fear and ye dinna lift a finger?"

"The men returned, Mairead! It was all well in the—"

"I will keep the sordid details tae myself and I will nae spread them tae the courts of Edinburgh or London, but I will tell ye, brother, ye winna allow Arran, his brothers or sisters, not one member of his family, nae even a cousin, if he has a good word tae say of him, in this castle or on yer grounds again. I winna stand for it. When the Earl of Lowden lived here he brought dishonor upon me, upon my children, upon ye, and now his sons are coming tae bring heaps more. It is because they believe ye are weak and they think ye are beneath them. I will nae stand for it again. They are nae allowed in the house."

"I am tae feud with the Earl of Lowden and his sons?"

"Aye, tae yer last breath, and tae yer son's last breath, for the rest of our family's bloodline we are nae tae consort with the Lowdens. Or I will tell the world how weak ye are."

"Fine, Mairead, sit down."

She sat, her chin raised, haughtily. Her hands folded in her lap.

He said, "Sean, do ye agree with Lady Mairead — we are tae cut all ties with the Earl of Lowden? This is yer Grandfather's title, these are yer step-brothers."

"They are naething tae me, they hae done nothing but disrespect our good name. Ye ought tae acknowledge that they are dishonorin' yer family."

The Earl lifted his fork and knife. "Good, then I will send a message tae Lowden telling them that he and his sons are nae welcome on the lands of Breadalbane. Twill be their loss, everyone kens I hae the best lands, and the more important title. They will be begging tae gain m'good graces in no time." He carved some meat and placed it in his mouth.

Lady Mairead nodded and muttered, "Good, finally. But brother, ye canna allow them in yer good graces, however they beg. If I visit again and hear that the Lowden family hae been in the castle, I will take all the money and power that I bestow upon ye and I will destroy yer reputation as well."

"Lady Mairead, I do nae believe it will come tae that."

"Good."

I looked peripherally, all of us were looking down at our plates. Magnus squeezed my hand under the table.

Lizbeth whispered. "Good lord, did mum finally get her way?"

Sean said, "Aye, she has, *finally*."

CHAPTER 33 - KAITLYN

*O*nce the Earl had retired, and Lady Mairead had gone to her room, we all relaxed.

Lizbeth said, "I hae never heard her take that tone with him. Och, twas impressive."

Sean said, "She is fortunate she inna spendin' a night in the stockade."

Magnus waited until Liam and Sean had their attention elsewhere and asked Lizbeth, "Lizbeth, do ye happen tae hae any of Lady Mairead's writings or books in yer possession?"

She said, "Ye mean like the books that she carries in her pocket?"

"Aye, I wondered if ye kent where she might keep them when she has filled them with notes?"

"Nae, I daena, but I think she would want tae keep them hidden, and though she trusts me tae keep her secrets, she kens it would be out of my hands. If m'husband wanted tae, he could force me tae divulge them. If the Earl made a point of searchin' m'rooms, twould be within his rights tae find whatever he wants, it is his castle."

Magnus nodded. "Aye, I thought as much. Kaitlyn and I suspect that Lady Mairead is in trouble and so we are lookin' for clues as tae where she is."

"Ye daena believe she had dinner with us just now, Young Magnus? That she has now retired tae her room?"

He shook his head, "But daena worry, Lizbeth, tis nae magic, we just want tae ken what is happening with her, what she might be keeping from us. Ye ken, she is always secretive."

She nodded. "She did tell me once that Paris is her favorite respite, the place she believed she was truly herself and absolutely independent. She said that if she went tae Paris she dinna hae tae answer tae anyone." Lizbeth stared off into space, nodding. "As a woman, who must often wonder about havin' things tae myself, I can understand that if she wanted tae hide something she would pick a place where she dinna hae a lord tae watch over her."

Magnus said, "Tis the way ye feel, Lizbeth?"

"Aye, tis nae a complaint about m'lord, Liam, but tis a statement of fact — he is m'lord. I would nae be able tae keep secrets from him if he asked."

Magnus said, "I never heard ye speak on it this way, sister, I thought ye were pleased with yer match."

"Och," she waved her hands, "I am verra pleased with my match, he is a fine husband, and I am fortunate that he dinna ask for m'secrets. He listens when I tell him my thoughts. He allows me tae hae my own opinions. I am blessed and full of gratitude that he is such a fine man."

At the end of the table, Liam and Sean were in a discussion and right then Liam growled. Lizbeth grinned and blew him a kiss. He caught it and put it in his pocket and continued speaking with Sean.

Magnus turned to me, "Do ye feel the same way, Kaitlyn?"

"What way, that you are a fine husband? You know I do."

"Nae, I mean, constricted in what ye are allowed tae hold ontae for yerself?"

"No, I don't really have anything that I would want to keep from you... but I don't think of you that way. I would just tell you. Like how I told you that I didn't have my knife earlier, I could have kept that secret, but I trust you that you will listen and... I think our rules are different."

"But ye would keep secrets if ye had one?"

I narrowed my eyes. "Are you just *now* realizing that I have my own mind and my own thoughts? I tell you everything, but also my brain is always working, if I told you *everything* you would drown in all the everything — be grateful I keep some of it private."

Lizbeth laughed. "Young Magnus, ye daena want a wife who is blank inside, a vessel for yer own thoughts, or *worse*, a mirror reflecting back everything ye want her tae be." She shook her head. "Nae ye would be verra ruined by a woman such as this—"

He chuckled, "Kaitlyn, daena listen tae anything I am about tae say, I am just playin' out the conversation: Lizbeth, I ken I would be hopelessly bored, I wouldna want it at all, but how would it ruin me? Our brother, Sean, assures me it is the best virtue in a wife for her tae be complacent and most importantly quiet in all matters."

She drank from her ale. "Och nae! Ye are such a man, Young Magnus, dimwitted and unaware. Canna ye see how much Kaitlyn does for ye?"

He laughed. "Oh I see it, I just wanted ye tae explain yer thinking on it."

"Ye would be absolutely ruined if ye dinna hae a wife who pushed back on yer ideas, Young Magnus. If ye did everything that came intae yer head and dinna hae tae discuss it with yer wife and consider yer bairns, ye would be insufferable, but the good news is ye would also be dead. Ye wouldna hae made it tae this ripe auld age."

"So my lovely wife's arguing is what keeps me alive?"

Lizbeth said, "Amen," and raised her glass toward mine.

Sean said, "What are ye speaking about down there?"

Magnus said, "Our sister is explaining tae Kaitlyn and me the importance of wifely virtues."

Sean said, "Well done, Lizbeth!" He and Liam raised their mugs toward our end of the table and Lizbeth bit her lip to keep from laughing.

The men who had forced Arran away returned later in the night, full of stories. The lead man was wearing a wool tam, with a piece of white yarn woven through it, in a crude attempt at a swoosh, mimicking a hat we had brought for Sean years ago. Magnus's eyes followed them as they strutted into the Great Hall. "Sean, where is Lochinvar, do ye think?"

"I daena see him." He called the men over. "Where is Young Lochie?"

The men laughed. "We lost him in the woods, when we were ridin'. He felt sure he could find his way home. So we gave him the chance tae prove it."

Sean groaned and asked Magnus, "Is this what I hae tae deal with now, Lochinvar is goin' tae always be brawlin', braggin', or bein' lost?"

"He is the age."

Sean sighed. "If he inna back by the morn, we'll hae tae go out and find him."

CHAPTER 34 - KAITLYN

*T*he doors to the dining hall opened with a crash and Lochinvar stood there, sword drawn, completely wet, glaring, and furious.

Magnus jumped up and went to meet him, and it was less of a greet and more of a stand and block Lochie from starting a fight over whatever had happened out in the woods. Lochie tried to push past Magnus.

Magnus shoved him up against a wall with his forearm against his chest. "Lochie, ye arna tae fight, toss down yer blade."

Lochie tossed down his blade. "They jumped me in the woods! They dinna give me m'horse back, I had tae run tae follow them!" He checked his arm. "I am injured!"

Magnus let go of him and checked his arm and their voices grew quiet. I glanced over at the long table where the men were boisterously laughing.

Sean went to go meet Magnus and Lochie at the wall.

Magnus returned and said, "Kaitlyn, will ye run for the first aid? He has a deep scrape on his arm."

I ran up to the room for my first aid kit. Then I returned and Lizbeth and I sat beside Lochie at a table, as he showed us his wound.

"Lochie, this looks painful."

"I hae had much worse, ye ken, someone is always wantin' tae beat me, but those men are arseholes."

I dabbed at it with an antibiotic wipe. "What were you fighting about?"

He was sullen, his furious eyes glaring down at the men who had deserted him. "They called Magnus a bastard."

I huffed. "I agree, they are arseholes. Did you tell him?"

"Nae."

"Good, thank you, it's hard on him, but also, you don't have to stick up for him. He has been dealing with it his whole life and he is a grown up, he can stick up for himself."

"They disrespected him, he is a king and they—"

I smeared some antibiotic cream on his wound. "You know, they don't acknowledge he is a king here. They have no idea. It's very tricky."

He scowled. "He is twice the man of all of them."

"I agree with you in everything you're saying." I applied a sterile bandage and adhered it with medical tape. As I pressed it to his arm, I asked, "What are you going to do?"

He gestured toward a dude at the far end of the room. "I'm goin' tae beat that man's smug smile off his face."

I sighed.

Lizbeth pushed a mug of ale closer to Lochie.

I said, "So here's the thing, you remember last night when the Earl said, 'Magnus are you brawling again'?"

"Aye."

"See, Magnus has been the man who *everyone* disrespects and that the Earl blames for *everything*. When I met him, Magnus was very concerned about his reputation, but through the years he has gained the respect of the men his age. Sean has become the head of this house and he is Magnus's brother. He is going to take ye under his protection, and Liam will as well. You can't brawl with the men anymore Lochie. It looks bad on Magnus.

You are a guest of Sean and Lizbeth, a family member of Magnus. You have to behave like it."

Lizbeth said, "Aye, and tomorrow you will work alongside Craigh. Ye listen tae him on everything. Ye do as he asks. He will guide ye."

"I daena want tae live here, Kaitlyn, will ye tell Magnus he ought tae take me with him? I can be a help, I promise."

I patted the back of his hand. "Magnus and I have to go to Paris and deal with something. While we are gone we need to leave you here with Sean."

"How long? How long are ye goin' tae leave me here?"

"I don't know—"

He folded his hands pleadingly. Then he shoved his chair back and dropped to his knees. "Please Madame Kaitlyn, would ye talk tae Magnus, I ken ye can persuade him."

I nodded, "I will talk to Magnus."

Magnus walked up just then with Sean and Liam. "What's this, Lochie is on his knees in front of m'wife?"

I said, "He was asking me for something, we'll talk of it later."

"'Tis a secret? I heard women keep secrets and a few hours later I am a witness to it!"

I laughed and smacked his shoulder. "Magnus, that's not what it is, it's just a private conversation for you and me to have later."

Magnus nodded, "I suspect I ken what it is." He addressed Lochie, "Where will ye sleep taenight?"

Lochie pouted.

Magnus said, "Boy, I am about tae knock the expression off yer face. I will ask ye again, where will ye sleep taenight?"

"Sire, I am nae going tae sleep. I will take the guard duty on the walls and then I will go tae work with Craigh at dawn."

"Good, it sounds a productive day, except ye ought tae go down tae the church tae pray at sunrise, then ye go work for Craigh. Hae ye had a meal?"

"Nae."

"Fill yer plate, then head off tae the walls so I might speak tae Kaitlyn."

Lochie stood and stalked off.

Magnus chuckled, shaking his head. "Och he is a pile of trouble."

Lizbeth said, "He is a verra good boy, Magnus, ye are confused on it. He has been fighting for yer honor against all those men." She gestured to the end of the table.

Sean snarled, "I will handle the men, Magnus, daena ye worry on it."

"Thank ye brother."

That night in our room. Magnus asked, "So allow me tae guess, Young Lochinvar was beggin' ye tae hae mercy on him?"

"Yes, he feels wronged that we are leaving him here. He doesn't want to stay."

"I think this is the best thing for him, he needs tae learn how tae blend in a family, tae follow orders, tae be turned intae a—"

"Are you going to say a warrior? Because that is—"

"Nae, I was going tae say a man."

I took a deep breath. "I disagree."

Magnus's brow drew down. "On what? On that he needs tae learn tae shew the men of the family some respect? That he needs tae learn his place?"

"Yes, I disagree with you."

"I never thought I'd say this but m'sister is a bad influence on ye with her high ideas on women."

"Jesus Christ Magnus, that is the most asinine thing you ever said."

He said, "Ye ken I am teasin' on that, but I daena ken how ye can disagree with me on something ye daena ken about. I think I ken how tae raise a young man tae adulthood in his clan."

"You might know more than I on that, but you don't know diddly-squat about raising a young modern man to adulthood in the year 2024. I bet I know a lot more about that, and the truth is, Lochinvar is a modern man. He has been ruined for the past, for better or worse. The other night when he stopped fighting it was because of an Eminem song! He has modern tastes, he can't live back in time and be happy or even content and... I think it's going to require happiness and wanting to please the people around him to make him want to behave. Who here does he want to impress?"

"I think he will grow tae admire Sean and Craigh and Liam given a chance."

"He respects and admires *you*. He admires Quentin and James and even Fraoch, he has adopted a clan, and now we've taken him away from it."

Magnus sat down on the bed with his elbows on his knees, shaking his head. "I daena think ye are right on it, Kaitlyn. He must learn tae get along in the world of men."

I sat down beside him. "What if he's already done that? He grew up in Dunscaith where his life was worth nothing. He trained to fight, he survived. Maybe he already knows how to get along with men, maybe he needs a different kind of lesson."

Magnus sighed.

"Is there anything else he can learn from fighting, besides maybe practice? Is there anything he needs to learn about stables? If there's anything that needs to be learned about getting along in a clan I bet you money Fraoch can teach it to him."

Magnus nodded, "True. If he can win over Fraoch he could win over anyone."

"It would be good for Fraoch too, he's old enough to be a big brother, he—"

"Historically he's likely old enough tae be his father."

It was my turn to laugh. "It would be good for Fraoch to

take on the role of Baldie, he would be good at that, he ought to be given the chance."

"I said the same thing tae Fraoch a while back."

"I think Fraoch would be great in that role and the truth is, the men were disrespecting you, Magnus. He's fighting for your honor, remember what it was like to have to do that every day? To wake up and have to prove yourself to everyone in the castle? And remember how you despaired that your father left you to do that, didn't claim you, just left you to be always scrapping about your honor? You're leaving Lochie to the same fate. He's been doing that at Dunscaith, he thought he had been rescued and now he's been told to do it again, by you, a man who he respects and you know what?"

"What?"

"He got down verra pleasingly, as your mother would say, and begged quite properly, and when you told him what to do, he listened. If you leave him here, he will do his best, he won't want to let you down, but we might be letting him down."

"Och, I daena like it when ye disagree with me like this."

"Because I am right?"

"Aye, ye are right on it." Magnus exhaled. "We will leave him here while we go tae Paris and look for Lady Mairead, and we will come back for him in a few days. Then we will take him tae Florida with us."

I kissed him on the cheek and hugged around his shoulders. "Thank you for listening!"

He pulled me back on the bed and leaned up on an arm and talked to my absolutely flat stomach. "Dost ye hear yer mother, wee'un? She is arguin' against me, but tis because her heart is so big so I hope ye will like her anyway."

I wrapped a finger in his curl and sprung it away from his face. "You really think there's a baby there?"

He kissed my bodice. "Aye, I ken it, Kaitlyn, daena ye feel it? The world has shifted, we hae a son comin'."

~

I woke the next morning and Magnus was already dressed and relieving himself in the chamber pot. I watched him as he moved around the room, readying for our day.

"You're already up?"

"Aye, I met Lochie at the chapel and we hae prayed then I told him about m'change of plans."

"Oh, good.

"I dinna credit ye, Kaitlyn, I am going tae tell him it was my idea. I daena want him tae think he can beg ye whenever he wants something. His wants might grow beyond yer empathy."

I nodded. "That makes perfect sense. I'd rather you get credit anyway. I wasn't trying to win, I just wanted to come to an agreement. Thank you for it."

"Ye're welcome, he was verra grateful, and seemed penitent on it. We will see if he continues in that way." He opened up one of our bags and placed a few of our things out on the bed.

"So we're leaving for Paris, I mean... If there is a baby, should I be jumping?"

"I daena ken."

"I mean, I have, right, before? I just got really nervous about it."

"We canna leave ye here, ye ken, for months, we need tae get ye home, we daena want ye tae give birth here."

"Last time I gave birth in a closet during a hurricane."

"Aye, but twas a twenty-first century closet, we daena hae antibiotics, nae, we hae the gold threads for yer head, and we will just do this one jump, then a jump tae get ye home and then we will do our best tae keep ye there."

"I like the sound of that."

"Me as well." He grinned, "But does this line of questionin' mean ye believe me?"

"No, but I don't mind the sound of it. We could begin to try."

"We daena need tae, ye will see, soon enough."

CHAPTER 35 - MAGNUS

*W*e time-jumped mid-morning, in a rare moment when the rain had stopped.

Lochinvar followed us tae the clearing, tae return our horses tae the castle once we jumped. I dismounted ontae a boulder because the ground was fair wet and muddy, then I pulled Kaitlyn from her horse and loaded our bags tae m'shoulders. I said, "Lochie, ye ken, be good, keep yer head down, help Craigh, sit with Sean at the table, daena brawl."

Lochie said, "Auld man are ye goin' tae keep lecturing me? I am wrecked from the hours of guard duty, then the prayin' in church, and workin' in the stables with Craigh, and now I am here for yer horses when I ought tae be looking for a warm young lassie tae be m'soft bed while I sleep."

Magnus's eyes went wide. "Och nae, Lochie! Nae young lassies! I will tell ye, when Colonel Quentin found the young lassie, Beaty, his attention made a promise tae her, and when he wanted tae come back with us tae Florida, she had tae come with him. Master Cook found Sophie and we had tae bring her as well. We are verra fond of Beaty and Sophie, but tis nae possible ye would be so lucky tae find another young lassie who we can time travel with — so if ye entangle yerself we will hae tae leave ye here."

Lochie clutched his heart. "I must choose between a woman tae warm my bed, or *cookies*? If I chose tae bed a woman I can nae longer ride in cars and nae television? Och nae, ye hae sent a chill through me, Magnus." Lochie's horse stamped left and right, splashing mud.

Kaitlyn stepped away tae keep the mud from hitting the bottom hem of her cloak, and I held her arm tae keep her from sliding from the boulder.

"Let the chill be yer warning, get some sleep on a bed of straw like the rest of the men, and then ye can time travel unencumbered."

Lochie pretended tae snore. "Ye're borin' me with the lectures."

I waved a hand, "Och, ye daena listen, but be careful."

"Aye, I will be careful and chaste and polite, and I will guard well and work hard and I will find a widow who wants tae be bedded and I will bed her. Lady Mairead might still be in residence in the castle, she might do."

I groaned.

Lochie grinned.

Kaitlyn said, "Lochie! You better stop saying things like that about Lady Mairead, or I'm going to think less of you."

"My apologies, Madame Kaitlyn, I winna do anythin' with Lady Mairead. I will nae go near her, but... I daena truly understand it, Magnus, how come Lady Mairead is here, but yet ye are goin' tae look for her?"

I said, "I explained it tae ye, there is a long line of time, and there are Lady Maireads at different times. Some old and some young, this one is a young Lady Mairead, I am searchin' for an older Lady Mairead. Dost ye understand?"

"Nae, I daena... and why is time a line, inna it more like a wheel?"

My eyes widened. "Och ye sound like Cailean!"

Kaitlyn said, "It seems like it might rain, we ought to go." She grabbed my forearms, "You ready to jump highlander?"

"Aye, mo reul-iuil, tis time." I twisted the vessel.

We landed in the far-away park on the edge of Paris, and then had tae wait for our storm tae clear and... there was nae one tae meet us. We hadna expected her, but with Lady Mairead ye always worried when she dinna show.

I slowly lumbered tae m'feet and looked down at Kaitlyn and gave her my hand. She pulled herself up with a moan.

I said, "I have risen quickly because first, I am verra hungry, second, twas a long visit tae the past and we need food."

She laughed. "It's all your stomach then?"

"Did I mention m'hunger?"

She said, "Yeah, let's get going." She shook out her body and we gathered our things. Stepping from the clearin' intae the woods and then up a slow rise tae get the view. Kaitlyn faced east and joked, "Where'd Paris go? There's nothing but woods and fields."

I gestured in the other direction, where Paris lay before us. It looked tae be just after dawn, which was an excellent time, because it looked as if it would be about three miles tae walk.

Kaitlyn pulled her cloak around her black dress. Neither of us had the right clothes for the fashion of the day, but we hoped the cloaks would help.

I knelt and brushed off our boots. We were both muddy though we had tried tae stay clean. She said, "Last time I was here I was a gentle-lady, with fancy jewelry and a fine dress, hanging out with poets and artists... this time I have on muddy boots, a medieval cloak, a plain dress, and—"

I joked, "A king, who is also in a sad state, a long slog ahead of us, but at least we hae each other." I pulled our bags tae my shoulders.

We walked down the hill through the woods tae a village with wide green fields and low rock walls, a road going past with a car sputtering by and a horse-drawn cart laden with sacks, going the other direction. The road was so slim they had tae slow tae pass without drivin' off intae a ditch.

We walked intae the village and up tae the first house with an open door. "Sir?" I called in.

The lady of the house, glanced, saw me there, and rushed, her feet thumpin' on the wood floors, out tae the back. We stood there waitin', able tae see clear through the house tae the fields in the back, until a man came around the house. He said, "Qu'est-ce que tu veux?"

I said, "Auriez-vous de pain pour deux voyageurs?"

His wife brought us a loaf of bread and I paid her from m'sporran. "Merci."

Kaitlyn and I walked out onto the road. "Thank God you remember French,"

I ripped the bread in half and passed her a hunk. "Twas crude, but I got the point across without having tae use gestures."

We leaned on a stone wall and shared the bread. Then a horse-drawn cart came up the road headed our way. I stepped out and hailed it, speakin' tae the man briefly, passin' him a coin, thankful I had thought tae bring them. He motioned toward the cart, the sideless flatbed, and in the center of it, a cask of... I dinna ken, because there was a lid upon it, but water had splashed around it. I called tae the driver, "What is in the seau?"

He answered, "Anguilles."

My brow drew down.

Kaitlyn asked, "What is it?"

"I canna think, let me..." I climbed ontae the small flatbed which had barely enough room for my arse, and tucked the bags I carried under my arms. The cart started tae go, leaving Kaitlyn standing on the road, laughing with her hands out, feigning incredulity.

I tugged on the driver's coat, "Och nae! Ma femme!"

He pulled the horse tae a stop and Kaitlyn jogged up. I patted my thigh and she climbed ontae m'lap. "Hold on, mo reul-iuil, tis gonna be a bump—"

The horse began tae move and the cart lurched forward, the cask splashed against my back.

"Anguilles… what dost ye think is in the cask?" The cart bounced and was more uncomfortable than a swayback mule and barely faster than our feet.

She said, "I don't know, but hold on," she twisted, holding on around my neck, and pried the lid up. "Oh my god, Magnus! It's writhing!" She dropped the lid.

"Och I ken the word — tis eels."

She wretched.

The cart hit a pothole and more water splashed down my back. She said, "Oh my god, what if one jumps out and gets on us!"

I joked, "I regret every decision I hae ever made."

We were let off at the gates of a large bustling market, streets and streets of vendors, baskets full of food, carts everywhere.

Kaitlyn put her hands on her hips. "*This* ought to be enough food for you."

We brushed each other off. Our route had taken us through busy city streets. I used the edge of m'shirt tae wipe black exhaust and dirty grime from her face. "Och nae, I daena ken if tis better, ye look like a chimney sweep."

"You do too, and you smell like the ocean." She wretched again.

I said, "Mistakes were made, thankfully Lady Mairead inna here tae see us."

We walked intae the market.

I scoped around tae see if we were being followed or

watched, I felt edgy bein' out in the open, with a hungry pit in my stomach.

We came tae a table where we purchased a loaf of bread with some spreadable soft cheese and then at another table I bought a pile of sliced beef. Soon enough we had full stomachs and a bottle of wine tucked under my arm for later. I asked for directions and then we strolled in that direction.

We arrived as the sun went high and it grew hot.

We stood on the top step in front of Lady Mairead's door. I joked, "Add tae our general look of uncleanliness, the stench, and we are verra ill-prepared tae appear on Lady Mairead's doorstep." I banged on the door.

Nae answer.

There was a window beside her door, we peered in and up the stairs, but twas dark inside. Below us was a gallery at street level, we looked through the window, it was dusty and looked unused.

CHAPTER 36 - MAGNUS

"*W*atch for trouble." I dropped our bags tae the stoop, dug through one tae pull out a piece of cloth. I wrapped it around m'hand, then with m'back tae the street, I punched the glass pane. I pulled jagged pieces free of the frame, and dropped them tae the ground. I reached in and opened the door.

"She is going to kill you."

"Aye." I ushered Kaitlyn in. "I am still trying tae decide if I ought tae risk rescuing her, perhaps I ought tae leave her be, twould be safer." I closed the door behind us then we went up the darkened stair tae her sitting room. The furniture was covered in sheets, the curtains were pulled, there was an eerie dust-filled, dim grayness over the luxuriously furnished room. "She haena been here in a while." I ran m'finger through the dust upon her secretary desk and began searchin' through the drawers.

Kaitlyn said, "It seems disrespectful to rifle through her things."

"I agree," I flipped through some old bank statements. "But I daena see how else tae find her. At first I just wanted tae live up tae my promise, now I am certain she is in trouble. I need tae find her."

"I think you're right, it's 1904, the year she was visiting Paris to see Picasso, we met with her here not that many months ago. You'd think she would be back, many times, but here she... it looks like it's been years."

"Aye." I sifted through some of her paperwork while Kaitlyn crept down the hallway

She called from a back room. "Magnus!"

I followed her voice tae Lady Mairead's bedroom.

"The bed was unmade, which was odd. And look!"

There were papers spread across the sheets, and a pen laying beside them. The bed mussed, as if she had been sleeping, writing, worrying... I picked up one of the pages. The top entry read:

I am very concerned, I believe Agnie has located this safe house. She seems determined to destroy me. I am set on the idea that I must_____

An ink-mark went down the page from the last word.

I flipped it over, there was nothing on the back. I passed it tae Kaitlyn, then scanned the next page. It was headed:

What do I understand about Agnie Macleod?

Kaitlyn read over m'shoulder, a list that included:

Ormr
Domnall
Dunscaith Castle
MacLeod Ranch, Montana.
The year 1872.

Circled a few times. Beside it, in looping hand:

Villa Magnifique. South of France.
1959.

Then ominously the words:

Can I trust Hammond?

Then:

I am no longer sure.

I passed m'mother's list tae Kaitlyn. "Och, do ye think?"

Kaitlyn looked down at it and shook her head, "I don't know, but if your gut and her gut tells you he's not trustworthy, maybe he's not?"

Magnus shook his head slowly. "I daena want tae beleve it, but I daena want tae be made a fool."

"He has been taking care of Riaghalbane for you for a long time."

"Aye."

"What was in it for him?"

"The only thing was that his life wasna at risk. If he was in line for the throne it was likely that someone would want him dead, so instead he allied himself with me tae survive."

"Maybe now that your kingdom is secure and your lineage strengthened, maybe he just didn't feel like his life was at risk anymore — he's just a cousin, right? Maybe what seems suspicious about him is his natural moving away from you. Maybe he's just breaking up with Lady Mairead. Maybe she suspects him because he's moving on."

"But someone brought me tae the kingdom and deposited me intae the middle of a fight with Ormr and Domnall, and without Lochinvar I would hae died."

I placed my hand on my injured shoulder, and moved the joint around in a circle. I barely noticed when I did it, but I did it whenever we spoke on that last arena battle.

She asked, "And we suspect Hammond did that?"

"He would hae been in a position tae do it, one of the few people in the history of the world. If it *was* him, it was a good plan. He wanted me dead, and he would hae gotten away with it." I shook my head. "This all means he has allied himself with someone else, which means..."

"Which means all those years of friendship are for naught." She looked around the room and then continued, "We should check on him first, right? We should go to Riaghalbane, find out. We don't *know*-know."

"Tis nae a we, Kaitlyn, I am taking ye back tae the rest of the family, then I will sort it with Hammond."

"I'm grounded?"

"This has gotten much more dire than it was before, mo reul-iuil."

"And we're no closer to finding Lady Mairead."

"We hae a list of places tae look, but I think I ken where she is."

"Really, where?"

"I think she is bein' held at Agnie MacLeod's Montana ranch in 1872."

Kaitlyn looked down at the list I had passed her. "How did you get to that point?"

I said, "Agnie inna going tae take Lady Mairead tae Dunscaith Castle, it is in Scotland. Although tis dreary, would be too comfortable for Lady Mairead even with the dreariness, also, tis verra important tae remember, Agnie would ken we hae *all* come tae Dunscaith. We ken tis her family castle. We ken too much about it. She winna take Lady Mairead there, scratch it off the list. The beach house in the South of France inna going tae be where they keep Lady Mairead, tis too pleasant, everyone likes a beach house. Scratch that off the list. Which brings us tae the ranch in Montana in the year 1872, it sounds like a horrid place for Lady Mairead, daena it?"

"It does: cowboys, dust, lawlessness, hanging trees, duels in the one road town — yes it definitely does."

"If ye wanted tae keep Lady Mairead at a place and time which would be purposely unpleasant for her, twould be the top of yer list."

"True that, besides, you know, Vesuvius. Or the Titanic."

I waved it away. "Och she would escape those, she is verra robust and relentless."

"Great description of her."

"The way tae really destroy Lady Mairead would be tae put her in a place with nae art, nae society, nae control over her life, and tae force her tae live in the dust of a terrible land. I ken where she is, now I just hae tae go get her. But I must deal with Hammond first. Or finding Lady Mairead may nae be the end of it."

There was a loud bangin' on the front door.

Kaitlyn's eyes went wide, she whispered, "Who is it?"

I quietly went tae the window and looked down at the front stoop. "A neighbor checking in. I did break the window."

"Oh true, man, that took the neighbors long enough, glad we weren't robbers, wait, are they going to think we're robbers?"

I moved to the stairs.

Kaitlyn whispered, "Careful!"

CHAPTER 37 - KAITLYN

I heard his low voice, speaking his halting French, and a few minutes later he returned upstairs. "I explained it, and somehow they believed me. They kent m'mother so we talked on her for a moment. I said I was her son, and he said he could see the likeness. They offered tae send a glazier over, I gave him money for the repair."

"That's a symptom of how handsome you are, they just offer to help. You've clearly broken in and they're all, 'can we send someone to repair the window, sir?'"

He laughed. "The money helped."

"Should we wait?" We looked around the space. "There's a lot of priceless art, we ought to wait."

"Aye."

The glazier came that evening to measure the glass and promised to return the next day. Magnus and I slept in the guest room and 'haunted' the house, leaving for the market at meals, then looking through books and opening a few drawers. I said, "It gives me a little trepidation that you're going through your mom's stuff."

"Lizbeth got in yer head about it, my mother has secrets

everywhere. She is secretive, I am her son, but I am also her lord. She ought nae keep secrets from me, it might kill me."

"I know but this is her sanctum, the place where she comes to keep all the things she really doesn't want you to know." I stood up and did some jumping jacks in the middle of the living room.

"What ye doin'?"

"Trying to get the blood flowing, we've been idle for a while."

He grinned and joined me in the middle of the living room, and we jumping-jacked together for a bit.

We wandered around the downstairs gallery, reminding myself why we had to wait for the glass to be installed. There was so much art in there: Two Picassos, a Cezanne, a Matisse and a Monet. Magnus looked around. "I am nae sure I understand. They *are* beautiful, but how come m'mother would lay down her life for them?"

I sipped from a glass of wine. "I don't really know, I mean, I know they will be worth a lot of money someday, but it's not just that, it's that they're important. I think she believes if she collects them she is important too."

Magnus nodded. "Aye, ye might be right."

Finally at midday the glazier showed up with the glass. We were relieved, but then he said he would return the next day to install it, we were disappointed. "This has been really boring, man, I miss the kids. I regret breaking in."

"'Tis m'mother's fault though, if she dinna hae so much art we wouldna hae tae wait for the glass."

"I feel like we are too nice."

I was teasing, because as I said it I was lounging on her fancy sofa, wearing her pearls, one of her robes, and had one of her books open and flat on my chest. Magnus and I had also figured out how to play the phonograph, so there was a weird rubber disc lazily turning, emitting something like music with terrible sound quality.

He grimaced. "This is supposed tae be music?"

"It was a marvel of its time, remember, if you had only ever lived in the eighteenth century and had heard this, remember how amazing it would have been."

"Tis hard tae imagine after havin' Chris Stapleton blarin' from the speaker while we grilled hamburgers by the loch in Maine."

I plumped the fancy, velvet pillow under my head. "Yes, a totally different experience."

That afternoon, I asked, "What if we're captive? What if we're in a tower, guarding the art, like the dragon? I might be confusing a few different stories, but you get me — what if we're trapped? I know! Let's go out and watch the sunset."

"I daena ken if it can be seen from the square."

"We'll be able to see the light change, come on, let's do it."

Magnus sat on the stoop, a glass of wine in his hand, at ease in a pair of slacks and a white shirt, and his boots. I was also wearing a pair of boots with a silk party dress that I had taken from Lady Mairead's closet. I had covered the dress in a silk robe and had a feather boa around my shoulders. I was eating a chocolate pastry, careful not to get any crumbs on the clothes. It was lovely out on the front stoop as the light changed.

Magnus said, "Times like this Paris seems almost pleasant, instead of a putrid cesspool of degenerate artists."

I laughed.

There weren't people in our square, but a main thoroughfare was just beyond and so I began to joke as they moved along, "He's saying, 'Oh ho! I'm fast-walking to the chimney-sweep convention.' And she said, 'Out of my way, peasants!' And then check him out, he's saying, 'I'm walking and I'm handsome, I'm handsome and I'm walking, I'm handsome and I'm walking.'"

Magnus took a sip of his wine. "Ye think he is handsome? I ought tae run him through."

"It's not me, it's *him*, he's the one saying it, look, you can see from the way he holds his head."

"Aye, he is verra fancy, he is definitely saying, 'I am handsome,' as he walks, ye are right on it. And that woman is saying, 'I am pretty and I am—"

"Careful, I will run *you* through with a sword."

"Och, ye might want tae but ye will never carry one."

"True, I suppose you are safe, but yes, that is exactly what she's saying. She has a parasol, there has never, in the whole entire history of the world, been a woman with a parasol who didn't have an overly fine idea of herself."

His eyes drew to the northern sky. It was behind our south-facing stoop, but he stepped out into the square to look. "There is a storm, near where we jumped."

"Oh, oh!" I scrambled up, rushed up the stairs, and took off the feather boa and put it in the box, wrapped in tissue. I took off my robe and hung it on the hanger, and wriggled the dress off over my head and folded it nicely into the drawer, also wrapped in tissue. I found my plain black dress and pulled it on.

I hastily made the guest room bed, and then remembered to replace the bedding over Mairead's bed, then rushed out to the living room and pulled the curtains closed. I grasped the heavy thick covering rolled up at one end of the sofa, and drew it out as a man's voice came up from downstairs. I raced to the stairs as it dawned on me — that voice belonged to Hammond.

I walked down. He said, "Hello, Kaitlyn." He didn't call me Queen Kaitlyn, which seemed notable, and he looked nervous, but it could have been because he had been left standing in the square and Magnus stood above him on the steps and hadn't invited him in.

"Hello Hammond, what brings you here? We were just leaving."

He explained, "I was just coming to check on Mairead... have you seen her?"

There was something about his facial expression when he said it that made him seem not curious about Mairead at all, but curious about what we knew.

Magnus said, "Aye, we just saw her at Balloch."

Hammond cocked his head. "Did you, good good... she was well?"

"Aye, verra well, ye haena seen her in a while? How long has it been?"

Hammond said, "I am... it has been a long—"

Magnus interrupted, "How did ye ken we were here?"

Hammond said, "Oh, I did not know, I was merely looking for Mairead and—"

I said, "That's a weird coincidence, we just picked a random date, how come you arrived in Paris while we were here?"

Magnus narrowed his eyes. "Did ye follow us here?"

"No, how would I... no, I just came to check in."

Magnus and Hammond looked at each other, then Magnus nodded. "How's the kingdom?"

"We have a lot to speak of, Magnus, perhaps we should—"

"Because now that I've ridden the lands of Ormr and Domnall, I think we are finally safe. It might be the first time the kingdom inna under threat. Possibly we ought tae return tae my kingdom and ye can relinquish the vessel, as I daena think ye need it anymore."

Hammond lowered his brow. "There is still much to do..."

"I'm wondering if you had any contact with Agnie MacLeod?"

There was a pause, then Hammond said, "Who?"

Magnus said, "Aye, well, we are both lookin' for Lady Mairead then, we ought tae look taegether, daena ye think?"

Hammond said, "You said you recently saw her, that's good

enough for my purposes. We should wait for her to reappear. In the meantime, perhaps you ought to accompany me to the kingdom, there we can..."

"*I* ought to accompany *you*...?"

Hammond shifted his feet.

Magnus scrutinized him, then exhaled. "If ye would like me tae accompany ye, anywhere, ye daena need Kaitlyn. Ye ought tae allow Kaitlyn tae travel on tae where she was goin', ye ken, Kaitlyn?" He pulled a vessel from his pocket and passed it to me.

"Oh," I said as I took it.

Magnus kept his eyes locked on Hammond.

Hammond asked, "Did you have somewhere you needed to be, Kaitlyn?"

"Yes, absolutely, I..." Was I supposed to go to the compound, that was it, right? Or Balloch, should I go to Balloch and get Lochinvar?

Hammond said, "It might be better if she came with us. Safer. There are dangerous things afoot."

"Nae, twould be better tae let her go..." Magnus added, "Dost ye ken, Hammie, what happened that caused me tae be dragged intae the middle of the arena?"

"Of course not. How could I...?"

"Indeed." Magnus said, "I will go with you, but I want Kaitlyn tae be given free passage, allow her tae travel safely, and I will do whatever you want."

"Magnus, that is not necessary, it is just…"

I said, because I thought there was just confusion between them, "Hammond is just…"

But Magnus shook his head, telling me to wheesht.

Hammond spoke into a radio he had fastened to his chest.

Magnus said, "What is that about? The men at the road?"

I hadn't noticed anyone at the road, but when I looked up I could see men entering the square. We were way outnumbered by about ten soldiers wearing black and gray camouflage. They all carried weapons. We were trapped and—

Hammond pulled a golden metallic strip from his pocket, it was similar to the choker I had once worn. "Magnus Archibald Caelhin Campbell, you are under arrest, you will need to come with me."

"Ye would assault yer king? Ye ken this is treason, Hammond, ye ken this means yer death. I believed ye tae be a cousin and an ally."

"You believed wrongly, I see now that your lineage is not my future, there is another path, one in which I have more power."

Hammond stepped closer. "Put your hands on your head." The men were closing in on us.

Magnus put his hands on his head. "Kaitlyn, run."

I turned, brushed past Magnus and fled into the house as he sprung forward onto Hammond. I raced down the three side steps to the small gallery and glanced back to see Magnus dragging Hammond in a headlock. I raced through the gallery, past all the fine paintings and shoved out through the back door, with Magnus right behind me, holding Hammond who was struggling to get free.

Magnus was yelling at the soldiers, "Get back! Daena follow us!"

I unlocked the door, flung it open, and raced into the alley. A dingy, mud-swamp kind of alley, with puddles and filth and grime — it looked like where everyone threw their laundry water, but also probably a few people pissed back here too.

I glanced left and right. Magnus yelled, "Twist the vessel! Balloch!"

I started to work the numbers, panicked out of my mind. The door behind us opened, men were running down the alley toward us.

"I know! I know! I'm trying to...!"

Hammond plowed his elbow into Magnus's side knocking him into the wall.

I rushed after them, twisting the vessel. "Hold onto me!"

Hammond was kicking and elbowing, it was hard to get

close to Magnus, to twist the vessel while holding onto Magnus who was in a massive struggle. I clamped my arms around Magnus's upper arm and as the vessel charged, as the wind rose and the thunder and lightning started, Magnus shoved Hammond away as hard as he could, but my face was pressed to Magnus's arm, and my tight hold had some of Hammond's jacket and so Hammond and at least one other man had hold of us as we ripped through time — the last bit of consciousness I had was Magnus yelling, "Wake up as fast as ye can, Kaitlyn!"

And then the searing pain hit my body and I was torn from the world of Belle Epoque Paris, in the middle of a storm. Repeating to myself a mantra, an urgent urge... get up get up getup getup getuupppppgetuuuupppppp

CHAPTER 38 - KAITLYN

*G**et up!*

I came to as I was being dragged by the arms through the leaves of an ancient forest. I glanced up at who was dragging me — Lochinvar.

I muttered, "Lochie?"

"Ye hae tae stay here, Madame Kaitlyn, stay down."

I mumbled, "Where's Magnus...?" as the sound of yelling voices came into my hearing. Was that Magnus's voice?

Hammond was yelling.

I turned onto my side, and patted down the leaves in front of my face to be able to see across the clearing, past the boulder, where Magnus was wrestling Hammond.

Magnus punched him hard and rose up above him, gripping his shirt and screaming into his face, "Why did you betray my family?"

Just past him Sean and Liam held another man, one of Hammond's soldiers between them. His head lolled.

Sean yelled, "Who are these men?"

Magnus said, "This man is m'General, the guardian of my kingdom, he is a traitor." He spoke to Hammond, "Why did ye betray me, what did they promise ye?"

Hammond struggled and tried to get up. Magnus held him down. "We are..."

Magnus screamed into his face, shaking him. "Who is we? Agnie? Tell me! Are ye comin' for my family? Are ye going tae take m'kingdom?"

Hammond spit in Magnus's face. "The kingdom is already ours."

Magnus climbed up, grabbed Hammonds wrists, and began dragging him.

Hammond yelled, "Where are you taking me?"

"Tae prison! A prison of m'choosing, ye will live out yer life in a cell!"

Sean said, "He is a traitor, Magnus, ye canna allow him tae live."

Hammond struggled free and scrambled up.

Magnus lunged on him, punching him to the ground again, holding him down, "Why did ye do it? Why hae ye betrayed me?"

Sean was yelling, "Tis treason, Young Magnus, ye canna allow treason! He will always be a threat tae ye, tae yer family!"

Magnus said, "Why, Hammond?"

Hammond yelled, "My life has never been my own. Agnie offered me a chance tae sit on the throne, this was my chance to change course!"

Magnus dropped off Hammond to the side, shaking his head. "Nae, och nae, Hammie."

Hammond dove onto Magnus, grabbed Magnus's dirk, fell back, and plunged it into himself. Magnus dove forward, trying to grasp the dirk away, but it was too late. The dirk was stabbed into Hammond, and the men were locked eye to eye until Hammond convulsed and fell back, dragging Magnus down on top of him.

"Nae!" Magnus bellowed, looking down in Hammond's face. "Nae!" He held Hammond's shoulders then bent close with his ear to Hammond's mouth. He listened to something Hammond said, then said, "Nae, nae, och nae."

And then collapsed back, sitting in the dirt beside Hammond, with his elbows on his knees, his head in his hands. His fingers gripping his hair. "Och nae, Hammie, nae."

And Hammond took a last gasping breath and died.

I scrambled to my knees and crawled to Magnus and sat down beside him. I put my hand on his shoulder and he shook it off. His face was wet from sweat and tears, his jaw set. He glared at Hammond and then looked at me as if he had just seen me there, he dropped his head to my chest and I held on to him.

I held Magnus while Sean, unceremoniously, stabbed the other soldier through, allowed him to collapse to the ground, and then Liam tossed his body beside Hammond's.

Sean came and stood over us. "Tis for the best Magnus, ye canna hae a traitor in yer midst, and ye canna reform him, ye winna be able tae trust him."

Magnus's voice from near my heart. "I ken."

"This was for the best. Tae jail him would hae meant tae always be guardin' him."

"I ken, he wanted tae die, his life has been at m'mercy. He had royal blood and nae way tae survive without protection from his king." Magnus wiped his eyes and put out his hand for Sean tae heave him up. He stood, tearfully looking down on Hammond. Then he put out a hand to help me up. And he and I both solemnly regarded the remains of the man who had been Hammond.

I asked, "What did he say to you at the end?"

"General Hammond's last words were, 'I beg yer forgiveness, Yer Majesty.'"

I wrapped my arms around his bicep and tucked my head there. Looking down on Hammond was heartbreaking, but my heart was still racing from the chase, and the fear of having him corner us, and the chill of how he had spoken to us. It had been as if he had cut himself off from all emotion and had grown cold.

I kissed Magnus's shoulder. "Should we pray?"

"Aye—"

A horse galloped up the path and pulled to the edge of the clearing, Lady Mairead, the younger one, shrieked, "What did ye do tae Hammond?!" She dismounted her horse and rushed toward us.

"He has died, Lady Mairead, he was a—"

She dropped to her knees and pulled Hammond's head onto her lap and clung around his head and shoulders. "Nae Magnus, ye canna, he was my Hammond, ye canna!"

Magnus said, "He winna yers for a long time, Lady Mairead."

She looked down into Hammond's eyes. "Nae, Hammond, ye must nae go, ye canna leave me. Ye promised tae always look after me — ye promised!"

Magnus just stared at the trees, blinking.

Lady Mairead sobbed. "What happened?!" She closed Hammond's eyes and hugged around his shoulders. "I daena understand what happened!"

Magnus's mouth worked before he said, "Lady Mairead, he has made an alliance with Agnie MacLeod."

Her hands trembled. She breathed raggedly, then she drew her hands away from Hammond's chest. She took a deep breath and shoved his head from her lap to the dirt.

She slowly stood.

And stared down on Hammond alongside us, her expression cold, her shoulders trembling.

Magnus said, "Sean would ye go for a cart? Kaitlyn, Lady Mairead, and I will stay here and pray."

Sean said, "Aye, Young Magnus," and he and Liam left the clearing, leaving Lochinvar to guard us as we prayed over Hammond's body.

~

Lady Mairead said, "I was about tae leave."

Magnus said, "We hae just been tae Paris, we were looking for ye, and we hae broken the glass beside yer door, we were waiting for a glazier tae repair it when Hammond arrived."

"What date?"

He told her the date we had been chased from Paris.

"I will oversee the repair."

"Daena interfere with us, please, we daena need the scene tae get any more complicated."

"Aye I ken, I will wait for the storm clouds tae clear."

She walked to the middle of the clearing.

"Ye are certain, Magnus, that Hammond had turned a traitor?"

"Aye, he admitted it, and he begged m'forgiveness, he has risked the lives of yer grandchildren."

"Ye are in hiding?"

"Aye, we hae a safe place now, but..."

She said, "Daena tell me. Ye ought tae hae some secrets from me, and if I am tae be captured and held by Agnie tis better for me nae tae ken the truth. I hae never relinquished secrets, but I also daena ken how much I can bear. I hae been tested, but everyone has a breaking point, even me."

Magnus said, "I agree, I winna tell ye."

"Good, but keep Archie safe—"

"And Isla."

"Of course and Isla and the rest. I forgot the timeline." She pulled the vessel from her pocket. "Magnus, thank ye for lookin' for me, ye are keepin' yer promise, I appreciate that ye are honorable."

"Ye are welcome."

. . .

We huddled together while the storm rose, until Lady Mairead had disappeared.

Magnus and I remained, quiet, praying for Hammond.

It dawned on me slowly, that night was on us. The woods around us turned dark as the sun went down, shadows slid across the clearing, occasionally Magnus wiped his eyes.

Finally, coming from the castle, we saw a small procession of riders, footmen carrying torches, and a cart. The bodies of the traitor, Hammond, and his soldier were loaded onto the cart without ceremony. Magnus and I held hands as we walked in the flaring torchlight, back to Balloch.

CHAPTER 39 - KAITLYN

*T*here he said, "I hae a great deal tae see tae, but, and I ken tis something I say much too often, but I am verra hungry."

"It makes sense, a full day has gone."

"Aye, if we were in the present day we would hae been fed three times a'ready, with treats tae get us through the turmoil."

I nodded, "Shall we go to the Great Hall?"

"Aye."

We sat at the long table, our plates piled with the remains of an earlier meal.

Lizbeth sat down first. "He was a very close alliance of yours, Young Magnus?"

"Aye, he has been... for how long, mo reul-iuil?"

"It's been about six years for me, maybe seven. I don't know, it's hard to keep the years straight."

"I canna count the years that he has been m'commander, my ally, or m'friend, it has been—"

Sean, Liam, and Lochinvar crossed toward us. Sean looked

heated, and sat down in a chair with a huff, "What are ye talkin' on Young Magnus?"

"I was telling Lizbeth about m'long history of alliance with General Hammond, I hae fought alongside him for a many years. I trusted him implicitly."

Lizbeth said, "And yet he turned on ye?"

"Aye, he turned."

Sean said, "This is yer problem, Young Magnus, tis always been yer problem, ye trust too easily."

Magnus said, "Tis true?"

"Aye, ye were always runnin' around here a young man, thinkin' ye had friends and allies, but who was fightin' for ye?"

"Ye were."

"Aye, because though ye were a bastard, ye were m'brother, and if ye sank in the estimation of everyone in the castle, ye took Lizbeth and me with ye, but twas *only* because we were brothers that I allied with ye. Twould hae been easier tae hae set m'self apart — but brotherhood kept our alliance. This is a tough lesson for ye, Young Magnus. Ye are a king, ye must make the men around ye prove their allegiance. Ye canna blindly trust them. Ye must be suspicious of all men and doubly skeptical of those with a claim tae yer throne."

I took a bite of a suspicious looking blood sausage and choked it down with a piece of dry bread.

Magnus had his forearms beside his plate. "I canna trust anyone?"

Sean banged on the table. "Of course not, ye hae tae keep yer son safe, yer kingdom. Ye canna trust anyone! but this is doubly true if they are hungry for power, ye must be skeptical of any man who claims tae be an ally!"

Magnus nodded. "I misplaced m'trust, he had proven himself, but I—"

"He was yer cousin! He had a claim tae the throne! Ye should hae been suspicious! More careful!"

It was chilling to watch Magnus staring down at his plate, like a young man, yelled at by his older brother.

"I thought I was careful, I believed he... I protected him."

"Aye, ye protected him, and then he turned on ye, ye brought him here, what if he had harmed yer family? Who else kens yer family is here?"

Magnus looked at the far wall, his jaw clenching and unclenching. "I daena ken. We hae an enemy in a woman, Agnie Macleod—"

"Och she is a woman, she is nae a concern."

"Our mother is a woman, *she* has been a concern."

Sean scoffed and waved his hand.

Magnus continued, "Agnie MacLeod is allied with a man named Ian the Troublesome."

"Och, he sounds like a detestable, pock-ridden, mewl-mouthed villain."

Magnus chuckled and ripped off a piece of bread, dragged it through his thick fish stew, and stuffed it in his mouth, chewing as Sean continued, "But ye canna trust anyone — how many men do ye hae in yer inner circle?"

Magnus shrugged. "About six. I trust them, I trust them all with my life."

"Ye ought tae make them swear their allegiance tae ye, tis a terrible thing tae find a traitor in yer midst. Ye ought tae cut them out before they cause trouble tae ye."

Magnus chewed and nodded. "How would ye say I do that?"

"Ye could threaten their—"

Lochinvar interrupted, "I disagree."

Sean turned, "Och nae, Lochie the Mewling, Maddening Midge has something tae say? He wants tae weigh in on his elders speakin'?"

Magnus raised his brow. "I see ye two were gettin' along well in m'absence."

Lochinvar scowled.

Craigh walked up just then and chimed in. "Lochie, ye

ought tae keep quiet, ye are tae be working and listening tae yer elders, or ye want another beatin' like I gave ye the other night?"

"Ye dinna beat me the other night, I had m'sword taken from me, twas nae fair."

Craigh laughed. "Ye are a wee midge, always buzzin' round, 'Twas nae fair'! I will shew ye fair, I will beat yer arse in the meadow for all the—"

Sean said, "We daena want tae see ye try tae beat Lochie the Midge again, the way he was carryin' on, we need some peace and quiet."

Lochinvar looked sullen.

Craigh nodded and walked away.

Magnus said, "I want tae hear what Lochie has tae say."

"I disagree with yer brother, Magnus, ye daena need tae threaten or require yer men tae take an oath tae ye, ye daena need tae."

Sean said, "Why nae? He has just been betrayed."

"Because Magnus is fair, his men will follow him because of it."

Magnus said, "Ye are supposed tae call me King Magnus, boy."

"Aye, my apologies, Your Majesty."

Sean huffed. "So a fairness from a ruler and suddenly all the men are goin' tae be trustworthy?"

Magnus said, "Yes, they would die for me and they ken I would lay down m'life for them. We hae battled taegether, but… I ken, if they turn, if they become untrustworthy, then they are dead."

Sean said, "This is the first sensible thing ye hae said on it."

"Sean, ye arna telling me anything I daena ken already. Ye forget I fought in an arena against m'uncles, my cousins, and m'half-brothers, and I hae killed them all tae gain the throne of Riaghalbane. I ken how tae take the measure of a man. The men I trust are proven. We are allies, much like ye and Liam, we are bound by family ties. I ken how tae keep a good man's allegiance." He looked down into his mug. "That being said, I daena ken where I went wrong with Hammond."

Lochinvar said, "Sounds like he became Lady Mairead's ally instead of yers."

"Aye, this is likely true, and now he is dead. I lost a long time friend on this day."

Magnus drank the last of his drink and shook his head sadly. "I ken ye are advisin' me from a place of brotherly care, and as m'elder ye believe yerself tae be in a position tae lecture me, but I am a king and a warrior and I daena need tae be told how tae form alliances nor how tae kill a traitor. I ken it. I hae lived it."

Sean said, "I ken Young Magnus, I wanted tae advise ye, and I... tis a hard thing tae see yer brother brought low by a traitor. I apologize for steppin' out of bounds."

"I ken and I thank ye, Sean." To soften his words, Magnus put his hand on Sean's shoulder. "I appreciate ye want what is best for me, ye hae been a good protector, ye kept me alive all those years—"

"Barely."

Magnus chuckled. "Thank ye for it anyway, but I hae had a long few days, with a great deal of turmoil. I think I will head tae m'room." He stood, saying, "Kaitlyn, will ye accompany me?"

I began to follow but instead rushed back to Sean and threw my arms around him. "Thank you for wanting to protect Magnus, you've always been a good brother to him."

He said, "Ye're welcome, Madame Kaitlyn."

I straightened, said, "Goodnight," and followed Magnus from the Great Hall.

In our rooms he collapsed on the bed and I crawled up beside him and put my head on his shoulder, wrapped around his chest, as he stared up at the ceiling in the pitch black night of our room.

He said simply, "Och nae."

Then he said, "I feel as if I hae let him down, ye ken? He has betrayed me, but twas at the end of a long life of servin' me, tis hard tae square it, and nae matter how I think about him in the sum of the deeds, he died by my dirk and tis... verra hard tae square."

I said simply. "I know," and then we clung to each other through the night.

The next morning Magnus oversaw the small funeral and burial of Hammond in the churchyard. The soldier had an unmarked grave, because we had no idea who he was, but Magnus paid for Hammond to have a gravestone with his name and the words, "Sleep on now, and take your rest." Which seemed fitting for his general and the man who had helped guard his kingdom for so many long years.

Magnus and I stood beside the grave for a time. Then he exhaled and squeezed my hand.

"Ye want tae go for a ride?"

"Sure."

We saddled horses and rode out toward the mountains and followed the path that rose up through the hills high above the castle. There, we climbed from our horses to look down on Balloch and the valley below. Magnus said, "Thank ye for ridin' with me, mo reul-iuil, I needed tae clear m'head."

"Sean was pretty tough on you last night."

"Eh." He shrugged. "He had his mouth working out a problem he was tryin' tae solve. As m'elder brother, he believed he was the one tae solve it, but he had forgotten I am a man, a king, and ken a great deal more about the world than he."

I nodded.

We stood shoulder to shoulder looking out on the view. His eyes swept the sky from the river and mountains to the north, and the hills to the south. "He wanted tae advise me as a strong eighteenth century man, but I am a twenty-fourth century king."

I glanced up at his face, stoic, his eyes, watchful. "You have always weighed his advice before?"

"Aye, he is verra wise, but he is using his wisdom tae be fearful, we ought nae be fearful based on Hammond turning, I daena think there is a lesson here at all, nae for me, except as relates tae m'mother — she ought tae hae treated Hammond better, but even within that code of conduct, he should nae hae betrayed me. But then what — I am supposed tae suspect Colonel Quentin now?" He shook his head. "Hammond and I are both descendants of a bloodline of kings, creatures battling in the muck and mire afore a golden throne. I had tae fight tae gain it, he survived by sitting beside it, we both did what we needed tae do, ye ken?"

I nodded.

"We were both tryin' tae survive."

He kicked a rock away. "Hammond was wrong. I am nae going tae let his corruption change me, tae ruin m'trust in my friends and family. I am nae goin' tae become sour and vengeful. I am goin' tae accept that sometimes shit happens."

I smiled. "That is so very modern of you."

He grinned, his eyes sweeping the valley. "M'transformation is almost complete. I'm near fully modern." He joked, "Now, next on m'agenda, avenge m'mother, regain m'kingdom with some proper bloodshed — verra verra modern."

"When are we leaving?"

"I think taenight, after the feast, perhaps if we get back early enough in the day we can hae another, better feast prepared by Zach."

"You can*not* get enough food these days."

"I daena think I hae been fully filled yet, the thirteenth

century is still here," he pointed at his stomach, "empty, needing sustenance."

He went quiet, then said, "Do ye remember me telling ye a story about being in the battle of the North Frontier with Hammond? We were waiting for a delivery of supplies. Twas delayed, and so we had tae kill and eat a squirrel. I was telling him about the squirrels here at home."

"I don't remember hearing that story."

"We spent many long hours talking about growing up."

"He will be missed."

"Aye."

We rode back down the hill, with Magnus quiet until he stopped his horse to say, "Dost ye hear that, Kaitlyn?"

I listened. "The distant woodpecker?"

"Aye." He looked around as if noticing that we were out in the woods for the first time.

I noticed he relaxed, breathed deeper.

He asked, "What tree is it...?"

Through the years he had taught me to see the trees, something that I used to never do... "That, my love, is an oak, one of the most important trees in this area."

"Aye, Black Duncan planted many of them and they are now a great deal of wealth for m'uncle. See the new wall, there?" He gestured with his head. "It has just been built." Our path took us down, nearing the loch shore. "That tree...?"

I said, "A hazel, and there, a birch. It's been a while, but I still remember."

He shifted in his saddle to look up and around. "We hae a fine day for a ride." He clicked for his horse and set us in motion, my horse following his down the path toward the castle. We had been in silence on the way up, talking on the way down — it was how I knew he felt better after losing Hammond.

After dinner, and a tearful goodbye with our family, Magnus said, as he and Lochie and I walked to the fields to jump. "I wonder if m'mother is going tae ever go back there?"

"To Paris? You mean, if she was free, not kidnapped?"

"Aye, it looks like she haena been there in a long time, and ye ken, it dinna look fun, there was only one bottle in her bar, nae signs of socializin', it looked dismal and dusty as if it had aged. I wondered if she had been lonely the last few times she went."

"Perhaps she and Picasso broke up? Ugh, the thought of it almost makes me sad for her."

"It makes me gleeful, but aye, tis a sorry thing tae see her safe house so dull."

"Well, here we go to our compound, I doubt it's dull at all, not with... how many people?"

Magnus said, "It feels like we had thirty-eight packed in that van."

CHAPTER 40 - KAITLYN

*W*e landed in a field without a structure in sight, just far woods surrounding us.

Above us, Quentin looked down from the driver's seat of a big pickup truck. "Hey boss, you back? Why'd you bring Lochie, thought he was living in the past?"

Haggis bounded out of the truck and frolicked in front of Magnus as he groaned and sat up. Haggis's tail was wagging brutally hard.

Magnus said, his hands up to protect himself from Haggis's licks, "I brought Lochie back, the eighteenth century did nae agree with him."

Lochie, from the ground said, "It sucked a dirty pigswill."

Quentin said, "Shhhh, no bad mouthing pigs."

I said, "How's the compound so far?"

Quentin put out a hand and hefted me to my feet. "It's fucking paradise, that's why no one else came, they're all living the Attitude Adjustment life."

Magnus and I climbed into the cab of the truck, Lochie sat on the tail, and Quentin drove us up a bumpy dirt road to the main house, a big two story lodge built out of giant timbers. It was a little like pulling up to Paul Bunyan's house.

"Wow!" I said, as Isla and Archie came barreling around the corner.

"Mammy!" They raced into my arms.

I dropped down onto the wood planks of the front porch and held them close. "I am so freaking proud of you, I know it was scary that I was gone, but I came back and now—"

Isla took my face in her hands. "Mammy, you do no have to keep talking, I want to show you the dock."

I hugged her. "Well, that is awesome." I stood up and joked, "I do not take that personally at all," and took her hand to go out to see the dock, even though I was still dressed like it was a totally different century.

Magnus and Archie followed us, Archie chattering. "There's two trucks, three ATVs, a couple of drones, all in the garage, oh! And there is a treehouse, it's so cool, and a bridge that goes across the lake to the island — you see the island? There's a couple of boats and Uncle James and Uncle Fraoch both race in the boats. It's really cool."

I said, "Are you in the boat while they race, or are you safely on shore?"

Archie started to answer and Magnus shook his head, teasing, "That is one of those questions ye daena want tae lie about, and ye daena want tae tell the truth — yer mum has a verra good imagination. Ye ought tae shew her how ye do it instead of telling her of it."

I laughed. "This is true, the image in my head of a boat race is a little like the Jackass movies. I doubt Aunt Emma would allow those kinds of shenanigans."

"Aunt Emma thinks the boat races are very fun."

"Good, then I know I will love them."

After paying our respects to the dock and giving appreciative compliments to the wide view, a big lake with a forest, our house on a peninsula jutting into the lake, a suspension bridge at the narrow end, we made it back to the living room and hugged everyone else hello. Zach gestured toward the kitchen doors, and asked, right away, if Magnus was hungry. I didn't need to be asked, because of course Magnus was, so we were both promised food.

Sophie and Emma came in from the gardens, followed by Zoe carrying a bucket with about a half cup of blueberries in it. Her face and hands were covered in purple stains. We hugged and Zoe said, "Booberries, AyWee?"

"Is that my name now?"

She nodded.

"Are you picking them, Zoe, or eating them?"

She nodded and pushed the bucket toward my face.

I took and ate a booberry. "Delicious!"

Isla said, "We can go pick, Mammy?"

"As soon as I change my clothes and eat something, right? I looked around. What time is it?"

"High noon, Ben was out helping James and Fraoch bring in the fish."

"So what do you think of the place?" Hayley pointed out a taxidermy deer head hung on the wall. "I call this dead-animal-country style." She looked around with her hands on her hips. "Isn't it lovely? It's a dying art, you know."

I asked, "Where's Beaty?"

There was a small side room beyond the main sitting room, like a separate smaller area for intimate conversations. A hand came up from behind a couch there, and waved its fingers. I heard the familiar snuffling of Mookie. I walked over and looked down. "How are you doing, Beaty?" Mookie had his head on her chest and looked up at me dolefully.

Beaty looked green. "Och, nae good, Queen Kaitlyn, the sickness of the morn is a lie, tis the whole day. I am full of gratitude for the blessin' of the coming bairn but..." She moaned and her hand went to her stomach. "Och nae."

I said, "Have you been eating marshmallows?"

She called, "Chef Zach! Can I hae another batch of treats?"

He stuck his head through the large double doors to what, I could see over his shoulder, was a restaurant-sized kitchen. "Treats?" He disappeared back through the swinging doors, and returned a moment later, carrying a tray of rice crispy treats and a spatula. He wordlessly pried up three treats, placed them on the plate beside her, then jogged back to the kitchen "Don't forget, it's hard for me to hear so if you talk about something important you need to talk loud or I miss out." He propped the kitchen door open when he went back in.

I patted Beaty on the arm. "Do you need anything else?"

"Nae, Queen Kaitlyn, I believe I will survive as long as I hae the treats."

CHAPTER 41 - MAGNUS

I made sure all the kids were out of the room, then said, "I hae somethin' I need tae tell ye: General Hammond is dead."

Their faces all expressed shock.

Colonel Quentin's eyes wide, he asked, "What happened?"

I considered telling him how Hammond had betrayed me, how he tried tae capture me, and I had escaped, draggin' him tae Balloch, and when confronted he had killed himself. But I dinna want tae ruin the history of Hammond's life, because he had been an ally and a friend for many long years. I took a slow, ragged breath, and exhaled. "He died tryin' tae survive. He had been forced tae take sides and, during a confrontation with me, he... he passed away." I shifted my feet and gestured into the distance. "I had him buried in the churchyard in Balloch. I will put a monument upon the spot when we are back in my kingdom of Riaghalbane."

Colonel Quentin said, "That sounds very complicated, are you okay, Boss?"

"Aye, twas verra complicated. I daena ken how tae feel about it, but I ken I mean tae honor him for the years of service he shewed me."

"Is there still a 'my kingdom'?"

I chewed my lip. "I daena ken."

James said, "Who will run your kingdom if your mom is gone, and you're enjoying life here with us? What if Agnie has taken over the future?"

"I have no idea, but we hae been livin' in the present and ruling in the future for a long time, we just hae tae—"

Lochinvar said, "This your 'we' again?"

"Aye, I hae been livin in the present and rulin' in the future — it required havin' Lady Mairead and Hammond tae watch over things. I daena ken how tae rule there from now on, there is a great deal tae figure out. I need tae find Lady Mairead, we ought tae do that first afore I go tae the future tae reinstate m'crown."

I glanced around. "Dost ye all agree?"

Everyone nodded.

CHAPTER 42 - KAITLYN

$\mathcal{M}$agnus and I went up the wide stair to our room to get showered. Our bedroom was big with sweeping ceilings, all built from giant timber. The beds were constructed from limbs of a tree, the mattress covered in quilts, weavings hung from the walls, plus, everywhere, taxidermied animals. The bathroom had a thick log door, like an entryway to a hobbit house, but inside there was a large modern bathroom with mirrors and good lighting and a big enough shower stall for the two of us.

We dropped our clothes to the ground. I turned on the water and we climbed in. He let the water roll down him and then pulled me close. "I would trade the water-stream with ye, but I want it the whole time so we hae tae share."

I let the water roll down my face and front, ducking my head in, against his chest to get the massaging water-stream centered on the back of my head.

"Remember when we were young and we would time-jump and there weren't kids to greet us, and we could recover however we wanted? But now we have to wear the old clothes around, and go see lakes, and visit and eat before we can change?" I poured some shampoo in his hand and some in mine and then we lathered up facing each other.

"Aye, I wouldna change a thing."

I laughed.

He continued, running his soapy hands over his chest. "Tis a blessin' and a hardship, tis how we ken we are the adults that we hae tae look upon a lake while Isla bosses us around even though our skin is still searing from the jump."

"True that. I wouldn't trade it either, I just marvel at our patience — we are the literal *best* parents."

He chuckled. "Aye, tis why I hae gotten ye pregnant once more so we can do it again. If we are this good we ought tae do it over and over."

I said, my hair covered in suds, as I watched him arch back to submerge his head under the water, "Now how am I going to rinse if you don't share?"

He grinned, water rolling down him. "I will share if ye get verra close."

I pressed forward. "But see, there is an issue, Master Magnus, your cock is up keeping me at a distance."

He said, "Is it now?" He straightened and pulled my hips closer, and said, "Tis only one remedy, we hae tae double up tae fit." He planted his feet wide and lifted me by my thighs to his waist and with our wet lips kissing under a stream of water, he pulled himself into me, and me onto him, and oh *god*, I wrapped my arms around the back of his head, one palm against the wall to steady us.

He said, "Grab the rail." I held myself up with the rail and kept stationary while his hips butted against me, my mouth against his neck, my teeth pressed to his skin, suppressing my moans, unsure how the sound would travel throughout the lodge. His fingers pressed into the flesh of my ass, and he plowed until he climaxed. Then it was just the scent of the shampoo mingling with the soap and the freshwater rushing down our skin as we relaxed and I exhaled with pleasure.

He said, "I think I will always hae a fondness for visitin' yer gardens with the shower on us. Tis a modern miracle with an act as old as time, tis verra nice.... How come nae one has invented a bed for the purpose?"

I kissed his neck. "What, a shower bed?"

"Aye."

"I don't know, maybe no one thinks it's a good idea?"

"Ye ken, there are whole playgrounds bein' built for cats, ye are sending men tae Mars, I daena think tis too far tae imagine ye might put a bed intae a shower for takin' yer wife. I canna hae been the first tae think of it."

I laughed.

He turned around and rinsed his front and his hair and then said, "I will leave ye the shower all tae yerself."

"Very kind of you, sir."

He climbed out, wrapped a towel around his waist, and brushed his teeth while I finished rinsing my hair, watching him through the glass wall: the way his wide shoulders stretched and his bicep bunched as he held the wee brush in his hand and furiously brushed it around in his mouth.

I dressed in a pair of sweats and a shirt that we brought with us from Maine and went downstairs and met Isla who immediately passed me a bucket. I said hello to Fraoch and James, back from fishing, to wave at Beaty, "How are you?"

"Fine, Queen Kaitlyn, better actually." She sat up. "Aye, much better." She scooped up a rice crispy treat and dazedly shuffled from her corner of the room, her hair a faded orange, sticking up all over. "Much better, but Chef Zach, ye ought tae keep the treats a'comin'."

Quentin said, "You were sick all day, now you're better in the afternoon?"

"Tis all day illness, Quennie, it means the bairn is goin' tae be a verra special girl."

Then Zoe rushed into my arms and I picked up Isla too and the little girls directed me along the shore of the lake, up into the hill, toward the bushes full of blueberries. "Mammy you do like this." Isla showed me how to pick one and drop it into the bucket. Zoe put one in the bucket and ate the next and we did that for a few moments before Hayley and Emma and Sophie joined us.

Zoe said, "Oh-fee help boo-berries," and climbed into Sophie's arms.

Sophie laughed. "Aye, Oh-fee loves picking blueberries."

Hayley said, "We better love it, we have been picking blueberries nonstop for days."

Emma said, "So, tell us the story of your trip."

I said, "Well, ultimately, we found a younger Lady Mairead, but not the current one, the one we are looking for, but we might have narrowed it down to some godforsaken ranch in the nineteenth century — heads up, Magnus'll probably be taking Fraoch and James and Lochie with him when he goes. I don't know about Quentin."

Emma said, "He looks pretty bothered by Hammond's death, is he okay?"

"I think he's okay. He didn't really go into it, but Hammond betrayed him pretty badly. I don't think he wants to think about it, so he's not talking about it, but yeah, it's very complicated. It's been a tough day. Tough two days... maybe only one day, I can't remember when I last slept." I looked around at the bushes and sighed. I was very exhausted and it was many hours until nightfall. "Speaking of... you want to keep picking blueberries while I go take a nap, Isla?"

"Mammy, you can't take a nap, it's a waste of your life."

"This is so true, but also, sometimes, a day in your life is so big and long you just have to rest your eyes for a minute."

～

I found myself lying on the bed in our room, staring up at the giant timber walls. *What a weird place.* Wondering like I so often did, *are we safe?*

It felt safe. It felt like a fortress. We were in a part of a state we had never been in before, a new place. I began to fall asleep when the door opened and Magnus, warm and big, climbed onto the bed. "Ye arna under the covers."

"I'm catty-corner to signify this is just a nap."

He dropped down beside me across the bed and snuggled his face against my shoulder.

I said, "You were sleepy too?"

"I canna remember when we last slept and I needed yer softness. A lot of the world seems hard right now."

I turned and wrapped my arms around his head and slowly we fell asleep in the middle of the day.

CHAPTER 43 - KAITLYN

*W*e woke up to the truck pulling up in the gravel by the front door and the sound of bags being dropped in the foyer, keys being dropped into the dish on the counter, Hayley, Sophie, and James returning from a supply run to Walmart.

Magnus said, "Sounds like we are up."

"Yep."

We went downstairs to see bags all over the entryway.

Hayley said, "We got two pairs of jeans for everyone, three shirts. Pajamas."

Quentin and James carried in yet another load of bags behind her.

She continued, "Shoes for all. It's all plain, and basic, but we can at least get out of these sweats we've been wearing for days."

Beaty called from the couch, "It all sounds verra ugly. I hae an Insta account, M'fans canna see me in ugly clothes."

Quentin said, "Beaty, love, you can't go on Insta right now. We're in level-four hiding again."

"I ken, Quennie, but... but... I hae tae hae cuteness, I hae tae." She burst into tears.

He comforted her on the couch, while the last of the bags

were carried in. Hayley said, "You're lucky I didn't let Sophie pick out the clothes, she settled on long prairie skirts."

Sophie laughed. "I thought they would be practical, if we are tae jump by surprise we might want tae be wearin' skirts."

Hayley said, "I get the practicality, but I *really* think we would look like sister wives and I am not down with that. This ain't no sister wives cult thing we have going here, just a loose conglomeration of families who love each other and wear sweats a lot and live in a compound."

James joked, "No kool-aid."

Lochie said, turning a pair of jeans around to look at the other side, "What is kool-aid?"

James said, "There is too much to explain in that sentence, but hopefully those will fit. We had to guess, everyone else had been measured already."

Magnus held his jeans in front of him and they looked a little wide because he was still thin.

After we had passed out the clothes to everyone, and most of us had changed into jeans and new shoes, Quentin went back to business, "Boss, can I show you the shooting range? We could use the practice."

We left the kids with Sophie and Emma and Beaty and loaded up in the big truck and drove down the dirt road. I rode in the cab with Quentin and Hayley. "All this land is ours?"

He said, "Hundreds of acres, yep, all ours, we can go hunting, but I thought maybe we'd brush up on shooting... I don't know, I think we need an attitude adjustment."

"Well, this is the place."

When we came to a stop Magnus, Zach, Fraoch, James, and Lochie all piled from the bed of the truck.

We were in a long field with targets at one end. Quentin passed out rifles and handguns. Lochie was fascinated by all of it.

We practiced shooting for a while, with so much ammo, then held a shooting competition.

The top three were Quentin, James, Magnus, then Fraoch, Hayley, me, Lochie and Zach who said he was not going to let it bother him. He joked, "I am going to try and focus on the fact that everyone still at the house would be behind me."

Quentin said, "I don't know, Zach, Beaty's a pretty good shot."

Zach groaned. "Well, shit, now I don't know if I'm in a good enough mood to make dinner."

Magnus said, "Och nae, Chef Zach, if ye want tae go again I will let you win. I dinna ken dinner was on the line."

We all laughed.

Quentin brought out a bow, "Katie, you wanna show off?"

"I'd love to." I carried the bow to the line.

In the meantime Fraoch reached in the back of the truck, and pulled out a battle hammer. "I haena seen one of these since we played with them back at Kilchurn."

Magnus said, "Ye were verra good if I remember correctly."

"Aye, tis nae as useful as a gun, but tis a good skill."

Quentin said, "That's why I put some in the truck, I thought you might have fun—"

While they were talking, I aimed, and let the arrow fly — thwak! Direct into the center of the target. Everyone cheered. I bowed. "Thank you, thank you, as Fraoch said about the battle hammer, a bow is 'not as useful as a gun' and not good for hand-to-hand combat, but if unarmored men are standing at a distance, and I have time to aim… they are *dead*."

"My turn." Fraoch wound up and slung the hammer. It roared down the field, smashed against my arrow, and struck the center of the target.

He put up a finger and said, "One."

I put down the bow to watch him.

He grabbed a second, cocked his arm back and released it.

The hammer flew down the field and struck right in the center, leaving a large divet.

He put up a second finger. "Two."

He returned to the truck, grabbed a third hammer, remained there, farther away, swung his arm back, and let it fly, striking the direct center. The blow cracked the target, leaving half dangling off. He grinned and said, "Three."

We all cheered.

Lochinvar said, "We all ken now not tae challenge the auld man tae a hammer fight."

"This Og Lochie, is verra true."

James said, "And this is why we don't let Fraoch near the tool box."

Fraoch rotated his arm, "Tis all from casting m'fishing line."

Quentin said, "You learned to throw a hammer like that from fishing? That seems unlikely."

Fraoch laughed. "Tis part of m'mythology. And the hammer skill is m'hidden talent, I wouldna want tae fight with a hammer man-tae-man, give me a sword, any day, but, like Kaitlyn, if I hae an adversary at a distance, they are dead."

Quentin gave us a pep-talk standing at the edge of the field after the competition. "We were pretty relaxed up in Maine, but now we know there is a threat, it has captured Lady Mairead, and it turned Hammond into a traitor. We can't ignore it. We are safe, but we need guards, we need to take our security seriously, and we need to practice our protection."

James said, "Again."

Quentin said, "Yep, again."

Lochie said, "How many vessels are there?"

Magnus said, "There are about twenty-six, by last count."

"How many do you have in your possession?"

"We have about six, here, there are more in the kingdom. We hae lost track."

Lochie said, "I think the losin' track might be an issue."

Fraoch nodded. "Never thought I'd say this but I agree with the new guy."

Magnus looked down at the dirt and grass under his feet and kicked some away thinking. "I had a strong safe in the kingdom and a secure guard, but without Hammond it has become verra dangerous. I daena ken what state the kingdom is in, or who is in charge." He looked around. "So aye, I agree, the safe in the kingdom is nae the best most secure place."

James said, "Well, we're in a fortress at the end of a dirt road in the middle of New York, in the middle of nowhere."

Quentin said, "There is a Walmart a twenty-minute drive away, it's less secure than you think."

Magnus said, "And tis built of wood, tis not verra secure, a stiff wind could blow it down."

Fraoch said, "We hae a sayin' back home, ye canna control the wind, ye can only control the sail—"

Magnus said, "What does that mean in this instance?"

"We may not ever hae a fortress strong or hidden enough, we ought tae be more adaptable, like a sail..."

Hayley said, "You think we should concentrate on the wind?"

Fraoch said, "Nae, not the wind, on yer boat, tis yer sail ye think on, the way ye prioritize."

Magnus said, "Aye, I think I understand what ye mean, we must batten our hatches, by that tae mean we hae a safe place here. Then we need tae reef the sail, tae do that we must go rescue Lady Mairead."

Fraoch said, "Exactly, then tae secure yer kingdom we hae tae cut off the head of the hydra."

My eyes went wide. "Except, maybe not that metaphor. Agnie used one just like it — she wants to cut the head off the hydra. In her case she was talking about Lady Mairead. I told her that was a stupid idea, everyone knows that if you cut off a hydra's head you only make it stronger, larger, angrier."

Magnus said, "Tis true, and I was followin' ye Fraoch until

ye mixed metaphors, I'm on a boat in the wind with a hydra? Who is the hydra in this scenario?"

"The hydra is Agnie, and whoever she has helpin' her."

Magnus nodded, "I am relieved for once the hydra inna my mother."

Fraoch laughed. "That old broad? She's no big deal. She just has tae be carefully watched because she can be wrathful. Tis easy tae deal with a woman with this sort of mindset, ye just hae tae nae cross her."

Hayley groaned.

I rolled my eyes.

Lochinvar said, "I think Lady Mairead is lovely."

Fraoch chuckled.

Magnus said, "Och, boy, ye hae tae guard against her. Daena let yerself be swayed by her charms, daena dismiss the wrath."

Fraoch added, "But she inna as wrathful as Agnie, Agnie might be the worse of the two."

"Aye, but still, ye must be mindful, Lochie."

Quentin began loading the guns into cases and then Lochie and James slid the cases into the back of the truck.

James asked, as he slid one of the cases in, "So what do we do first?"

Magnus said, "We jump intae Montana in the middle of the nineteenth century and we cut the head from the serpent and rescue Lady Mairead."

Quentin said, "All right, and who's going?"

James's arm shot up in the air. "Me me me! Pick me!"

Quentin said, "All right, James gets to go be a cowboy."

"Only if I get a horse."

Magnus said, "Ye are hired, ye can jump intae Florida first, and grab Sunny, Thor, and Osna. I hae been worried on Sunny, I bet he hasna had a proper ride since Fraoch brought him home from thirteenth century Scone. Then ye will meet us in Montana."

James said, "Sick! This is exactly what I'm talking about, a *good* adventure."

Zach joked, "I'm staying here, I know I know, you're all surprised, but I have never wanted to go to the old west, that sounds like a real crap place. Though I do like to watch a good western, I don't like my chances living through it."

Fraoch said, "I will go or stay, whichever is m'better place."

Magnus said, "Fraoch, Colonel Quentin, James, and I will go. Lochinvar and Chef Zach will remain here. They will both be armed, Lochie will keep watch. Colonel Quentin hae ye come up with emergency plans for the household?"

"Yes, indeed, I will get Lochie informed about what that looks like."

Hayley said, "And me, I mean, you already told me, I know the emergency plan, I mostly mean, I will also take guard duty while you're gone. Lochie and I will trade off."

Fraoch said, "Lochie best be on his best behavior, nae funny business."

Lochie said, "Och nae, I am on m'best behavior, Frookie, I will take verra good care of yer wife." He grinned.

Fraoch said, "I hae changed m'mind."

Magnus said, "I think we need ye Fraoch, ye can trust Lochie. Canna he trust ye Lochie?"

"Aye, I am verra trustworthy, I take guard duty verra seriously, especially when chef Zach is in the house, we must protect him at all costs." Magnus and Lochie fist-bumped.

Hayley said, "I want to go on the record that it's not just Lochie who decides to be on his best behavior. I am a full member of the guard. I will be armed, I am married, and I am not to be accosted or tried in any way, got me, Lochie?"

"Aye, Madame Hayley, tis all been one big tease, ye are verra above m'station anyway, I wouldna insult ye with—"

Fraoch said, "What the hell is goin' on — are ye really discussing this? I am about tae whip ye soundly."

Magnus said, "Fraoch calm down, everyone is teasin' ye.

James and Quentin we will need ye tae look at the maps and help us come up with a strategy for attack."

Quentin clapped his hands together and rubbed them. "Can we go to the kingdom and get a helicopter, something really mind blowing?"

"Nae, I daena think we can access any of the weapons, we daena ken what is happening in the kingdom, it may be bleak. We must use what we hae tae extract Lady Mairead."

Quentin said, "I think we have two ATVs in the storage in Florida, when you pick up the horses, James, check and bring them."

James pretended to cry. "You don't understand how happy this all makes me."

Magnus said, "Be careful though, we are sendin' ye alone, there may be trouble."

Quentin said, "Use stealth."

James said, "Trouble? There won't be no stinking trouble. But I'll be stealthy."

We went back to the house for dinner, followed by watching Star Wars. We lay around on the furniture, with rough wool blankets pulled over our legs in the lofty great room of the main lodge, a fire in the hearth. It wasn't cold outside, just a little cool, but the kids cuddled with us anyway.

The next morning my goodbye with Magnus was short. This was just for a day. It was dangerous, but it was one of those missions that needed all of us to partake in bravery. I smoothed the coat across his wide shoulders and said, "I'll always be your harbor from the tempest, you know where to find me."

"Aye, I will see ye on the morrow."

We kissed, and then he left the lodge for the jump-spot and he was gone.

CHAPTER 44 - MAGNUS

*A*fter a great deal of planning, we jumped, and arrived west of the ranch so the sun would be behind us as we approached. Our landing spot was in a location along the West Boulder River about five miles upstream of the MacLeod ranch, behind a range of prairie-grass covered hills. We were in a valley, dotted with deep green forests, the horizon made up of blue snow-capped mountains. We found a place hidden behind a tree-covered rise, and set up a rudimentary camp for the night.

The wind came up, whippin' the high branches of the Aspens. Colonel Quentin said, "This is good, the wind is coming from the east. They won't smell us coming."

Fraoch sneered, "Aye, but I can smell their stench on the breeze. How will I sleep?"

Quentin said, "I guess you want first watch?"

The night sky was flung with stars, cold and clear. The land hummed from all the life upon it. The aspens clattered in the wind. I asked, Fraoch, "What dost ye think of this night?"

"Remember when we used tae sit under a medieval sky in

the thirteenth century? And I told ye that it felt as if we were at the oldest point in which a man could live? This feels older."

"Aye, tis only the nineteenth century, but I was thinkin' the same thing."

The sun rose and warmed the land, an orange light upon it all. Fraoch said, "Twas m'turn tae sleep but the birds are squabblin' and raisin' a racket." From a distance, we watched the designated jump spot for another storm, and the arrival of James Cook.

His storm rose about high noon, and when we arrived at the spot, we found James lying in the dirt, beside him: Sunny, standing, stamping furiously; my two other horses, Osna and Thor; and James's truck, his big truck with the verra large wheels.

Colonel Quentin muttered, "Holy shit, he brought his truck."

I greeted Sunny, "When was the last time we saw each other, Sunny boy?"

I stoked down his neck and he nestled his muzzle against my chest. He whinnied.

"Aye, I agree, it has been too long."

James slowly regained consciousness and moaned and sputtered and spit dirt from his mouth, then slowly sat up with his head in his hands. "It's like the worst kind of hangover."

Colonel Quentin said, "Um, James, what's up?"

James was bleary-eyed. "What do you mean? Oh," he glanced over his shoulder. "You mean my fucking, badass truck?" He smiled. "That's because I thought it would be sick. Isn't it awesome?"

"You went to Florida for horses and ATVs, where are the ATVs?"

"I have no idea, it was weird, I went to the storage unit and it was empty. I know there were two ATVs there, right? I just don't know where the hell they are. Did we leave them somewhere?"

Colonel Quentin said, "I don't know, it's like, vague... bottom of a ravine? You don't remember?"

"Nope, that seems like something that would be memorable, but anyway, the gun box was basically empty except for some explosives. I grabbed what was there; some of our camping equipment; got the horses from the stables, Debbie at Amelia Stables says hi, by the way; then I thought, shit, this is going to suck, we're going to be in cowboy times with three horses and four men, that doesn't seem fair; so I thought about what else would work, and lo and behold, the Ford Raptor, big enough to be a stupid idea, perfect enough to be just what we need. I'm going to drive right over the ranch, what's it made of, mud and sticks? I'm going to park right on the roof."

Fraoch said, "Ye woke up in a fine spirit."

"I am in my element. Let's ride!"

We kept the ridiculously large truck there while we worked out a plan, climbing a nearby hill and using the binoculars and thermal imaging monocular tae watch the ranch, an assortment of low wooden buildings: a larger house surrounded by small shacks, a stable, and a tiny hovel near the shore of the snaking river. Colonel Quentin said, "It looks to be about twelve men not including the ones who might be away right now."

I asked, "Dost ye see a woman among them?"

He passed me a monocular and I scanned the rest of the lands, looking for a holding cell or jailhouse. I dinna see anything.

Colonel Quentin said, "I see a person at the riverbank, three men at the stable, and others milling around. We have to assume they have weapons. How else would they survive homesteading here in this desolate place?"

"What weapons do they have?"

Colonel Quentin squinted. "It looks like the usual long rifles and side arms of the period. But at this distance, it's hard to be sure. We ought to assume they have more."

James looked around, "This is awesome!"

Colonel Quentin still looking through the binoculars, said, "Yeah, we heard. Did you hear what I said about the weapons?"

James said, "Yeah, I heard you," quietly he added, "still think it's awesome."

We reconvened by the truck.

"Who wants horses?"

James said, "Shit, I can't decide, truck or horse? Truck because it's badass? Or horse because it's legit? And this is my one big moment in the..." He kicked gravel. "What do you think, Quentin?"

"I think you're shit at horse, you ought to do truck."

"I got a lot better at horse — you know what, horse, a cowboy on a horse. Will you take the truck?"

Colonel Quentin climbed in the truck bed and pulled a rifle from the gun box and clamped it onto a tripod. "Sure, I'm the best shot anyway." He looked through the box. "You did bring a whole lot of explosives." He ran a hand over his hair and tossed us each a radio. "Here's what we're going to do."

He stood elevated on a low rock and drew a diagram in the dirt with a stick. "You're going to move to this position, coming in from the west." He marked an X.

"I will place explosives here. The sound of my engine will draw them over, the explosives will hopefully wound or at least distract, then I will set up a long range rifle here." He marked a second X.

"You will already be headed in. This way, I take out any people left, or the men returning to the homestead. Got me?"

James blinked. "Wait, if the sound of the engine draws them

in, but you are exploding things, and then going to there." He pointed at the second X. "They will hear the truck moving to there, right?"

Colonel Quentin said solemnly, "Yes, they *would*, but I won't have the truck when I move from there to there."

James grimaced. "Nah dawg, are you going to blow up my... ? Shit, that is not good news."

Colonel Quentin said, "You're the one who brought the explosives *and* the truck."

"Dammit. Yeah, but... shit. Okay, fine." He put a hand on the hood of the truck. "There were some good times, right Big Truck? Good, good times." He shook his head. "I did not think this through, but fine, yeah, yippee." He circled his fist in the air. "Sacrifice my truck to save Lady Mairead, cool cool."

I said, "I will make sure she kens the sacrifice so she can ignore it." We all chuckled.

Colonel Quentin passed us each a bullet-proof vest and we pulled them over our chests. We each grabbed our helmets and a pack. We each had a radio strapped tae our belt.

Colonel Quentin put his earpiece in his ear. "This is an improvement on the necklace radios I had Hayley and Katie use, those were the worst. I could only listen and not say a word while they went rogue."

James said, "So if I go rogue you'll be bitching and complaining in my ear the whole time?"

Colonel Quentin said, "Nah, I'll just shoot you, this is the Wild West, you know?"

James said, "I get that's supposed to be a threat, but I've never been so happy, wait, say it again, but say, 'string you up' this time."

Colonel Quentin rolled his eyes. "If you go rogue I will personally string you up, asshole. Now let's get back to business." He adjusted his radio and spoke intae it. "Testing, one two...?"

I said, "Three." We tested that our radios were connected, our earpieces the right volume, our mics strong.

We each had a combat rifle, a sidearm.

We each had a vessel.

Colonel Quentin said, "If we get moving, we will get there when the sun is right, ready?"

CHAPTER 45 - MAGNUS

I led Fraoch and James around the perimeter of the ranch tae the southwest corner, where they remained tae wait for the signal while I continued on. James said, "Shoot straight, Magnus. Damn, I have always wanted to say that."

I said, "Aye, shoot straight, Master Cook."

Fraoch said, "Aye, and stay low, ride fast."

I rode along a path where the forest met the high prairie grass tae the bank of the Boulder River, and found a grouping of pine trees tae hide behind, and waited. I watched the landscape: undulatin' hills speckled with boulders and outcroppings on a tapestry of greens. In the high sky there was an eagle, glidin' on the wind. Between the grassy knolls the jays were jeerin'. There were a great many similarities tae the highlands — it felt familiar.

I heard in the distance a low rumble, the engine, faintly. I raised my gun and through the sight watched the homestead: men were watching west toward the sound, then they called to each other, jumped on horses, and headed that way. I counted the men as they rode, then swept my sight back toward the river, men ran toward the buildings, and then in their midst — a woman.

From the distance, she did look a bit like Lady Mairead in build, but this woman had a wild look tae her, gray hair stuck out around her head. She walked slowly, the walk of someone unafraid, someone not expected tae protect the homestead.

I climbed on Sunny and waited until there was a verra loud explosion from the west, and a large column of smoke and flame rising intae the sky. In my earpiece, Colonel Quentin's voice: "Your truck said goodbye."

I set my horse tae charge.

Sunny's hooves thundered across the ground — tae m'left, Fraoch, headed north toward the stables, James, with a billowing dust cloud was farther away. We were all headed tae the homestead.

I thundered along the river, scanning right and left and then saw a man, crouching behind a boulder. I fired, killing him as I passed, noting first: he had a modern weapon. I spoke intae my mic: "Modern weapons."

Ahead of me a drone lifted from the roof of the main building.

Intae the radio, I asked: "Colonel Quentin, ye see it? Drone."

The drone exploded intae pieces. Colonel Quentin's voice emitted from my earpiece: "Got it."

I heard a faint shift in gravel. I swung Sunny around and stilled him, and listened, a man was climbin' the river bank. I found his spot, aimed, and as soon as his head rose over the bank, fired, killing him with a shot. I turned Sunny away from the river toward the homestead, catching a glimpse of Fraoch as he fired intae the rear of the main building. "Got him, Fraoch?"

"Got him!"

"How's it going, Master Cook?"

"Killed two, holy shit, this is insane!"

Shots were fired from the windows of the house. A long low building, smoke rising from chimneys at both ends. I dropped from Sunny and ducked behind a wall, leaned out, took a shot, missed, ducked back behind the wall and then shot again. A man yelled.

I charged the house on foot, making it tae the door. "Front door!"

Fraoch yelled, "Backdoor!" I heard gunfire through the house.

I snuck a look inside: a dark interior, dust floatin' in the sunlight from the door, the smell of smoke from the hearth.

My back pressed tae the wall, I concentrated. The world had slowed, I gained m'battle focus.

I smelled the stench of a man.

I settled m'breath and heard his fast breathin' on the other side of the wall, inches away.

I concentrated on that spot, drew in a deep slow breath, then spun around the doorjamb, and fired—

He slumped dead tae the ground.

The creaking wood of the footsteps as a man emerged from a back room, we exchanged fire, and I shot him through the head — blastin' him back against the wall.

Fraoch's voice: "Got him?"

"Aye." I walked through the room, steppin' over bodies, checkin' behind furniture. "This room is clear." I crept down the hall and checked through the first door. "Two rooms clear."

James's voice: "Holy shit, there are three here!" The sound of shots rang through the radio.

Fraoch's voice: "Headed that way, Quentin ye see them?"

Colonel Quentin's voice: "I have one in my sights." A distant gunshot fired.

James's voice, broken with static, then: "...splashed the wall with his brains, two to..."

I crept down the hall to another room, the wooden boards creaking and shifting under my weight. I entered, gun first around the corner, slowly, listening. There were bunks here — a man rushed me from behind. He was on me. A blow tae my head.

A second of confusion as my eyes lost focus.

I plowed m'elbow back, knocking the wind from him, and fought blow-tae-blow against him until I had him down and senseless.

I disarmed him, scanned the room, then yelled intae his face, "Where is Lady Mairead?"

He whimpered.

His eyes glanced past my shoulder. I turned tae the open window in time tae catch a glimpse of muzzle flash.

I lunged off him, behind a bunk. Bullets chipped the wall overhead.

The man lumbered up tae flee, I fired and killed him before he made it tae the door.

I said: "Fraoch — man outside!"

"Busy!"

I exhaled, crept through the room tae the door. "Bunkhouse clear."

Shots were fired at me from the back of the stable. I dove out, firing, making it tae a small outbuilding, yelling: "Colonel Quentin! Can ye get stable boy?"

"He's hidden!"

"Och nae!"

I waited.

A strange man's voice emitted from my earpiece: "Come and get me, Magnus Campbell."

James's voice: "...who the fuck... why are you... on our channel, asshole?"

"I'm your worst—"

His words were cut short with a gun blast.

James's voice: "...'Our Worst' is dead... stables clear."

I entered the small outbuilding, checked the corners and behind the sacks of grain. "Storeroom clear."

Then James's voice: "Fuck!"

Fraoch's voice: "He's got James."

Colonel Quentin's voice: "Who? Who has... is that him? Northside of stables?"

Fraoch: "Aye, I am blocked."

Colonel Quentin: "Okay, steady, James, you cool, can you duck?"

James voice, "He's got me — no I can't fucking duck!"

Another strange man's voice: "Drop yer weapons!"

I snuck toward the stable, where I crept tae a position far behind the man who was holding a struggling James. I quietly loaded a fresh magazine.

It smelled of horse and hay, the land around us eerily quiet. I aimed my rifle, *steady steady—*

A gunshot sounded through my earpiece.

Och nae, who was shot...?

I kept m'sight on the man holding a gun on James, *focus.*

Fraoch's voice: "Quentin? Quentin?"

There was nae answer.

Focus, Magnus.

I took the shot, exploding the man's head against the building, his body slumped tae the ground.

James scrambled up. "I'm good! Thanks! Headed for that last asshole!" He charged around the corner.

I asked intae my radio: "Are ye checkin' on Quentin, Fraoch?"

"Headed that way!"

I ran tae the last outbuilding, enterin' rifle first around the doorjamb intae the darkened room, tae see Lady Mairead risin' unsteadily from behind a cask. She was wearin' an oversized dirty and ragged sackcloth gown. Her hair was a pale gray fluff around her face. She looked weakened and verra auld.

Her voice wavered, "Magnus? Magnus, ye came?"

"Aye, Lady Mairead, we are—"

Gunshots outside. She clamped her hands over her ears.

James's voice: "Got him."

I spoke intae the mic: "I found Lady Mairead."

She sank tae the floor, her hand clutching her heart.

"Aye," I crouched beside her and patted the back of her hand. "Aye, of course I came, ye dinna think I would come?"

She burst intae tears. "Nae, I dinna think anyone would come."

I sat all the way down and pulled her head intae my lap and she sobbed against my shirt. I comforted her while keepin' my eyes on the surroundings, and askin' intae the radio: "Eyes on Quentin yet?"

Fraoch's voice, the sound of his horse, Thor, galloping: "Nae yet."

Lady Mairead weakly asked, "Did Hammond come?"

"Nae, Lady Mairead, Hammond inna here. How long hae ye been here?"

"Over a year, it has been... verra difficult."

Her head fell back and she looked up at me, her face weathered from the brutal climate. "How did ye find me?"

"I broke intae yer house in Paris and found some of yer notes, ye had a list of places ye thought Agnie might use, I narrowed it down."

She reached up and tucked m'hair behind my ear. "That was verra smart, and also correct, this was the only place Agnie would put me, because tis a shithole as ye kids say." She chuckled. "I am *verra* hungry."

"Och, I hae been there." She felt verra frail, as if she might break in my hand.

A voice came through the radio, "I hae Quentin, he's unconscious, wound on his shoulder."

"James?"

"I see him headed this way."

"Ye three go ahead and jump, I will bring Lady Mairead with me from here."

I asked Lady Mairead, "Dost ye need tae gather any more of yer... anything?"

"Help me up." She was unsteady on her feet, leaning on me as we made our way tae an armory. She pointed at a drawer.

Inside was a pile of gold-shot rocks. I unzipped my pack and shoveled them in. I hoisted it tae m'shoulder and pulled a couple of guns off the walls. She opened a few more drawers and found a vessel in one, wrapped in cloth. "Dost ye see, Magnus, even with riches, they choose tae live a mean and base existence."

She passed the vessel tae me.

I asked, "Anything else?"

"Nae, this is all they had of merit. Agnie is head of a family of cruel uncivilized brutes."

I led her outside. "There is something I need tae say tae ye."

"Aye...?"

"Hammond betrayed us, he is... he is dead. I had him buried in the churchyard at Balloch."

Her knees buckled and she fainted clean away.

I lifted her tae m'shoulder and carried her tae Sunny, who was wandering around in front of the house. Tae the west I could see a storm in the sky, Fraoch and James headed home with Colonel Quentin. I held the horse's reigns wrapped around my wrist, and used m'vessel tae jump us tae our new compound.

CHAPTER 46 - KAITLYN

Zach and I were standing guard at the gate across the driveway, while Hayley and Lochinvar drove to pick up the returning warriors. The kids were all in one place, inside the house, until we gave them the all-clear. Their lives these days were so full of running around like little banshees that it was hard to get them to stay inside, we made promises of treats.

A loud clash came from in the house, and Zach laughed. "Man, I'm afraid if they stay inside much longer they're going to break a wall."

"Did you see Ben climbing yesterday? He made it to the ceiling!"

He said, "The timbers make great footholds. It's tempting."

The truck came barreling down the road with dust billowing up behind it. Zach and I hurriedly swung open the gate and Hayley continued on, waving her arm for us to follow.

Zach closed the gate while saying, "Go ahead!" So I ran after the truck, catching up to it as they pulled up on the gravel in front of the house and whipped onto the lawn. James and Fraoch jumped out. "Quentin's hurt!"

"Shit!" Emma and Beaty rushed from the house, kids came

out too, though they weren't supposed to. We all stood on the porch as Fraoch carried Quentin up the steps.

Emma walked alongside, with her fingers on his neck, checking his pulse.

My heart sank. "James, where's Magnus?"

"Not sure, sorry, we were separated, last thing he said on the radio was that he had Lady Mairead and was headed here." He dropped his bullet proof vest and helmet on the porch.

"What's happening with Quentin?"

Fraoch said, "I found him unconscious, och, I hope he is well, he has blood here." He placed Quentin down on the rug in the living room and Emma looked all around to see where the blood was coming from. "Get scissors!"

Fraoch pulled out his dirk and began cutting away at Quentin's shirt. We found that his shoulder had been grazed.

Beaty got down on her knees beside his face. "Wake up Quennie, wake up!"

I ran to get the first aid kit and put it beside Emma who shoved Quentin on his side and pressed a clean cloth down on his shoulder.

Quentin moaned and then gasped and startled awake.

"What the... where am I?"

Fraoch said, "Ye're in the compound, ye hae an injury."

"Who is sitting on me?"

"That would be me," said Emma.

"I wondered if it was Mookie."

"She is savin' yer life, Quennie. Mookie is watching ye, he is worried on ye."

Quentin smiled, his face pressed into the rug, he entwined her fingers in his.

Emma said, "Well, your shoulder might match Magnus's, you'll be twinsies..." She peeled back the cloth and glanced.

I was chewing my fingers. "How long until Magnus gets back you think...?"

Everyone was very quiet in answer.

. . .

Then Lochie ran in from outside, "I just got the horses to the stable, and there's another storm!"

Zach looked at the monitor, "That's Magnus's vessel."

Lochinvar glanced around, then reminded us, "I canna drive!"

"Oh right!" I ran for the keys. "Who has the keys?"

Hayley yelled, "Me! Follow me!" She and I ran out and climbed in the truck, Lochie jumped in the bed, crouching, as Hayley drove us at top speed into the middle of the storm, with a high buffeting wind, and a torrential rain whipped up from the nearby lake and the gray clouds of the day.

The windshield wipers made a loud flap flap flap. We pulled up to the clearing with rain pouring down, the wind whipping, and two drenched people lying in the mud. Beside them was a horse that shifted, rocked, then stood.

Lochie jumped from the truck bed, wind buffeting him sideways, he fought against it to reach the bodies. I forced open the door and jumped out into the storm and followed him.

I knelt down beside Magnus and smoothed his hair back from his face. He was alive, just semi-conscious, but beginning to stir. I unclasped the chin strap on his helmet and pushed it off his head.

In the mud beside him a person was facedown. *A woman? Lady Mairead?* She seemed too small, and was wearing what looked like was once a white night dress, but was now covered in mud. Most confusing, her hair was grayed at the roots, about five inches out... I pushed her shoulder, because I couldn't believe I was really looking at Lady Mairead, lying in a mud puddle.

I shook Magnus's shoulder gently. "Babe, wake up, please..." He spluttered awake.

I burst into tears and collapsed against his bullet-proof vest. It was suddenly very clear that this had been dangerous, and my nerves were jangled, we had been waiting, he hadn't come home with the others, Quentin had been shot, and… and…

His arm went up around me. "Kaitlyn, are ye cryin' because ye're happy tae see me, or because I died? Please let it be the first."

"The first." I wiped my face on my arm, put my elbows down beside his ears and kissed him. Then I wiped rain from his face with my fingers and kissed him again. The storm was dissipating, the deluge over, now just a light sprinkle, but it was too late, we were soaked through.

I glanced over at Hayley, nudging Lady Mairead with her toe. She whispered, "Hey, Mags, what's up with Meemaw?"

Lochie said, "Och, she is near lifeless."

Magnus said, "She has been through a fuckin' ordeal. How is Quentin? Did Fraoch and James make it home?"

I said, "Quentin is awake, his shoulder is wounded, but looks like it will heal, Fraoch and James are home, safe."

"Did Sunny make it?"

"Sunny is standing under that tree."

Lochie said, "Lady Mairead, are ye well enough tae move?"

She moaned, "I daena think I can ever be well enough again."

"Och, ye are a tragedy." Lochie hefted her up and carried her tae the truck.

I pulled Magnus up, he stretched his back and said, "Ye go ahead, I will ride Sunny tae the house, he has had a long day, we ought tae talk it out."

Everyone was shocked at the state of Lady Mairead.

Lochinvar carried her into the house and a hush fell over the room.

He said, "Dost we hae a bed for her?"

Emma pointed down the hall. "We have the guest room at

the end." All of us looked at each other as he carried her down the hall.

I shook my head. "I don't want to be the person to take care of her, please don't make me."

Emma said, "I know, I get you."

Sophie said, "Tis my turn, I will help her." And she followed Lochie to the guest room.

Beaty said, "Quennie, I just remembered that her room daena hae shampoo and... promise me ye winna die while I go help with Lady Mairead."

He chuckled. "I will not die, this is a scratch Beaty, I'm going to be fine."

She put her hands on her hips. "Nae Quennie, ye must be a wee bit injured, ye cannae die, but ye ought tae let me take care of ye."

Quentin said, "Fine, Beaty," and then he moaned, "Don't leave me!" He stretched out a hand, acting desperate.

She folded her hands together and looked on him lovingly. "This is why I love ye, because ye *need* me." Then she said, "But I *must* go see tae Lady Mairead." She asked Emma, "Will ye put hair dye on yer list for her? She will be verra anxious about how she looks."

I said, "How long do you think she was there? She looks so much older."

Zach said, "I don't know, my guess is, over a year."

Beaty said, "Och nae!"

Emma passed Beaty an armful of shampoo, conditioner, and soap, and Beaty padded down the hall toward the guest room.

Magnus stomped up the front steps after his trip to the stable, Haggis at his feet, children swarming around.

As he came through the door he asked, "Where is Lady Mairead?"

"In the guest room down the hall."

"She will need tae be fed." His eyes fell on Quentin lying on the sofa, his shoulder bandaged. "Och nae, what happened tae ye?"

Quentin noisily slurped some juice through a straw then said, "Some asswipe decided to sneak up from behind, he's dead, but he shot me first, luckily he didn't have good aim."

"Ye were unconscious?"

"I think I hit my head, it hurts like shit."

James said, "His helmet has a dent."

Quentin called into the other room. "Zachie! Can I get something to eat?"

Magnus was still wet.

I asked, "Want to go get changed?"

"Aye."

That night we ate a large meal while the men told us about their mission.

We needed to make plans, but Magnus shook his head. "Nae, we will wait, Lady Mairead is restin', and we want her tae be a part of the discussion, until then we need a good night sleep and, of course, guards on the walls."

Lochie took first guard, with Fraoch sleeping early then waking and taking second watch.

CHAPTER 47 - KAITLYN

*I*n the middle of the night we heard Lady Mairead wailing from the end of the hall. "Naeeeeee, NNNNNaaaaeeeeee! Nae!!"

Magnus's eyes were open, but he seemed frozen as if he were worried about what he might see if he went.

"Stay here, I'll call if we need you." I jumped up and dutifully left.

Lady Mairead was in the living room, and looked lost, "Nae! Nae!" She was reaching around as if she couldn't see what was in front of her. "Nae!" The oversized nightshirt she was wearing made her look too thin, and her bare legs looked spindly. She was more wrinkled, looking much older. "Lady Mairead, are you okay?"

She shrieked, "Nae! Where am I? Daena kill me!" and swung at me. I backed toward the wall.

Lady Mairead screeched, "They took everything from me!"

Sophie rushed into the room and put her arms around Lady Mairead as she struggled. "Lady Mairead, please calm yerself, ye hae tae still yer mind, love," she drew her toward the couch, sat down beside her, and held and soothed her.

Magnus entered and sat in the chair opposite.

Lady Mairead said, "They hae taken everything from me! I lost everything!"

Sophie smoothed the back of her hair. "Were they terribly vile tae ye?"

Lady Mairead nodded. "They were evil, aye, but I can escape from evil, but they stole everything, the art, m'youth, the kingdom. Och nae, Hammond!" She sobbed.

Magnus said, "Lady Mairead, hae they taken the kingdom, ye are sure of it?"

I pushed forward a box of tissues. She took one and messily blew her nose. "If they turned Hammond they must hae." She drew in a staggering breath. "Is he truly dead?"

Magnus nodded.

He looked weary, and very worried.

Isla padded into the room. She said, "Grandma Wady Maiwead, why are you crying?"

"Because the world is a cruel place, granddaughter, ye must be prepared tae accept that ye will hae a life of naething but unendin' cruelty."

Magnus said, "Mother, tis nae true, ye are goin' tae scare Isla."

"What is there for her, but a house hidin' in the woods, in a godforsaken land? Hae ye seen the news of this time, Magnus, ye ought tae heed the warnin'!"

Magnus said, "I am nae heedin' any warnings and I am nae livin' in fear, this is a waystation while I consider m'options—"

"What options! There are nae options! They destroyed the art, Magnus! They destroyed me!" She began to sob again, very dramatically.

Magnus said, "Mother, do ye need a meal?"

"What is the point of it? I might as well die, old and unloved."

"Och." Magnus exhaled. "Mother, dost ye need a meal? And ye will call me a king."

She raised her chin. "Aye, King Magnus, I need a meal."

"Good, now I tell ye tae pull yerself taegether, I hae never kent ye, in the history of yer life, tae spend the night sobbin' about what ye hae lost. I ken ye lost a great deal, but ye must gather yer strength."

"I am auld! I am weak!"

Fraoch's voice from the opposite side of the room. "Lady Mairead, dost ye want Agnie tae win?"

She shook her head. "She is a detestable witch."

Isla climbed into my lap, giggling, and whispered, "Destble witch."

Fraoch drew near and sat in a chair across from her. "Then ye must eat a meal, rest, and gather yer strength for the coming battle, ye canna allow her tae win."

"She is too strong."

Magnus said, "Nae, she is nae too strong. I hae been thinking on it while I rode Sunny tae the house and put him away in the stable. Agnie is verra weak, she is just malevolent, what is it ye said, Kaitlyn? Ye called it Chaotic Evil."

I said, "Yep."

Zach stuck his head through the door to the kitchen. "Exactly! Chaotic evil, that's exactly what she is — and food is almost ready."

Magnus continued, "She is focused on ye, so she seems strong, she has had one purpose, tae see ye pay."

Her voice was small when she said, "She made me pay so much."

"Aye, it has been too much. But she miscalculated and has overplayed her hand, focusin' on ye, and in return what hae ye been focused on?"

"Staying alive."

Magnus said, "Afore that — ye were living with artists, and opening museums, and guardin' a kingdom, she is a jealous wee midge tae yer royal mastery. She is naething tae ye. She tried tae break ye, are ye broken?"

"I feel like it."

Zach put a plate of food on the table beside her. "Your favorite, marmalade covered toast with two poached eggs. This is a start, more if you're still hungry."

She said, "Thank ye, Chef Zach," then she took a bite and chewed and said, with a slight tremble to her chin. "Tis verra good, ye made it perfectly."

Magnus watched her chew, then he said it again, "Are ye broken, Lady Mairead?"

She exhaled. Then she raised her chin and met his eyes. Her eyes were the only thing about her recognizable, no makeup, her skin tanned and peeling, her hair a gray halo with a faded-brassy color five inches from the roots, very thin, looking as if she would gain ten pounds just by moisturizing her skin.

"Nae, I am nae broken, this has just been a minor setback."

Magnus said, "Good because we need ye."

She scoffed. "I am nae sure what use I will be... I am nae broken, but verra weakened. What do ye expect me tae do?"

Fraoch said, "We need ye tae be there tae dance upon her grave."

She gave him a weak smile. "That canna be easy for ye, but I agree, for that purpose, I will make sure tae be strong enough tae tie on m'dancing shoes."

While she ate I ushered Isla out of the room to go to sleep.

CHAPTER 48 - MAGNUS

*T*was my turn for guard duty so during the night I had been walkin' the perimeter, taking the view of the edges of the land, admiring the fine maples growing there, leaning on the gate for a time. There were cameras at the far corners, but we dinna want tae rely on the cameras alone, we walked everywhere, watched everything. Now, as the dawn brightened the forest I stood on the dock with a view of the road ontae the property and the fields on the other side.

The lake was still and quiet. The birds singing in the trees.

The sun cast a pale orange glow across the land and the light was verra beautiful. I turned back tae look at the house, strong and large enough for all of us, appointed with all the best of everythin' and more than we needed.

The front door opened and Chef Zach strode down the steps carrying a mug of coffee out tae me. "You looked thirsty."

"Ye read m'mind, Chef Zach — it has cream in it?"

"Yep."

I took a sip. "Perfect." I rested m'hands on my gun, strapped around m'shoulder. I was wearin' a camouflage coat because the mornings were chilly, but the sun was already warmin' up the place.

Colonel Quentin came from the house. "Hey boss, ready for me to take over?"

"Aye, but I think tis James's turn?"

"Beaty is nauseous and when she's nauseous I get nauseous, so I ought to get out before she starts..." He made a retchin' noise and held his stomach. "I think it might be too late."

Zach chuckled. "You have sympathy morning sickness? Oh no, are you going to be like that dad on Good Morning America who had sympathy labor?"

Colonel Quentin's eyes went wide. "That could happen? No, no, tell me that doesn't happen." He held his stomach. "Ugh, I feel sick."

I joked, "Colonel Quentin, seems ye are putting on a bit of weight as well, tis truly a sympathy pregnancy ye are havin'?"

Colonel Quentin said, "Very funny, I'm here to take over the watch, unless you want me to go in and lay down beside Barfing Beaty?"

"Nae, ye can hae the watch."

I returned tae the house with Chef Zach, takin' off my coat because of the warmth and putting it in the front closet and placing the gun in the gun box.

Then I came tae the main room. "Where are Kaitlyn and the bairns?"

Zach said, "A bunch of them followed Katie to the side lawn for an exercise class."

I filled my mug with more coffee and cream and went tae see.

There was Kaitlyn on an exercise mat spread upon the grass. Sophie, Lochinvar, Hayley, Emma, and all the bairns were on mats as well. Even wee Zoe was upon a mat tryin' a Warrior Pose.

Kaitlyn grinned. "An extra mat for you, Magnus."

I chuckled. "I think ye were layin' in wait." I put my mug on the rail and went tae my place on a mat and moved intae a Warrior's Pose.

Then she had us go intae a Downward Dog. Lochie asked, "What madness is this?"

I had m'arse up in the air and Isla came over, crouched down, and turned her head almost upside down. "Da, you look funny."

Katilyn said, "Now put your right foot forward into the World's Greatest Stretch."

I put my foot forward and whispered, "Isla, ye are supposed tae be doing the stretch."

She whispered, "I'm hiding behind you so mommy won't see me."

Kaitlyn said, "I can see you..." Then she said, "...and back to Downward Dog."

Isla climbed my calf up to my back and draped herself across. "I'm doing Downward Dog on Dada."

I grabbed her legs, pulled her off, and rolled her giggling down to the mat. Zoe tackled us.

Archie said, "I don't think you're doing it right, Da." I put out an arm. "Yer ma winna mind if we are a pile on a mat as long as we are having fun."

Kaitlyn said, "This is so true. Exercise is for serious or fun, both are valid — now another flow, starting..."

Zach came out, "Who wants smoothies?"

The kids all ran past him into the house, cheering happily.

I called after them, "I want one as well, but I hae tae finish m'workout!"

Chef Zach asked, skeptically, "What move is that?"

"The Exhausted Warrior Pose."

He laughed.

Kaitlyn said, "Now that the kids are gone, you *have* to finish."

"Och nae," I teased, following her in the movements. "What dost ye think, Lochie?"

He said, rolling his arms back, "The women persuaded me this would help with battles, but I think it is tae make me weak.

Who needs tae touch their toes? Tis nae a thing that ought tae happen."

I said, "Aye, if ye are touchin' yer toes ye arna battlin' correctly."

Hayley said, "That must be a relief, Lochie, because you can barely touch your knees." She went over and pressed on his back and he dangled there.

Kaitlyn doubled in half, and showed him, "See, like this."

He grunted, his fingers a foot from the ground. "I canna do it, Madame Kaitlyn."

I tried tae touch the ground between my toes and with strainin' got my fingertips tae graze the mat.

Kaitlyn had her hands on her hips, her head cocked to the side. "Well, it's a start."

I joked, "I hae a great big piece of m'body up front here, at the fold, tis difficult tae get past it."

Kaitlyn teasingly huffed. "*That's* your excuse?"

Lochie tried to bend forward again. "Tis my excuse as well."

I said, "Ye canna use that excuse in front of m'wife, Lochie, yer excuse is that ye arna good at it."

We all laughed.

CHAPTER 49 - KAITLYN

e finished our workout and then went in for smoothies and granola bowls then Magnus requested eggs and then bacon and toast, and then joked, "We had a starvation breakfast topped with the usual ordinary breakfast."

And Zach joked back, "It was a nutritious, light breakfast topped with too much food for second breakfast."

Lochinvar said, licking his fingers, "I verra much like the idea of second breakfast, if ye daena get up from the table between tis just one verra long meal."

Fraoch and James came in from fishing then.

Fraoch said, "Ye are having second breakfast without me?"

Chef Zach said, "First breakfast devolved into second breakfast without anyone getting up from the table."

Fraoch rubbed his hands together happily.

While we were eating, Lady Mairead shuffled into the room, wearing a thick robe. She looked like a hospital patient who shouldn't be out of bed.

We all went quiet. She raised her chin, and slowly made it to the closest chair, the one that had James in it. He jumped up, "Pardon me, Ma'am." He pulled the chair out and once she sat down, pushed her chair in, while Sophie busily removed James's dishes.

Lady Mairead asked for oatmeal with fruit and brown sugar, Zach rushed away to the kitchen yet again. Emma placed a handful of vitamins beside her napkin.

Magnus nodded at Lady Mairead. "'Tis good ye are out of bed."

"I am nae sure how long I will manage it, but I thought ye might want tae see that I am recovering and I will be well soon."

She unfurled the napkin and pressed it across her lap.

After she quietly ate, she stiffly rose from the table, "I am tired, Sophie, will ye attend me tae my room?" Sophie jumped up from her chair and took her arm and supported her as she left down the hall.

Emma watched them go. "I'm running to the store, I will grab some hair dye for Lady Mairead, anything else?" And we began making a list.

Later that afternoon, it was up to me to take a cup of tea to Lady Mairead because no one else wanted the job. I took a deep breath and carried it in, placing it on the bedside table, "Emma sent it."

I turned to go, but she said, "Would you sit, please, Kaitlyn?"

I sat in the chair beside her bed. She was leaning on a bank of pillows that had a towel draped over them to protect them from the auburn-colored hair dye that Beaty and Sophie had applied.

She daintily took the cup to her lips and sipped.

I asked, "How are you?"

"I am recoverin', Kaitlyn, twas a verra dark time."

"A year?"

"Aye. Tis tempting tae ask Magnus tae go rescue me earlier. I would prefer tae hae it happen *before* I caught the eye of George MacLeod, who stunk tae high heaven and had nae teeth," she gave a small sad smile. "But tae be rescued earlier might loop and set the timeline off, something terrible might happen." She picked at the blanket that was spread over her lap.

I said, "George MacLeod sounds horrible."

"Aye, fortunately he had enough power on the homestead tae keep the rest of the men off me, but I had tae put up with his gruntin' upon me in exchange. I find solace in that he is dead now, shot by my son. I warned him the day would come." She exhaled. "I am a woman, I can accept a horrid man gruntin' upon me in exchange for my safety while I wait tae be rescued. He smelled of horseshit and sulfur, but a proper bath removed his stench."

I said, "Thankfully you couldn't get pregnant."

"I am thankfully too auld for that. Though sadly, I am unsure if I will be able tae..." She sighed forlornly. "How will I enjoy my friendship with Abby if I arrive there and I am a decade older than she remembers me?" She shook her head. "And I had a lover, a wonderful lover in Cornie, and now he winna even recognize me."

"We dyed your hair, perhaps you're not giving yourself enough credit and—"

She gave me a wry smile. "Kaitlyn, I always give myself more than enough credit, ye ken tis one of my most endearing traits." She dropped her head back. "I miss Hammond verra much."

"Me too, I am so sorry he is gone. I... I know he was very important to you."

"He was my... I relied on him for *everything*. I am unsure how..." She shook her head. "I find myself at a low moment, in my son's guest room, dependent on him, grateful for my rescue, and now for what...? How will I manage?"

"I have never known you not to have a plan, we... we saw you, back at Balloch, you were younger."

She sighed. "I was everywhere at one time. I could do anything, I had a great deal of power. To be young again, it breaks my heart." She flicked a piece of something from her bedding. "Has Haggis been in here, upon the bed?"

I sighed. "Haggis roams far and wide." Then I said, brightly, "We have a kingdom to run, we need you for that. You will have power again."

She waved a hand. "Och nae, I ken for certain, the kingdom is nae ours tae run. We must fight again — and the art museum! Dost ye think the art museum is still there, Kaitlyn?"

"I honestly don't know."

"She destroyed so much art, twas horrible tae see it lost tae history, nae one will ever see the beauty of it." She asked, "How is Elmwood? Is it...?"

"It's gone."

She dropped her head back on the towel. "I think I need tae rest."

I stood. "We will figure something out, Lady Mairead, we will, we just need to—"

She narrowed her eyes. "Ye are with child again."

I screwed up my face. "No, not — did Magnus tell you to...?"

I sank back down in the chair.

"Ye can see it, Kaitlyn, *anyone* can tell."

"Well, if I am, then it has only been a few days, it's not... no, I'm not..." I suddenly wondered if I should have asked Emma to get a pregnancy test from the drug store.

"Well, it took ye long enough tae fulfill yer duty tae Magnus, ye hae been lax about it. I will pray tonight that it will be a son."

"Fine, pray all you want, I'm not stopping you." I huffed.

"See this is what you do, you have these moments with me, where you seem chill—"

"Chill?"

"Yes, where you seem considerate, almost kind, but then you switch and say or do something very mean, so cruel — it's unsettling."

She smirked, "Tis part of m'charm."

I huffed.

She took another sip of her tea. "Ye remember when I first spoke tae ye about how ye ought tae get married and rule yer family?"

"Yes, you told me I ought to pick a man who suits me and who furthered my aims, and I must marry him. Then I could rule a household."

"Twas before I kent ye were going tae be married tae Magnus. I advised ye tae be a strong woman who ruled her husband, without considering it might be my son and I never dreamed ye were going tae be as good at it as ye are. I hae always found it unsettling that ye hae taken my spot at the head of the family, ye should hae been incompetent. I can never forgive ye for having been so triumphant." She tilted her head. "Even when your triumph has led tae good outcomes for my son and grand-children, I still feel spiteful for it. *But...* I hae grown tae respect ye." She shrugged. "I wish I could be more selfless, but tis hard tae find comfort in that my son's success has come more from you than from myself. And now... now I am auld, I am beaten, ye ought nae hate me as much as ye do — ye hae won. Tae hate me..." She shook her head. "Some might find it near gloating. Tis unbecoming of a queen."

I exhaled. "I will try not to gloat." Then I added, "I might not be a queen anymore...."

"Yer husband will ride intae battle, he will win the kingdom for ye and yer coming son—"

I interrupted to say, "Archie. Archie is in line for the throne. I adopted him, he is my son."

She exhaled. "Of course, Archie is next in line. But it daena hurt tae give Magnus a son, tae carry on the bloodline for him. I warned ye tae do it, long ago, but ye had tae take yer time." She dropped her head back on the pillows. "I am verra tired, will ye excuse me tae rest?"

"Gladly."

I walked out into the living room full of everyone. "Store run tomorrow?"

Emma said, "A few days, I think, what do you need?" She turned the pad of paper and pen toward me on the table.

I wrote: pregnancy test.

Archie ran up. "Mammy add sour gummies to the list." He pointed, then read aloud, "Pregnancy test, what's a pregnancy test?"

The color rose on my cheeks. "It's a test to see if someone is pregnant with a ba—"

Magnus across the room began to, loudly, roar with laughter. "Ha ha ha!"

Beaty from her position, lying flat on the far couch, called, "We daena need one, Madame Kaitlyn, I already ken!"

I gulped.

Emma said, her eyes going very wide, "Wait, are *you* pregnant?"

"I don't know, but other people seem to think—"

Magnus laughed so loud he doubled over holding his stomach. "Who else kens? Ye spoke tae m'mother! Did she tell ye? Ha ha ha!"

"Magnus! I will have you know, I am getting the pregnancy test as a *precaution*, so I can prove to you *and* your mother that I am *not* pregnant."

Hayley said, "Oh no you don't, this is the final straw, you,

Mister Fraoch, are getting a vasectomy pronto, this pregnancy is infectious."

Fraoch looked all around the room. "Aye, seems tae be some fae magic inflictin' the women of the family."

James said, "What the hell is going on? What's so funny Magnus?"

He wiped his eyes. "Och, I will let Kaitlyn tell ye. I want tae hear her say it."

"Magnus told me that he got me pregnant the other night, and he was wrong, you can't know it, Magnus, that's not how it works—"

"Tis how it works with me, I kent it the moment I bedded ye."

I rolled my eyes. "He told me he could tell, and I told him that was impossible and now he has conspired with his mother to *also* tell me that she thinks I am pregnant."

Magnus put his hand on his heart. "I dinna speak tae m'mother on it, she said ye are pregnant because we can all see it."

I put my hands on my hips. "This is outrageous!"

Magnus said, "Sophie, what do ye think, does Kaitlyn look pregnant tae ye?"

Sophie said, "I daena want tae overstep, Madame Kaitlyn looks upset by the attention."

I said, "I am only pretending to be upset, because I know I am right. It is impossible to know if someone is pregnant, and definitely not right after having, um... you know... *relations*. You can speak freely, but if you side with Magnus, I retain the right to say that you've been coached ahead of time."

"Ye do hae a high color and a softness that I think lends ye tae bein' pregnant."

I glanced at Hayley who had a laptop in front of her. "What do you think, Hayley, is Magnus conspiring against me?"

"I am not even playing along with this, I am researching vasectomy docs."

"Jesus Christ."

Zach said, "Now you're eating for two? Yikes, my grocery list keeps doubling."

I turned to Emma. "Help me, talk some sense into these people."

She shrugged. "It's scientifically impossible for Magnus to know you were pregnant from the first day—"

"The first minute! He seems to think he got me pregnant just by his..." I glanced around, and whispered, "You know... *movements.*"

Emma giggled. "Well, that is unscientific, but then again... sometimes you just know and maybe Magnus just... maybe he just knows you so well. It's romantic if you think about it."

Zach joked, "So Magnus, since you have the power to make the baby, what sex did you make?"

"I made a boy, I—"

Archie said, "Yes! A boy! Ben, there's going to be a baby brother!" They started jumping up and down, so Isla and Zoe started jumping and wiggling beside them.

I huffed and set my face in a comical frown. "Now the kids are involved in this pseudoscientific feeling you have that you just *performed* a baby boy. Quentin, did you know when you got Beaty pregnant? And do you know what sex it is?"

Quentin said, "I did not know, but then again, it's my first time, maybe I was inexperienced. Now that I look back on it it was clearly that night, you know the one... right Beaty?"

"Och aye, Quennie, twas the night, definitely, and I am carryin' a girl, ye can tell because I am wretched and I want tae eat..." She put her hands over Mookie's ears and mouthed: *meat.* "Tis how the mother tries tae feed the daughter, tae strengthen her for the coming adversities. Everyone kens. Are ye cravin' steak?"

"Of course I'm not craving steak! This was *at most* five days ago!"

Magnus grinned. "Five days ago, I got ye pregnant with a son, I am verra proud of it."

Everyone laughed.

Emma said, "Well, it's still early to pee on a stick, I think, we want to really know-know, but it's not too early for prenatal vitamins." She pulled a bottle from the shelf and dumped some in her hand.

I comically scowled while I chewed and swallowed them down.

CHAPTER 50 - KAITLYN

*W*e decided to wait for a while, for Lady Mairead to regain her strength, and we had plenty of supplies, so we put off shopping, and buying a pregnancy test. I also wanted to wait until there was no chance the pregnancy test would be a false negative or positive.

But finally I couldn't wait any longer, and Emma returned from the store with one. I said, "I want privacy with Magnus, will you all please, *please*, pretend like nothing is happening here?"

Everyone agreed. I drew Magnus by the hand down to the bathroom off our bedroom.

We didn't speak, he leaned against the bathroom counter.

I tore the box apart and dropped it in the trash, then pulled the stick from its wrapping and pulled down my pants. I sat on the toilet, put the stick between my legs, and urinated on it.

In that position I said. "I'm afraid to look, I don't know how I feel, I wasn't trying, you know, I..."

"I ken, we dinna talk about it afore, we hae been busy about our lives."

"And we have such full lives. Archie's next in line for the

throne; Isla's regal enough to be a badass warrior queen, and so... they are enough, you know?"

His face softened into a warm smile. "Ye ken, Kaitlyn, we daena need another child, but winna it be wonderful tae hae another, anyway?"

I smiled back. "It really really would." I took a deep breath. "So what I'm saying is you are probably mistaken, don't be disappointed, now that we've decided that we would like to, we can start—"

"Mo reul-iuil, just take the stick from between yer legs and look at it."

I said, "Yes, fine... but it has to sit for a bit I think..." I pulled the stick from between my legs, "Wait, what's the plus mean?"

He teased, "I canna imagine."

"The plus means pregnant, right? Is that what it means or does it mean you're in the clear, maybe it means I'm not pregnant?"

He fished the box out of the trash. "The wee cross upon the stick means that God has given ye a bairn."

"A baby? We're having a baby?" I tossed the stick in the sink, pulled up my pants, and threw my arms around him. "We're having a baby?"

"Aye, mo reul-iuil, I told ye, we are havin' a bairn."

"Oh my god, oh my god, oh my god," We kissed. "We're ready for this, another one?"

"Aye, we are ready."

"It's still very early, maybe we should wait to...?"

He laughed. "They are all waiting to hear!" He raised his voice, and boomed loud enough for the whole house to hear, "Did ye hear? Kaitlyn is pregnant!"

A cheer went up from the living room. "Told ye, mo reul-iuil. I am always right, ye ken."

I teased, "I forgot about how you crow when you've gotten

me pregnant, that cocky thing. I thought that this time, since you're an old dad already, you'd be less cocky."

He pulled me closer, my face against his neck, our voices quiet in the harsh light of the modern bathroom. "Och nae, I think I will be more cocky, mo reul-iuil. Ye ken, this time it was sheer prowess that got ye pregnant."

I kissed his throat. "Sheer prowess?"

"Aye, twas m'cock that decided it, ye canna argue, ye hae tae allow me tae crow. If ye think on it, m'cock daena get nearly enough celebration."

"You mean overall or day to day?"

"Day tae day. Tis frowned upon tae hold it up and hae others remark upon its talent. This is the one day when men can say, 'Och aye, look what I hae accomplished!'"

"So here's the thing, my love, this means we'll have three kids, that's us *each* with one on our horse and then...? But I suppose Archie can ride alone now..."

He patted his chest over his heart like a beat. "Och, I love ye, mo reul-iuil. And Archie can ride on his own. Isla can ride with me, ye will carry the bairn, we will make it work, and ye forget I can drive now."

"I almost did forget that. Okay, that was the only downside, the rest of it is just happy good news, except..."

He lifted my chin with the crook of his finger and looked down into my eyes. "I ken ye are worried, I am as well. We are rentin' a compound tae hide and we hae a kingdom that has likely been lost, we hae an enemy, and our best asset, the Lady Mairead, is down for the count. Aye, there is a great deal tae worry on, but ye ken, we always hae some kind of drama—"

I chuckled, "Oy, do we have so much drama."

"Now is the time for celebratin' our new bairn." He grabbed my ass and squeezed it with both hands and pulled my hips close and kissed my lips. "Twas a fine arse this morn out on the lawn greetin' me when I returned from guard duty."

I pulled away. "Let's go out and let you properly crow."

He pushed away from the bathroom counter, took my hand, and we left our rooms.

When we got to the living room Emma's was the first face I saw. "Really, truly? Another baby? We're going to have two babies at almost the same time?"

I nodded. "I can't believe it, we'll be about a month behind Beaty, I think."

Beaty poked her head over the back of the couch, her hair was mussed, she was a shade of sickly green. "Yay! We are twinsies, Queen Kaitlyn, our bairns will be like siblings."

I folded my hands together. "They will be so freaking cute! We can put them in matching clothes!"

Hayley said, "Ugh, more babies, seriously? My gift-buying bill has just skyrocketed. I see you're all acting like this is the most positive thing in the world, but you need to think about the aunts and uncles, this is a *lot* of extra work for us."

Fraoch laughed. "Och aye, I will need a bigger boat if I am tae take them all fishin', how many will it be? A dozen? I will need a verra big boat."

I said, "Dear God, I hope Beaty and I aren't carrying eight children!"

As the nieces and nephews ran through the room, he said, "Wait, there are only four nieces and nephews here aready? How come it feels like so many more? Everywhere they go they are a mob."

The kids mobbed him and wrestled him down to the ground.

Archie asked, from the bottom of the pile of kids on Fraoch's stomach, "What are you talking about?"

Magnus said, "We were announcing to everyone that yer ma is goin' tae hae another bairn."

"This is really happening?" Archie climbed from the pile. "And it's definitely a boy? Oh man, I hope it is a boy."

Isla put her hands on her hips, her face frowned. "No one asked me first."

Magnus said, "Ye canna ask first, Isla, ye hae tae accept God's will. Tis a bairn and we are goin' tae rejoice in the blessing."

"Will I have to share Angelica with the baby?"

Magnus said, "Who is Angelica?"

Isla rushed across the room, plucked a doll from a basket, and rushed back. "Angelica."

"Och nae, tis yer bairn, Isla? Ye winna hae tae share yer bairn."

"Good. Because I don't like to share my babies. Tell Zoe she can't hold Angelica." She tossed the doll down and came over to sit beside me. Behind her, Zoe picked Angelica up and dragged her by the ankle around the room.

Magnus asked, "Anyone else hae any questions on the coming bairn?"

Isla said, "Will Aunt Beaty's baby and our baby be brothers?"

Magnus smiled. "All of our bairns will be brothers, even the sisters."

Archie said, "You don't look pregnant, how do you know?"

"I took a test." I held up the stick, "Don't touch it, I peed on it — but see that mark?"

Ben's eyes went wide. "You *peed* on it?"

"Yes, but that's not the point, see the mark? That means I'm pregnant."

Magnus said, "But ye ought tae tell them about *why* ye took the test…"

I said, "They were here, they know, I took the test because your father told me that I was going to have a baby."

Magnus rolled his hand.

I continued, "And I didn't believe him, but he was absolutely right."

Magnus chuckled. "The message here, Archibald, is yer da is always right."

I rolled my eyes. "You are sometimes right. In this one

moment, I will concede that you always know when I am pregnant before I know myself. It's infuriating."

Magnus shrugged, "Tis also verra romantic: I love ye, and I canna take m'eyes from ye, and so I see yer changes. Ye are irritated with me for doin' what ye ken I canna help."

"That is a very good point, and I love you too."

Emma said, "So when's your due date? When did you conceive?"

I grinned, "October 20, 1708."

Emma said, "Uh oh, um — how many days ago?"

"Like twenty-one?"

"Looks like your due date will be in late July, if you don't change your timeline in any way."

"Maybe we ought to etch marks into a clay tablet that I carry in my pocket and count the days that way."

Zach rubbed his hands together, and said, "So we'll have a celebratory meal, but once I go in the kitchen don't keep talking about big things out here. I can't hear you from there and I don't want to miss anything."

Emma said, "I'll FaceTime you if anyone else shows up pregnant."

CHAPTER 51 - KAITLYN

*L*ady Mairead entered the room.

Her hair was dark auburn again, swept up in a French twist. She had applied makeup and looked younger and healthier, although thinner than usual. She was wearing a well-designed pantsuit, as if she was going to a luncheon of the G-8 summit.

She announced, "I am nae pregnant, in case anyone was wondering," and smoothed down the front of her suit. "Thank ye for ordering the clothes for me, Madame Emma. It feels verra fine tae be well dressed again." As she said it her eyes trailed over the rest of us, wearing casual clothes, some looking an awful lot like pajamas.

Emma said, "You're welcome."

"What is the conversation?"

Magnus said, "We are announcing that Kaitlyn is with bairn."

She sat down at the table. "Of course, I mentioned it tae her weeks ago, this is yer usual 'announcement', Magnus? Something we all ken already?"

He laughed. "We all kent it, but I still get tae announce it, tis part of being a king. I get tae do whatever I want. I can make proclamations and make them a grand thing, such as this, 'I hearby announce that after many long days m'mother has finally gotten out of bed.' See? Tis verra regal sounding when a king says it."

She huffed and asked Zach for tea and not tea from the machine, a proper tea from the kettle. Then she added, "This is why I wanted tae speak tae ye, Magnus. And though I believe sometimes it ought tae be private, I am sure ye will expect *everyone* tae hear."

"About what, the tea kettle?"

"Nae the kingdom — pay attention, Magnus, your kingdom is gone. We hae tae come up with a way tae regain it."

Fraoch said, "Tae play, for one moment, devil's advocate, do we?"

She said, "Of course we do, there is imminent danger tae the—"

Magnus stood, "Madame Sophie, would ye mind taking the bairns outdoors for a time?"

"I would love tae. Bairns! Let us go tae the bridge and play m'favorite game, throwin' sticks intae the current."

Beaty said, "I want tae come, I feel so much better now." She climbed from the couch and followed Sophie and the kids outside.

Magnus said, "Now ye can speak on the danger, Lady Mairead."

Lady Mairead said, "I hae always believed that without the kingdom we arna safe, or rather, ye, Magnus, and your progeny, arna safe. If someone else is in control of the future, Agnie and this Ian person, *they* are in control of all the information that exists on Magnus. So tae answer yer question, Fraoch, if the tables were turned, if there was a family who were once on the throne and they were overthrown — what would ye do, if ye had been the overthrower?"

Fraoch said, "I canna be sure. I would weigh all that I kent on the family tae determine the danger they would be tae me and deal with them accordingly—"

"Let's say they are a danger tae ye, let's say, for the sake of argument, that their family is run by a strong patriarch, who has proven himself lethal in the arena, and a powerful matriarch who wants her children tae sit on the throne—"

I said, "You are the matriarch in this scenario?"

Her brow went up, "Nae, ye are the matriarch, Kaitlyn, in all things, I am merely the auld woman who is allowed the governance of the kingdom when ye canna be bothered."

I said, "See? This is how it goes with you, a compliment and then a stab-in-the-back, it's infuriating and exhausting."

She said, with her chin raised, "Tis my way, I canna be expected tae worry on yer emotional reaction, we hae more important things tae do —"

I interrupted to say, "*My* emotional reaction? Part of the reason we are in this position is because you were overly emotional about some paintings!"

Lady Mairead glowered, then exhaled. "Tae *continue*, Fraoch, if this were the type of family that was opposed tae ye, what would ye do — deliberate?"

"Nae, I would act."

"Magnus, would ye make sure the overthrown king and his family wouldna seize power again? Ye saw with the Scottish pretender and his bloodline that he and his heirs were *always* trying for the throne. Tis the way of it, would ye allow for it?"

"Nae."

"Would ye kill the father?"

"Probably."

"Would ye kill the sons?"

Magnus looked uncomfortable, he shifted and said, "Aye, if I deemed it necessary."

"Well, ye are about tae hae two sons. I think ye see the danger they are in."

"I do, I see it." Magnus shifted again. "What do ye propose we do?"

"I hae been thinking on it long, we must go tae war."

Magnus groaned. "War? Och nae..." He folded his arms, his brow drawn. "Tae think on the many lives we might lose, ye daena hae a better plan? Ye hae been thinking long and this is the best ye hae? War? And where will I get these men tae fight the war?" He shook his head. "Nae, nae, I canna expect men tae die for me, what if I challenge Ian tae an arena battle?"

"Ye hate arena battles! Ye hae removed arena battles from law!"

"Yet somehow, I keep havin' tae fight them..."

Lady Mairead continued, "This is nae an issue anyway, Ian would never accept a challenge from ye, why would he? He has the kingdom, he has seen ye in the arena, he kens ye are lethal. Tis out of the question. Ye must come up with another plan."

He said, "Ye are right — I daena understand how Ian would accept the challenge." He tapped his fingers on the top of the table.

"And though ye hae won many times, there is always a chance ye will lose, Magnus, ye canna expect tae never be bested."

"But I am tae declare war with only a few friends and brothers around me? I might lose that as well."

"Ye hae more than that. I hae associates on the inside, they will be waiting to hear from me."

"Who?"

"Burton and Wallace."

Magnus nodded. "I always kent Wallace was in yer pocket."

"He inna in my pocket, he is in yer pocket! I hae demanded his allegiance, but his loyalty is tae your throne."

"Fine, I see yer point. But two men daena make an army — will we hae enough soldiers tae wage war?"

"Aye, with Wallace and Burton loyal, we begin there, we show strength, we build an army, we wage war."

Magnus shook his head solemnly. "Ye make it sound so easy."

Quentin said, "I've been at war for a long time, and I agree with what you're saying, there is no way Ian is accepting a challenge from Magnus. He will say no. We have to wage war, take your kingdom back by force." Quentin added, "Though I do kind of wish he had... I don't know, a sense of duty?"

Magnus chuckled, dolefully. "The man who has usurped m'throne inna working from a place of duty, or honor, or ethics, or morals."

Quentin said, "Yeah, you're right, I suppose — so we make war and kick his ass."

Lady Mairead said, "Good, we are in agreement: my son, the king, winna die in the dirt of an arena like a bull with a sword stuck through him, like a beast."

I grimaced.

Lochinvar was licking a nacho-flavored chip. "Och nae, here I was listenin' tae the conversation and thinkin' I would get tae fight in the arena. I had a whole plan: I would put m'self forward tae fight for Magnus, so he wouldna die, and I would be victorious and we wouldna need a long war, we could just hae one fight." He tossed the chip in his mouth, chewed it, and brushed his hands off. "I am disappointed."

Magnus drew his brow, and shook his head. "Lochinvar, ye wouldna be fightin' for me in the arena anyway, never again, nae in a battle that Ian is definitely *nae* goin' tae accept."

Lochie said, "Why nae? If there was going tae be an arena battle, it ought tae be me. I am well-suited for killing, I am trained, and as they say, bloodthirsty. I was told once that I hae a brain good for battlin' but not much else. I took it as a compliment."

Magnus chuckled. "There winna be an arena battle, but even if there were, I am nae comfortable with the idea of another man fighting my battles. Donnan had me imprisoned, forced me tae fight for him, tis a brutal and cruel thing tae ask another man tae die. Nae, put it from yer head, and tis immaterial. There is nae way Ian the Troublesome will accept the challenge. I wouldna if the roles were reversed. We must plan for war."

Magnus had been leaning on the table, he straightened up and adjusted his shirt as he spoke.

Lochie plucked another chip from the bag, crunched it, and licked his fingers. "I honestly wouldna mind, Magnus, I want tae fight. If it means ye would get tae keep the kingdom, and the bairns would be safe, then bring it on. I am like the em-and-em-man, I hae one shot, ye ken, or I blow."

Zach and Quentin high-fived.

Magnus watched Lochie, and slowly shook his head. "I am nae Donnan, I canna force a man tae fight for me. I winna do it. Nae, ye can stand down, Mr Em-and-em Man, there winna be any arena battle. We will hae tae find ye something tae do with a full war—"

Lochinvar said, "Fine, but if ye need me, just ask, but daena wait too long, I am goin' tae get fat." He poked his stomach out and patted it like a drum.

Lady Mairead said, "Then we are at war."

Magnus said, "Aye, it sounds as if tis our only option."

Lady Mairead raised her tea cup. "Tae gain peace we will need war. Tis the usual order of it. Then I will again take over the guardianship of the kingdom. I will be even better suited than I once was, because I hae naething better tae do, I am auld now and must sit my aching bones upon a throne because nae one wants me around."

Magnus joked, "I see ye hae regained yer wonderful disposition."

I said, "I'm sure after a wee rest you will be back to your old galavanting around."

"In the meantime, I will guard over the kingdom for ye."

Magnus looked around the room. "Who will come?"

Lady Mairead spun her spoon in her cup, daintily, "Ye ought tae bring Lochinvar, because he ought not stay here anymore."

Magnus stopped still. "Why not?"

She raised her chin.

"Why not?"

"Naething tae think on, he is from the future, he ought tae return there."

We all stared at her squinting. She raised her chin even more. I swear we could hear the cuckoo clock on the wall mark the seconds with a tick-tock while we were silent.

Magnus said, "What dost ye mean? He is connected with us somehow?"

Lady Mairead looked around and then whispered, "Aye... he *becomes* connected."

Magnus huffed.

She continued, "I daena want tae ruin anything, but Lochinvar is awaited by his future. He daena hae tae live here with Magnus while he lives out his happy ending here in this..." She looked up at the timber walls and ceiling and shivered. "Log cabin."

Hayley put her hands over her ears. "Ugh, spoiler alert."

Magnus said, "This is a million-dollar log cabin, ye canna disparage it. There is a stuffed bison in the corner watching over us as we eat dinner, tis a first rate castle."

"All I am saying is some proper stone and more fine glass wouldna hurt." She added, "Lochinvar, ye are from the future, we ought tae return ye tae it."

"What time?"

"The twenty-four-hundreds, and I am nae telling ye anything else upon it."

I noticed Magnus counting with his fingers tapping on the chair.

Lochie said, "Even if I beg?"

"Especially if ye beg, tis unbecoming, and I winna put up with it. Ye ought tae grow up and be a man."

He joked, "Whatever m'future holds will there be cookies?

Because when Mags took me tae the past there were nae cookies and twas frightful. I dinna like it one bit."

"If we regain the kingdom for Magnus's bairns and their progeny, then ye will hae all the cookies ye want."

Lochie grinned. "One more question, if I am tae just accept that ye ken my future, and ye arna tae divulge it tae me, if I am nae tae ken anything, tell me this, when I call Mags an 'auld man' am I right in it?"

"Aye, he is verra auld compared tae ye."

Lochinvar stood from where he was leaning, similarly to Magnus. They didn't look much like each other, he was pale and ginger, Magnus was dark haired — their main similarity was in the jawline and the shape of the eyes. Lochinvar said, "Good, I will call him grandpa."

Magnus said, "Och nae, tis nae the way it works. We are half-brothers, meaning we are the same generation, else we are naething."

Lochie laughed good-naturedly, "All right, auld man, I winna call ye grandpa, just auld man, we daena want tae confuse the timeline. " He clapped Magnus on the shoulder. "We need tae prepare for war. But all this talk of sweets has me hungry, can I get something, Chef Zach?"

"Help yourself."

Lochie left the room and Zach said, "So, speaking of brothers, are you saying that Lochie becomes *more* connected with Magnus's family in some way? Is he also a part of your family a bit further down the road?" He grimaced. "That's a whole lot of Donnan DNA."

Lady Mairead huffed. "I canna expect ye tae understand, Chef Zach, ye arna royal. Magnus and Lochinvar are half brothers from different centuries, Lochinvar is from the twenty-fifth century, Magnus is from the seventeenth they have different mothers. By the time ye get down tae the great-grand-children ye daena hae tae worry on it, and this is the way of royals anyway. In the history of the world there are always bloodlines being shared from one tae the other."

Emma said, "So you're saying that Lochie is going to be a part of Magnus's timeline farther down? By marriage, to one of the great granddaughters or some—?"

Hayley asked, "Is it Rebecca? Oh my god, is Lochinvar Sophie's dad? Or... or... is he James's grandson?"

Lady Mairead glared.

I said, "Hayley, read the room, we aren't talking about it, we aren't guessing, we're trying to be discreet."

Lady Mairead said, "I will endure nae more speculation—"

Zach said, "I have one more question, though, I get the 'why' you want to take him to the future, he's *from* the future, because he's originally from the twenty-fifth century, it's his place and *already* it's been done. He should be there, but you're doing it now — how did he become a part of Magnus's family the first time?" He gestured to his brain exploding.

Lady Mairead said, "I daena ken what might have happened tae Lochinvar in other timelines, our interference has changed the history of the world, but also has given us power beyond any ever wielded." Her face looked drawn and tired.

She finished her speech with, "*Whatever.* I am nae God, I daena hae all the answers." She stood. "I am tired from the conversation, I think I will go lie down."

Magnus said, "Ye drop a bomb on us and then walk away?"

"How else would ye hae me do it?" She smirked, "A lady should always sweep from the room leaving everyone behind with their expression slack-jawed, tis how ye are best remembered."

"Ye ought not meddle in the future, as a matter of morality. I remember once ye told me that ye dinna go tae the future because ye dinna want tae learn too much. Now it seems ye are interfering in the lives of yer descendants on the regular."

"I daena *want* tae learn about my descendants, and twas an accident how I found this out... but it is written. Lochinvar lives in the future. More important tae us, we need tae fight a war, live tae see peace once more and yer bairns tae grow up, and for ye tae live long — all the while driving me mad."

Magnus smiled. "Did I drive ye mad while we were rescuin' ye?"

She said, "I am grateful for the rescue, twas a verra hard thing tae be stuck in the past and I was well aware that twas likely yer dreams come true tae hae me safely absconded with—"

I interrupted with, "Like when you had me kidnapped? Or when you left us to live a whole year in the sixteenth century, where, I might add, there is not much of *anything*?"

The other people in the room watched from her face to mine then back to her's.

She nodded, her eyes moistened as if she might weep. "Aye. It might hae been easier tae hae revenged against me by leaving me there, I ken ye considered it — I daena take it lightly that ye rescued me anyway." She stared directly ahead. "I ken all of ye might hae had a reason tae leave me, and I am sure ye argued the case. I am relieved ye dinna win, and for the part ye might hae played in Magnus's rescue of me, I thank ye."

She brushed off her front, and with uneasy steps left the room.

I said, "Did she just... did she just *apologize*?"

Magnus said, "Nae but she came verra close. And she thanked us for the rescue so ye ken, I think we ought to celebrate with a feast—"

Zach said, "No! No food yet, I've been standing out here listening for..." He looked at the clock. "So long! Everyone stop talking about important things or I will never get lunch made."

I said to Magnus, "Besides, I think you have many decisions to make, like who goes with you, who waits?"

"Aye, maybe an afternoon spar, while I think? Anyone want tae come spar with the young Lochinvar?"

As if on cue Lochie stuck his head through the swinging

door to the kitchen with a half-eaten popsicle in his hand. He asked, "Did I hear ye say spar — are we sparring?"

Magnus nodded. "Colonel Quentin, Fraoch, want tae come spar with the lad?"

Quentin said, "Not me, injured shoulder, but I'm happy to referee."

Fraoch cracked his knuckles. "Aye, I want tae spar with him verra verra much, I think that could be m'favorite thing — the anticipation is wondrous."

Zach said, "I'll be here sparring with a brisket."

Magnus, Fraoch, Lochinvar, and Quentin left, talking about weapons, and what they ought to take with them to the future. I watched them go and then my eyes settled on Hayley. "We doing this again?"

"What, the war, or the baby? Because both are equally 'not cool'."

"I meant the war, I already knew your thoughts on my coming baby and I don't need to hear about it, because, dum-dum, you are a great aunt and you ought not to talk smack about wee bairns, because they might grow up to hate you."

She gasped, a hand clutching her heart. "How dare you!"

I playfully shoved her shoulder.

She went back to scrolling through web pages, pouting a little. "They are literally all I have, those nieces and nephews, don't tease me like that. I would die for them. I would also buy presents for them."

"Fair enough, all I'm saying is Beaty and I are going to give you two more to die for and to spoil."

"Ugh, the shopping is endless." She tapped the enter key pointedly. "There, I put some stuff in a cart, let me get Emma to explain how to check-out on the down-low."

She left the room. I peeked at the laptop: the shopping cart for an online toy store held a big science kit for the boys, some doll clothes for Isla's doll, and a smaller doll for Zoe. The window peeking out behind the shopping cart was a website for a local urologist.

She returned with Emma.

I said, "You really are shopping for vasectomy doctors, *seriously?*"

She sat down. "Yep, one hundred percent. Fraoch is in agreement and Quentin said he thought it would be safe to make the appointment. There's a local doctor, and we have some fake credentials we're going to use since we're in hiding, yet *again*."

"I would apologize but since this is your bitch mother-in-law, Agnie, stealing our throne, not mine, I don't have to."

She laughed. "Your bitch mother-in-law is being weird. I don't trust her."

She's not being weird, she's just defeated. It's hard to watch, but if I had to guess, she's about to rise again.

CHAPTER 52 - MAGNUS

"*S*o what's the procedure?"

Fraoch said, "Tis a snip, ye ken, a wee cut, inside the verra large shaft."

James chuckled. "Is that how Hayley explained it to you?"

"Aye," his brow raised. "She is a good judge of size."

Lochinvar's eyes were wide, holding his hands over his crotch.

Colonel Quentin said, "Are you sure, Fraoch?"

"Aye, Hayley and I made a deal from the verra beginnin', we dinna want the heartache of bairns, and we might hae eventually grown out of it from boredom, but we are surrounded by bairns, so we are able tae keep our promise tae each other."

I clapped him on the shoulder and joked, "Tis too bad ye are giving up all beddin' forever."

Lochinvar said, "I think I need tae sit down." He wobbled, then he fainted, slumpin' tae the dirt.

Fraoch nudged him with his toe. "Og Lochie, wake up!"

Lochinvar startled awake and looked around. "What happened?"

Fraoch said, "Ye hae become a woman, so fearful ye dropped

intae the dirt. I am nae pickin' ye up, ye'll hae tae pick yerself up if ye are going tae talk with the elder men."

Lochinvar groaned and lumbered up. "It went verra dark, I canna believe ye are choosin' nae tae bed yer—"

Fraoch laughed. "Lochinvar, Og Maggy is just joking with ye, I hae explained it now, eight times, it winna harm me. I will still be able tae properly bed m'wife."

I shuddered, "Och, with yer willy shorn in half? I daena think so."

Lochinvar gasped, "Och nae," he turned white as a sheet again.

Fraoch groaned.

James said, "Mags is just kidding, Lochie, they don't shear it, it's more like cleaning a fish, they just flay it and—"

Fraoch groaned and put his hand over his cock.

Lochinvar looked unsteady on his feet.

James said, "Look around, we all have our hands over our cocks."

We all laughed.

I asked, "How long will ye be in the hospital?"

Fraoch said, "The physician told me the process would take about twenty minutes, and then I can go home soon after. I think gettin' m'tooth implant was much more trouble."

James left one hand over his crotch, and put the other over his mouth. Then he said, "All kidding aside, it's going to be fine, no worries. When's the procedure?"

"Day after tomorrow."

CHAPTER 53 - HAYLEY

*Q*uentin drove us to the small medical center, we parked at the far end of the parking lot, and sat on the back of the truck while Fraoch went inside, by himself, to check in.

I chewed my fingernails, Quentin stood looking a little like a bodyguard while we waited.

A few moments later he came out with forms and I filled them out on the hood of the truck.

He said, "I joked with the lady, I asked if the physician's sword arm was steady, and ye ken what, m'bhean ghlan? She dinna think twas funny, she dinna understand me." Fraoch's eyes went wide. "Och Hayley, I am tae hae a surgery on m'incomparable cock, and they canna even make a joke about swords?"

I said, "It's not the comedy we need, though I do get that it would be nice to have a little bedside manner. Give her a look from me."

I dotted an i on the form and passed him the stack. "Make sure to tell the doctor that joke, he might appreciate it."

He strolled back across the parking lot to the medical center.

Quentin said, as he went in the door, "There he goes, our boy is locked and loaded ready to go."

I said. "His dick is not a weapon!"

"That's not how he thinks on it."

"True, but he's a human and there is a scalpel aimed at his private parts and we ought to just… I don't know, be quiet and show some respect to the moment."

"Absolutely."

I said, "Besides, you're partly responsible, with your baby making."

He grinned. "You knew everyone was going to make babies, it was inevitable and Mags is on his third."

"Yeah, I always knew I would be surrounded by babies. The deluge is still a shock. I didn't know we would want the vasectomy so urgently, but here we are."

He nodded. "Here we are."

He reached into a cooler in the truck, pulled out a couple of sodas with one hand, and passed one to me.

"You're going to make a good dad."

He said, "You think? My dad was shite, you think I'll do better?"

"Oh hell yeah, sheesh, you are not going to be anything like your dad or your stepdad, look at you, the kind of guy who takes care of all of us, and you remember to bring sodas."

We both took a sip.

He said, "I'm going to walk the perimeter."

"Always gotta be on guard?"

"Yep."

He disappeared around the corner.

I scrolled through my phone, which was boring — we weren't supposed to use social media, but I had an old anon account that I used to use to argue on Twitter with morons and sometimes I used it to look at other people arguing without actually arguing myself. I got a little sidetracked by something going on with Ryan Reynolds and then I heard a gunshot.

I dove to the ground.

Fuck, fuck fuck. *Go in the building, or get in the truck?*

Another shot. I crawled around the truck, shoved open the door, climbed in, slammed the door, and checked my gun — *there's one in the chamber, safety is off, trigger discipline.* Keys were in the ignition.

A barrage of shots.

It sounded like it was coming from behind the building and I had been looking up Ryan Reynolds, I was the worst fucking person in the world. People ran from the front of the building.

I climbed down and asked the closest person, "What's happening?!"

She wouldn't say, which freaked me out. Was it happening around back with Quentin, with an injured shoulder? Or inside, with… an unconscious Fraoch?

Another gunshot.

I had to help Quentin.

I ran across the parking lot, weaving through cars, to the edge of the building — *hold on Hayley, keep your shit together, don't be scared, just get to the corner.*

I peeked around to see what was going on, but was buffeted back by a gale force wind. I put my arm up to block my eyes, and was forced to take a step back. The dumpster was back there, trash filled the air in a tornado of whipping winds, the top of the dumpster crashing up and down, almost as loud as a gunshot, but… I couldn't convince myself it hadn't been real — it *had* been gunshots.

Now there was a storm.

I fought against the wind, but couldn't get closer to the center of the storm. *But maybe Quentin was inside getting Fraoch?*

Fraoch had to be done with procedure, he might need help.

I rushed back around the building, and ripped open the front door to find nurses and patients rushing around terrified. I grabbed the sleeve of the closest nurse. "I'm looking for Fraoch MacDonald! Have you seen Fraoch MacDonald?"

The woman's eyes darted toward the back room. I shoved down the hall toward the examination rooms. A nurse behind me declared, "You can't be back here, why are you—?"

"Where is Fraoch MacDonald? He was here, where is he?"

Her face went ashen. "He should be there!"

I shoved open a door and looked around.

I spun around. "Is that the back door?" Without waiting for an answer, I plowed against the emergency door, setting off an alarm.

Out back there was nothing, no one, small gusts, a sprinkling rain.

I turned back into the medical center, adding to the scurry, asking everyone, "What happened?! What happened?!" and stumbling toward the front door where people were running and in the distance, police sirens headed this way.

I had to leave before the police arrived.

Ugh.

What if Fraoch and Quentin were kidnapped?

I needed to get away. I needed to look for them. I needed to see Magnus, I needed to...

I hopped in the truck, started it, and drove from the lot, shaking so much it was difficult to keep to the lane. I called Katie's phone and put it on speaker almost driving into oncoming traffic.

Katie answered, I said, "Hey," and burst into tears.

Her voice, "What's going on, talk to me, what do you need...?"

I stuttered and blubbered and sobbed but managed, "Quentin and Fraoch... gone... shooting... backdoor and I tried.... And the police were coming—"

"Oh no! Are you on your way? Don't hang up. We'll be waiting for you by the gate."

I could hear the comforting sounds of Katie explaining, and

Magnus's voice, low and calm, James in the background asking, "What the fuck...?"

And then they were waiting while I was driving, so many miles back, feeling scared and sorry for myself.

CHAPTER 54 - KAITLYN

A few hours later, in the middle of the night, Hayley, Beaty, and I were sitting on the porch of the lodge, looking out over the lake. Hayley and I were holding hands, Beaty had her head in my lap, Hayley had a can of soda, but I could tell she really wanted a bottle of whisky, and in times like this we needed Quentin here to be smart with her about it.

We had sent Magnus, Lochinvar, and Lady Mairead to the kingdom to get Fraoch and Quentin back.

We were being quiet. Zach stood beside us, armed, a gun in a holster, watchful and nervous. James was out by the gate across the road.

Hayley and I would take over watch from him, but first I needed to sleep, but before that I had to help Hayley, so I was sitting up, keeping her company, and comforting Beaty.

I asked, "Getting tired?"

Beaty nodded, her head rubbing up and down on my thigh.

Hayley said, "I don't know if I'll ever sleep again. I freaking drove my husband to a doctor's appointment and now he's gone."

She sighed and put her head back on the porch wall. "This sucks."

"Yes, it does."

Zach said, "I'm going to go inside and relieve myself, back in a minute."

He left us on the dark porch, a cool night, stars in the sky.

I said, "It's always hard when Magnus leaves, and definitely harder when he's been taken away, I don't know what to say except I've been there. I know it sucks to hear someone say that, because it seems to make light of your predicament, but I don't mean it like that at all. I just mean to commiserate, and to say, the good news is that though this has happened to me, we also got Magnus back. Do you hear that, Beaty? We always get Magnus back. We'll get Quentin and Fraoch back, we will. Magnus and Lochinvar and Lady Mairead have gone to Riaghalbane and that's their mission — get Fraoch and Quentin back."

Beaty's voice was small when she said, "His shoulder was injured, Queen Kaitlyn, he ought nae be enduring any terrible privations. I am verra worried on him."

"Me too, sweetie, me too."

Hayley said, joking with that end-of-the-world dark humor common in the trenches, "Fraoch's dick was broken, I am super worried about it."

"Me too, sweetie, me too."

She said, "You're worried about my husband's dick?"

"I'm worried about your whole husband for you, his dick especially, but they said he was in the recovery room, at least his vasectomy was finished. He was probably just a little loopy still, a little numb in the crotch, this is good news."

Her chin trembled. "Why did I insist on doing the procedure now?"

"Well, you know, you wanted control over one thing in your lives. You and Fraoch have been at the whim of our dramas and you had one thing you wanted to do for yourself. You wanted to get it done. I don't think you should blame yourself, you had a safe place, a guard."

"I was scrolling through Twitter!"

"Without logging in, good lord, you are riding the pity-train. Chill out, stop blaming yourself, we need to get from self-incriminations to a proper broken-hearted waiting. He will be home, they will both be home."

"You know what we were going to do tonight?"

"What?"

"Put a bag of frozen corn on his crotch and watch a movie in bed."

"That's why you're holding the thawed bag of corn?"

She nodded at the bag dripping in her lap, dolefully. "When will they be back?"

I said, "Three days. That's all we have to wait for."

CHAPTER 55 - KAITLYN

*W*e waited three days, then at sundown the fourth day, we saw a storm. James drove the truck at top speed, with Hayley in the passenger side.

Zach and I stayed to guard the house.

I had been carrying a gun for days, trying to be a mother, cool and fun, also trying to be a security guard while there seemed to be threats all around us, scary, which made me uptight — those two were hard to jibe, so I snapped at Isla and then apologized. She cried and carried on and I truly regretted the whole conversation and only got out of it by being a bad mom and bribing her with candy. This whole thing was too complicated. I could not be all these things at once, and do any of it properly. But I had to guard well.

I got a call, I put it on speaker.

James said, "High alert, keep your eye on the house, only Quentin here."

I looked at Zach. "Only Quentin."

"Sounds like he thinks more people might have come,

maybe they're hiding some—" He gulped. "I'm going to check around the house."

I stuck my head in the house and told Beaty, "Quentin just jumped home."

"Och aye, thank the lord." She climbed up from her knees where she had been praying for hours every day, with a plate of rice crispy treats beside her, ever since Quentin and Fraoch disappeared.

The truck drove up to the house.

James jumped out, went around to open the passenger door and help Quentin climb out, placing a shoulder under his arm to support him. "Steady buddy, come on, one foot after another."

Beaty grasped Quenton's other arm, "Quennie, will ye survive it? Please please survive it, Quennie."

We held the front door and they carried him to the living room sofa.

He was gaunt, his clothes filthy. Beaty unbuttoned the top of his shirt and pushed the collar down to see his shoulder — it had healed with an ugly scar.

He groaned and held his stomach. "I'm going to hurl."

Zach passed a bowl. Beaty said, "If ye hurl, Quennie, I will hurl with ye, I am nae—"

He retched, gagged, and threw up in the bowl. Beaty began retching and threw up in the bowl. Zach threw his hand over his mouth and groaned.

Emma said, "Are you kidding me, Zach, you're being such a baby!"

He said, "You can't blame me Em! He's…" He put his hand over his mouth and groaned.

Hayley said, "Quentin, what's going on, why are you alone, where's Fraoch?"

He lay back, done throwing up. "They still have him, they sent me to Magnus with a message and told me they didn't give a shit if I came back. Magnus sent me home."

James sat down on the chair across from him. "Are we safe? Should we go further underground?"

Quentin nodded. "Yeah, we've got to get out of here."

James stood. "Okay, peeps, you know the drill, grab your things." People began rushing around.

Zach asked, "Where we headed?"

Quentin said, "Back to Balloch, year 1709. They have guards there, we need more guards, we are not enough."

I said, "Do we have time to talk, what about Magnus, what's going on…?"

Quentin sat up with his head in his hands. "I don't have time to talk about it, we got to go, grab your stuff. We'll talk when we get to Balloch." He heaved himself up and swayed.

Zach said, "I am getting you some food, some vitamins — you look like hell."

Beaty said, "Chef Zach, will ye bring enough crispy treats?"

I turned to the kids. "You heard Uncle Quentin, grab your things. We're going to see the cousins!"

I threw clothes and toiletries into bags, and then in the kids room met Sophie, stuffing toys into bags. I asked, "Are you frightened?"

"Verra, but I am glad we are goin' tae a time I am comfortable in. Or… I suppose I ought nae say that, this is a *verra* comfortable time." She tossed a stuffed animal into the bag. "But everything here is new, I daena understand most of it. At least there I winna hae so many questions."

"Your world will be upside down here, mine is upside down there. Though I guess I'm getting more used to the past now."

She pulled a garbage bag of toys up to her shoulder and left the room. I watched her go, thinking about how much this sucked and... wasn't it frightening that it had become so commonplace? We had done this now so many times that we were used to fleeing in fear and it was awful it was so casual. We had normalized fear and I didn't like it one bit.

We needed a place to be at home for a while, all of us together, without assholes trying to make us pay for past wrongs.

If you thought about it, this was all Lady Mairead's fault.

She had been locked in a revenge-thing with Agnie for *centuries*.

Of course, it was also her fault that I met Magnus in the first place.

I stuffed the last of Isla's clothes in a bag and hefted it down the hall to pile on the rest.

We just needed to settle. I needed to rest: after all, come to find out, a baby was coming.

Magnus needed to come home.

I glanced over at Hayley standing forlorn in the middle of the room. First, Magnus needed to bring Fraoch home.

CHAPTER 56 - KAITLYN

$\mathcal{W}$e were worn, frightened, and in pain when we arrived at Balloch and so I barely remembered getting from the clearing to the castle.

Sean had been there, Liam, the older man Craigh, our stuff had been loaded up, the women and kids in a cart, along with Mookie the pig. Hayley and I walked beside the cart, for lack of room, with Haggis guarding me. Quentin looked exhausted, but remained behind with James, watching over the supplies and Magnus's three horses, until the men could return with the cart for our things.

I was relieved to find out the Earl was away. So there was room for all of us, without the hassle of dealing with him.

Lizbeth greeted us warmly, thrilled we had come. It had been long months since she had seen us, and she had been worried. She was more worried when I explained why Magnus wasn't there.

"Och nae, Young Magnus is always at war with someone."

"It's the excitement of being a king I suppose."

"Aye I suppose it is."

She began directing everyone to different rooms: Zach and Emma had one, Quentin and Beaty, another, James and Sophie, one, and Hayley would stay with me and my kids, plus Ben, in Magnus's room. Haggis, too.

Magnus's room had a sitting area at one end and plenty of floor space, so we planned to meet there. Lizbeth promised to direct the men to deliver our bags and boxes up to this room. Sean would stable the horses.

We shuffled around, still a bit fuzzy, as our bags were carried up and placed in piles. We didn't want to start conversing while the men bustling around might overhear, so we were quiet, dazed — the night's meal wouldn't be ready for a bit, and we... we sat around the room, surrounded by giant garbage bags of our things, in a kind of shock.

Finally, it was all here, we were all present, I asked, "Quentin, I have to know, I'm about to fall down from exhaustion, scared, worried, horrified, what's going on? Why isn't Fraoch with you?"

Quentin was sitting on the gun box, looking gaunt. "It's a fucking long story."

"Also, easier question – how long were you gone? Because you look like you were gone for a—"

"About six weeks."

I blinked in shock. James was staring, wide-eyed.

I sat down on the nearest bag of stuff, losing my balance in the process, and struggled to right myself. "Let's hear the long story."

"Ian the Troublesome has taken the throne, he's calling himself Ian I, and Magnus is at war."

"I hate that guy. He has a shit name." I rolled my hand, "Sorry I interrupted."

"Ian and Agnie are working together, ruling the kingdom. They have most of the army on their side, but boss has men on his side, an army of loyalists, though their numbers are small. They are attempting to retake the throne. He said they have men on the inside as well. Once they gain control of the south, they plan to move in, surrounding the capital—"

Hayley asked, "Where's Fraoch in all this?"

"Um…well, that's complicated, Hayley, I don't know — he's captured, he was in the cell beside me, but they took him away a couple of days after we arrived. When I spoke to Magnus about it he said Fraoch has become a commander, he's on Agnie's side."

"I don't believe it."

"Yeah… Magnus thinks that he has one of the gold bands around his neck, probably… I mean, I'm sure of it, it's the only way he would cooperate with them. Or maybe they're threatening him, using *us*." He gestured with his head toward the kids.

"How did you get out?"

"Magnus negotiated for me, he captured one of their generals and traded for me. He tried for Fraoch, Hayley, I can see it in your face that you're pissed — he tried to negotiate for Fraoch, but Fraoch refused—"

"Like he said, 'I refuse,' or…?"

"I think Ian refused for him, by letter, but they let me go. I'm sure Fraoch arranged that and probably got me free so I could help Magnus."

Hayley said, "Fraoch would never do it unless there was a threat against…" She jerked her head toward the couch where the kids were huddled watching a movie on an iPad.

I nodded. "I agree, it must be a big threat, or he's got the gold band around his neck, something." Everyone nodded in agreement.

Hayley chewed her lip, "So what's the outcome? How do we get him home?"

"Magnus needs to gain more ground, capture another high-profile commander. Ultimately Boss needs to win the war."

She dropped her head back on the couch. "I want to go get him."

"You can't Hayley it's—"

"I want to go get him, he's in way over his head, he needs to be rescued. Magnus can't just leave him—"

"Magnus isn't leaving him, every moment, in every plan, in

every situation, Magnus is thinking about how it will affect Fraoch. Magnus is worried, very worried, but he is implementing a plan to try and take the kingdom, while keeping Fraoch safe. You can't interfere, it will just get more complicated and dangerous for Fraoch. Hell, Ian the Shithead didn't even want me, but still Magnus had to fight for weeks, take a city, capture a general — weeks to get me out. It's going to take time, we just have to wait."

James asked, "Does he need us?"

Quentin shook his head. "We're spread thin. He wants us to stay here and watch over the family. The issue though..." He glanced over at the kids, on an iPad, their faces glowing blue. "The issue is we can't use the vessels to go resupply. Magnus told me no jumping."

Archie looked up with his eyes wide. "No resupply, uncle Quentin? What about when our iPad runs out of power?"

Ben said, "What? Our iPad will run out of power?"

Emma said, "You kids lived in the past for a whole year, you know what it's like, you can do it."

Archie said, solemnly, "We should save the juice." He clicked off the iPad and Isla burst into tears.

"But I wanna watch the movie!" She ran over and collapsed across my lap. "Mammy, Archie won't let me watch the movie!"

I was too overwhelmed to answer. I just patted her hair and did my best to comfort her while my mind was freaking out. "But Magnus can come see us, right? He can be here in three days. The three day protocol has been our plan for years."

"He will do his best, but any time travel draws attention to where we are."

"But they know we're here, right? This is a known base of his family."

"Remember that protocol Hammond and I came up with called Melodious Cave? It's in operation now that Magnus is out of power, it's hiding records of you, creating a shadow, and creating extra noise to keep you hidden. It should work until..."

"Until when?"

Quentin shrugged. "I don't know, it could stop working, we have no idea how long it will last. What I *do* know is we don't want them to turn the vessels on remotely and find us. We need to hide the vessels well away from here. But other than that, we should be good. We still have the monitor, right?"

Chef Zach said, "Still the best theft ever."

Ben's eyes went wide and said, "Daddy did you steal something?"

"Oh, no, little guy, not at all, it was more like this evil dude stole something from Uncle Mags, and I had to go get it back… think of it like National Treasure, I was like Nick Cage."

"Who's Nick Cage?"

Zach said, "Grug from the Croods movie — fuck," he looked at Emma, "what are we teaching these kids?"

She sighed. "Terrible language and nothing else right now, we've literally been on the run every day for the past couple of years."

"They'll be fine, I'm toning it down, one f-bomb a day won't kill them, and Ben and Archie can read. I brought a stack of Harry Potter books with us, it's going to be okay." He rubbed his hands together. "This is all going to be good. I will go downstairs to the kitchen this week and become reacquainted with cooking in the eighteenth century, so we don't starve. It's going to be great."

I frowned. "No coffee?"

"I forgot to pack it, so yeah, no coffee, not until Magnus fixes the future-future."

"But definitely before the babies come, right?"

Quentin said, "Oh… yeah, definitely, of course…"

But he seemed uncertain.

CHAPTER 57 - KAITLYN

*T*hat night at dinner, Zach put down his plate and arranged his lanky body over the bench and sat down. "Guess who's here? Auld Eamag! She moved back after Kilchurn caught on fire and has been here working for the Earl. Isn't that great news? First thing she asked me for was coffee though, and yeah... I got no coffee, but I did bring a big Tupperware of rice crispy treats, but no coffee. What was I thinking? But honestly, I thought we would be able to come and go."

I wanted to share his enthusiasm for Auld Eamag, but I had just finished the last bite of blood sausage and oats and was pretty sure that was the meal that would kill me when it was my time to go. It was horrid and impossible to feel upbeat about, even when a familiar face was cooking it.

I gulped and looked around and everyone seemed to gulp. Zach said, "But we can't travel, we have to make the best of it, right? Right."

We morosely nodded.

Quentin said, "James, want to ride with me tomorrow to hide the vessels?"

"You well enough?"

"I will be, and I promised Magnus I would do it as soon as I got here."

James said, "Tomorrow it is."

Sophie looked around at all our faces. "I ken ye are disappointed that ye hae tae live here with these deprivations, but we hae done it before — back at Kilchurn. We were verra happy for a time, perhaps if we hae goodness in our hearts and mind—"

Hayley said, "But Fraoch isn't here, or Magnus, or... even Lochie."

"I ken." She smiled comfortingly at Hayley. "I ken tis nae the same, but what I am saying is this is my own time. I am returned tae the eighteenth century, tis familiar. I will do all I can tae make it comfortable for ye. We will hae fun, I promise. We are surrounded with friends and family, enough food, the finery of this castle, under the auspices of the Earl. We are verra fortunate. Ye made me feel welcome at yer home for a time, I will return it by sharing some of my favorite parts of living here. I will do everything tae make ye comfortable."

She seemed very earnest and everyone else seemed kind of dejected, so I decided to whip up some excitement. I said, "So what you're saying is you will be the tour guide and our games director?"

"Aye, ye ken how ye bairns love tae toss the sticks intae the water at the loch? We will do that here, we will come up with adventures and we will ride horses and twill be verra merry. Ye daena need tae worry, I hae it all under control."

I grinned, "You sound very modern."

She laughed. "Och, I am so modern, Madame Kaitlyn, ye ken, I am using a positive outlook. Twas something I learned about while we were in Maine, from a magazine in the bathroom. I learned about positive outlooks and how tae apply lip liner tae make yer lips full. Boyfriends like it verra much."

"Well, see, I do feel better already." I put down my fork. "Here's the thing, everyone, we just need to settle in. Magnus is not going to waste one moment away. He will be working the whole time to get back to us, and he will miss us desperately so we just have to hang tight, get along, and be cool with each other. Zach is going to try and get Eamag to make better food. Sophie is going to keep our spirits up. Beaty is going to build a baby. Emma is going to take care of Zoe. Archie and Ben are going to play with their cousins and Isla is going to keep me company, a lot. Lizbeth is going to keep Hayley busy so she won't worry about Fraoch. James and Quentin are going to carry the vessels away. Is that everyone?"

Isla said, "What are you going to do, mammy?"

"Well, I don't know, Isla." *Worry, freak out, cry, feel sorry for myself.* "Maybe in the morning I'll go to the chapel and pray."

Beaty said, "I will go with ye, Queen Kaitlyn."

Sophie said, "I will as well."

I nodded, "Good, let's do that."

It was odd waking up in the chilly morning of the eighteenth century in Magnus's room with Isla on one side and Hayley snoring on the other. I nudged Hayley to turn her over, and put my finger to my lips to tell Isla to wheesht.

She giggled and ran to the corner to pee in the disgusting chamberpot, while I put my feet down beside my bed and sat for a moment, wiggling my toes on the chilly floor. There was hardly any light, a grayness signaling rain. I got up, stretched, *ugh this mattress sucked, and there had been no Magnus-chest for a pillow.* I was a little irritated that someone had taken my mattress, but… I didn't truly blame anyone, it was too precious to sit in a room unused. I padded over to the chamber pot and relieved myself and shook my hips to dry.

We hadn't unpacked the gear yet, we thought we had at least one roll of toilet paper there, but we ought to ration it. We had really been idiotic when we left, too fast, too carelessly, and thinking we would be able to travel whenever.

Quentin had probably known, but he had been wiped out, freaked out, his only thought getting us to safety. I couldn't hold it against him.

I was grateful to Lizbeth for our clothes. She had given us a pile of skirts and bodices, and tartan wraps. I had asked, "How will we repay you?" It was dawning on me that we were modern refugees, thankful that the castle could afford to take us in.

I looked back at Hayley, still trying to sleep. She pulled the pillow, really just a sack of feathers, over her face to block the dim light. I dressed, thinking about having Magnus tie and untie my bodice laces and how, through our years together, that was one of the most intimate parts of our lives. After finally getting myself laced up, I went to the sitting area, where Isla was on the boys' bed waking them up. Archie and Ben had been sleeping with their heads at opposite ends.

Archie had an arm thrown over his eyes and as soon as he saw me he said, "This bed sucks."

I said, "My love, there's nothing to do but get used to it, as soon as your dad comes for us we will have a soft bed and — imagine how happy we will be? And how lucky — your cousins will never have that chance."

"Yeah, I know, I should be grateful and consider myself lucky, but the bed still sucks."

I chuckled. "Yes, both those things are true."

He hefted himself up to go relieve himself in the chamber pot in the darkened corner. "Don't look, Isla!"

"Why I want to look at your wee-wee, Archie?"

"I don't know, just don't look over here, and Mammy, this toilet-thing sucks too."

"There's the garderobe at the end of the hall. That's a win-win because no one will have to carry a bowl of piss out of the room."

He sighed while he relieved himself.

I said, to no one, "Well, we are off to a great start."

· · ·

At the end of the hall I met Beaty who said she felt better. She was not nearly as nauseous. She added, "This is a good thing because the rats hae eaten all m'crispy rice treats. "I am sorry Queen Kaitlyn, they arna good tae eat now, and if ye are ill…"

"Oh, do not worry about it, Beaty, for *sure* Magnus will be back for us, *long* before my morning sickness comes on."

CHAPTER 58 - KAITLYN

*M*agnus did not get back before my morning sickness started about six weeks in.

The only saving grace was that it was cool inside the castle. I dragged a chair over to a wall in our room and sat with my forehead pressed to a smooth stone. Something about the solidity and the chill kept me from throwing-up. Also, luckily, my morning sickness was better than the last two times, but I still spent many hours during the day with my forehead pressed to that wall, alone.

Hayley spent a lot of time at the spinning wheel. Sometimes I went up to the workroom to help her, but it was a quiet work. Spinning put her 'in the zone'. Most days the kids spent their time with Emma, Sophie, and Beaty watching over them. I visited the nursery, but the boys were too busy to care if I was there. So Isla and I would play house, or mommy, or store, or some such game, with Zoe doing her best to be a part of it, but most days I helped Lizbeth in the running of the house.

Lizbeth was skilled at this job, and had done it for so long that there was an ease to it. Scheduled tasks, little drama, but a whole lot of walking. I liked this work because it was methodical and important, and I was good enough as an assistant to be able to take some of her load, when I wasn't completely nauseous.

One day, about twenty weeks in, we were lugging a bundle of cloth across a room, and she said, "We work verra well taegether, Kaitlyn, I am grateful for ye. Ye understand the pace at which we need tae work, tae hae that perfect balance—"

We dropped the bundle to the floor. I dusted off my hands, and blew hair from my forehead.

"The perfect balance between…?"

"Being busy enough tae nae hae tae be idle."

I asked, "You don't want to be idle? "

She laughed. "Nae, what am I tae do? Go tae the nursery and watch my daughters and nieces carry dolls around?" She scoffed. "The world would hae me follow my sons and nephews intae the hills around the castle and watch them play fight and get intae the kind of trouble I ought tae talk them from? Who am I tae talk them from it? Yer husband and my brother were such trouble at this age and I never could talk them from the trouble of it. They would hae fought me on it, and they turned out wonderful men." She put her hands on her hips and blew hair from her warm forehead. "Nae, I must be busy so I can leave the bairns tae be as they want, besides that, if I grow bored…" She smiled. "I will dream on chocolate."

"Me too, I miss chocolate so much."

She looked wistful. "It has been months since I had some last."

"So so long. I will never travel without it again, from now on, when I come, I will have an armful of giant chocolate bars." I gestured how big one would be.

She said, "They make them so big? Then aye, this is a promise I will hold ye tae." She added, "Ye are beginnin' tae show."

"Really?" I looked down at my middle. "It doesn't seem like it. I wish Magnus was here."

"Ye are showing, and I do hope for yer sake that Young Magnus returns in time. Ye are a strong woman but ye are verra needy, all of this is beyond ye."

I feigned horror. "What?! I'll have you know I am very strong and not needy at all. Not... I mean..." I sighed. "I am very needy, I hope it's not in a weak way. But yeah, I really want Magnus back, I do need him. I miss him."

Living in Kilchurn we had melded times, we brought things together and mixed it up, but here, now, we lived in the eighteenth century with eighteenth century means. We ran out of batteries on our electronics, bit by bit; we ran out of toilet paper; then we had no toiletries left; and we were completely free of caffeine or sweets. I desperately missed all of it. It was like living in the sixteenth century with Magnus, but without his good humor and without his guidance. He was usually our guide to this world, or Fraoch. Now we had Sophie and Beaty to help, but they had no power, they couldn't really change anything for us.

Sophie and Beaty were like two sides of a coin. Sophie could only tell us tae accept our fate. Beaty was inclined to not accept. I would catch her with her hands on her hips huffing at the broom, or scowling as a rat scurried across the floor. "Och nae, tis a disappointing outcome." She and Sophie stayed with the bairns or sat in the weaving rooms at the looms.

James and Quentin worked for Sean, argued with each other, and went out for long rides, hunting, or out to the islands, fishing. Zach went with them if he wanted, or could go to the kitchen, making it his personal mission to cook better food.

It was difficult to make it better. We ran out of spices very early on. It was cold and rainy and we were growing weary of the... all of it.

I, for one of the first times in my life, had a routine. I woke, helped the kids start their day, went down to help Lizbeth with her duties — most days these were commonplace chores, organizing meal service for the house, making the shopping lists. There were merchants and farmers to meet with. We would spend days planning and ordering and buying cloth, we met the men as they returned from the hunts, went to the docks to see the catch, and kept track of the harvest, there were many people to feed, and the past year had been very cold, we had to keep our stores always in mind.

At first Lizbeth had the pens that we once brought and we used them to make lists, until they ran out of ink. The last mark from the last pen had made me cry. The finality of it. I had sat with it in my lap for quite a while, just thinking about how easy it was to replace a pen in the twenty-first century. Most desks had a cupful, but here... it was insurmountable.

I said to Lizbeth, "I am so so sorry, I didn't mean to use the last of the ink."

She nodded, solemnly, "Och, twas a wondrous thing tae hae it, but like all things, tis fleeting, we must go back tae using a quill pen."

"Or memorizing, since a quill is a huge pain in the arse."

"Aye, it truly is."

Twice a week Lizbeth met with Burness who ran the Earl's gardens. He provided grain and vegetables. Then we met with Malcolm who kept the Earl's animals. Lizbeth spoke to them at length, their voices elevated, arms waving as they spoke. She remained calm and haughty, not unlike her mother, and then the two men would leave, seemingly exasperated. The first time I asked, "Are you placing an order? They sounded angry."

"Tis more like they are telling me I canna hae what I want, but I am telling them I want it anyway. They are always set tae win against me, but they always give me what I want in the end. I think tis a game with them, but they are always at it, with nae chance of winning — Och! I hae a secret, Kaitlyn!"

"What is it, oh, is it Magnus—?"

"Nae, how... nae, not Magnus, tis something else, but I am nae going tae tell ye, twill come at the market the day after tomorrow."

Life was so routine that I forgot about the surprise until we were at the market and Lizbeth left my side while I was looking at some very fine cloth, wondering if we needed it for a nice dress for... She returned a few moments later with a sack. "A gift for ye, Kaitlyn."

I sniffed it, dark, rich, aromatic. "Is it coffee?!" My eyes wide, I buried my face in the sack. "It's coffee!" I pinched a bit and put it in my mouth. "Awful, bitter, oh my gosh, it's the greatest gift I've ever been given."

"I kent ye would love it, I heard there was some around and tis expensive but we need the pleasure of it, daena ye think?"

"I do, I think we need it so so so much. Thank you!" I threw my arms around her and hugged her tight. I dried my tears of joy and asked, "What else do we have to do here today?"

She said, "Naething, we need tae return tae Balloch and tell Eamag that she needs tae put the water tae boil. She will be thrilled, she developed quite the taste for coffee."

We hooked arms and went up the path.

CHAPTER 59 - KAITLYN

*I*t was a freezing cold morning in mid February when I felt the baby move for the first time. *Oh. Hey little one.*

I was sitting in a chair beside Hayley while she was spinning and I had been staring out into space, thinking about nothing but how cold it was… and how long it had been.

I said, "I just felt the…"

She was concentrating. She said, "If you're going to complain about the cold one more time you are kicked from the tower room, this is a no-complaining tower room."

"It's not really a tower room."

She pointed at the door.

"I'm the only one who will hang out with you and you're going to send me away?"

"I want to be alone, I want to feel sorry for myself, I want no complaining."

"Fine, I'll go talk to Emma about it, you can spin by yourself."

I felt the flutter again, low, under my belly button, like a little parasitic-something tiny had taken up a spot on my host body, or to be less horrible, like a baby was there, a baby Magnus had known was coming and he wasn't here to meet the first quickening.

The hallway was cold, my wrap tight around my shoulders, my shoes echoing in the stone passageway, a dim light coming in through an open window. I stopped there to look out at a gray heavy sky. It would be raining again, soon, but for now a gray mist hung over the green grass.

As I passed along the upper hallways, I loved running my fingertips along the stone. There was a groove, almost smooth, a tiny bit of a vibration as my fingers traced between two stones and then across the face, to another groove — I imagined the fingers that probably did this for years before me, and how it did seem to be a worn path, and how cool would it be to see this castle years from now — would that groove be there? Would it be even deeper? My groove, from walking to and from my room, dragging my fingers along.

I was headed to the stairwell, where I would meet someone to walk down with me, allies in twos.

It had been so long since I had been up on the walls, a place meant for men. We women were to stay in the inner halls, up and down and around on the stairs... I found Emma with Lizbeth and Beaty with Mookie beside her, talking in the hall.

Beaty had a hand on her hip and a rounded stomach. When I caught up I smiled widely. "Guess what?"

"What? Was there a storm?"

I sighed, "No, and we all really need to stop asking 'guess what' excitedly. My heart keeps breaking, sorry about that. I felt the baby move!"

They all pressed a palm against my stomach and after a moment shook their heads, but then Beaty let us place a hand on her middle and we waited until her baby started kicking. She grinned. "I think it might be twins, it canna be only one bairn. There is so much kicking she keeps Quennie awake!"

Lizbeth laughed. "How does Colonel Quentin ken the bairn is kickin'?"

Beaty said, "He curls up against m'stomach with his face pressed right here. He can feel it all and he must talk tae me about it all night: 'Beaty did ye feel it?' 'Beaty what dost ye think she is doin'?'" She huffed. "Och I am worn out from it. Dost ye see, Lizbeth, my brow is wrinkled from the — where is Quennie? He is supposed tae kiss me when I am in a mood…" She turned and began wandering down the hall with Mookie at her heels.

Lizbeth said, "Wait for us, Madame Beaty, ye arna tae walk alone."

We followed her downstairs and I asked, "How do you know you're having a girl?"

"I can tell, Queen, I mean, Madame Kaitlyn, because I hae a great deal of belchin' from the gas, which is a sure sign, because girls are light and airy compared tae boys, ye ken, tis science."

I chuckled. "Where did you learn 'it's science'?"

"On TikTok, Madame Kaitlyn, ye can learn everything ye want tae learn there. Dost ye miss it? Och nae, I miss it so — see? Here is another mood swing. I need Quennie tae give me two kisses now or I may never recover." Then she frowned. "I am sorry tae say it Queen Kaitlyn, I daena mean tae make ye feel bad. I ken King, I mean Lord Magnus inna here. I hope it daena cause ye sadness tae hae me speak on kissing Quennie."

"Don't worry about it, Beaty, I am sad, but it is never caused by you."

Emma said, "All this baby talk is making me think I need to brush up on my birthing skills. I've never attended a birth in the eighteenth century."

Lizbeth said, "Och, Kaitlyn has, she was elbow deep in an eighteenth century birth, thankfully, as I dinna think I would pull through. Twas with God's help and with Kaitlyn's deft handiwork that she turned the—"

Beaty's eyes grew wide. "Tis a chance of the bairn nae…? Och nae, I need tae go pray on it."

Lizbeth said, "While ye ought tae pray, Madame Beaty, I am

understanding what Colonel Quentin meant by your moods the other day."

I teased, "He said you were having mood swings that were going to kill him."

Beaty said, "There is naethin' in m'mood that would kill Quennie except surprise, if he pays attention tae me, he will nae be surprised. He ought tae ken when I hae m'forehead creased like this…" She furrowed her brow. "Tis because I need tae sit down, and I just need a kiss — I am very easy ye ken." She put her hands on her hips and huffed. "Now I think I ought tae go get m'kisses and *then* I can go tae the chapel and pray."

We all walked down the steps to find Quentin for Beaty.

CHAPTER 60 - KAITLYN

A few weeks after that, Quentin called a meeting. We sat in chairs in a circle in the Great Hall, much like we used to when we lived in Kilchurn. "I want to go... I need to... we need stuff for the birth, this is... we need stuff, right, Emma?"

"Um... yes and no, I mean, her sister and her cousins all probably gave birth here and she was—"

Quentin said, "Beaty, do you want to hear, or cover your ears and hum?"

"If ye are goin' tae talk on birth, Quennie, I am going tae cover m'ears." She placed her hands over her ears and hummed with her eyes closed.

He whispered, "One of her cousins died in childbirth."

He told Beaty, "You can take your hands off your ears, Beaty."

"I ken what ye were sayin' Quennie, but I am glad ye kept me from hearin' it, if women who are with-bairn hear evil tis easy for darkness tae overtake them."

Quentin looked queasy. He swallowed. "You hear that? We have *darkness* coming, we have a drafty castle and not an OB-

GYN for centuries. And *darkness*." He mopped his brow with a shaky hand.

Emma said, "There are midwives, and Kaitlyn and I have a little bit of—"

He said with a grimace. "What about, *compli-cations*? I mean," he turned to James, "what would you do?"

"I have no idea, I think I would get a vessel and park her in the lot outside of the hospital, but then again I know nothing about this."

Emma sounded irritated when she said, "Why are you asking James?"

Quentin said, "I don't know, just taking a poll, I—"

Zach put up his hands. "Look, dudes, this is… you gotta let the women plan this, you can't be deciding to throw your woman over your shoulder and take her through time to the hospital, you gotta balance the needs of the baby and… did I say it right, Em?"

"Yes." She exhaled, then she softened. "I get you, Quentin, you're scared, I just get riled up when we aren't asking *Beaty* what Beaty needs."

"Beaty doesn't know, Beaty has never given birth before and… Yeah, I'm freaked out."

I said, "But we aren't supposed to leave."

Emma said, "I could get Lizbeth to help procure some things for the birth, so we're ready."

Quentin ran his hand over his shaggy hair. "Antibiotics? Oxygen?"

"No, I doubt we could… What's in the first aid kit?"

Hayley said, "Let me get the kit, I'll be right back."

She returned a few minutes later with the suitcase-sized first aid kit, and passed it to Emma.

Emma rummaged through it. "We have antibiotics for infection, here." She flipped over a package. "Still in date. We have bandages, we have…" She flipped through. "We have some of what we need…"

Quentin looked at Beaty, took her hand, and squeezed it. "Then that's fine, right? We're good, we're not supposed to leave, so yeah, this is going to be fine."

Emma said, "We have a while until her due date, for sure Magnus will be back by then."

James said, "Unless…"

Quentin said, "Fuck you, James."

"We need to think about the real possibility that if something happened, we wouldn't know."

Quentin said, "Okay, I'm calling the meeting over, because the rest of this conversation is just going to get depressing."

I said, a hand resting on my rounded stomach. "Magnus is fine, Magnus is waging war, Magnus is going to win the war, regain his throne and we have one job, to wait, to not leave our hiding place. It's the only thing he is asking of us, so it's what we need to do."

Everyone nodded and we got up to go about our day.

James and Quentin went on a long hunting trip, and returned looking refreshed. Beaty was relaxed.

We were all good until a month later, Quentin called another meeting.

Hayley met me at the top of the stair. I asked, "What do you think he wants to meet about?" My fingers trailed along the stone of the circular tower stair as we walked down.

"He's freaking out again. I saw him earlier at breakfast, he was in a cold sweat."

"Okay, yeah, he's really upset, that's good to know. You didn't say anything to get him freaking out?"

She chuckled, "Not this time, I've been on my best behavior. No, this is all him. Possibly James, though, they are always needling each other."

Quentin had the chairs in a circle in the outer gallery, the one filled with rugs and large paintings of the ancestors. He had pushed the ornate chairs into a ring around the sofa, but he didn't sit. The rest of us perched on the uncomfortable satin covered chairs, favorites of the Earl that he'd ordered from London.

Quentin put his hands behind him and paced back and forth, his coat form-fitting, his kilt sexy, his boots modern, a sword at his hip, as always.

He started to speak.

I interrupted to ask, "Where's Beaty?"

"She stayed in bed, and this is… this is what we need to talk about. This is… I'm not taking no for an answer — I'm taking Beaty to a hospital."

We all watched him.

Then I said, "Okay, yes, I agree."

He stopped mid-pace. "You agree? I had a whole speech."

"Scale of one to ten, ten being frantic, how bad do you want to take her to the hospital?"

"A ten."

"Then gather your things and go."

Quentin said, "Oh my God, thank you." He dropped into the empty chair. "Thank you, okay." He wiped his eyes. "I had this whole thing about how Magnus would not want me and Beaty to be—"

My eyes misted over. "You are correct, Magnus would *never* want you to be this nervous, or for Beaty to be in this position. If he had any idea it would be this stressful for you he would never allow it to go on like this — how do we make it safe?"

"I was thinking… she's bedridden right now, but it's still early, right, Emma? Is it *too* early?"

She said, "Not really, with the right care…"

Lizbeth walked up just then. "Ye are speaking on Madame Beaty? I was thinking ye needed tae discuss it, she looks tae hae a pallor. I daena want tae overstep but I believe she is having trouble."

Quentin nodded and clapped his hands on his knees. "Exactly, I'm going to take her to a hospital. I'll go to the one in North Carolina, I was stationed there back in the day. I know my way around."

Hayley said, "I'll go with you. And before you say no, you need a second, and no one else ought to leave, but me... I can leave."

I said, "Are you sure? It's dangerous."

"I'm sure. If he doesn't have a second, we won't know what happened. If he and Beaty stay there, I can come back to let you know. It makes perfect sense. We need James and Zach here, you'll be down to the two of them, guarding all of you."

"And Sean and Liam and all the Balloch guards."

"You know what I mean. I'll go. I need to be useful, I'm going crazy not knowing what's happening to Fraoch."

"No benders. No going rogue. No taking up with a street gang and fancy party-dueling in the road."

"Never, except the street gang, I've always wanted to do something like that."

Quentin said, "We're decided? 'Cause I'm leaving now."

A few minutes later he was carrying Beaty down the steps of the castle and I was shocked. I knew she hadn't been feeling well, but to see her carried out... she looked very unwell. She muttered that her head hurt terribly, and Emma said, "Hopefully it's not preeclampsia."

James and Hayley and Sean would pull them by cart to the clearing.

I asked, "You have your wallet? Your phone?" as Quentin passed through the gates.

He nodded. "And I have her passport."

I hugged Hayley goodbye. She said, "If Fraoch comes while I'm gone tell him not to move, I'll be right back, I'm trying to be a good auntie."

"I'm proud of you."

I didn't get a chance to hug Quentin, he was busy, worried, frantic. If ever a man needed a hug it was in times like this, but he didn't need the weakness of it, he was in commander-mode: his eyes focused, his plan firm. He was going to jump, he would get up fast, he was going to call a car and get Beaty to the hospital.

And then they were gone.

I went up the steps to the open window on the upper floor and watched the hills over the castle. I could see the clearing from here, a pale dip in the deep green of the woods. My hair back, a head covering, a tartan wrap, long skirts, a loose bodice over my rounded stomach, I had become a part of the eighteenth century. I was wistful, as my friends left for the twenty-first century, but I didn't want to go, not really, not if it put my family at risk. I was safe, secure, grown used to a rare cup of coffee with some raw milk and the horribly bland food, the interminable boredom of the long days and nights.

A storm rose over the woods.

In three hundred years a storm would rise over the woods in North Carolina.

I said a prayer that we were the only ones who would notice.

CHAPTER 61 - HAYLEY

*Q*uentin washed as much medieval grime as he could get off in the bathroom of the hospital and went into the exam room with her, then he met me in the waiting room. I felt entirely too *medieval* to sit in one of their chairs. He said, "She needs to have the baby, they say she's close enough to her due date so they want to induce — you have any idea what I'm talking about?"

"No, not… I'm just your hired gun, not your doula. I don't know, sounds like you're having a baby today."

"It's three and a half weeks early. They said it was good she came in…"

I clapped him on the shoulder. "See, you did good, you followed your instincts—"

"What if something happens? What if something is wrong with the baby? What if jumping made it go…"

I said, "All I can think of to say is 'wheesht'." I hugged him. "From what I hear, now that you're having a kid, you're going to be asking, 'what if…' for the rest of your life. I hear it doesn't get easier. If you had listened to me you would've never done it, but you ignored my sage advice and now your wife is about to give birth."

He wiped down the front of his clothes.

He was wearing modern street clothes that had been in a bag since we had jumped to the eighteenth century, months ago.

"I gotta go in."

"Yep, you go become a daddy, I'll be out here—"

"Guarding the door. No twittering or whatever you call it."

"Of course not, no way, I have learned my lesson."

He stalked into the delivery room to be with Beaty.

I was called in, hours later to meet the baby, a wee boy. He was very small. Quentin was beaming. He looked like he could breathe for the first time in months. He couldn't take his eyes off Beaty, holding his son, and he was mopping his brow and laughing.

"Och, I thought we were… phew, hey, Hayley, I have a boy, do you see, a son!"

I said, "He's awesome, look at him, so small, but Beaty, not sure what's going on, you assured me it was going to be a girl!"

"I always kent it would be a boy, I dinna want tae take the surprise away from Quennie."

He chuckled. "I am very surprised. This morning I was in the eighteenth century thinking the world was ending and now I'm in a North Carolina hospital with a son. Holy shit. Phew."

I went for food for us in the cafeteria and then went back to my place in front of the doors, because Beaty would be staying in the hospital with the baby for watchful reasons, and the baby couldn't leave until it could eat, put on weight, do some other thriving things.

I called and got Quentin and me a hotel room, so we could trade off sleeping there, visiting Beaty, and guarding the door of the hospital. Quentin was still a bit of a wreck but now it wasn't the coming babe. Now it was keeping Beaty and the baby safe, while maintaining a normal facade so that the hospital didn't freak out about us. So I stood in front of the hospital, a little like a guard, near their regular hospital security guard, and then I sat in the lobby facing the door, while Quentin sat with Beaty and the baby, trying to get the baby to sleep and eat like a regular human. Then I went back to the front door when I got bored.

And I was very bored. The hospital's security guard was standing beside the planter on the left side of the door, I was leaning against the planter on the right.

There was a weird man walking through the parking lot. He looked homeless and a little like he was staggering. He beelined to the front door, swayed, looked up at the hospital sign, bleary eyed, and said to me, "You got some booze?"

"Nope, and you might want to rethink it, dawg, it'll kill ya."

"Fuck that, don't care, got money?"

The security guard said, "Hit the road unless you've got business in the hospital."

He swayed and turned away, then staggered toward me and fell against my front, but then stood, "Sorry, dude," as he staggered away.

I looked down — on my lap was an envelope.

Written on the front were the words, Colonel Quentin, in what I recognized as Magnus's looping hand.

Magnus!

Kaitlyn was going to be thrilled — he was alive!

I stood straight and looked around for anyone who might have given the envelope to pass to me. No one, just the staggering guy, I yelled, "Hey! Where did you get this letter?"

He waved my words away, irritated, "Don't know what you're talking…" He disappeared behind a truck.

The security guard said, "You don't have to keep it, no one's supposed to pass out leaflets here, it's trash."

"Yeah." I said, "Will you be extra watchful for a moment? I need to go talk to someone inside."

He looked confused, because I was not a fellow guard, or his boss, but said, "Sure," anyway. We had been standing in front of the door for a long time together that day.

. . .

I found Quentin beside Beaty's bed. She had the baby on her chest and was beaming, a tray of food in front of her. "They are feedin' me, Hayley, I am the luckiest. I wish I could take a box tae the bairns at Balloch."

I said, "Me too, I had McDonald's. I think Kaitlyn is going to cry, speaking of crying." I shoved the envelope against Quentin's chest.

"What's this?"

"A note, a homeless guy gave it to me, looks like Magnus's handwriting," but Quentin had already torn into the envelope.

He looked down at the letter. Then he flipped it over and wiped the corner of his eye. He read it again and then handed it to me.

It read:

Congratulations, Quentin and Beaty, on the birth of yer son.
I canna wait tae hae a bowl of ice cream with ye tae celebrate.
Yours, M.

I said, "He's alive."

"Yep. And fucking all-knowing." He turned and looked around at the corners of the room. "Is he here?"

"He's probably just seen the birth listed in the… shit, I ought to go back out and guard."

"Yep, and speaking of the birth, we need a name, don't we, Beaty?"

"Ye can name him, Quennie. Ye are the father, tis yer choice. Besides, I named Mookie, tis yer turn."

He laughed. "Now I'm really glad I didn't argue for my name choice for Mookie then, or you might name our son, Mookie."

She said, "I might be silly, but I am nae goin' tae name the son of Quentin after a pig. I would name him something strong and biblical, he would get a hero's name."

"I always liked the name Noah."

She beamed at him. "That is perfect, Quennie, Noah! I love m'wee Noah, he built the ark for the animals, tis a wonderful name. And we can put a saddle on Mookie and put the bairn on top and take photos for m'Insta."

Quentin chuckled, "Someday, as soon as Magnus has secured the kingdom, you can post as many photos of wee Noah on a saddle on Mookie as you want. I, along with your Instagram fans, definitely want to see that."

I said, "So you and Beaty need to stay here, right? When should I head back and tell them the baby is here? Or do you need me as a guard?"

He looked down at the note in his hand. "I think this means that we're close. Why don't you head back? I got us, here, until the bairn is ready to travel or we'll drive to meet you somewhere — everyone is coming back here, right? To present day, eventually?"

I looked around. "Seems weird to call this present day when most of our family is in a different century. So what are you going to do?"

"What any soldier does when he's at home, sharpen my swords — you know, relax." His eyes drew to the baby's face.

"You're going to sit around watching the baby all day every day, and next time I see you you'll be all, 'Sword? What's a sword?'"

"Never." His eyes didn't leave the baby's face.

"You love him so much, right?"

"Aye, it's uncanny how it happened so fast."

Beaty kissed the baby's forehead and looked softly into the baby's eyes, it was like she didn't hear a word we were saying.

I slapped my hands on my knees. "Well, this is my cue to go where there's less baby adoration going on. See you on the flip side."

I left the room, looking back to see Quentin kissing Beaty's hand.

I stopped at the grocery store and filled bags with coffee, chocolate, candy for the kids, so many cookies, and presents for everyone... then I stood at the checkout and thought about it — I could go to the past, deliver presents, tell the gang that Quentin had a baby. *Or* I could go to the future-future and try to help Fraoch.

He was... he needed me. Maybe Magnus needed my advice, maybe he wasn't considering Fraoch, if Fraoch was still not recovered, maybe he was dead, maybe I needed to...

But I kept thinking about the lesson I had learned, Fraoch saying to me, *Quentin is workin' verra hard tae keep us all safe, he daena sleep, he strategizes, and he needs tae ken where people are. He takes good care of us, of the bairns, and we owe it tae him nae tae let him down.*

I put everything into shopping bags, and got a ride to the edge of the next town over, walked out into a field, and set the vessel for jump, headed to the eighteenth century clearing.

I didn't like jumping alone, but I did it anyway.

CHAPTER 62 - KAITLYN

$\mathscr{T}$he excitement of the presents was over — the imported, modern-day coffee was gone, the candy hadn't lasted a day, and the chocolate was barely remembered. We knew a baby had been born, Noah, but we hadn't met him yet. And I was big as a house and irritated.

The only bright spot in this whole thing, Magnus had sent a note to Quentin. Hayley had reported that it said: *I canna wait...*

We took that to mean he would see us soon.

Hayley and I sat in my sitting room in the chairs, a fire going because I was cold even though it was July, a gloomy gray July, rain outside, a chill through the castle.

She said, "We're lucky we came *this* year, because last year was the coldest year in the history of cold years, like in the history of cold, it was the coldest. That's why it's still colder than any sane person would want, even though it's July—"

"That's the hundredth time you've told me that fact." I shifted my ass, worn out from sitting on a poorly padded chair.

"Fine, I told you already, but don't tell Quentin about it, I was standing in the checkout line at the grocery story and looked down at my phone, next thing I knew I was seeing that statistic, like I scrolled by accident, but I caught myself, then I turned off my phone, because that was not good—"

"You've said that now, a hundred and four times. Nothing about this is lucky." I pulled my fur tighter around my shoulders. "Besides Lizbeth said this has been a really lean year at the market, she's worried about food. So yeah…" I stared off into space. "We are not lucky at all. But a reminder, if we are found, it's because you accidentally scrolled."

"God you're grumpy, and I know it was a risk, and I would feel like shit, luckily that hasn't happened — when the hell are you having that baby? I can't take your mood."

I frowned. "Who can tell? I think soon. I think any day now. Emma remembers. She works the calendar. I just grow babies and pine for my husband. Let's talk about something else, how were the French fries?"

"I barely remember, it was weeks ago."

I pretended to cry.

She chuckled. "They were epic, I dipped them in a milkshake."

"I hate you. Tell me about the Big Mac."

"It was so big, so mac, but actually made my stomach hurt."

I sighed. "Do you think Magnus is alive?"

"Yep, a letter, remember?"

"What about Fraoch?"

"I have no idea."

"What did the note say again?"

And then we were talking over the note again, bored out of our minds, trying to read the future from our position in the long ago past.

CHAPTER 63 - KAITLYN

$\mathcal{T}$wo weeks later we had a bit of warmth, Isla and I went for a walk through a field, basking in the sun. Farther along, I could see Archie and Ben and the cousins chasing each other through tall grass. I enjoyed watching them, the light glistening on their skin, their yells and cheers as they raced.

I looked down at Isla, picking wildflowers. I crouched down and put a daisy in her hair, and breathed in the fresh scent of her. As gross and medieval as we got, the littles still smelled yummy. "Want to feel the baby roll around?"

She put her small hands on both sides of my stomach and giggled. "It's a silly baby. Hey baby, I'm your big sister, you have to be nice to me because I am in charge."

"Is that how it works?" I pushed a lock of her hair behind her ear and put a flower there, but her ears were so wee and soft they didn't want to work so hard.

"Of course, mammy, I am in charge of Zoe and all the bairns, everyone knows, especially my baby, I am in charge of him specially."

I kissed her forehead. "You're sure it's a boy?"

"Sophie said it, because you eyes are bright, mammy, little girl babies take all your brightness for themselves."

I said, staring into her bright pale blue eyes, "I have never heard that but when I think about how bright you are I realize that must be true."

"Da says it's a boy too."

"Do you miss your da?"

"Yes, but he be here soon, because the baby is coming."

I grinned. "How'd you get to be so smart?"

"I your daughter."

"True that." We high-fived then stood from our place in the tall grass and meandered toward the castle, but then I saw the men above us on the wall waving their arms. A man yelled down...

What?

I looked back over my shoulder at the sky, dark — it was a distance away, but there was a storm in the sky. Shit! I picked up Isla under my arm, awkwardly, and hustled toward the gate, dropping her down because she was too heavy, grabbing her by the arm and dragging her along — "Hurry, hurry! Isla, go fast!"

"I go fast mama!"

She was not going fast enough.

I neared the gate as Sean and Liam thundered past on their horses, Sean said, "Get in the gates! I am goin' for the boys!"

Isla and I made it into the gates, then turned around to see Sean and Liam rounding on the boys, leaning down, hoisting the boys onto their horses, and ferrying them to the castle, and dropping them at the gates. "Inside! Close the gates!"

They turned and charged off in the direction of the storm, taking with them about ten men.

Isla clung to my skirts, Archie stood stoically near me, but I looked down and saw the fear in his face. I took his hand, we went to the far side of the courtyard, under the shadowy overhang of the upper floors, and waited to hear what was happening.

This hanging out was against protocol, but also, I had to know what was happening,

We waited.

The men called orders to each other down the walls. I could see James at the corner holding binoculars to his eyes, watching east.

Zach passed. "You're supposed to be in the nursery."

"I can't, I need to, I will go if I… I need to know."

"Fine, pretend like I didn't see you, I'm going to go check everyone is in their battle stations, I'll come back down in a moment."

I watched all the activity of a castle battening down. There were many merchants here, the men had gone up on the walls, the women were taking cover along the interior edges of the courtyard, animals milled around, and carts, stacks of bags, and baskets were left laying around.

The men were at the work of being guards on high alert. I had been here long enough to know many of their individual personalities — there was Yungly, who raced around for the older men. Drach-dim had a grim expression as he stalked by and scowled at me, and Trochench, who always looked confused, was headed away from the walls. I asked him, "Do you know what's happened?"

He stopped and scratched his head, "Nae, I daena ken, but… I am tae get…" He looked left and right. "More guns."

"Then go to the armory! I'm sorry I kept you!"

He walked away, not as purposeful as I thought was necessary. Then Yungly raced by him, shoving through the people who were milling about the courtyard, went to the armory, returned with guns, skirted Trochench, who was meandering around some pigs, yelled, "Hurry!" And took the stairs two at a time.

Archie said, "Should I help carry guns up to Uncle James?"

I held him close to my side. "No, this is your job. We're supposed to be away from the guns and gunfire—" I stopped talking as men started yelling, guns were aimed, yelling from below, yelling from above, it all sounded so dangerous, so imminent. I clutched the kids' shoulders and clamped my eyes but then the guards swung the main gate wide, a horse rode in, a man — Magnus! — he spotted me, dropped down from his horse, and shoved through the people and animals all around the courtyard.

His clothes were a uniform, but not his king uniform, the uniform of a soldier, in a gray camouflage, big boots, straps across his chest and bag of gear on his back. His face was dark from dirt and grime and soot. He held a helmet from the strap and tossed it to the side, then he was there, in front of me, he threw his arms around me and hugged me so tight. In my ear, "Och, och nae, twas so… och I wanted tae see ye."

I buried my face against his neck, his stubbled jaw — he smelled of effort and smoke, exertion and war, sweat and dirt, mingling to a kind of mud on his neck. His thick arms holding me so close, bound, his excitement to see me in his strength as he held me to his body. I kissed his jaw and then his lips and with our lips pressed, his hold tight, he said, "I dinna miss it?"

"What…?"

"The birth?"

We both looked down, between us. "Och aye, ye are as big as a tank, mo reul-iuil. Ye are as fine a sight as I hae ever seen."

"And I won't be giving birth for days now."

He chuckled. "I think ye might want tae listen tae me on it, I got here just in time."

He pulled away from my arms and knelt down to hug the kids who knocked him down to his bottom, as they liked to do. Isla climbed in his lap, Archie sat beside him. I dropped down to the ground on his other side and Isla told Magnus about picking flowers in the field as if that had been the only thing we had done in the whole long nine months that we had been away. Archie was quiet and just held on.

I dropped my head to his shoulder, wide and strong, how I had missed it. "Where is Fraoch?"

"He's still captured."

I exhaled. "So how long are you here? We haven't won?"

He kissed my forehead. "Not yet, the war has been long, mo reul-iuil, but we hae almost taken the city. We hae exerted a tremendous force upon him, collapsed the supply lines, blocked the trade routes, but it has been slow-going and continues on…"

Everyone came down from their hiding place in the nursery and sat down around us in the dirt. Zoe and Ben crowded up to Magnus. Hayley asked, "No Fraoch?"

"We hae much tae talk about, Madame Hayley, about Fraoch… but…"

"He's still alive though, right?"

"Aye, he is alive, we will get him home, but… can it wait for a moment? I daena want tae talk of him with the bairns present. Tis complicated…"

Hayley nodded, hugging her arms around herself. "Of course."

He asked us, "Quentin and Beaty didn't return?"

We shook our heads. He nodded, "Good, we dinna want tae risk the time travel."

Hayley said, "I traveled though, and—"

"Were there any threats on ye here after ye traveled?"

Hayley said, "No, I was pretty panicked, but no."

"Good, then they dinna find ye for it. I dinna want tae hae such a strict rule, but I felt I had tae, even though I hae broken it."

He shook his head. "I was in the command tents, near the battlefield, and – Lady Mairead told me the date ye…" He squeezed my hand. "I told m'self I couldna come, that it would be a risk, and twas the worst time tae leave the war, but m'heart decided for me, I rode away from the troops tae the woods and twisted the vessel and now I am here. I dinna think on it, I just did it. I had tae see the bairn."

Isla said, "You are silly, Dada, the bairn is not a bairn, the bairn is inside mammy's stomach."

He put his hand on my rounded stomach and grinned. "Aye." The bairn rolled through my stomach. "Och, dost he hear me?"

He bent over, causing Isla to shift and be playfully squished, and to giggle merrily, while her face was pressed to my midsection. He pressed his face to the folds of fabric on my skirt. "Hey Bairn, ye are happy tae hear me?"

The baby moved, a mound rolling from one side of my stomach to the other.

I smiled at my husband, he returned it, his teeth white in a broad smile against his dirty skin. I said, pushing hair back from his forehead, "You look like you've been through smoke."

"Ye ken me, mo reul-iuil, I am always tae put out the fires, but we daena need tae talk about war, nae now. Let's just sit here and let me enjoy yer great big body for a moment, this fine roundness, the comin' bairn, and Isla needin' hugs and Archie." He hugged the kids until they squealed with joy.

The others stood and left our circle, leaving us be, except Ben who needed to get a hug too. Then Zoe. Then we just sat together in the dust of the courtyard, on a fine day with a high sky, and the castle settling down from the excitement of a high alert.

We finally got up from our huddle and went to our room and Magnus changed and washed his hands and face in the bowl. The kids had gone off to look for Ben, and now Magnus and I were alone.

He asked, "Has it been verra hard?"

"Yes, but nothing like your experience, I'm not at war, I just… it's not fun waiting, and we don't have anything good— I'm not complaining though, it's not war. We survived."

He pulled me back on the bed. And then chuckled at my rounded stomach. "Tis verra big!"

"And so uncomfortable, I have to lie on my side." I rolled over to face him. He turned to face me. "Has it been very hard what you're doing?"

"Aye... but tis almost over." His hand went on my stomach and the baby kicked again. "Och, he wants all of m'attention!"

I said, "You seem so convinced it's a boy. You know, Beaty tried so hard to guess and she ended up totally surprised. It was a boy, Noah, by the way."

"I ken, and are ye comparin' my prognosticating powers tae the ones of Madame Beaty?"

I raised his chin from where he was looking down at my belly. "Did you sneak a peek at our future, Magnus? Have you gone to the future and asked if we have a son or daughter, do you know?"

"Nae, I promise, we hae hidden ye, I couldna look ye up without riskin' yer location, so this is all guess work, but I am right in it. We already hae a girl, of course tis a boy."

I chuckled and we kissed, then I said, "You have to wash up, even more. There is no touching me from the waist down as filthy as you are."

He said, "If ye kent how desperate I am ye wouldna push me away even for one moment. Ye would feel sorry for me, my want would bring ye tae softness and ye would take a gentle kindness tae my plight. It has been a long time without ye, and tae see ye all round like this, och nae, I canna wait."

"I am not softness, I am firm, take off all your clothes." I climbed off him and went to the pitcher of water, poured some into a basin, and taking the rag beside it, wrung it out in the clear water and then returned to my husband.

He stood in front of me, majestic and naked, and I washed him, starting in his mid-parts and down his legs and he said, "Och nae, tis ticklin' and ye are... hurry, mo reul-iuil, ye need tae… I am sorry I came tae ye so filthy, but och nae, I need ye…"

I washed his cock and balls and around his stomach and his legs, and went slow and teasing, "But what about here, my lord, you might want me to take my time here…"

"Och nae, ye are… call me m'lord again."

"What do ye mean, m'lord, ye want me tae call ye, Master Magnus…?"

And then that had been too much for him to take. He lay down and pulled me to lay down beside him, he pulled up my skirts and in the spoon position entered me from behind, *say it again…* his hand on my stomach, his breath on the back of my neck, in my hair…

"What, m'lord? You want me, Master Magnus?"

"Aye…"

I gripped his hand and groaned from the pleasure of it, enjoying his desperate want and his building excitement, his taking of me out of desperation, desire, needing the closeness of me…. Out of his mind, he groaned, once more…

Yes, m'lord.

He climaxed and drew me closer, his arms tight around in a full body hug as he grew soft between my legs and slid free with his mouth on my shoulder. He sighed. His palms pressed to my stomach. "I daena ken if I will ever get enough of it, I am so sorry I hae missed it, mo reul-iuil, I canna believe I…" His voice broke and he held on, quietly for a long time. Vulnerable, trying to regain his composure.

Finally, there was a knock on the door. I rose and answered, it was Lizbeth passing him some clothes through the door.

"Thank you, you think of everything."

She said, "I hae few charms, that is the best of them."

· · ·

I watched him dress, slowly, in his normal, eighteenth century attire, wrapping the tartan around a loose shirt.

I said, while fixing my hair, "Sex is usually the best way to get a baby to come, so maybe it worked…"

He grinned as he pulled on his socks and boots.

I said, "I know Hayley is desperate to talk to you about Fraoch, we should go down."

"Aye."

CHAPTER 64 - KAITLYN

We gathered in the Great Hall. It was mid afternoon, so no one else was there. The nightly meal wouldn't be served for a couple of hours.

Everyone sat at a long table.

I said, "It's weird not to have Quentin here, I'm used to him being in charge of all things modern security."

James said, "I'm doing my best, but he's definitely got the mind set. I think I'm not security minded enough, not modern enough, not soldier enough."

Magnus said, "Colonel Quentin is irreplaceable, nae one of us could take his part."

Hayley said, "Imagine how bored he must be in North Carolina."

James said, "He's probably working in the secret service for the president by now."

Magnus clutched his heart. "He would do that? Och, twould make me so jealous."

We all laughed.

Magnus leaned forward in his chair, holding my hand under the table, his thumb stroking the back of my hand.

Hayley said, "Enough of the small talk — what's going on with Fraoch?"

"He appears tae be sidin' with Agnie and Ian—"

"I do not believe it, there is no way he would side against you."

Magnus's head hung down, finally he said, "Aye, I agree, they must be holdin' something over him, Lady Mairead believes they are threatenin' his nieces and nephews, or he might hae the golden band around his throat, I daena ken. But tae an outside observer he looks verra much as if he is on their side—"

"He's not though, he would never."

"Aye, I ken, he is a prisoner, and he is bein' coerced. I believe he has a plan, he must — he might be gaining intel, lookin' for weaknesses, but he haena communicated with me on it. I am in the dark on it."

"Great," she huffed, "he's still alive though, how do we rescue him?"

"'Tis nae so easy, Madame Hayley. He has... he has raised arms against me. In the war he has led an army against m'own. We are locked in a tragedy. I am waitin' for him tae lay down his weapon and turn, tae kill them, but he haena."

"...yet. He will. Unless he is unable to do it. You know him, Magnus, if he isn't doing it it's because they have something over him, he needs more time..."

Magnus nodded, "I agree, I am just tellin' ye, that the situation is too complicated for me tae simply mount a rescue." He rubbed his hands together and then clasped mine again. "We hae been fighting in the borderlands and there was..."

He told the story of the war, about how he began the fight with a small group of loyalists, and then they gained control over a battalion, and then soon enough their numbers had grown to an army, and finally, after wins and losses, setbacks that had demoralized the men and some very dark times, they were fighting in the city, street by street. Now the city was mostly conquered.

I asked, "What next?"

"I daena ken. I hae sent Ian a demand that he surrender. We are waitin' tae hear his answer."

Hayley said, "How long has Fraoch been held now?"

"Many long months. Long enough tae change a man."

A tear rolled down Hayley's cheek. "He winna change, he just..."

Magnus said, "I ken, I am countin' on Fraoch bein' hard-headed and immutable."

I gulped and asked, "So Lochinvar has been a help to you?"

"Aye, he has fought alongside me, and has been an astute and strategic commander. That is nae tae say he haena driven me mad with his demeanor. He is like having an army of midges around yer face — tae bat them away gives them the scent of ye and makes them gather more. Lochie is irritatin', overly vain, and incessantly talkin', when I tell him tae go away he becomes worse. I hae tae turn off m'ears or I will grow mad from his bellyachin'. 'But auld man, ye daena ken what ye are doing,' he is always fighting me on everything."

Hayley frowned. "I hate this situation. None of this is Fraoch's fault, he is being held, he can't stay there until the war is over. They'll kill him, you have to rescue him."

"I daena see how."

"Then you are leaving him to die and I hate you for it."

He nodded. "I ken, I am just a messenger, but I ken ye will need tae blame someone and it is likely tae be me."

"If you hadn't..."

I said, "What, Hayley?"

"Nothing."

I said, "That's great, Hayley, blame Magnus, he's been at war for months, I don't think..." my voice dragged off as I thought...

What is that feeling in my midsection?

I let out a long low breath.

Magnus's brow drew down as he watched me then he smiled briefly and then said to Hayley, "Ye can blame me, tis a burden that someone must bear and I think it may as well be me. Fraoch has been taken, he has been forced tae… he has killed m'men, it has been…"

"You can't blame him for it, Magnus, it's not his fault!"

"I ken. I daena blame him, I just canna get him free from his captors, so day after day I am at war with a side that he is on. This is heartrending." He let out a long breath. "Fraoch and I lived beside each other in the mire on the edge of a medieval battlefield, we would lay down our lives for each other— and now he has come verra close tae killing me—"

"He's come close to killing you?"

"Aye, nae directly, but he has given orders. I barely escaped with my life."

"How do you know?"

"Men have left that side, come tae join me on my side. They told me that he is in the strategy meetings."

Hayley said, "So what's your plan, Magnus?"

"We daena hae one yet—"

"Promise me, Magnus, promise me you will rescue him, promise me you will not let Fraoch die."

"I will do m'best—"

"That's not good enough, you have to promise me. He loves you, he's a brother to you. I just, I don't know what to do, but you always keep your word, promise me you won't let Fraoch die."

Magnus sat quietly then nodded, "Aye, I give ye my word."

"Thank you." She sat quietly. "He would do the same for you if the roles were reversed."

"I ken he would."

Magnus turned to me. "Ye are awfully quiet."

I chuckled, and then doubled over with a contraction.

Everyone jumped from chairs.

Emma asked, "You want to go up to your room?"

"No, I think I ought to walk around for a bit, this is going to take hours — I am a million miles away from a hospital, I just ought to walk around, I think, get my mind off it." Magnus put out an arm and we walked slowly from the Great Hall.

It was a little like a promenade: I, on my man's arm, parading around for all to see, though I was not wearing finery, and the purpose was less Bridgerton and more Grey's Anatomy. I had on the long skirts, a tartan wrapped around my shoulders. Every little while I stopped, gripped Magnus's hand, and breathed through a contraction, then I would say, "I'm fine," and we would walk a big circle down the long galleries, through the halls, out to the courtyard and around, back to the galleries, every now and then looking up to see Lizbeth on the upper gallery looking down, checking to see how I was. Emma occasionally walked up, casual-like. "How's it going?"

"Not um… fine… it's going…" I bent over, gripped Magnus's hand, and breathed in and out in puffs.

"Maybe you ought to go up to your room now?"

"No, there are so many hours left, so many, I can't… the kids will miss me and—"

Magnus chuckled.

Isla came up, "Mammy, you having the bairn?"

I puffed out air. "Yes, Isla, I'm having the—"

"Good because Archie said I couldn't play with them and I need the baby now."

"That's not really how…" I puffed out air. "You could play with Zoe. She's with Sophie."

Isla rolled her eyes. "Zoe is not big enough, mammy, she does not understand how to play."

I glanced at Emma, she said, "Zoe *is* kinda boring right now, but she will be your bestie, just give it time."

She said, "I don't want to give it time, I want baby to play with me."

I puffed out air. "You know… I think Isla ought to go… find… um someone to hang out with…."

Emma rushed Isla away to take her to Archie and Ben. Magnus said, "I think ye are verra close, mo reul-iuil."

We had taken two steps when I bent over again.

"Not true… this is…. *hours*." I waved a hand to get him to be quiet.

Lizbeth showed up a moment later. "I think ye ought tae be in yer room, Kaitlyn, tis time for Magnus tae leave ye?"

"No… Magnus… no leave… no."

She laughed. "Magnus! She wants ye tae stay! Hae ye ever heard of such a thing?"

He said "I caught Isla when she was born."

She laughed merrily. "Ye are always full of jests, Magnus, indeed, ye are tae 'catch' the bairn."

He said, "I did! I did catch the bairn. I was at the birth."

Lizbeth laughed again and wiped her eyes. "We hae clean sheets and water in the room, whenever ye are ready, Kaitlyn."

"No, I need… I am…. I am waiting for…." I rolled my hand to show that I was waiting to go to my room.

Lizbeth said, "Och, I can see ye are verra competent, but ye ought tae get tae yer room long *before* ye give birth on the Earl's rugs here in his gallery."

Magnus said, "Ye ready tae go up, Kaitlyn?"

"No, one more time… around." We started walking.

In the courtyard my water broke. "Shit, that was…" I meant to say, lucky, but lost my train… *what?*

Magnus's face swam into my focus. "Kaitlyn? I'm takin' ye upstairs."

Magnus had an arm around my back and was carrying me up, my feet barely touching the ground as I floated. He got me halfway up the stairs until I grabbed the stair rail and… "Stop, hold on… oooooh…"

I pressed my forehead to the wall, holding the rail. Magnus held his arms around me protectively to keep me from falling. I had a doozy of a contraction there. "Baby… here…"

He said, "I daena think so, Kaitlyn, the last bairn was born in the closet, ye daena want tae hae this one in the stairwell, tis too common."

I said, "Besides... stairwell where we... have sex."

I thought it was funny, he chuckled, said, "Yes, we do and the hallways, we need to get you to the—"

He lifted me cradled in his arms. I was under a wave of a contraction, my head lolling. "Just want down."

"I ken, just let me get ye there—"

"Down..."

"Almost in the room."

He hustled me down the hallway to the door and pushed it open. Emma and Lizbeth were there, waiting. I said, "Hey, bed...we have sex... there, too."

Emma laughed. "What are you talking about?"

"I can't remember." I dropped onto the bed as a massive contraction hit.

Lizbeth put her hands on her hips. "Young Magnus, ye are goin' tae remain in the birthing chamber?"

"Aye, I missed all the rest of it, ye canna expect me tae be the last tae meet him." He grinned.

Lizbeth said, "I will never understand ye, tis verra sweet, but ye will lose the magic."

"How can I lose the magic when I am going tae see a bairn come clean out of her? Tis God's majesty, ye canna make me look away."

I said, "Magnus, stay..." I tugged at the tartan but it was wrapped and tucked into my skirt waist. I raised my hair off my neck and mumbled, "Off, this..."

Magnus untucked the tartan and unwrapped it.

Emma said, "The thing is, Lizbeth, last time she gave birth we didn't even have to do anything but just let her carry on."

I held my arms up while Magnus pushed my skirts down, leaving me in my long shift. He crouched down to untie and pull off my boots.

Another doozy contraction. I gasped, "Mountain. Ben Cruachan!"

Magnus tossed my second boot to the side. "What ye want me tae do?"

"Sit."

He sat on the side of the bed and I draped over his back and then when a contraction hit I rose up over him using his shoulders as my altar, kneeling down, rising up, muttering prayers and laments, then I said, after a riotous wave of a contraction had blown through, "I am so mad at you."

I collapsed, my arms draped over his shoulders, my cheek pressed to the back of his head.

"How come, mo reul-iuil?"

"Daena sweet talk me."

"How come?"

"You did this. I hate you... I will never forgive you"

"Och, ye daena mean it, ye are just passing a bairn through yer body, ye will forgive me when ye lay eyes on him."

I roared through another contraction, raising up above him, then dropping down to rest and then raising up and dropping down. Then I moaned as I said, though maybe not out loud, *I'm pushing...*

Magnus said, "Ye sound different, what is happening?"

A contraction seized me again and as Emma and Lizbeth rushed across the room to get to me I felt a baby slide down to the bed between my legs.

I weakly said, "Bairn."

Emma lifted my shift and said, "Oh my god! There's a baby! You literally just dropped a baby right there!"

She and Lizbeth worked between my legs while Magnus held my arms secure on his shoulders because my legs were shaking so much I thought I would fall right over. Emma wrapped the baby in a linen cloth and held it beside me as Magnus and Lizbeth all helped lift me and lay me down on the bed. I said, "All of this whole place is disgusting."

Emma said, "True that."

They placed the baby against my chest.

Oh.

He was loosely wrapped in cloth. "Hey beautiful, what are you doing? Did you just get born?"

I sobbed, happy tears, streaming down my face, "Magnus do you see? I made you a boy!"

He grinned. "I do see — ye did, but hae ye even checked yet?"

"I don't have to, I just know! He looks just like you!" But I moved the fabric aside to see his parts. "He is a boy!" I laugh-cried, almost hysterically. "Thank God, his nose would have been so ridiculous on a girl."

Emma pulled a clean sheet over my lap. "You literally went through every emotion right then."

"I pushed a whole baby out, oh my god, did you see?"

Lizbeth said, "Nae, I missed it! I was so busy thinking ye were going tae be at it all night that I missed m'nephew coming!" She wiped her eyes. "I am verra pleased I was here, I dinna think I would ever see yer bairn born, Kaitlyn. I am glad tae hae been a part of it though I dinna help in any way."

I said, "You did exactly what I needed, you were here, in case I needed you."

Magnus put his arms around me, nestled his face against my throat, a small huddle of us, wrapped around the new bairn. "I love you so much, Magnus."

"I love ye as well, mo reul-iuil."

"Please don't hold any of that earlier against me."

"I would never hold any of it against ye. When ye battle ye hae tae hate someone, better me than the bairn."

"I love him so much! Do you see? He is so perfect."

Magnus pressed his lips to my cheek and nudged my lips up to meet his mouth. He kissed me and then drew away. "I will go find the bairns and bring them tae see their brother."

I joked, "While I deliver the placenta!"

Emma said, "Fun!"

CHAPTER 65 - KAITLYN

*T*he children crept into the room, their eyes full of awe, and stood at the edge of the bed to look at the baby. I said, "Let me see your hands." Isla and Archie put their hands out. "Go wash your hands and then come and meet the baby."

They ran to the bowl and Emma oversaw them washing their hands, then they returned and I patted the sides of me. "Climb up." Isla curled up so that she could kiss the baby's head, and Archie could hold his hand.

I said, my voice a whisper, a fire crackling on the hearth, the sun lowering, "This is your brother."

Isla said, "A brother?" Her voice was full of awe. She kissed his head and said, "I always wanted a baby brother."

Archie said, "Me too."

Magnus sat down beside Archie and looked lovingly down on the new bairn and I had, yet again, happy tears rolling down my face.

Archie said, his hand looking like a big-boy hand clasped around the newborn's fingers. "What's his name?"

I looked at Magnus. "I don't know, it's been — I didn't really believe I was pregnant, so I didn't really…"

Magnus said, "I want tae call him Jack, after yer grandfather."

"Oh." I met his eyes. "Oh, I would really like that."

Magnus said, "Good, it's a strong name and it means he is named after a good man."

I said, "But it's also a variant of John, are you okay with naming your second son after the Johns you know — the Earl for one, my father for another?"

He said, "My stepfather as well, but this is because it is a common name, we canna hold any man against the name — we will call him Jack, and we will ken he was named for yer grandfather. Tis a good name. Then we need another fine name tae add tae it."

Isla said, "Spider-Man!"

I giggled, "You want to name your baby brother Jack Spider-Man Campbell? Well, there are no bad ideas, we'll put that on the list."

Magnus said, "How about John Duncan Campbell and we will call him Jack. Duncan was the Campbell who built all of our best castles, so he seems a good strong name for the builder of walls."

I thought about how I had once upon a time nursed the Duncan who had built those Campbell castles and smiled, "You do like high strong walls."

Isla said, "Spider-Man climbs walls!"

We all laughed.

I grew tired and so Magnus shooed the kids from the room.

I slept for a bit, curled around the baby, nursing and dazedly sleeping, then I heard voices from the other room, Magnus speaking to Lizbeth and Sean.

Lizbeth's voice, "I just want ye tae ken, Magnus, ye are wrong in this…"

Sean said, "Careful Lizbeth, ye are out of line."

"Nae, I am nae, I am advisin' him, as is m'way. I hae heard him make promise after promise and I am worried on him…"

My ears pricked up. I listened intently.

She said, "The promise to Hayley, I heard it and I was shocked, and I am verra worried, Magnus. Ye need tae ken, ye canna promise tae keep Fraoch alive, ye make too many promises and ye will kill yerself meeting them."

Magnus's voice, quiet and tired sounding. "How dost ye ken I am makin' so many promises?"

"I listen, I hear things, ye ken how it is. Ye are grateful I do, so I can advise ye, Young Magnus, as I advise Sean when he needs it."

Sean said, "Brother, ye ought tae listen, I suppose, she winna stop until ye do."

"So what are ye advisin' me on? What are all these promises?"

"The one that is a mistake is that ye hae told Hayley that ye will save Fraoch's life. Tis a promise ye canna keep if ye are tae keep yer other promises: tae yer wife, that ye will provide for yer family; and tae yer children, that ye will guide them tae adulthood; tae me and yer brother that ye will keep us safe and…" Her voice became less stern and more jesting. "Keep our mother busy and away from meddling with us."

Magnus said, "I dinna live up tae that promise — I rescued her, she was absconded away but has been returned, much older than she was, a bit of a hit tae her self-esteem—"

Lizbeth said, "Aye, Kaitlyn was tellin' me, ye hae seen her brought low… I daena ken whether tae marvel at it or feel despair, she has always been the strength I aspire tae."

"Daena worry, she was brought low, but she is recoverin' her strength. She is helpin' command an army. Ye will see, she will be here tae harangue ye soon enough, so aye, I dinna keep the promise of keepin' her away. She will return."

"I never asked tae never see her, just tae see her less often." She huffed, I imagined her pacing with her hands on her hips.

She said, "Ye need tae take yer promise back, tis worrisome, tis upsetting, ye are tae stay alive for yer family, but also tae fight for yer throne, ye are fighting against an enemy who wants ye dead, but ye are supposed tae keep him alive. Hayley does nae understand what she is asking. She is asking too much."

Magnus was quiet, then he said, "Tis verra complicated."

"Tis nae complicated, is it Sean?"

Sean said, "Nae really, all ye hae tae do is win the fight tae restore yer crown. Tis straightforward, ye canna consider anyone who stands in yer way."

"Even a friend?"

Lizbeth said, "*Especially* a friend. Ye hae tae honor him by granting him the respect of being loyal."

"How so?"

"He is captured, but he is acting, ye say? He is nae imprisoned, he is strategizing. He has a threat against him, and he has a plan of how tae behave. He might be building trust. He might hae a plan tae escape, he might hae a plan tae overthrow his guards. These plans might involve his livin' or dyin' so ye canna interfere, or ye might ruin his plans."

Sean said, "This is a good point, dost ye see how tae rescue him?"

"Nae."

"Is he between ye and yer throne?"

"Aye."

Lizbeth said, "He is in an untenable position — ye need tae pray, Magnus. Tis difficult tae hae someone ye love and admire before yer throne but ye must harden yer heart tae him. Ye must win yer throne for yer sons."

Sean said, "Aye, I agree with Lizbeth on it. Ye should tell Hayley that ye canna promise tae spare Fraoch. If he is trying tae keep yer sons safe, he might be willing tae die tae do it."

Magnus said, "Ye ken what Fraoch used tae say? 'Ye canna

control the wind, Og Maggy, ye can only control yer sail,' I believe ye are right, the winds of war are blowin', and he canna stop them, but he can adjust himself tae ride it. I must do what needs tae be done and nae worry on him. At the end of the day, with prayer, we will hae both weathered the storm." He added, "Though Madame Hayley might kill me."

Sean said, "Make sure she inna armed when ye talk tae her about it."

I gulped and kissed the baby's hair, he was a couple of hours old and already there were hushed conversations, threats and battles, his life was in danger.

This was a big problem with time: our days were a slow progression, one after another; but when your enemy was in the future they could look back on your life, the whole progression of it, and see it as a block of time. They could choose a moment of that time, a day in your life, and attack. It was horrible. I would never grow used to it. And though I hated when Magnus went to the future to fight, I understood — keeping the kingdom was critical.

CHAPTER 66 - KAITLYN

*L*izbeth entered the room and saw me awake, "I am sorry ye overheard us."

"No, it's okay, I appreciate what you said. He should keep himself safe. He thinks of everyone else too much."

She fluffed my pillow. "He ought tae think of ye more. I was wrong, ye arna needy, ye are a queen. I am verra proud of the way ye hae given birth tae my new nephew." She beamed down on the baby. "Sean and I are going to go. Magnus is tired and ready tae sleep. Emma will check in on ye." She kissed me on my cheek.

She turned to go but then she stopped. "Lady Mairead has really aged?"

"Aye, she looked a great deal older."

Lizbeth sighed. "Her youthfulness had given me hope, but the years come for us all."

She left the room and Magnus and Sean spoke for a few more minutes, their voices low and rumbling, then Sean left as well.

Magnus came and lay down beside me. "I was bein' lectured

by my siblings, and yet, all I wanted was tae come lie beside ye and Jack."

He picked up Jack's foot and kissed it. "He was inside ye, nae a few hours ago."

"It's a miracle."

"Aye."

I was propped up with all the pillows, he was lying flat. He looked up at me. "Ye heard the conversation?"

"Yes, you're in a very difficult situation."

"I ken. I hae a man behind enemy lines, and every part of me wants tae liberate him, but I hae tae win the throne tae do it, and the path tae the throne lies across his body."

He rose up and put his head on my shoulder. I kissed his forehead. "Just be safe, highlander, you are the love of my life and you're too important."

He said, "I am goin' tae sleep beside ye, but I will leave on the morrow."

"You have to go so soon?"

"I snuck away, taking a break while m'men are still at war, and we hae had a great many losses — we must finish the fight, mo reul-iuil, so I can come home for good."

"How many days…?"

"Three." He stroked his fingers down Jack's face, "Daena ye grow up too fast, wee Jack, I will be home verra soon…"

We fell asleep, a light sleep, then woke up to adjust. Magnus turned on a flashlight he had brought, for a dim light. I was nursing Jack while Magnus lay with his arm on my thigh, his cheek against my shoulder. I said, "You and I are even more entwined now."

"Aye, a son will do it tae ye."

I chuckled. "How so — how a son more than a daughter?"

He said, "Tis m'chromosomes." He raised his head, "Tis the right word?"

"Yes, you mean the Y-Chromosome? The one that makes you a man?"

"Aye, ye daena have Y-Chromosomes, they come from me, and then when I make a boy in ye, and ye grow him, ye arna growin' a woman, same as yerself, ye are growing a man, ye are growin' my son, tis a gift of yer body, and I am verra grateful for it."

I said, "I think I am deeply offended, but also, not, that was sweet in a misogynist sort of way."

After a moment I asked, "So you think that you put a boy in me and I'm just like the host body that grows him and then gives him back?"

He chuckled, "When ye put it that way it daena sound how I meant, I dinna mean it quite so crudely."

I said, "Have you heard of sex selection, my love?"

"Nae."

"The idea is that females select males to be fathers to their children. So the men have to prove their fitness to the females. Males change and adapt to please females, you never heard this?"

He said, "Nae."

I rolled my hand. "So the body of one, female, creates the mind and body of the other, male, who then changes the mind of the first, the female. We are in a spiraling dance."

"Ye are less the host and more the creator?"

"Exactly."

"Yet I hae the Y-chromosome, and I was verra creative when I took ye in the hall all those months ago."

"This is true, I think we ought to focus on the spiraling entwining dance."

"Aye."

"Though I did just create a whole baby and pushed him right out of my va-jay-jay."

"Ye did, ye are a wondrous person." He rolled over and

buried his face in my side, his arm around us. "Tis times like this when I am in awe of ye as a creator and reminded that I am but a destroyer."

I wrapped his hand in mine. "That is not true, look at the family you have built."

His voice vibrated against my side. "Ye haena seen the destruction that I hae wrought tae regain m'throne."

"I'm sorry. I was ribbing you about who is better, who creates who, and... I'm sorry. You've been at war and I didn't mean to discount you."

"Tis all right, I understand, I wanted tae see ye and tae hold the baby at his beginning, It was the most important thing in the world tae me. The war couldna keep me away."

"I love you so much."

"I love ye as well, mo reul-iuil."

His worn, strong hand enclosed mine beside our new baby and we both slept again, and woke up again.

He got up to get me a cup of water, and steadied me as I went to the chamber pot to relieve myself.

I asked, "Are you sure you didn't bring me some maxi pads or some towels or... diapers — please, just some diapers?"

"Nae, I was an arse about it, Madame Campbell, I raced away without tellin' them. Luckily I had this flashlight in m'gear, but other than that I thought only of m'self. I am sorry I dinna bring ye chocolate."

"I want chocolate so much, you must bring it when I see you in three days."

I returned to the bed where he was leaning on a pillow holding the baby in the crook of his arm. "Oh love," I climbed across the bed and it was my turn to put my head on his shoulder. "I could look at you hold him for hours." I watched Jack sleep in Magnus's arms for a moment then said, "But I miss him already, let me have him back." He chuckled and passed me the baby.

Then we went quiet again, companionably quiet, watchful over the baby. "He's perfect."

"Aye."

"You were so right, you did get me pregnant, and now look."

He chuckled. "Told ye, ye ought tae always listen tae me, I am right in everythin'."

"Says the man who just had a lecture from his sister and brother."

He raised his lips to kiss mine. "I am right about most everythin', the rest is told tae me by m'sister."

"I will agree that Lizbeth is right in many things, and she is right in this... please don't make promises you can't keep. Stay alive."

"I will keep m'promise tae ye, Kaitlyn, I will do m'best tae come home."

He kissed my shoulder and we fell asleep.

At dawn the baby nursed and I lay on my side watching my husband remove his long shirt and replace it with his camouflage uniform. He said, "Daena tell Sunny I was here, I haena spoken tae him, he might feel slighted. I will make sure I see him when I return in three days."

"I won't say a thing." I added, "Do you need me to talk to Hayley before you go?"

"Nae, ye just do all the mom things, I decided I am goin' tae ask Madame Hayley tae go with me tae Riaghalbane, tae the war. I think she ought tae see what transpires, so she inna surprised, whatever happens. I think when she sees what we are up against, she will understand."

CHAPTER 67 - MAGNUS

I walked down the hall tae Hayley's room, and knocked. When she stuck her head through the door, I asked, "Ye want tae go?"

"Where, to the future? To where Fraoch is? Hell yeah."

She left the door open and rushed around the room. "What do I need?"

"Clothes for a warfront if ye hae them."

I waited for her in the hall. She had a bag and was wearing a pair of pants. Twas scandalous in these times, but the men of Balloch were used tae the strange costumes, the odd comings and goings of our family.

She and I strolled out to the clearing, and set our vessel tae jump.

We woke in a clearing, with Lochinvar standing over us saying, "Ye hae decided tae return, King Magnus? Hae ye brought a grown son tae fight with us?"

"Nae, but I saw him born!"

"Och aye, twas a fine lad?"

"Aye, he is verra fine, large in all the ways ye want in a son."

Lochinvar put out a hand and hefted me up. "Why did ye bring Madame Hayley?"

"So she can help make decisions about her husband."

We climbed into an armored car tae ride tae the front lines. Lady Mairead gave Hayley a glance as she climbed into the back seat, then said, "First, Magnus, we thought ye were dead, I am relieved ye hae returned unharmed. Ye ought not tae frighten me."

"Ye kent where I was, because ye slyly mentioned the date m'bairn would be born. He is good by the way, a fine lad, born hours ago — both mother and bairn are doin' well, thank ye for asking." Our armored car was in the middle of a fully guarded motorcade, four in front, four behind. I added, "And I ken nae tae frighten ye, at yer advanced age it might mean yer death, but ye are exaggeratin'. *Again,* ye kent where I was."

She smacked my shoulder.

Then said, about Madame Hayley. "Also, sometimes, Magnus, ye ought tae ken, too many wives are a trouble."

I chuckled, then turned around tae speak tae her. "Ye mean women, too many women? Ye are verra often so insulting toward everyone ye include yerself in it."

"Ye mark my words, Madame Hayley will insert herself in yer business tae yer detriment."

Hayley said, "I will not, I'm just here to see Fraoch, once he sees me he will lay down his arms, he—"

She said, "Madame Hayley, I will only say this once, Fraoch is a good man, and he is being held. He is behaving in a way that is counter tae his nature, so ye hae tae assume there is a threat upon those he loves. Laying eyes upon ye might not turn his mind, and it might make him too confused tae carry on with his plan. Ye canna just strut past him and hope tae end a war!"

Madame Hayley said, "I am just trying to help. I just need to be here so I know what is going on."

I turned around once more, "Ye canna blame Madame Hayley for comin', ye canna blame her for wantin' tae see her husband, ye canna blame her for tryin'. We are in an unprecedented time and we face an enemy who is holdin' a man who has lived with me, with us, for many long years, who has shared Madame Hayley's bed. Ye canna blame her for wanting tae try tae liberate him from his captors."

Lady Mairead said, "Ye are right, I canna blame her, my apologies, Madame Hayley."

Hayley sat quietly, staring out at the landscape as it passed. "What's to stop me from going to Fraoch right now?"

I turned around in my seat. "It would mean crossin' the battle lines, goin' tae the enemy camp, and riskin' becoming captive yerself. Ye canna consider it."

"What if I went—"

"If ye go it would be tae yer death, dost ye think that is what Fraoch would want? Och nae, I was just telling my mother that ye werna goin' tae cause trouble and now ye are wonderin' about marching up tae the enemy gates?"

She shook her head. "I was just trying to figure out how to help."

I exhaled. "If ye are held against me, the fate of the war would be settled, we would lose, and Fraoch's life would be in even more danger. Nae. Do I need tae put ye under guard?"

"No, you're right, it wasn't a good idea. You can trust me."

Lady Mairead said under her breath, "As *always*, I was correct on it."

CHAPTER 68 - HAYLEY

I was irritated, confused, dismayed, all the feelings that meant: very upset. Especially after having pissed off Magnus. I watched out the armored car window as we rode along a newly cleared road through dense woods. There were felled trees to the side, then the woods gave way to the city, streets full of tanks, buildings in rubble.

The city was a ruin for miles.

Magnus's army, tank after tank, armored cars, a mighty opposition filling the city streets, all pointing one direction. Beside the main thoroughfare we were on, stood a directional signage, an arrow pointing ahead:

Caisteal Morag, seat of the kingdom of Riaghalbane.

As if it was pointing the way for Magnus's army.

One of the largest buildings ahead of us had a gigantic projection facing our front line: the flash of a photo of a king wearing an ornate crown, the words Ian I. Then the command: Lay down your arms. The flash of the king again, then more propaganda: If you surrender you will receive amnesty.

It dawned on me that Magnus was a mighty fucking important man and that this war was a real war, and a huge fucking deal. I mean, I knew he had said as much, but it took seeing it to really believe it. Everything was trashed too, like the battles had lasted for a really long time. Our car rolled through the war zone: soldiers looked exhausted, injured, their uniforms filthy, their faces dirt-covered, their boots muddy. In the distance, in front of us, gunfire, far distant explosions. I was handed a helmet and ear protection.

We climbed from the armored car and were hustled into the large command tent, surrounded by a barrier of rubble, protected by tanks and soldiers. I was trying not to look as shocked as I felt, but I was very shocked. I couldn't believe Quentin was missing this, but all of a sudden Quentin walked up, "Hey! Surprise!" He did jazz hands.

Magnus hugged him. "How are ye here, Colonel Quentin — is the bairn all right?"

"Yeah, Noah is great, I lived in that hotel room in NC for weeks and got, I'm not too proud to say, a little stir crazy. Plus Beaty really missed Mookie and the kids, so as soon as the baby was cool we jumped to meet everyone at Balloch. I had missed you, so they sent me here to this date, I arrived earlier this morning."

Magnus said, "Did ye meet Jack?"

"Yep, he and Noah are going to be great friends."

"Aye, and ye were nae needed anymore?"

"Beaty wants me to help you, honestly she was sick and tired of having me underfoot."

Magnus said, "So ye hae become acquainted with the battle plan?"

"I'm looking over it — your army is massive. I was studying the troop formations, and the engagements. General Wallace told me you're waiting for a response from Ian. You demanded he surrender?"

Magnus said, "Aye, it haena come yet?" He scowled and gestured toward the projection. "Ye see he continues tae run this disinformation campaign. He is claimin' tae hae won, though by all signs he has lost the war."

"Yeah, your troops are bone-weary, it sucks to have that crap blaring at them. But we'll be at the gates of the castle soon, and—"

"Aye, but… how much loss of life can we take?"

I asked, "I'm sorry to interrupt, but… you said our army will be at the gates of the castle? Then we will, what…? What will happen to Fraoch?"

Magnus shook his head, "I daena ken, Madame Hayley, Fraoch is there. There are also prisoners of war in the cells on the castle grounds. I hae loyalists embedded in Ian's cabinet. If I attack the castle, I would be attacking men who fought for me, who hae been feeding me information. How is that a way tae repay their steadfastness? We need Ian tae accept my demand he surrender."

Quentin scowled. "There is a chance he won't accept."

"Aye, I agree, even though I hae taken the borderlands, the eastern provinces, the western fields, the industrial section, and the ports — there is a chance he winna surrender, because he is an arse."

I asked, "What happens if he doesn't?"

"Then we hae tae continue through the city, with a growing path of destruction, and lay siege on the castle, and I daena want tae hae tae do that. I am half in jest, but I just rebuilt that castle. I daena want tae destroy it if I daena hae tae."

Magnus pounded his fist against a post of the command tent, setting it to shaking. He grasped it to stop it. "Och nae, I wish I had strong walls."

His eyes scanned a video of the front lines. I could hear the battle raging in the distance and the repetitive incantation: *Lay down your arms… if you surrender you will receive amnesty… lay down your arms.*

He said, "I see these men, at the end of long months of battle, and I am asking them to continue on, tae fight more. We have been facin' down the kingdom's war machine, it has been brutal. I ken it looks like we hae won, but it has been verra diffi-cult tae get here tae this point."

Quentin stood beside him. "I can see it, it looks like it's been a bitch, but remember, the darkest time usually happens when the goal is within reach."

Magnus said, "Aye, I agree with the sentiment, though much of war is dark, tis hard tae judge the contrast, there haena been a lot of light."

I threw my arms around Magnus's shoulder in a big hug. "I'm really sorry about earlier."

"Aye, Madame Hayley, I am as well."

"I get that the promise you made to me might be impossible to keep. I just... you know."

"I ken, we need Fraoch tae survive this. I will do m'best tae that end, thank ye for not keepin' me tae the promise."

"This is all so hard."

"Aye, tis a verra hard thing, but we will figure it out."

Quentin said, "Something happened...?"

Magnus said, "She was considerin' all options and things got heated between us. We are good now, aye, Madame Hayley?" He put out his fist.

I said, "Aye," and we fist-bumped.

Nightfall was coming on. I was shown into the barracks, assigned a cot, and I fell into a fitful sleep. You might think that being near Fraoch would help, but frankly, it made it worse.

CHAPTER 69 - MAGNUS

*W*e met inside the command tent in front of a video projection, a map of the kingdom, with my troop movements shown in symbols and arrows. A messenger had arrived carrying a letter from Ian the Troublesome: the usurper calling himself Ian I.

He had declared that he wouldna surrender.

I was exhausted and had a great deal of worry weighin' on me, and Lady Mairead was in a rant that I had tuned out, until I heard her say, "...and now Ian is refusing tae surrender..."

"Aye, he is goin' tae make me destroy everything." I tossed the letter from the pretend king tae the table and dismissed the messenger who had delivered the news.

I looked off, my eyes resting on a pile of rubble, a city building reduced tae dust. We had been destroying the city street by street. The people were becoming refugees — but yet, he refused tae surrender.

General Wallace entered and changed the video tae one focused on the battlefield before us. "We have news from our reconnaissance team, Your Highness. Our men have surveyed the city between here and here." He pointed at our front line and then at the castle. He said, "Do you see these markers, King Magnus?"

"Aye, the red and blue ones?"

"The reds are the schools, the blues are the hospitals. Most of them are new."

"Och nae, are they full of...?"

"Yes, fully working, there are kids, there are wounded, it is—"

Lady Mairead said, "He is a monster."

I said, "There is nae path forward without endangering those lives?"

General Wallace shook his head. "We have yet to find one, but I have gathered the commanders, we will come up with a new plan."

I said, "Off the top of yer head, a new plan would mean...?"

"Commander Richardson was there when I heard the news, he believes we should move forward anyway. He is developing a plan in which we disregard this information. He will present it at the meeting."

I scowled. "This is... This would make me a monster as well."

General Wallace said, "I will be recommending we turn around." He pointed tae the region behind us. "We would reconvene here, near the port city, resupply, move up through the west."

I said, "How much longer would we be at war?"

He exhaled. "I will need to work the numbers and—"

"Guess, I winna hold ye tae it."

"It will take months."

Lady Mairead said, "That is it! This is enough. We must end this—"

"But he winna surrender!"

"I ken!" She jabbed at a letter. "He has refused yer demands, with insolence, I remind ye, and so we must take it tae the next level. We will demand an arena battle!"

My eyes widened. "Now ye are takin' the other side!"

"A woman is *allowed* tae change her mind, based on the information at hand... we will challenge him tae the arena and once the battle is won, ye will—"

"Ye think twill be easy as that? I daena see how he will allow himself tae be challenged. This man winna surrender, he will put a hospital in front of an army — what will make him willing tae lose a kingdom at the end of a sword?"

Lady Mairead said, "Magnus, ye hae brought him tae his knees, most of his men hae left him, he is beaten—"

I waved her words away. "I ken all of this aready, but yet, now, it seems I must turn around."

I asked Colonel Quentin, "How many men did we lose in the last offensive?"

Quentin said, "Hold on, I'm new here... but..." He held a command screen and scrolled through information. "...it looks like your army took a lot of casualties... I do know, from interviewing soldiers, that morale is low. I'll speak with Captain Burton about the details."

I waved it away. "I daena need the details right now, I was interested in the idea of it, there are 'a lot of casualties, morale is low.' This is the information I wanted." I exhaled. "Yesterday we were winnin' the war, now we are expected tae turn around and lose ground?"

Lady Mairead incredulously put out her hands. "This is exactly why we need tae challenge him—"

"What would make Ian accept our challenge?"

Colonel Quentin said, "Any man who would put hospitals in front of an advancing army knows he is losing, and doesn't want to look weak. You are winning. He'll want an out. I say challenge him publicly. He will look weak if he doesn't accept."

"Ye agree with Lady Mairead?"

"Yes, it makes me uneasy, but here we are."

I turned to General Wallace who had begun the war under Ian and had come tae my side early on. He had more knowledge than many of us about Ian. "What dost ye think, Wallace?"

"Ye mean whether he will take a challenge?"

"Aye."

He said, "Ian has a ridiculously high opinion of himself."

Lady Mairead said, "I agree, he is an insolent upstart, I ken it because he challenged ye, Magnus, many times before, he daena ken his own place."

Wallace nodded. "He does not want to seem weak and he will not accept failure. If you challenged him publicly, with fanfare, he would not refuse. He probably thinks he will win."

Lady Mairead said, "He is overly sure of himself, and inadequately informed of his own shortcomings, tis a public service tae run him through with a sword."

I said, "So I publicly challenge him tae an arena battle for the kingdom and we can stop this bloodshed and street-by-street warfare, this horrible morass of death and destruction? Ye think we can finally end this?"

Colonel Quentin nodded. "He ought to be a man and surrender, but instead he's going to surround himself with human shields? It's time to end it, call him out."

Wallace said, "I agree. To fight forward is abhorrent, and the alternative, to lose ground, is unacceptable. This is the way."

"So how will I go about it?"

Colonel Quentin said, "You've never been on this side of the challenge before, huh?"

"Nae."

"General Wallace and I will prepare the challenge documents, we will take over the news channel, and announce it. If he refuses he will look like a weak-ass loser."

I ran my hand down my face. I was so tired, we had been fighting for so long. Even with the break tae go tae Balloch, I hadna really slept. I stretched out m'injured shoulder, feeling the tightness and the ache I had grown tae live with. I was nae sure I was ready tae fight. "All right, prepare the documents."

Lady Mairead said, "Ye daena need tae stretch yer injured

shoulder, ye will be putting forward Lochinvar tae fight in yer stead."

Lochie rubbed his hands together. "Good, at long last some fun. I will fight for ye, Magnus, tell me when and where."

I groaned. "Nae nae, this is not — we had this argument already. I winna ask another man tae fight for me. Lochinvar? Och nae, this is a terrible idea." I paced down the room, then considered, "And what is stoppin' Ian from doing the same thing? As soon as we challenge him he will come forward with his most skilled fighter—"

"I will still beat him."

"Aye, ye are verra lethal, we ken this, why would I put a man forward, a son of Donnan, *himself* in line tae be king?"

Lochie shrugged, "Not sure I would want the hassle frankly, Magnus."

Lady Mairead said, "Magnus, ye are the king of Riaghalbane. Magnus I. Ye canna barrel around arenas swinging yer sword for all the world tae cheer, ye must be more... *royal*. Ye will hae a second tae fight for ye, it is perfectly regular. Donnan did it all the time."

Magnus said, "Exactly, I wear the scars of being Donnan's second. Ye are asking me tae tell a young man tae lay down his life for me, as if I am Donnan, demanding allegiance. He is my brother, he has already fought for me in the arena once. I daena think I can ask for it again, and, tis concernin' tae hae someone who is in line for the throne fight for it. What is tae stop him from takin' the throne for himself? What if he promises now, and waits until I am auld, and then challenges me. He is young, he will hae sons one day."

Lady Mairead said, "I believe he is trustworthy because of the reasons I laid out for ye earlier."

Lochinvar looked from her face tae mine. "I *am* trustworthy, ye dinna need tae discuss it."

Magnus said, "Lochinvar, I ken ye are trustworthy, but a kingdom is a verra powerful prize. Tis the biggest prize in the world and would turn the most honorable of men tae the darkness if twas within their grasp. I ought tae fight for m'own kingdom, then ye winna be corrupted by—"

Lady Mairead said, "I ken of what I speak. Ye can trust Lochinvar tae fight for ye, it involves bloodlines and ancestors. I hae seen the future and yer future is um... *tied* tae one another."

I raised my brow. "Ye ken of what ye speak, fine, ye hae been seein' the future. Who dost ye think Ian will put forward tae fight? I will give ye one guess."

She narrowed her eyes. "Are ye suggestin' he would put forward Fraoch?"

"Aye, tis a certainty."

Lady Mairead said, "Nae, he wouldna — would he? Nae, he wouldna trust him. He would put forward someone else."

I said, simply, "We disagree."

"We do, but we canna focus on that, we put forward our warrior; he will put forward his own."

"And when this goes down, ye expect me tae watch from the sidelines...? Hae ye met me?"

"I hae met ye, I hae seen ye override yer good sense tae be the man who handles *everything*. Ye will need tae allow Lochinvar tae handle this one. We will challenge the man Agnie has settled on your throne and ye will put forth Lochinvar as yer warrior. Ye are a king, not a dueler, not anymore. Ye are more civilized than that. *Finally*."

CHAPTER 70 - MAGNUS

*W*e sent the challenge by messenger tae the king, as was traditional. Then at the same time we made contact with our man inside the royal news station and asked him tae run the challenge all across the kingdom. It had been dangerous for him tae do it, he had likely lost his life in the action, but he had been successful taking over the projections, and for a few glorious moments it was broadcast:

Magnus I challenges Ian tae an arena battle for the kingdom.

My soldiers cheered as if we had won the war.

Quentin, Lochie, and I watched the projection without cheering, this might be a chance tae end the war, but it meant a battle, and a grave risk tae Lochinvar's life.

~

Within the hour I received a response: Ian had accepted the challenge.

~

I called Lady Mairead, General Wallace, Colonel Quentin, Lochinvar, and a few of my other commanders tae headquarters. I asked for Hayley, since the arena battle now involved her.

I leaned against a table. They were all standing around me.

I announced, "Ian has accepted our challenge. We will hae a fight in the arena for the throne. We hae exerted pressure, challenged Ian the Arsehole, and he has agreed tae our terms. I hae put forth Lochinvar tae fight. The battle has been scheduled in the books."

The men around me applauded.

But Hayley, her lips pressed, asked, "Who have they put forward?"

I raised my brow. "Ye ken."

"Fraoch? Oh my God, they put forward Fraoch? No!"

Quentin said, "Fucking-A, this sucks."

Lochinvar shook his head, looking down at his boots.

Hayley looked pale. "Lochie against Fraoch, to the death? What are we going to do? How do we stop it?"

"We daena, Madame Hayley. Our path forward means either a great many innocent lives lost, or turning around and losing ground, or an arena battle. This way there are only two men decidin' the fate of the kingdom, two lives at risk. And there will be only one death."

Hayley said, "So if Fraoch wins the battle it won't be that big a…"

I glanced at Lochie and shook my head. "Fraoch canna win against Lochinvar, Madame Hayley. Lochie has a foolhardy bravado, he lacks fear, he is an accomplished warrior, he daena feel pain, and he has the near immortality of youth. Fraoch has lived long enough tae ken he wants tae try tae keep on living. Tis a weakness tae nae wanna die. Lochie daena even consider dying, twill never cross his mind. He is the better warrior because he daena hae any fear at all."

Under my words, Lochinvar shifted, his jaw set. He nodded in agreement.

Quentin said, "Fuck."

I continued, "And I hae been fighting alongside Lochinvar now for months. I hae seen him fight."

Hayley said, "So you're taking his side over Fraoch's?"

"Nae, never, I am nae taking anyone's side. I am just tellin' ye, Madame Hayley, that ye canna count on Lochinvar losing: m'throne, m'family's kingdom, Archie and Isla, all of our safety, tis all dependent on overthrowing Agnie and Ian. Lochinvar canna lose. And he winna, he is brutal."

I exhaled, "...and I'm worried, even if they were evenly matched, Fraoch wouldna want tae kill Lochie. He daena like the boy much, but I hae seen he has a soft spot for him. Tis hard tae live with someone and tae want tae murder them."

"Lochie shouldn't want to kill Fraoch either!"

"Aye, but he is a machine when he fights, Fraoch is all heart."

Hayley was agitated. "Exactly! *You* should fight him in the arena, Magnus, you won't kill him, he won't kill you. It's the perfect plan, right?"

"Ye are right, I wouldna be able tae kill him." I leveled my eyes on Hayley. "Would ye want me tae die at yer husband's hand? Tis something ye could live with?"

She leaned against the table and pouted. "No. There's no... no."

"If I die at yer husband's hand, who would protect Archie and Isla and wee Jack?"

She shook her head.

We heard gunfire and a loud explosion coming from a few streets over. Quentin gestured for us tae pull our ear protection on.

I met Commander Burton's eyes. "What is that?"

He looked down at a screen. "Our west flank is attacking a munitions factory, the last. This will greatly reduce their capabilities and it was right on schedule."

There was another loud explosion and more gunfire.

I asked, "Do we need tae move?"

"No, sire, we have the guard stationed, though..." He looked at the map. "Let me deliberate with Connor at the front and confirm we are in the clear." He left the tent.

We waited for the explosions to wind down.

Hayley said, "What are we going to do?"

Commander Burton asked, "If Lochinvar refuses tae kill Ian's man, do you think Ian's man would spare Lochinvar? Do you think it is possible?"

I said, "I daena see how. If Fraoch has a plan I canna guess it."

Commander Burton said, "Fraoch must know he will die by entering the arena."

Hayley said, "Lochie, is there anything you can do? Please, I beg of you, please, please don't kill him."

His brow furrowed. "What dost ye expect of me, Madame Hayley? This is a fight tae the death, are ye askin' me tae die? Because Fraoch will be fightin' tae kill me. If I daena swing he will swing on me — remember when I took his spot at the breakfast table? Tis like that, but far worse. Ye are asking me tae die, Madame Hayley, I am sorry, I canna choose it."

I said, "Madame Hayley, think about what ye are askin' of Young Lochinvar. Ye hae never been in a fight tae the death — there inna usually time tae pull oneself back from bloodlust — Ye must see, Madame Hayley, what we are up against."

She nodded. "Yeah, I see it. But we know Fraoch, he is on our side. He... he must be— " Her chin trembled. "He might send you a signal, Lochie, he might have a plan. I know I haven't been in a battle to the death, but maybe if Lochie starts defensively, and watches Fraoch's moves, maybe he would see that Fraoch isn't trying to kill him. I still believe Fraoch has a plan. Just give him, I don't know, like five minutes. If Lochie is this good at fighting, he could probably wait a few moments before he goes in for the kill, right?"

Quentin handed her a tissue and she dabbed her eyes. "I see

how hard it is, and — Lochie, I know you and Fraoch were often at odds, but he doesn't want you to die, please, *please*, just look for signs."

Lochinvar said, "Aye, Madame Hayley, for you I will watch for signs."

CHAPTER 71 - HAYLEY

*T*he day was long, I had nothing to do but worry. Wishing I could see Fraoch, talk to him, tell him goodbye, but Magnus had been right. I wouldn't be able to live with the possibility of making this situation worse.

Plus Fraoch had a plan.

I didn't know if his plan meant he would survive. But I hoped so.

We gathered for a meal of stewed greens, mashed potatoes, and a Salisbury style steak. Quentin said, "I miss Zach, this food is shite."

Magnus said, "Aye, the food at war is horrible, I canna wait tae get home."

I ate quietly. Everyone here was going to go home to a family, waiting babies, except me. I was going to be all alone. I glared at Lochie. He was quiet and thoughtful. He had been training all day. Training to kill Fraoch.

While the men talked, I considered killing him.

I had a gun.

I glanced up and Quentin was giving me a look. "Whatcha thinking about, Hayley?"

"Murder and mayhem."

He said, simply, "I can see, but the thing to remember is you have men from every century here, they've tried war, spy-craft, subterfuge, negotiation, and now an archaic arena battle, all the while trying to figure a way around Fraoch, a way to solve this in which he survives, and this is what they've come up with. You have a long slow march of war with all that death, or this. You might want to accept—"

"How can you be so chill about this?"

"I am not chill. I am losing my shit, but what is it going to help if I do it publicly, *anything*?"

"No, nothing."

"Yeah, I'm not chill, Magnus is not chill, Lochie is not chill. We are all very un-chill." He took the last small bite of his ration. "If you still want to try murder and mayhem, you have to go through me."

A messenger ran into the command center, "General Wallace, Colonel Peters, King Magnus, you have to see something!"

We all went out to stand in the street surrounded by a large crowd of soldiers all looking up at the large projection, which had changed from the usual propaganda to a new kind.

Now on a black background the words:

Ian I

vs.

Magnus

And then it shifted to Fraoch holding a hammer, he looked badass, and I had never been more afraid for him.

I watched Magnus's face, stoic, as he watched the video, Fraoch glaring down on us, shifting his hammer from hand to hand.

I blinked. I glanced around at the giant war machine, the surrounding army, the weapons, the signs of months of battle and war, the men all facing a frontline, a projected piece of propaganda, all glaring at their common enemy, my husband.

I exhaled.

Fraoch's voice amplified. "Are ye ready tae fight, usurper? Just you and me in the arena, boy, hammer tae hammer."

Ugh. There would be no way to talk Lochinvar down now—

But then I glanced at Lochinvar and he was grinning, "Ye see the sign, Madame Hayley? Ye asked me tae look for it, dost ye see it?"

"No, what sign? What do you mean?"

He asked Magnus, "Do ye see it?"

"Aye, I see it, Lochinvar, I am relieved tae see it."

I said, "What? Relief — what? Do you see it, Quentin?"

Quentin said, "Yes, absolutely, you can't see it?"

Magnus said, "The hammer is Fraoch's specialty, Madame Hayley. He is carrying it as a sign tae Lochie, remember what he said about it?"

Lochie said, "He said he would never use it in hand-to-hand combat, he would only use it for distance."

Quentin said, "He would never pick it to fight Lochie in an arena."

Magnus said, "He chose it tae throw it. He's planning on a target — but Lochinvar, we need tae behave as if this is still a true challenge tae the death. The soldiers are watching me for m'response, will ye crow for their morale?"

Lochinvar said, "Aye, of course, besides killing, this might be m'greatest talent."

He set his face in a glower and stepped in front of the crowd. With his eyes on Fraoch's image he rolled his neck, shook out his arms and legs, and pounded on his thighs. He bellowed, loud enough for the soldiers around him to hear, "Och aye, see that, men? Tis the face of a dead man."

A soldier from the back yelled, "Lochie! Can ye take him?"

"Can I take him? Och aye, I am goin' tae kill this man, Fraoch, and return the throne tae our true ruler, Magnus I."

They cheered.

Lochie climbed on top of a tank and put his arms out, "Tomorrow Ian the Bawbag's man will meet God at the end of m'weapon, and Magnus will once more be seated on the throne!"

Magnus kept his expression impenetrable, as he watched Lochie crow.

The soldiers cheered.

This whole army, all these soldiers, they were desperate to see Lochie win.

Lochinvar jumped from the tank to stand beside me. He bumped his shoulder against mine, "Tis goin' tae be all right."

Quentin put out a low fist and I bumped my fist down on it.

Magnus nodded. "I see a glimpse of a gold band on his neck, Lochie, dost ye see it?"

"Aye."

"Lady Mairead will show ye how tae get it off, ye must remove it the first chance ye hae."

Quentin said, "A ceasefire has been called, now we just get Lochinvar ready for the arena."

The night was long. Quentin told me to stay close, so I shadowed him, and then when I was too tired I went to lie down in my cot.

Quentin's cot remained empty all night, because, as he said, "Who can sleep?"

I could not sleep. I stared at the ceiling thinking about Fraoch and what his plan might be and how the hell it would work and all the ways he could die.

Quentin came in near dawn and sat on his cot. "This whole thing is so crazy, we're dealing with the advisory board that runs the arena battle, but are they neutral, or on Magnus's side or on Ian's? We have no idea. When I've seen these battles before it's always from the king's point of view, with the challenger's army sitting outside in case they win the throne. Spoiler, they never do — Magnus is impossible to beat, but he's not the king. Lochinvar is not Magnus. Their fighter is Fraoch. He has a plan. We don't know what will happen."

I said, "We have to be ready for anything. We have to keep Fraoch alive."

"Aye, and I've been talking in circles all night. Around the commanders I'm talking about winning the battle, around Magnus and Lochie I'm talking about supporting Fraoch's plan, a plan we're only guessing at. Tomorrow, Hayley, not one word about the sign from Fraoch. Not one word about how he might have a plan."

I said, "Yeah, we have to pretend like it's a full battle, it still might be, we don't know-know."

He scrubbed his hands up and down on his face. "I'm worried and exhausted."

I said, "Me too."

"But just between us, it's not as tiring as being around a newborn for weeks."

I laughed.

CHAPTER 72 - MAGNUS

*C*olonel Quentin and I walked Lochie tae the arena door. He was mentally and physically prepared for a fight tae the death, I watched his jaw set, the coldness forming behind his eyes. I had said my piece: how he was tae work *with* Fraoch instead of against him, but I dinna truly ken which Lochinvar would do. In the heat of battle he might be unstoppable. This was always a possibility.

And the time for talking was over — we had soldiers alongside, a load of armor carted between us. I was quiet. This felt verra familiar, tae be led tae the arena, and I couldna square the feeling with the idea that this young man would be fighting in my stead.

Had Donnan ever felt a moment of regret for havin' me kill so many men in his name? He had forced me tae kill brothers, a cousin, an uncle. I glanced at Lochinvar, his eyes up, his jaw set. He had a bounce tae his step. He was energetic, lookin' forward. I felt heavy and worn beside him.

My fears for Fraoch and for Lochinvar were based in experience, for me these fights were nae a philosophical act — I had lived through them. I knew what it was like tae kill a man while a crowd cheered. It caused a deep psychic and moral disturbance.

Castle guards searched us for unauthorized weapons and then sent us through the tunnels tae the waiting room. We had hours left before the battle would begin.

Trays of snacks and drinks were spread across a table. The soldiers accompanyin' us partook of some food, but Lochie refused. He faced the door, sitting in a chair sometimes, watching his hand dance with a sword-fight playing in his head, or sometimes standing, bouncing and shifting — his focus never wavering. He said, "Nae, I want tae stay hungry." He pounded his thighs and shook them out.

Colonel Quentin said, "You want to have calories to burn, though."

"I will be all right, I am Historic, I am at m'most vicious when I haena been fed."

Lady Mairead and Hayley arrived and it was nearing time for us tae take our seats.

"Dost ye want me tae stay with ye until the battle begins?"

"Nae," He bounced from foot tae foot. "Go ahead tae the skybox, I will join ye as soon as I hae handled him."

I clapped him on the back. "Thank ye, Lochinvar."

He nodded.

Lady Mairead put a silk scarf printed in the Campbell tartan, in his shirt pocket. "For luck." She kissed him on the cheek.

We banged on the doors tae signal to the guards that we were ready tae go tae our seats and were escorted down a back hall toward the door of our skybox, Lady Mairead noting as we walked, "Along that corridor is our *royal* skybox, Magnus."

I ignored her, having other things on m'mind: life and death and friends and enemies.

She continued, "Arna ye incensed that they hae stolen our skybox? I had just had the seats recovered with a fine silk!" She stopped still, her eyes wide. "Dost ye think Agnie has the class tae keep them clean?"

Hayley's eyes went wide. "Why are you focused on the *skybox* at a time like this?"

"Because this, Madame Hayley, is the final insult, and I hae—"

"Well, I'm not listening to any of it, Fraoch is about to fight to the death and..." Hayley took a deep staggering breath. "Stop distracting me. I need to focus."

"Aye, ye must focus, we *all* must focus — Agnie has won, she has taken everything from me: first Donnan, then Hammond, my youth, the kingdom, years of stress, always siding with my enemies against us, and now she means tae drive a blade through Young Lochinvar using the arm of your husband. I have *plenty* that I am dealing with."

Colonel Quentin held the door open for us and we entered the skybox.

All around us, the videos of the crowd were focusing in and out, a hundred thousand faces, a stamping cheering howl that pained m'ears.

Lady Mairead looked wildly around the box. "Och nae, dost ye see this, Magnus?" She wiped a finger along the rail. "There is grime and dirt! We are being treated like the poor relations put up in the worst room."

I took a seat.

"Ye are going tae sit there, as if all the arses of the kingdom haena sat there before — the unwashed entourages of the losing sides of your challenges... Och! I daena ken if I can..." Her eyes swept across the side windows. "There is a smear, it haena been washed!" She fanned herself and then her eyes focused onto the larger, royal skybox higher up along the wall.

"Agnie is sitting in my skybox!"

I said, "Ye kent she would be."

"Ye daena ken what I ken and what I daena ken — ye are ridiculous! A *king* allowing himself tae be ushered intae a small grimy skybox! Tae sit upon a common chair. I am nae standing for this!"

She yanked the door open on the skybox and left.

Colonel Quentin said, "What the fuck does she think she's doing?"

I couldna help a bit of a smile. "I hae nae idea, but I believe she is goin' tae create chaos and that is a good thing."

He asked, "Should one of us go with her?"

I said, "She works alone. We should leave her be."

We all went quiet with our individual worries. I was waitin' tae see what would happen and verra worried on the comin' battle.

Colonel Quentin said, "Are you okay, Hayley?"

"Not really."

"Yeah, me neither."

CHAPTER 73 - MAGNUS

*A*lone door opened at the far end of the arena and Lochinvar stepped out ontae the field. The crowd went wild, cheerin' and jeerin' equally.

Hayley leaned over the front rail, craning tae see the door at the opposite end of the arena. "When will Fraoch come out?"

I said, "It will take a moment. If ye make them wait, it helps yer side."

She gripped the rail. "This is freaking me out."

Lochinvar was wearing armor, heavy and strong. He had a weapons rack beside him. Two hammers. He stood within arms reach of the rack, and stared at the door.

Colonel Quentin said, "Do you think he ought tae say something to the crowd, Boss? While he has them to himself?"

"Aye, winnin' over the crowd is a good strategy." I stood, leaned over the rail, and yelled across the arena, "Lochinvar!"

He turned tae face me, and bowed with a sweep of his arm.

I said, "Safe battles, m'brother."

"Aye, Yer Majesty, I will do m'best for yer throne."

The crowd cheered, wildly, stamping and blowing horns, their videos focusing in and out around the walls.

I returned tae my seat.

Colonel Quentin said, "Perfect. Agnie and that Ian dude look pissed."

"Good, I winna look over there." I adjusted my uniform coat and slouched down in m'seat tae look as if I did nae care about the battle. "Though do tell me if Lady Mairead jumps intae their skybox, I want tae see all the theatrics."

He said, "I've got one eye on the field, the other on that box."

The door at the opposite end of the arena opened and Fraoch stepped through. He raised an arm and walked proudly up tae his own weapons rack. The crowd chanted, "Fraoch! Fraoch!" Stamping their feet and blowing horns.

I watched him for signs of deceit, *was he going tae throw the battle?* I couldna tell, except... as his eyes swept the arena they went past Hayley without pause.

She said, "What the hell was that?"

Colonel Quentin said, "Don't let it bother you."

I said, "Aye, Madame Hayley, that is a good sign. If he was actin' from fear he would hae met yer eyes, he would hae tried tae signal me. He has a plan and it is going the way he expects."

Fraoch said, his voice booming above the crowds, "My name is Fraoch MacDonald, m'father was a MacDonald of Glencoe, I fight for him!" The crowd had been cheering but they faltered and went silent.

I glanced from the corner of my eye as a man's voice emitted from the royal skybox. Ian the Troublesome had stalked to the rail and spoke loudly, "Fraoch, who do ye fight for? I believed twas for yer mother and yer king."

Fraoch kept his eyes on the far arena, he said, "Aye, Yer Majesty." Then he stalked tae his weapons rack and pulled off a hammer. He tossed it from hand tae hand checking the balance. He picked up the second hammer and tossed it up, flipping through the air, and caught it easily by the handle. He looked tae be checking the heft.

I watched carefully, he was pretending tae inspect the

hammers but from the corner of his eyes he clocked the position of the guards near the doors, Lochinvar's stance and distance, and then verra quickly, almost imperceptibly he glanced at the skybox.

The arena was filled with a verra loud clamor.

Hayley yelled, "Fraoch, I love you!"

He nodded, and without lookin' up at us, tapped his chest with the fingers of his right hand over his heart, lightly, and then put his arms out, and boomed, "Are ye ready tae fight, boy?"

"Aye, auld man, ye ready tae die?"

Fraoch laughed, "Och nae, I am Fraoch, I never die, I am near invincible—"

From the skybox there was a commotion.

Colonel Quentin said, "Uh oh, something is... they're looking at the door, do you think Lady Mairead is trying to get in their skybox, holy shit, she is wild!"

I glanced. Ian was up on his feet, Agnie was up, they turned toward the door at the back of the skybox.

My eyes returned tae Fraoch, who spun so fast it was breathtaking — his arm went from his side, and a hammer was loosed, hurled, barreling across the sky, slammin' intae the head of Ian, and smashin' his skull with a burst of blood splatterin' across the wall.

The blow felled Ian over the back of a chair.

A scream went up from Agnie, screams and mayhem from the video-projected crowds. Agnie dove ontae Ian's body, as a second hammer slammed intae her shoulder, knocking her back.

I looked down at the arena floor, Fraoch was clutching at his throat. He looked like he was suffocating, his face turning purple. He fell tae his hands and knees clawing at the band. Lochie ran toward him, holding his hammer — Hayley shrieked, "No! Lochie, don't hurt him!"

But Lochie swung the hammer at a guard, knocking him stumbling away. He made it tae Fraoch, guarding over him.

They were surrounded. Lochie swung the hammer around, clearing soldiers away. "Get back! Get back!"

"Holy shit!" Colonel Quentin yelled over the rail, "Everyone drop their weapons! Drop your weapons!"

I glanced at the royal skybox: Lady Mairead had forced her way through the door. For a moment she was struggling with Agnie, they fell over the chairs, clawing and swinging at each other, but after a tense moment ye could see a flash of steel in Lady Mairead's grip, and then her arm plunged forward intae the stomach of Agnie.

She stabbed again and again.

Then she drew herself away from Agnie's clutches, blood everywhere, with her dirk juttin' triumphantly from Agnie's body. Her lifelong adversary was dead.

Lady Mairead's act of murderous vengeance had been projected throughout the arena. The blood-thirsty crowd cheered. Lady Mairead shoved Agnie away and stood. She nudged the bodies of Agnie and Ian with her toe, tae make certain they were dead.

Then she smoothed down her hair with a bloody hand and raised her chin, standing in her skybox, verra proud of the moment.

She gave me a nod.

Gunfire sounded, my eyes swept the arena. Lochinvar was on Fraoch, grasping the back of his neck, takin' off the band. More blasts.

Colonel Quentin said, "No one is fucking dropping their weapons!"

Guns sounded from both ends of the arena. Quentin yelled, "Down! Down! Down!"

Hayley and I dove behind the bulletproof rail. Bullets sprayed the wall above us.

I yelled over the ruckus, "The soldiers daena ken who tae take their orders from, the usurper has been overthrown! I need tae get down tae the floor."

The handle on the door was shaking, then fists banged on the door, then General Wallace's voice: "Yer Majesty, let us in!"

Colonel Quentin crawled over, unlocked the handle and General Wallace led guards in tae protect us.

Below us, the gunfire slowly ceased, but then men were yelling. I looked down with an exhale, Lochinvar was loudly crowing, holding up the gold band. "How's that, auld man? I saved your arse! I could hae killed ye!"

Fraoch yanked off his helmet. "Did not, boy, I saved yers by nae killin' ye."

Lochinvar shoved Fraoch on the chest, he barely budged.

Fraoch stepped up tae Lochie's face. "Take yer helmet off, face me like a man."

M'soldiers were filing in tae secure the arena, they were encircling the fight. Colonel Quentin muttered, "Uh oh, tensions are fucking *high*."

Lochie threw his helmet to the side and charged Fraoch with his shoulder aimed at his gut. Fraoch groaned on impact, the blow sent him stumbling back. Soldiers cheered. Millions were watching from home, clamoring for more. Fraoch wrestled Lochie intae a neck hold—

Colonel Quentin commanded, "General Wallace, we need to protect both the idiots, we need everyone down there." And we all raced out of the skybox, down the hall, down the steps, and out intae the arena.

By the time we were down there, Fraoch had a bloodied lip, Lochinvar had black eyes — they were prowling around each other, encircled by battle-thirsty soldiers, spurring on the fight. Lochinvar dove on Fraoch—

I ordered m'soldiers intae the scrimmage tae drag the men apart. Lochinvar yelling, "Ye canna fight me, auld man? Ye must hae soldiers protect ye?"

But Fraoch broke free from the soldiers grip and dropped tae his knees. "Yer Majesty, Magnus I, King of Riaghalbane, I forfeit the challenge of Ian I!" A camera-drone hovered above his head, filming his words, projecting them on the large screens. "I hae been forced tae fight for the usurper, on threat of death tae yer descendants, and I humbly beg ye tae grant me amnesty and as the next in line for the throne, the stepson of Ian, the son of Agnie, a son of Donnan, I relinquish all claim tae the throne. I surrender and beg yer mercy upon me."

I crossed tae him, and stood in front of him, and said, "Och aye, Fraoch, mercy is granted." I put m'hand on his shoulder. "Thank ye."

He nodded. "Ye're welcome."

Lochinvar put his hands out and bellowed, "The arena challenge between Ian and Magnus is over! Fraoch, fighting for Ian has ceded the challenge, Ian the usurper is dead. I, Lochinvar, fighting for Magnus, have won! Long live the King!"

More of my soldiers were streaming through the doors. Outnumbered, the soldiers who had fought on Ian's side began laying down their arms, shoving them away, and kneeling.

I waited, watching, as a wave of men lowered themselves, until I was encircled by men on their knees. Twas a relief tae see it, an army brought tae their knees with the blow of a hammer.

This moment meant nae more bloodshed. Drones swooped and circled, filming the event. There was a hush in the arena and on the projections of the audience as we all waited for the last man tae kneel. Then I said, "Do ye men, the soldiers of Ian the Usurper, surrender?"

They responded, "Aye, King Magnus."

"Aye," I said, nodding, then I put out my arms as I used tae do when I was victorious in the arena. "M'name is Magnus Archibald Caelhin Campbell and I am the King of Riaghalbane, Magnus I, and I accept yer surrender. The reign of Ian I is nae more!"

The audience went wild, chanting, "Magnus, Magnus!"

I smiled and waited for the chants tae subside, then said, "I declare that the kingdom of Riaghalbane will hae three weeks of feasts tae celebrate the end of the battles!"

The soldiers erupted in jubilation. The projections took up the chant again, "Magnus! Magnus!"

I waited for the uproar tae subside, and the drone tae swoop down and focus upon me. I announced, "The occupied regions are once again reunited with the loyalist-held zones, I declare us a unified kingdom, a people undivided. I, the king of Riaghalbane, Magnus I, declare the war over! We are, once again, one land under God and throne!"

The cheering was thunderous.

Hayley shoved through the crowd tae Fraoch and they embraced, whisperin' in each other's ears.

Lady Mairead walked out ontae the arena floor tae stand beside me. She was wiping her hands on a formerly white handkerchief. There were blood splatters across her dress, and a smear of blood down her cheek.

She said quietly, "Well done, Magnus." Then she called out, "Master Fraoch!"

He turned tae her. "We did it, Lady Mairead."

"Aye, we did, and I am in the mood tae..." She put her hands on her hips and began tae sway, then she took some steps and began tae really dance.

Fraoch grinned and joined her, hooking his arm around hers, they danced around each other. Then they stopped. She hugged him.

I went tae Lochinvar and hugged him hard, a pat on the back, and then I joined Fraoch and put a hand on each of his shoulders. "Och, I thought ye were lost tae me."

He said, "I thought I was lost tae ye as well." And we embraced each other for all those long years of friendship, and for the loss of all these months of war, and the fear of havin' lost each other, and the happiness of havin' won, and longer for Fraoch survivin'.

After a moment, Lochinvar rushed over and threw his arms around us both. Fraoch said, "Och, the boy is overcome with emotion like a wee lass."

Lochinvar said, "I am huggin' ye so ye daena look like two staggerin' auld men comfortin' each other after a night of drinking."

Fraoch laughed and yanked Lochie intae a friendly headlock, rustling his hair, until Lochinvar said, his voice higher than usual, like a lad's, "Let me go!"

Fraoch let him go with a push, laughed, and then Fraoch and Lochinvar bear-hugged.

I heard Fraoch say tae Lochie, "Thank ye for nae killin' me."

"Ye're welcome, auld man."

Fraoch pushed Lochinvar aside and yelled, loud enough for all tae hear, "God save the king — Magnus I!"

A chant began, *God save the king, God save the king...*

I returned tae Lady Mairead's side. "How are ye? Ye are verra still, are ye injured?"

She was standin', her chin raised, her hands clasped in front of her. She said simply, "Agnie is dead, I hae killed her, I hae finally won."

CHAPTER 74 - KAITLYN

On the third day, I was up, dressed, with Jack slung in a plaid that wrapped around my front, anxiously awaiting my husband. I had promised myself that I was not going to talk about it with my children, or the other people at the castle, because I was a grown up and I would wait, patiently, without dragging everyone else into the possible heartbreak. But as soon as the kids were awake, it erupted from me, "Guess who comes today?"

And then it was all anyone could talk about.

And the day was long, dragging, seriously slow, but then... finally... a storm darkened the sky.

James, Sean, and Liam rode to meet the newcomers in the clearing, taking additional mounts and a cart, just in case.

I had a walkie-talkie that Quentin had left and after about a half hour of staring down at it, it buzzed with static, and then my husband's voice. "Mo reul-iuil, are ye there?"

I burst into tears. And nodded.

His voice to someone, "I canna tell if she is there."

I pushed the button. "Yes! I'm here!" I sobbed.

"We hae won the war, mo reul-iuil, we are done, I..." Static, then he said, "Everyone is accounted for... we are all okay... a moment, we are laden with gifts..."

I clutched the radio and cried.

We were all gathered in the courtyard when they rode in through the gates, Magnus, Fraoch, Hayley, Quentin, Lochinvar, Lady Mairead, along with a horse-drawn cart full with sacks and crates, and James, Sean, and Liam alongside.

A cheer rose up.

Magnus jumped down from his horse and hugged me around wee Jack, Isla and Archie clinging to our legs.

"You really won the war?"

"Aye, and Lochinvar fought Fraoch in an arena battle too! Somehow we all came through victorious." He peeled back the fabric on my front and leaned down to kiss the top of Jack's head. "He is a good bairn?"

"The best."

Magnus picked up Isla in the crook of his arm, and lifted Archie and they all hugged for a moment.

I said, "Lochinvar! You came too?"

"Aye, I begged off from goin' tae a future year that I hae never known, tae come visit my family. I missed the bairns."

I hugged Fraoch and Quentin and everyone in a circle, just hugs and laughter for a long time, hurried explanations and bits of details as we greeted the travelers. Then I said "So many stories, I can't wait to hear them."

Magnus grinned, his smile broad, "We will feast, and we will gather the chairs in the Great Hall and we will tell ye the story."

And that's how we came to be together in the Great Hall, a fire roaring, minstrels in the corner, playing what sounded suspiciously like the melody of a Beatles song, Lochinvar and Fraoch standing in front of us telling the story of the arena battle. Hayley jumped up from her seat to add from the perspective of an audience member, with Lady Mairead adding her part, recounting the murder of Agnie with a copious amount of glee, and I looked around at the circle: Lizbeth beside Liam; Sean intently listening with a pile of the cousins in front of him; James with his arm around Sophie; Quentin, holding wee Noah in his arms, Beaty beside him, patting Mookie on the head; Zach beside Emma, Zoe on her lap; Ben and Archie sitting together on a chair, enraptured by the story of murderous battles, oh how I wished I could keep the danger from them; and Magnus, holding Jack in one arm, Isla on his lap, Haggis sitting beside his knee; and me, a Hershey's kiss melting in my fingers.

We had come through this together, each of us with a role, working to keep us all alive and here we were, more of us than before. I felt so full of love for my family that it felt like it might burst my heart, watching all of them.

Once the story was over, Lady Mairead stood. "I would like tae say a prayer for my son, the king."

Sean said, "What about yer son, the *not* a king?"

She scoffed, but she was smiling. "Fine, I will say a prayer about my other son as well."

Lizbeth said, "And what of your daughter — I am nae tae be included in the prayers? I might need them the most, I think, as I am regularly keeping all the sons alive."

Lady Mairead laughed. Lochinvar passed her a glass of wine.

Fraoch said, "Since I am newly orphaned, I could use a prayer as well."

She said, "Och, we may as well make it for one and all."

She put out her arms and we all enclosed hands in a circle and closed our eyes.

Lady Mairead said, "Oh Lord our heavenly Father, high and mighty, King of kings, Lord of lords, the only ruler of princes;

most heartily we beseech thee with thy favor tae behold King Magnus: his wife and his children; his sisters and his brothers; his cousins, nieces, and nephews; all and sundry friends," She waved her hand around, "and the ones who hang around him, and *especially* his gracious and wondrous mother, entreated, once again, tae guard and guide the kingdom while her son, the king, once again, *relaxes*."

I opened my eyes to see she was mischievously smiling. I glanced to my right to see Magnus grinning.

"Tae replenish King Magnus, his family, and especially his mother, that I mentioned afore, with the grace of thy Holy Spirit, endue them plenteously with heavenly gifts; grant them in health and wealth long tae live; and strengthen, with the help of his brothers, tae vanquish and overcome all their enemies. Amen."

We all said, "Amen."

Magnus joked, "I suppose ye are verra pleased with that one?"

Lady Mairead said, "Of course, twas a perfect prayer for—"

Magnus said, "Is this true, hae we entered a new age with ye as the 'wondrous mother'?"

She batted his shoulder. "I hae always been wondrous, Magnus, but that prayer was for our family as we are on the cusp of greatness."

Magnus looked around. "Aye, I agree, tis a wonderful thing tae be surrounded by all, with new bairns born, battles won, wars finished."

He raised a glass. "Here's tae our future! May our prayers ascend tae the heavens, may good health and fortune rain down upon us, may we roll on the wheel of time taegether — slàinte!"

We all raised our glasses in agreement. "Slàinte!"

Then Magnus smiled at me.

Yes?

Aye.

He leaned over and kissed me, between us holding Jack, Isla, and Archie. I stroked my fingers down his cheek. "I love you, Magnus."

"I love ye as well, mo reul-iuil, want tae go for a walk?"

CHAPTER 75 - MAGNUS

I carried Isla, while Kaitlyn carried Jack, and with Archie between us, we strolled out tae the fields.

Isla said, "Where we going, Da?"

"I hae presents for ye, but we must be in a special place tae get them."

She said, "Oooh. I like presents."

Then after a few steps she said, "I forgot to get you a present, Da."

I chuckled. "I daena mind, wee—"

"Let me down." She dropped tae the path, reached down, and picked up a green leaf. "For you!"

I said, "Och, tis just what I wanted. This is an oak leaf — ye will see, I hae a present that will match it."

Her eyes went wide. "I knew it was special!"

We came tae the edge of the woods and followed a well worn path and continued on for a while until we came tae a stone outcropping. I climbed up tae the top of it. Archie scaled up tae stand beside me. I helped Kaitlyn up, and then lifted Isla by her hand. We looked out upon the landscape.

I pointed tae the southeast. "Ye see that spot, children? Tis where Caisteal Morag will be built someday, centuries from this point in time. Yer da has been fighting a war for our kingdom — I hae finally won. I am the King once more." I dropped my satchel tae the stone and rifled through it. "I was standing on the walls of Caisteal Morag and looked out on this spot and thought that what we needed was a forest, right here." I pulled out a box and a hand shovel and passed them tae Archie.

"Three oak seedlings is yer present, Archibald. I found the acorns and started them, I think we can plant them right over there — the beginnings of our forest."

Archie pulled up the lid on the box and found the bags with seedlings in them. "Cool! Those were acorns?"

"Aye, ye only need tae dig down this far." I gestured the depth and hopped off the boulder tae mark the three places. "One for Jack, one for Isla, one for ye."

Archie began digging in the spot I had picked out.

I said, "And for ye, Isla, I brought this." I handed her a small rock with a hole through it. "It is a verra good rock, when ye hold it, ye will be reminded I am thinking on ye. And if ye hold it up and look through it, everything ye will see on the other side will be magical."

Her eyes went very wide. "Really?"

"Aye, try it."

She put the rock up tae her eyes. "Da! It works, it all very magic."

I said, "I told ye."

Then I pulled out a present for Jack, a wooden three-ring chain I had carved and sanded for him during those long nights of war when I was too worried tae sleep.

I peeked into the plaid wrapping Jack, wound around Kaitlyn's shoulders, "Och, Jack, ye are asleep, ye are missin' the presents."

Kaitlyn said, "I'll hold it for him." I passed her the chain.

I said, "Did I forget anybody?"

Kaitlyn put her hands on her hips. "Me?" She laughed. "But don't worry, no problem, it's fine, I just..."

I chuckled and passed her a thin box. "I am teasin', I wouldna forget ye."

She lifted the lid.

"Tis just a small thing, a pen—"

She clutched it to her heart. "It's not small at all, it's so important, so necessary."

"I thought tae put a jewel on it, tae hae it made of gold, I wanted tae... Ye would deserve it, but I kent ye would understand — the pen itself is precious, and more importantly, tis made tae be used. I was thinking we could use it tae add Jack tae the register in the chapel, tae put him in the official historical record."

"Thank you, I love it, it's perfect, and I have a present for you, too... kind of a re-gift. Hold out your hand, close your eyes."

I held out my hand and something small was placed into it. I opened my eyes. "A key?"

"To our house in Florida. We get to go home now, right?"

"Aye, as soon as Jack is ready we get tae go home. Thank ye, tis perfect." I put the key in my sporran.

And then Kaitlyn sat on the boulder in the sun with Jack sleeping contentedly in her arms, and Isla recounted all the magical things she could see through the stone, and I helped Archibald plant the seedlings: three trees that would grow intae a mighty forest, on a land that someday in the future Archibald would rule.

~

The end.

Except...

EPILOGUE - RANULPH

EILEAN A' CHEÒ, 1604

I waited for the storm tae end, m'horse stampin' angrily at bein' stopped so near but forced tae keep within the trees.

The gale whipped around the clearing, the trees lashing in the onslaught — a windstorm of blowing debris, obscuring m'view. Twas a brutal blast, but finally, almost as fast as it had grown, the wind faltered and died down.

I told m'men tae fan out through the woods, searching the area, guardin' as I rode intae the clearin'. There was a mystery tae what might lie within — sometimes men, sometimes dangerous men with a guard nearby.

I circled the clearing, then, hearin' the signal from m'men that the area was secure, I rode intae the center.

The vessel lay in the mud. I dismounted, nudged it with m'boot tae make certain there was nae vibration, then I tentatively picked it up. I wiped it free of muck and noted the markings. I had discovered the pattern and now knew how tae decipher them.

I dropped the vessel intae the sack knotted at m'side. I unsheathed m'dirk and carved another notch intae m'belt.

Aillain's voice behind me, "Ye found another?"

"Aye — it makes six." I sheathed m'dirk.

His horse stamped in the mud, splashin' around. "One more?"

I mounted m'horse and nodded. "One more and then I will be ready tae avenge m'father, Samuel, and regain his throne."

THANK YOU

*T*here will be more chapters in Magnus and Kaitlyn's story.

If you need help getting through the pauses before the next books, there is a Facebook group here: Kaitlyn and the Highlander

I would love it if you would join my Substack, here: Diana Knightley's Stories

Thank you for taking the time to read this book. The world is full of entertainment and I appreciate that you chose to spend some time with Magnus and Kaitlyn. I fell in love with Magnus when I was writing him, and I hope you fell in love a little bit, too.

As you all know, reviews are the best social proof a book can have, and I would greatly appreciate your review on this book.

THE KAITLYN AND THE HIGHLANDER SERIES

BOOKS IN THE CAMPBELL SONS SERIES...

Why would I, a successful woman, bring a date to a funeral like a psychopath?

Because Finch Mac, the deliciously hot, Scottish, bearded, tattooed, incredibly famous rock star, who was once the love of my life... will be there.

And it's to signal — that I have totally moved on.

But... at some point in the last six years I went from righteous fury to... something that might involve second chances and happy endings.

Because while Finch Mac is dealing with his son, a world tour, and a custody battle,

I've been learning about forgiveness and the kind of love that rises above the past.

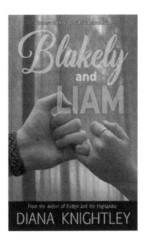

We were so lost until we found each other.

I left my husband because he's a great big cheater, but decided to go *alone* on our big, long hike in the-middle-of-nowhere anyway. Destroyed. Wrecked. I wandered into a pub and found... Liam Campbell, hot, Scottish, a former-rugby star, now turned owner of a small-town pub and hotel.

And he found me.

My dear old dad left me this failing pub, this run down motel and now m'days are spent worrying on money and how tae no'die of boredom in this wee town.

And then Blakely walked intae the pub, needing help.

The moment I lay eyes on her I knew she would be the love of m'life.

And that's where our story begins...

THE SCOTTISH DUKE, THE RULES OF TIME TRAVEL, AND ME

Book 1

Book 2

SOME THOUGHTS AND RESEARCH...

Characters:

Kaitlyn Maude Sheffield - born December 5, 1993

Magnus Archibald Caelhin Campbell - born August 11, 1681

Archibald (Archie) Caelhin Campbell - born August 12, 2382

Isla Peace Barbara Campbell - born October 4, 2020

Jack Duncan Campbell - born July 31, 1709

Lady Mairead (Campbell) Delapointe - Magnus's mother, born 1660

Hayley Sherman - Kaitlyn's best friend, now married to Fraoch MacDonald

Fraoch MacDonald - Married to Hayley. Born in 1714, meets Magnus in 1740, and pretends to be a MacLeod after his mother, Agnie MacLeod. His father is also Donnan, which makes him Magnus's brother.

Quentin Peters - Magnus's security guard/colonel in his future army

Beaty Peters - Quentin's wife, born in the late 1680s

Noah Peters - Born June 1, 2024

Zach Greene- The chef, married to Emma

Emma Garcia - Household manager, married to Zach

Ben Greene - born May 15, 2018

Zoe Greene - born September 7, 2021

James Cook - former boyfriend of Kaitlyn. Now friend and frequent traveler. He's a contractor, so it's handy to have him around.

Sophie - wife of James Cook. She is the great-great-granddaughter of Lady Mairead, her mother is Rebecca.

Lochinvar - A son of Donnan.

～

Sean Campbell - Magnus's half-brother

Lizbeth Campbell - Magnus's half-sister

Sean and Lizbeth are the children of Lady Mairead and her first husband, the Earl of Lowden.

Grandma Barb - Kaitlyn's grandmother

Grandpa Jack - Kaitlyn's grandfather

General Hammond Donahoe - guarded the kingdom of Riaghalbane for Magnus and Lady Mairead.

～

The Kingdom of Riaghalbane, comes from the name *Riaghladh Albainn,* and like the name Breadalbane (from *Bràghad Albainn)* that was shortened as time went on. I decided it would now be **Riaghalbane.**

～

The line of kings in Riaghalbane

Normond I - the first king

   Donnan I -

Donnan II - Magnus's father, murdered by Kaitlyn Campbell in the year 2381

Magnus I - crowned August 11, 2382 the day before the birth of his son, Archibald Campbell, next in line for the throne.

Some **Scottish and Gaelic words** that appear within the book series:

dreich - dull and miserable weather

mo reul-iuil - my North Star (nickname)

osna - a sigh

dinna ken - didn't know

tae - to

winna - won't or will not

daena - don't

tis - it is or there is. This is most often a contraction 'tis, but it looked messy and hard to read on the page so I removed the apostrophe. For Magnus it's not a contraction, it's a word.

och nae - Oh no.

ken, kent, kens - know, knew, knows

mucag - is Gaelic for piglet

m'bhean - my wife

m'bhean ghlan - means clean wife, Fraoch's nickname for Hayley.

cù-sith - a mythological hound found in Scottish folklore.

cù - dog

Locations:

Fernandina Beach on Amelia Island, Florida, present day. Their beach house is on the south end of the island.

Magnus's homes in Scotland - **Balloch**. Built in 1552. In the early 1800s it was rebuilt as **Taymouth Castle**.

Kilchurn Castle - Magnus's childhood home, favorite castle of his uncle, Baldie. On an island at the northeastern end of Loch Awe. In the region Argyll.

The kingdom of Magnus I, **Riaghalbane**, is in Scotland.

His castle, called, **Caisteal Morag,** is very near where Balloch Castle once stood, near Loch Tay.

~

True things that happened:

November 7, 1929 Abby Aldrich Rockefeller did indeed have a big party for the opening of the Museum of Modern Art.

And **Cornelius Vanderbilt Whitney** was a real person.

This is the dress Kaitlyn wore, designed by **Madeleine Vionnet** from 1927:

The silk scarf Agnie wore was designed by Accornero de Testa for Rodolfo **Gucci** to be given to Grace Kelly. It was called, Flora.

ACKNOWLEDGMENTS

Thank you so much Cynthia Tyler, for your bountiful notes, for reading through twice as you do, your edits, thoughts, historical advisements, and the proofing. You are so good at noticing, like when you pointed out that Kaitlyn would *not* be drinking a Martini at the Museum of Modern Art opening in 1929, because it was Prohibition. Got me.

I loved when you said, in response to Magnus and Kaitlyn's conversations on the high walls, so much so that I added a line like it to the story:

Cynthia Tyler
5:51 AM Today

Space aliens is ALWAYS the answer.

From language, to grammar, to landscapes and interiors, to the one million and one times that I get lay, lie, to lay, to lie, and lying vs laying wrong — I'm filled with gratitude that you're so good at this, thank you.

Thank you so much David Sutton for your abundant notes. You are so great at keeping the characters consistent with their archetypes, especially Fraoch, you always champion him, including my favorite:

And for calling me out on 'cranking' open car doors, saying:

Thank you heaps for your help.

~

Thank you to Kristen Schoenmann De Haan for your notes about what you love and what you didn't. I dove back in and rewrote, tightened, reorganized, and you were, as always, right, so much better now.

An example of the love:

For still being here after so many books, thank you thank you thank you!

~

Thank you to Jessica Fox, I loved when you said, "I love the comic relief throughout as I learned that the more I laughed the bigger the plot twist that was to come." I never thought about that, it's my conduct code. And thank you for this:

> "Things I loved: the talk of giving eighteenth century kids diabetes, Magnus's shopping spree. "What is the point of livin' without bears with wee hats?" is the next merchandising product idea. "How dost ye create the storms? Tis yer flatulence?" would be hilarious as a sticker..."

Thank you for still reading after all these years, all these books.

∾

Thank you to *Jackie Malecki* and *Angelique Mahfood* (the admins) for letting me watch your 'chapter dashes' (reading at the same time) and for helping me keep timelines, family trees, and details straight!

∾

And a very big thank you to Keira Stevens for narrating and bringing Kaitlyn and Magnus to life. I'm so proud that you're a part of the team.

∾

And thank you to Shane East for voicing Magnus. He sounds exactly how I dreamed he would.

∾

Thank you to Gill Gayle and Emily Stouffer for believing in this story and working so tirelessly to bring Kaitlyn and Magnus to a broader audience. Your championing of Kaitlyn means so much to me.

~

And more thanks to Jackie and Angelique for being admins of the big and growing FB group. 7.8K members! Your energy and positivity and humor and spirit, your calm demeanor when we need it, all the things you do and say and bring to the conversation fill me with gratitude.

You've blown me away with so many things. So many awesome things. Your enthusiasm is freaking amazing. Thank you.

~

I have a new venture, Patreon, and thank you to those of you that followed me there whether it's fan level or 'I love Liam and Blakely' tier, or both. Thank you for being a part of the magic, Anna Spain, Kathi Ross, Betsy Chapman, Jackie, Angelique, Paula Seeley Fairbairn, Diane Porter, and Sandy Hambrick for being the very first.

~

Which brings me to a huge thank you to every single member of the FB group, Kaitlyn and the Highlander. If I could thank you individually I would, I do try. Thank you for every day, in every way, sharing your thoughts, joys, and loves with me. It's so amazing, thank you. You inspire me to try harder.

And for going beyond the ordinary and posting, commenting, contributing, and adding to discussions, thank you to:

Anna Fay, Bev Burns, Azucena Uctum, Lori Balise, Mariposa Flatts, Debra Walter, Ellen McManus, Tina Rox, Dev Daniel, Anna Spain, Dianna Schmidt, Fleur Garmonsway, Dawn Underferth, Debi Mitchell- Kirchhof, Linda Rose Lynch, Diane Cawlfield, Kathleen Fullerton, Carol Wossidlo Leslie, Michelle Lynn Cochran, Jo Clair, Mary McCormick Brennan, Teresa Gibbs Stout, Diane M Porter, Lillian Llewellyn, Carolann Hunt, Thủy Purdy, Sherri Hartis Hudson, April Bochantin, Karen Scott, Veronica Martinez, Kim Glenn, Shanni Hendler, Denise Clements, David Sutton, Ashley Justice, Joyce Fleming, Carol Stevens Owen, Veronica Basco Juneau, Karin Coll, Maria Sidoli, Christine Ann, Mitzy Roberts, Joleen Ramirez, Cheryl Rushing, Jenny Thomas, Lindsey Molloy, Alisa Davis, Makaylla Alexander, Tara Smith, Susan O'Neill Mottin, Carolyn Carter, Renée Stringer, Maro Andrikidis Hogan, April McCoid, Maria Linkerhof, Marni Elizabeth, Leisha Israel, Roxanne Smith, Sharon Maggart Brase, Brittany Hill, Reney Lorditch, Michelle Wimberly Dorman, Linda Jensen, Liz Leotsakos, Melissa Fondren, Margot Schellhas, Jackie Briggs, Enza Ciaccia, Crislee Anderson Moreno, Marie Smith, Christine Cornelison, Lydia Lagunas, Susan Sparks Klinect, Marilyn Rossow, Patricia Ashby Davis, Harley Moore, Elidyr Selene Brynelis, Sherrie Simpson Clark, Linda Carleton Stoops, Patricia Howard Burke, Stacey Eddings, Sharon Crowder, Dianna Metroff, Nancy Blais, JD Figueroa Diaz, Deborah Carleton, Lauren Scarlett-Johnson, Amy Brautigam, Kathy K Cox, Thunda Quinn, Diane McGroarty McGowan, Diane Patricia, Luz Hernandez, Deb Herbert, Dorothy Chafin Hobbs, Joann Splonskowski, and Jan Werner.

When I am writing and I get to a spot that needs research, or there is a detail I can't remember, I go to Facebook, ask, and my loyal readers step up to help. You find answers to my questions, fill in my memory lapses, and come up with so many new and clever ideas... I am forever ever ever grateful.

This round I needed to be reminded about the cloaking shadow program thingy, April Bochantin remembered *"...book 12. Chapter 50. Uaimh Bhinn (melodious cave)..."* for me.

Also if the Earl had a nice mattress, Ellen McManus said, no. And Lori Balise reminded me when Quentin was made a General.

$\sim$

And when I ask 'research questions' you give such great answers...

_____

I asked:

Agnie, a fellow time traveler, likes to dig under Lady Mairead's skin: she has arrived uninvited to a party at an art gallery in NY,

she is trying to ruin everything,

AND she is not even dressed appropriately for the year, 1929, showing her disregard for everything historical and properly civilized.

Absolutely disrespectful.

What is Agnie wearing?

There were so many great answers, but I went with Lauren Scarlett-Johnson's, 1970s Gucci.

She said:

Lauren Scarlett-Johnson
Why do I suddenly envision Agnie in 1970s Gucci? It's a dress, but full blown colors and mismatched patterns, knee-high boots, and leather jacket? Lady M is clearly in black and sequins so the full blast of color, chunky heels, and leather are a blast into the future that makes Lady M see red. Yep... totally see it, and because it's Gucci, which was starting to become popular in the 20s, but not the known brand it'll become, Lady M is thoroughly pissed. (I also may have read House of Gucci and the history is fascinating. ♥)

Especially once I discovered the Flora silk-scarf to go with it. Ultimately I decided that the worst part of Agnie being dressed poorly would be for her to be dressed out of time, and Lady Mairead would recognize the scarf, immediately.

I asked:

I need (I think) a desolate ranch land in the past. A place with a cool history. Possibly cowboys. Wide open spaces.

Tell me the ranch or town name — the location. (US state, the Scottish borderlands, the Australian outback, etc.) Give me a range of years that the place was active, and what's cool about it.

First I picked Jerome, AZ. And so I want to thank Beth Foist Whitlinger and Shelby Brawley for the suggestion. Trouble was, I then found MacLeod Montana, and that seemed even more perfect.

I asked:

Magnus is going to visit Balloch (Sean and Maggie) and Lizbeth (and Liam) and the nieces and nephews) (also the Earl) and he needs to take them some gifts.

He is in present day, NY City and has walked down to a liquor convenience store/with green grocer next door.

What does he take?

There were so many great answers and I want to thank everyone: Alana K Mahler, Alicia Jay, Alison Caudle, Alison Goodwin Simpson, Amanda Ralph Thomas, Amy Brautigam, Anna Fay, Becky Montie Preston, Carol Wossidlo Leslie, Christine Cornelison, Christy Neff, Dana Phillip Baucom-Langer, Dawn Goodnature Miller, Deeanne McKenzie Pugh, Diane Cawlfield, Diane McGroarty McGowan, Dorothy Chafin Hobbs, Elizabeth Lockyear, Gabrielle Joles, Harley Moore, Jessica Mitchell Guill, Joann Splonskowski, Kaci Conaway, Katie Carman, Kristie Comer Matthews, Lillian Llewellyn, Linda West, Lisa Hogan Sanabria, Margo Machnik, Mariposa Flatts, Marlene Villardi, Marni Elizabeth, Megan Muckey, Michelle Lynn Cochran, Mitzy Roberts, Nicola Murphy, Patricia Howard Burke, Rochelle Hopkins Fitzpatrick, Rose Mikkelson, Sandy Hambrick, Stephanie Laite

Lanham Summers, Thunda Quinn, Trisha Lynn Smith Spears and Trista Strait.

If I have somehow forgotten to add your name, or didn't remember your contribution, please forgive me. I am living in the world of Magnus and Kaitlyn and it is hard some days to come up for air.

I mean to always say truthfully, thank you. Thank you.

∼

And thank you to Debi Mitchell-Kirchhof for the post about hag-stones. It came just when I was trying to decide what present Magnus would bring for Isla.

∼

Thank you to *Kevin Dowdee* for being there for me in the real world as I submerge into this world to write these stories of Magnus and Kaitlyn. I appreciate you so much.

Thank you to my kids, *Ean, Gwynnie, Fiona,* and *Isobel,* for listening to me go on and on about these characters, advising me whenever you can, and accepting them as real parts of our lives. I love you.

ABOUT ME, DIANA KNIGHTLEY

I write about heroes and tragedies and magical whisperings and always forever happily ever afters.

I love that scene where the two are desperate to be together but can't be because of war or apocalyptic-stuff or (scientifically sound!) time-jumping and he is begging the universe with a plead in his heart and she is distraught (yet still strong) and somehow — through kisses and steam and hope and heaps and piles of true love, they manage to come out on the other side.

My couples so far include Beckett and Luna, who battle their fear to search for each other during an apocalypse of rising waters.

Liam and Blakely, who find each other at the edge of a trail leading to big life changes.

Karrie and Finch Mac, who find forgiveness and a second chance at true love.

Hayley and Fraoch, Quentin and Beaty, Zach and Emma, and James and Sophie who have all taken their relationships from side story in Kaitlyn and the Highlander to love story in their own rights.

And Magnus and Kaitlyn, who find themselves traveling through time to build a marriage and a family together.

I write under two pen names, this one here, Diana Knightley, and another one, H. D. Knightley, where I write books for Young Adults. (They are still romantic and fun and sometimes steamy though because love is grand at any age.)

DianaKnightley.com
Diana@dianaknightley.com
Substack: Diana Knightley's Stories

A POST-APOCALYPTIC LOVE STORY
BY DIANA KNIGHTLEY

Can he see to the depths of her mystery before it's too late?

The oceans cover everything, the apocalypse is behind them. Before them is just water, leveling. And in the middle — they find each other.

On a desolate, military-run Outpost, Beckett is waiting.

Then Luna bumps her paddleboard up to the glass windows and disrupts his everything.

And soon Beckett has something and someone to live for. Finally. But their survival depends on discovering what she's hiding, what she won't tell him.

Because some things are too painful to speak out loud.

With the clock ticking, the water rising, and the storms growing, hang on while Beckett and Luna desperately try to rescue each other in Leveling, the epic, steamy, and suspenseful first book of the trilogy, Luna's Story:

ALSO BY H. D. KNIGHTLEY (MY YA PEN NAME)

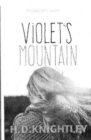

Bright (Book One of The Estelle Series)

Beyond (Book Two of The Estelle Series)

Belief (Book Three of The Estelle Series)

Fly; The Light Princess Retold

Violet's Mountain

Sid and Teddy